HER‹

THE SPEAR OF DESTINY

HEROPLOT

THE SPEAR OF DESTINY

SCOTT HARVEY

Everyone has their heroes, and I too have mine.

To my wife, Maria. My greatest friend and the light in my heart. Your love and belief are the two strongest things that I know. I could never have written this book without them, or without your unwavering support. For everything that you do, and for all that you are, thank you could never come close my love.

To Gabriel, who was forced to fight from his very first breath. You have endured more than most could, or should ever have to in your short life, and overcome every obstacle without ever giving in. Your smile was a shield that remained constant, even at the thought when all seemed lost. Your courage is superhuman, and beyond anything that I have ever experienced. The world is yours, and I know that you will always use your powers to keep your little brother safe.

And to my father. My heart is aching, and it always will, until I see you again.

PART I

All good things

GRADUATION DAY

The vibrating hum of a cell phone was the only sound that came from number five Upper Fant Road. On any normal day, the purr could continue for hours; at least until the battery was flat. But today wasn't a normal day, and as the hum continued, a croaky voice begrudgingly spoke out.

'Argh... w-what time is it?'

The voice fell silent as the eyes of a young student flickered, then squinted as they met the bright sunlight that poured in through the Venetian blinds.

As the phone continued its dance on the side, a hand reached out from under the duvet; searching for a snooze button, a pause button, an off button, or any other type of button for that matter, so long as it would make the noise stop. But it didn't. It was relentless. And somewhere during the half-hearted search for peace and the gradual awakening of the first few brain cells, something pricked his distant memory. Faint at first, followed quickly by shock, then horror, before a dash of panic forced a reaction to all and a body to bolt upright in bed.

'Oh no… no! It can't be… I can't be….'

It was a young man. Not the rugged well-built kind, the kind that appears in fashion advertisements, all pouting and brooding. This young man was scrawny; what some might call thin, or others more politely call frail. In fact, whichever way you wished to describe him, he was, without doubt, clearly lacking substance. His hair was dark and terribly messy, as if it had been dragged through a hedgerow and made into several bird's nests along the way. Hunched over with red and bloodshot eyes now strained and open; his face was etched, contorted in pain.

The windows hadn't been opened for some time, giving a thick feel to the air in the room. It had that distinctive old people smell; stale and stagnant, like you only find when visiting your grandparents house. As the young man yawned, the flavour from a mixture of laundry, a blocked sink, and mouldy food left on half eaten plates, touched his dry lips.

Eew! he thought, stomach clenching. He closed his mouth to block the unhelpful stench, when suddenly, the lingering taste of beer reminded him of the night before.

'Oh no…' he moaned yet again, as he placed a hand on the side of the bed to try to steady himself, hoping that the room would cease in its endless spinning.

'M-make it stop! Please, *m-make it stop!*'

His cries were in vain. The carousel that his head was riding continued to turn. Round and round it went, faster and faster it spun, dizzier and dizzier he became, until he realised that the pounding that he felt inside wasn't from the sound of the vibrating cell phone; it was from something else entirely. The previous evening, he had been drinking with his good friend; his best and only friend in fact. It was only a bottle or two of beer, but then it only took a bottle or two of beer to destroy his fragile little body and reduce it to this whimpering mess.

He lowered his right hand towards the dresser beside his bed; his fingers touching upon an open empty wallet and greeting the discovery with a groan of displeasure. They edged tentatively across the splintered varnish, like a spider that gently finds its way, before stopping at a pair of spectacles. Thick and black rimmed; the type that made eyes appear larger than they actually were. The kind that may have looked cool and hip at one time or another, but that was a time that had long since passed. As he put them on, his eyes finally found focus, and he could see the thrumming phone with the display that shone far too brightly for even a fleeting glance.

'Oh no... no, I knew it.'

His head continued to spin, as more of his body began to function and he felt the sudden dryness of his throat. It was arid and parched; scratched for moisture like the dry coarse sand of a beach baked in the hot midday sun, long after the tide had gone out. He needed water, any form of hydration so long as it came quickly. Then, without warning, his brain alerted him to another, less favourable fact. His bladder was full, close to bursting, and as much as he needed to drink, his need for the bathroom was all the more. Determined to stand, the young man summoned every ounce of energy left in his body. So much effort for someone of skin and bones; for someone who wasn't so very tall at all.

'Argh!' he grumbled.

His feet touched the hardwood boards, sending a freezing shiver up his spine. It echoed throughout his body, as he shuddered from the unexpected chill and the anguish of yet more pain to bear. Reluctantly, his right foot took an unsteady step forward, and as it did so, landed upon a pillow which offered a respite of relief. Perhaps this day wouldn't be so bad after all?

Luck, it seemed, was on his side. But then luck is far from loyal, and as he aimed to take another step, the pillow slid beneath him like a banana peel on a waxed floor. He fell forward; his hands barely managing to break the fall and unable to stop his spectacles from catapulting across the room.

'Oh, that's brilliant,' he said sarcastically. 'Just brilliant!'

Face down with his bladder pressed hard against the floor, he was blind once again as the phone continued to taunt him.

'Where are they…? M-my glasses?' he murmured. A voice spoken as much in exhaustion as it was in desperation.

He turned his head to the side, trying to look around, but it pounded harder than before. It thumped like a drum and the rhythm served only to compound his blindness, adding further to his suffering. He would need to raise himself, at least to his knees, if he was going to be able to search and find them. In a small, open plan apartment, it shouldn't take too long. After all, how far could they get? That being said, it's surprising how the largest of things can remain hidden in even the smallest of places, and as his search grew, so too did his frustration.

'Come on… where are they? They should b-be here!'

Little by little he scoured the floor, like an infant on all fours learning to crawl until the vibration of his phone was interrupted by a ringtone.

'James!'

The young man's face changed; alleviated and lit up. "James" was obviously a magic word, like that used by a hypnotist as it had a profound and instant effect upon him. His priority was no longer the bathroom, but to get to the phone instead, and he jumped, as he leapt to his feet.

In any event, magic should never be used without some thought of caution, for not only did the young man forget what he was doing, he had also forgotten where he was—beneath a cupboard in fact. And as he stood, with all the speed of an Olympic athlete, his head cracked like a log as it slammed into the corner of it. Startled, most definitely shaken, he was not to be deterred; he was going to get to the phone, to speak to James, and nothing was going to stand in his way.

Clutching his head, he moved back across the room as he followed the vibrating sound, sat down on the bed and answered.

'James....' he said downcast, head throbbing.

'What's up, buddy?' replied an overly enthusiastic voice.

'W-well... I... erm—'

'I'll swing by and pick you up in thirty. It's going to be awesome, Eddy. Just awesome!'

'In thirty? W-wait! No. I... I need at least....'

But it was too late, James had already hung up.

He didn't like to be called Eddy. It sounded far too common for him. Like the name of some street thug or boxer from a Hollywood movie crying "Hey yo, Eddy! How ya doin'?" His name was Edgar. Edgar Spear. Soon to be Dr. Edgar Spear, actually. Just as soon as he found those spectacles and got ready for his graduation.

It had been four hard years of study for Edgar, and he was looking forward to starting his residency at Massachusetts General Hospital, or "Mass Gen," as it was more commonly called, in Boston. It meant leaving the West Coast and moving to the other side of the United States, but it was all going to be worth it for his dream to finally come true.

Edgar had always wanted to attend Harvard University and study medicine to become a surgeon. At least, that was what he had managed to convince himself was true. For as long as he could remember, he had told everyone that if his parents had survived the car crash, then they would have made sure that he got in. They would never have allowed him to go anywhere else. But this, like his passion for surgery, was just a delusion; a case of self-deception and not true at all. The real truth was that Edgar just didn't have the grades for Harvard, or the money for that matter. However, if the truth failed to fit with Edgar's stories, or gave a less than perfect impression of him to others, then Edgar would simply change it; change it to something else. Something better. Something more befitting his masquerade. In other words, he would lie. And Edgar did lie, exceptionally well. Since in Edgar's eyes, he was, and would always be, perfect; never to blame, and never, ever, at fault.

Born in Renfield, a small town in Butler County, Missouri, Edgar was raised mainly by his mother, as his father was never around.

Edgar enjoyed and thrived in the intimate life of a small-town community, where his close group of friends looked out for each other. That was until suddenly—at the age of ten—after his parent's accident, when Edgar was sent to Port Larsen in Ventura County, California, to live with his grandfather. In stark contrast to Renfield, Port Larsen was a hive of activity and was anything other than intimate.

While Edgar's parents were warm and loving, it would be fair to say that Edgar's grandfather was not. He was a hard man. A God-fearing man. The kind who froze other men and made the hairs on the backs of their necks stand on end whenever he stared icily down from his large mountainous height. Empty of love and emotion, he showed Edgar little time and gave him even less encouragement. It was his duty to take his grandson into his home and ensure that the Spear family name continued. And Edgar's grandfather did his duty but nothing more, because his life, his time and passion, were consumed by his work. A small company that he owned at the harbour; where real men worked and laboured hard to earn an honest day's pay by loading and offloading cargo from boats and freighters.

As the years passed, Edgar never really settled and made very few friends. He was always the outsider, kept very much to himself, and as a result had become increasingly introvert. "Trust issues," the psychologists called it. Certainly, the bullying that he endured at school only made matters worse, and as he grew into a teenager, it became clear that he was not going to inherit his grandfather's physical presence, nor his mother's benevolence. Perhaps it was because his grandfather saw so little of his daughter in Edgar, or perhaps because Edgar had himself unwittingly inherited many of his father's traits, that the emotional distance between the two had only grown and pushed them further apart as the years went by. Edgar was, in reality, a grandson by name only. The result of a marriage between his grandfather's beautiful daughter, and a short, weasel-like salesman that travelled the country selling tobacco.

It was, in actual fact, somewhere around his seventeenth birthday, after watching a documentary entitled, *America's Richest Doctors*, that Edgar made the surprising and somewhat unexpected decision to become a plastic surgeon. Prior to this he had told various people that he was either going to be a writer, a sculptor, a photographer, an architect, an editor, a prosecutions attorney, a professional skier, a professional golfer, a helicopter pilot, and even at one point, a stockbroker. In fact, the only thing that Edgar's imaginary career choices had in common were that none of them involved helping anyone other than himself. Still, the life of a plastic surgeon, tightening the skin and lifting the faces of Hollywood's celebrities was a profession that would offer him the lifestyle he so richly deserved. The cars, the money, the fame, all his for the taking, and he wouldn't have to do much more than a little nip here and a tiny tuck there. So, at the age of twenty-one, Edgar completed a Batchelors degree in Human Anatomy, the first step on the ladder of his career. Having said that, Edgar had no head for heights and the idea of injecting fillers and sucking fat out of thighs for the rest of his life soon became a depressing thought.

Thankfully, it was around that time that a follow up documentary, *America's Richest Doctors Part II: The Money and The Power* was released, and Edgar knew that the reason why he was so unhappy at the thought of becoming a plastic surgeon, was because he was always meant to be a brain surgeon. A neurosurgeon. A man who saved lives, who gave something back, and who by strange coincidence was also number one on the list of *The Money and The Power*. So, when Edgar shared his newfound dream for the future, it was perhaps hardly surprising that his grandfather dismissed the idea as nothing more than the latest folly.

To become a neurosurgeon would be no easy task. Edgar would have to enrol at medical school and that required funding. He knew that although his grandfather never cared to admit it publicly, deep down he still clung to the faint hope that one day Edgar might come to work at the company and Calhoun Carriers would survive for another generation, at least. A future that to Edgar, spelt a fate that was worse than death itself.

Since he moved to Port Larsen, on the rare occasions that Edgar ever spoke to his grandfather, it was only for whenever he needed something. If he was going to get what he wanted now, then Edgar would have to make a sales pitch. And like all good salesmen, Edgar had quickly learned that one combined with charm was the fastest way to close the sale; to make the deal and get what he wanted. However, Edgar also knew, that this time no ordinary pitch would suffice. If he was going to succeed in bringing his grandfather around to his latest vocational notion, then he would have to pull out all the stops to do so. It wouldn't be enough to simply get his grandfather's permission. He would have to get his grandfather's blessing and support. That would be the only way to get out of Calhoun Carriers, once and for all. He would have to convince his grandfather that his mother's wish—no, her dream—yes, that was much better.... His mother's *only* dream was that he would one day become a surgeon, save lives and help all those who needed him. That this was all she had ever asked of him and was all that she ever wanted for him. Of course, this was never his mother's dream and she had never said such things, but why should Edgar care? It was the lie that he needed to sell to get what he wanted. Now he would pitch it as often as necessary; day and night, over and over, set to repeat until the lie became the truth. Until his grandfather would not only believe that she had said it, but also imagine the very way in which she did.

'Typical,' his grandfather would remark. 'That she would want you to waste time on people who have no money. She was too good for this earth. Too good.'

His grandfather would say that a lot. That God had taken his daughter because she was just too good, when maybe it just made it easier to live with the pain of losing her.

'I'm only trying to honour her memory, grandfather—to make her dream come true,' was Edgar's standard response. Always lying. Always manipulating. Knowing only too well how to play upon his grandfather's only weakness; the undying love that he held for his daughter. And yet despite his charming charismatic prowess, everything hadn't always gone Edgar's way. His grandfather was still his legal guardian and being so meant that he had to make decisions on Edgar's behalf. Edgar might well have sold his grandfather the lie about his mother's wishes, but he couldn't control what his grandfather was going to do with it. Or more precisely, where he was going to live that lie. Despite Edgar's pleas to move and commence his medical studies on the East Coast, his grandfather chose instead The University of California. San Francisco, to be exact. After all, the tuition fees were half the price of Harvard's, so there was never an argument for suggesting a move across the country, and if Edgar didn't agree, well, there was always the alternative....

In spite of his noted protests, Edgar unhappily consented to his grandfather's decision. In doing so, he knew that it meant remaining; staying trapped in California. But now that his time was at an end and he had gained his residency at Mass Gen, Edgar was finally off to Boston. Free of this life. Free of his grandfather. Free of this university, and the lie for his being there. Today was the last day. Today was graduation day.

A reflection of light from the floor struck Edgar's eye.

'M—my glasses!'

He hurried over, knelt down and put them on. With his vision restored, colours turned into shapes and Edgar's attention was drawn to several drops of blood. He reached out to touch one. It didn't feel tacky or sticky, like the way old blood does; it was warm. Edgar stood up and walked towards the bathroom, and there, in the mirror, he saw a large gash on his forehead. He checked it quickly. It was deep. Not deep enough for stitches, but enough to make for a terrible graduation photo, nevertheless. He removed a Band-Aid from the medicine cabinet and covered the wound, trying to close the gash as best he could. Filled with a sense of pride as he stood back to view his work, Edgar was convinced yet again, as if he had ever been in any doubt, that he was indeed going to become the world's greatest surgeon. He reached behind to turn on the shower and get ready for James's arrival, never taking his eyes off the mirror as he waited for the water to warm. Suddenly, an acute pain in his abdomen meant that he was going to have to wait to continue admiring his handiwork, as the need to relieve what was left of last night's celebrations had become a medical emergency.

Edgar was still buttoning his shirt when the buzzer rang out on the intercom. It was an old mechanical buzzer where the metal had become rusty and worn, so it made a dull warbling noise. It was a horrible sound. One of those you were always glad to hear the end of. It rang for a second time, and Edgar continued to ignore it. He might well have begun to feel human again after his shower, perhaps even alive, but he was in no condition to begin multi-tasking.

The buzzer rang again, then again, and then again. Convinced it was someone trying to get into the building, Edgar grew angry. He often got angry. He had a short temper and hated it when people forgot their keys, or their visitors rang his buzzer by mistake. It wasn't his responsibility to let tenants or their visitors in; people should take care of themselves. So, he walked towards the intercom, prepared to speak his mind.

'Yes!' he shouted through the speaker.

'Eddy. It's me. Buzz me in, dude.'

Edgar pressed the entry button and less than a minute later there was a knock on the apartment door. Still half-dressed, he unlocked it and the door flung open.

'Eddy!'

A young man slid past him and across the floor like a skater on ice. His short, mousy blonde hair was well groomed, and his quiff so moulded with clay that not a single hair moved. He was around Edgar's age and height, but that was where their similarities came to an end. This young man exuded confidence. Dressed in expensive fashion labels, he was hip, he was cool; he was the one and only James Munro.

'Come on, brother! We gotta roll!'

'Y-you said thirty minutes, James.'

'Yeah, yeah, I know. I was just fooling, man. I was already parked outside.'

James began to turn back around towards Edgar; the door still open behind him.

'Dude…! Come on! Time is money and I can never get enough of either. We gotta roll!'

As usual, James talked a lot and as a result, it usually took his eyes a little longer to process information because his mouth was always moving.

'Dude…!' he exclaimed, pointing to the Band-Aid on Edgar's forehead. 'Woah… what the… I mean… what happened to your…?'

'I know. I… I was down at the Deli when t-two guys came in to rob the place.'

'Dude…! Seriously?'

'Yeah. I g-grabbed a tray and hit the one guy in the face. But the other guy w-whacked me with his gun,' said Edgar with a certain, albeit false air of humility.

James's mouth fell open. 'With his gun?'

'Yeah. Some kind of p-pistol. So, I—'

'Pistol? Dude…! That's bad ass. You're so bad ass!'

James reached into his pocket and took out his cell phone.

'Hang on man… I gotta get this out there.'

James held up the phone and began to film Edgar, as James himself narrated the video.

'Yo, people! This is Eddy *Bad Ass* Spear, and you don't wanna mess with this dude. He just took out two gangsters on the corner of Steiner and Sutter—'

'Erm... actually, there w—were three of them.'

'No way! Did you hear that? Three gangsters just got served a whooping with a side order of *Not today hombre*—and like right before his graduation. People, seriously, he's like Steven "The Spear" Seagal!

'He's my home boy and doctor to be, so don't be late for your appointment or The Spear will get serious and amputate your ass!

'This is James Munro and I gotta go!'

James waved at the camera and stopped the recording on his phone.

'Wow dude! This is awesome!' said James, never once looking at Edgar. His eyes fixed firmly on his cell phone, making sure that his video was uploading. A few seconds later and his attention returned.

'It's out there now, dude,' he said, delighted with his spur of the moment footage, before turning off the phone and putting it back into his pocket.

It was quite a testament to Edgar that despite suffering from the effects of a hangover and in the midst of getting dressed, his response to the day's first question was to lie and fabricate a story where he was the hero.

'Dude...! Come on... you're not even dressed. We gotta roll. Grads in an hour and we gotta get set up first.'

'Set up?'

James failed to offer a reply. In fact, he hadn't listened, nor even heard Edgar's question, and had already gone back to the door.

'Dude...! Seriously? Three of them? You're so bad ass. You're just *so — bad — ass!*'

Edgar continued tucking in his shirt and quickly flattened his hair down.

James looked at him and smiled. 'You're beautiful, baby. Now come on... let's roll!'

'W-wait.... I... I need my gown!' shouted Edgar as he ran back into bedroom.

'Oh yeah, dude...! Can you imagine...?' James laughed. 'I mean... like if you forgot that thing?'

'Ok,' said Edgar, clutching his graduation cap and gown. 'Let's go!'

On the way down the stairwell, James's cell phone beeped constantly, alerting him to new messages. He reached into his pocket and took out the phone and as he did so, his eyes lit up. He smiled so broadly that his face could barely contain his excitement and he shouted out to Edgar.

'Oh my God! Dude... you're off the chart... you're off the freakin' chart! Ten thousand views in like sixty seconds? You're viral man. You're freakin' viral!

'Check this out. Profile breakdown shows seventy-two percent female. Ninety-four percent under twenty-four. They love you, dude. The ladies love you!'

Overwhelmed, James stopped dead in his tracks.

'Listen to some of these comments: *"Dr. Bad-Ass is in session!"* Oh, and here, listen to this one: *"The doctor just delivered a clean bill of health!"* Oh, and this one. You gotta hear this one, Eddy, this one's my favourite. Check it out: *"He ain't Eddy. He's Evil!"*

'Dr. Evil man. You're like Dr. Freakin' Evil. I love it!'

The two friends continued down the steps, out to James's car. It was an unusually warm winters day with no wind or rain, so James took advantage of the weather and left the hood down.

'We gotta do like a follow-up... seriously,' said James, as he reached into the glovebox and pulled out a pair of aviator sunglasses. 'Eddy, you're my new star. Like my super Spear star!'

He grinned, lowering his head and coolly slipped the shades on; raising an eyebrow to confirm his look as he nodded in the rear-view mirror.

'Well... I... I'm not... I mean—'

But before Edgar could say how he felt, James interrupted yet again.

'Dude...! What's with that...? You gotta stop with this stuttering. You always stutter when you're stressed. People think there's like something wrong with you man. You know... like you're... like backward or something?

'You've graduated with honours. You're the smartest guy I know, and you're top of the class. You're probably gonna be like the best surgeon *ever.* But seriously... dude... you gotta learn to speak. You gotta get an attitude—get with the program.

'I've told you like a thousand times, everything's online. Your life. Your likes. What you do. Where you go. Who you meet and where you meet—it's all out there. All of it. Why d'you keep fighting the system? Dude... you can be anything you wanna be online, and you sure as heck won't have to worry about that stutter. You just gotta get a profile set up... start sharing the love.

'Check it out... even now, everything I'm doing is uploaded and shared. The people know what I'm doing and who I'm with at all times. I'm like—*truly connected.*'

'And you're not worried...? That you're with m-me?'

James paused for a moment, turned to Edgar, then peered over the rim of the frames.

'Uh, hello! You just blew the ratings off my chart. *Kapow!*

'Right now, the only dude I wanna be with — is — *you!* Do you have any idea what you're doing to my profile? I'm like your *only* friend in the whole world. People be like, how cool is James Munro to know that guy?'

A few stop signs later and James pulled into the parking lot of the university.

'Ok… come on… let's do this!' said James, as overly dramatic and enthusiastic as ever.

He jumped out the driver's side, not bothering to open the door, and pulled out his cell phone yet again, eager to check the status of the video.

'No – way! Dude… you're on like forty-nine thousand! You're the hottest thing that's *ever* been on CaliChat. You're spreading like crazy—you're a forest fire, man! Like everyone at uni has seen this already. No one can believe you took down those gangsters.

'Dude…! Listen to this: *"Is that stone face Spear? For real? Guy's a secret psycho!"* They love you, man. The world loves you!' screamed James, as he punched the air with joy.

When they entered the main building, several students recognised Edgar and began to clap. Their applause gained momentum, along with the attention of other students as more and more joined in adulation of the have-a-go hero. People were everywhere and cheers rang out in crescendo around the corridors, while James stood calmly aside, filming the spectacle. Edgar was surrounded, devoid of his senses and struggling to adapt to his newfound fame. He was rooted to the spot, drowning in adoration as a vibrant flash of yellow caught the corner of his eye. It shone like a golden eclipse; as mesmerising, as the sun itself. And he watched as it floated effortlessly through the crowd, like a warm knife carving its way through butter. It brushed past each face, turning helpless heads as it drifted by. And although hidden, almost entirely obscured, Edgar knew exactly who it was. There was only one girl who possessed such sublime power. One woman who had the ability to seduce and subdue every man in her wake. It could only have been, Hadley Jones.

Since enrolment and the first time he laid eyes upon her, Edgar had dreamt of the day when Hadley Jones might recognise his existence. She was always surrounded by boys, they hung on her every word and more often than not, had fallen by her second. As she moved through the crowd, he could barely believe what was happening.

There she was, at the front, enchanting all with her smile, and none more so than Edgar. The light in the corridor above her head lit her hair like a halo, creating a glow that enclosed her heavenly frame. She wasn't of this earth. She couldn't possibly be. She was an angel who had come with a message for Edgar, and he stood helpless, captivated in wait of her delivery.

'You're a hero.'

The applause died down and the clapping subsided. It made no difference, it was only background noise, a distraction from the goddess that had bewitched him. If only time could freeze this moment, then Edgar could live for eternity. But a push from someone in the crowd pulled him suddenly back to earth. His mouth dropped open, no words came out, and Edgar's stuttering returned.

'I... I... I'm sorry...?'

'You're a hero. You're my hero, Edgar.'

He looked down, his face flushed crimson. He could pinch himself but for fear of ending this dream. Less than an hour ago Edgar was fast asleep and now Hadley Jones had just called him her hero. Surely there must be a God, and for whatever reason, that God loved Edgar. As he looked up, he once again tried to speak. Determined this time to say something cool; something funny. To not become another victim of the magic that was Hadley Jones.

'I... I'm no—' began Edgar, as a hand reached out from nowhere and ripped the Band-Aid off his forehead.

'Ow!' he screamed, to gasps of shock.

Hadley's smile recoiled and her spell was broken. What happened? Who did that? Why would they? And then, from the stunned silence, a voice shouted out.

'He ain't no hero—*he's a fraud!*'

Edgar turned to stone; surrounded by hundreds, isolated and completely alone. A student jostled his way to the front, opposite Hadley, and pointing directly at him.

'I was at the deli this morning!' shouted the accuser as he turned full circle to the baying crowd. 'There was no robbery. There were no gangsters and there were no guns. Spear's a phony…. Look at that cut… that ain't from no gun. He probably cut himself combing his hair!'

A second passed; a second that to Edgar felt like an hour. Standing like the emperor in his new clothes, unveiled and exposed, there was nowhere to run and nowhere to hide. A sole snigger echoed through the air. The smallest of giggles. Uncomfortable at first, inviting the others to join; as they did, the horde began to laugh, and their laughter rang out in chorus. Their howling was loud and boisterous. Not the kind so often heard after an anecdote or funny story, but the kind that leaves bellies aching and struggling to breathe. The infectious kind. It grew louder and stronger, became stronger and louder still. Until finally, with the force of a tsunami that devastates everything in its path, Edgar received its full brutal impact. Their derision raced through the corridors without restraint, and it ridiculed him without mercy. Deceived and made foolish, Hadley slapped Edgar across his face; the crowd roared all the more. His dignity stripped bare and humiliation now complete, everything, absolutely everything, was filmed by James.

Desperate to run, but no one willing to move; the entertainment was priceless, and the crowd wanted their money's worth. Edgar pushed, then he shoved, lashing out like a wild animal hopelessly trying to flee from his captors, enjoying the torment of their prey boxed in. He lowered his head and tried furiously to forge a way through. Forwards and onwards, pressing farther and beyond, there would surely be an end to this unruly mob? Then, having made small headway, he spied an opening and barged as hard as he could towards refuge.

The classroom was empty. Edgar slammed the door on the euphoric crowd behind him, who were not yet aware of his escape. He slumped onto a stool, his head in his hands; contemplating the stark realisation of a life that was sullied from a lie now exposed. There would be no way back from this. No story or falsehood that could rescue him now. His reputation was in ruins. He wasn't just a laughingstock; he was the butt of the joke, and one that was shared by all. Moments later the door opened, and James entered before turning the lock.

'Dude! Dude! You're so... I mean... you're so—'

'Screwed?'

For the first time in four years Edgar interrupted James, and for the first time since they'd met, James was speechless. It was the first time his mouth was unable to complete what it began or find the words that it needed to say. But then today was a day for firsts. It was the first time that people had ever heard the name, Spear. The first time that his lies were seen for what they were. And the first time that Edgar had truly understood just how alone he really was.

'Everyone's going to think that I lied,' said Edgar, still trying to convince himself that his story about the deli was true.

James took out his phone which was beeping wildly and unlocked the screen.

'Oh dude... I got over sixty thousand already.'

'Y-you got...? W-what did you say? You got... sixty.... D-don't... don't say you just filmed all that?'

He shrugged, with an unapologetic smile. 'Dude... I had to. You know that. It's my duty.'

'Your duty?' screamed Edgar. 'Your — *duty!*' shouting even louder. 'What about the duty to your friends?'

'Dude... I have over two hundred thousand friends.'

'No. Not your stupid online friends. I mean your *real* friends. What about me?'

'I keep trying to tell you. It's all online now. These are my real friends.'

Edgar turned away in disgust. He was hurt, he was wounded, but most of all, betrayed. The one friend he was sure that he had. The one person he believed he could rely on. The only one who was there for him, who should be there for him, had now done this to him. How could he? How dare he?

He tried to think, to analyse, to try to find a way out of the situation.

Yes, he thought, that was it. That was how this happened. This was all James' fault. Edgar was just a victim. He had done nothing wrong. It was James, James who had done all this, who had got him into this situation. And as so often, and so many times before, Edgar's lies once again began to manipulate the truth. Because if Edgar was guilty of anything, it was friendship, of trusting his only friend.

'Look dude… you remember our first day here. They all looked at us like freaks. No one would talk to us. People ignored us. They wouldn't sit with us…. Before I built CaliChat, no one wanted to hang with me—'

'I did!' roared Edgar, like a volcano on the very brink of eruption.

'You did because no one else would hang with you…. Look, dude… we needed each other back then. That's all. It's nothing personal.'

'Nothing personal? *Nothing – personal?* There's five hundred people out there laughing at me because you posted a video on your stupid site, and you have the nerve to stand here and say it's not personal?'

'Woah…! Woah, dude… calm down!

'CaliChat's not stupid and those people aren't laughing at you because I posted a video. They're laughing at you because you lied about the deli—'

'I never lied!' screamed Edgar, still trying to persuade James and himself of his innocence.

James shrugged again. 'Makes no difference. There's sixty thousand members who think you did. So, what you did or didn't do doesn't matter anymore. The truth—the real truth—the truth that people buy… that's out there, dude… and that truth says *you* lied.'

For the first time in Edgar's young life, he was up against a force far greater than himself. And on this day of firsts, Edgar had yet to face another. The power of online opinion was a power far greater than any lie that he could ever spin in person. Nothing would convince the hundreds outside, the thousands online, that he had stopped three imaginary gunmen earlier that morning. This time, for the first time, no one would believe him. James was right; it was the truth that people buy, and in this new reality, Edgar needed time to adjust. A time where he fell silent; where James saw his friend despondent and resigned to defeat.

'Dude... let me tell you something. Something I've never told anyone before....

'When I launched CaliChat, it only took a couple of students to set up their profiles—to start chatting—for me to be able to see everything they liked. Seriously... a few lines of code was all that it took, and I could see *everything* they were doing.

'When someone went somewhere and posted photos, I went online and found different photos. I'd put them on my profile to show that I'd been at the same place. After a while, I didn't even have to go online... I just automated it all. So, when someone checked into a place, the system would check me in four hours later. And if someone went to a concert—gave a positive review—the system would write one from me, as if I'd been at the same show.

'Do you understand? Do you understand what I'm telling you...?

'I created a different profile of myself for every user on CaliChat, so every user saw a different me whenever they logged in. The *perfect* me. Every time someone checked their friends list, I was always there—right on top—recommended as the most likely friend to total strangers. These were people I had *nothing* in common with. But I knew everything about them. Who they talked to, what they talked about, and where they went...? Then, when they saw my profile, they believed that I had more in common with them than any of their real friends.

'You know, it didn't take long before people wanted to be friends with me. Not because of who I was, but because I was friends with other people—the same people they wanted to be friends with. I just made my own popularity, that's all. I mean, if this guy says I'm ok, and that guy thinks I'm cool, then I must be, right?'

James stood up and walked around a desk. He was nervous, clearly debating and unsure of whether he should continue with his confession.

'It's the same today as it's always been…. Making a friend request now, it's no different to the way they used to write letters of introduction—back in the day…. It's just an endorsement… it's *all* about endorsements…. Endorsements build trust. Trust gets you friends. Friends build you a network. And a bigger network makes you more interesting.'

James stopped pacing and stared at Edgar.

'In the end, Eddy, the only question worth asking is which network will you join…? Whose side are you on?'

Edgar looked perplexed; the undertone and hidden meaning of James' words causing his confusion. He blinked, their eyes unlocked, and James continued his slow saunter between the desks.

'It's like a cycle—like a giant wheel you just can't get off. You know what I mean? The more friends I got, the more people I could reach. The more I could reach, the more influence I got. Understand?'

'Eddy… do you understand what I'm telling you? What *all this* is about?'

James stopped.

'Yo! Eddy… are you listening?'

Edgar looked up from the floor.

'Influence—it's about influence. I started to get into people's heads. Where everything gets bought and paid for by the companies who want to use my influence. My car. My phone. My clothes. *Everything*. I mean like *everything*. Nothing costs me a dime. Seriously… even the food I buy.

'I share a photo of me eating a Hersey's bar and the sales of Hersey's go up. That kind of power comes at a price... If Hersey's don't pay, then I eat a Snickers, a Mars, a KitKat, until someone pays me for advertising their product. I don't have to like it. I do it because I get paid, and I get it for free.

'That's what it's about.... What — *all* — this — is about. It's free enterprise. Pure and simple. The social economy—and I'm a social millionaire!

'The more CaliChat grew, the more data I got. I'm not talking about terabytes, Eddy. I'm talking about crazy amounts of data—like data about everything. Every kind of habit, routine, opinion. You name it—I got it. Tons and tons and *tons* of data—all stored, doing nothing. But then something interesting happened.... You know by seeing what people like, you can actually see what they don't like. By seeing what they click on, you can just as easily see what they don't click on. By following what they comment, you can follow their thoughts. So, those gaps in people's profiles. You know—the darker side—the Yin of their Yang. It starts getting filled in through A.I.— all working from that data.

'You see, it's simple.... If you control the data, you influence the user. If you influence the user, you *control* the user.

'I had no friends, but now I have more friends than anyone I know. You know why? Because I'm the perfect friend, Eddy—I'm automated, but I'm real too, so no one questions what I'm doing or why I'm doing it.... Sure, I created CaliChat, but I also use it. I post regularly, so no one suspects a thing.'

James pointed to the masses outside the classroom, and his face turned cold.

'All those people, Eddy... all those users out there... they all use CaliChat. I give them what they want, and in return, they give me what I need. It's not rocket science. It's just supply and demand, so don't judge me. People wanna believe they're getting a free lunch, but someone's gotta tip the waiter, and it's about time you woke up and smelt the specials.'

Edgar could no longer contain himself. His lips trembled and quaked, then erupted in rage.

'And they call *me* a phony? You're the biggest liar of all, James.

'You pretend to be so easy going with all your "dude this" and "dude that" drivel. You put on this show and you play this charade. You try to fool everyone, but in the end, you can't even fool yourself.

'Look at you... you're nothing more than a common, two-bit thief. As fake as your stick-on veneers and that cheap plastic smile.'

James wasn't entirely appreciative of Edgar's reaction to his confession. Perhaps he had hoped that Edgar would see the real purpose of CaliChat, and that social sharing was only about manipulation. Influence and exploitation. Perhaps he had hoped that Edgar might join him; he was, after all, an expert manipulator. Nevertheless, any such hopes were dashed as soon as Edgar released his fury, and if James looked sinister before, then it was nothing compared to how he looked now.

'I am *anything* except "common." I don't fool myself about a thing, Eddy. This is the new world. You're either a player or you get played.'

'And that's it, is it? You played me? You film me and post it on your network, and no one points a finger at y—'

'I give them what they want. Things to discuss. Gossip to share. Distractions from their boring mundane lives. The vultures don't shoot the messenger, Eddy. They just wait for him to deliver a new story so they can feed off it. And I'm bigger than any story now... *I am the story....* You know why? Because I don't just control the user, I control the narrative. That's why.'

James's honesty was broken by the loud banging of palms upon the classroom glass, as other hands tried the knob of the locked door. It was a signal, a reminder for him to go back to the performance, and like a switch or mood that swings from one extreme to the other, James was acutely aware that eyes were upon them. The chameleon, almost schizophrenic, was a man of many faces, none of which were real to Edgar.

'Dude... come on! We gotta get ready for the ceremony.'

But Edgar's rage had barely begun to find its true form. It was venom; pouring through his veins, and its intensity grew greater the deeper and further that it spread.

'We've got to *what?*' screamed Edgar. 'Are you crazy? Have you forgotten what just happened? Did you *see* what happened out there? Did you hear them...? See their faces...? I'll *never* go out there again.

'Do you really think I'd walk onto a stage now—to collect a piece of paper—with everyone laughing at me? Are you out of your mind?

'I'm done with this place. I'm done with this city. Done with these people. And I'm *done* with you, James. So, go put that in your story. Post that on your site. Add that to your comments. Do whatever the hell you like. Because I – am – *done!'*

The silence between them was crippling. James didn't dare to respond, not in front of the faces that were pressed against the glass; the eyes that stared in from outside the room. Edgar rose to his feet, his face empty of emotion, stiffened and lifeless from the poisoned anger that clutched at his heart. He stared blankly out of the window, out across the car park, his back towards James.

'You were right about one thing,' said Edgar, his voice now calm and deliberate. 'I *am* a brilliant doctor, and I *will* be a brilliant surgeon.... By the time I'm finished, the whole world will know the name Spear.

'They'll ask to see me... crawl on their hands and knees— begging to be treated. They'll plead with me to help them—to save them—to give them hope and a future. But I won't. I won't give them anything.... *Nothing*—nothing except pain and suffering. When I'm finished, every person outside this room will regret the day they dared laugh at me.'

Edgar returned his soulless stare to James.

'And every person inside this room will regret that they ever knew me.'

His hand took hold of a book from the desk beside him, and he clenched it tightly, squeezing it tighter as his eyes drove deeper into James.

'When I'm done with you, Munro, you won't have any friends. No one to read what you say or watch what you post. No one to care about what you do or where you go. No one to fool. No one to cheat. You won't have anyone... you won't have anything. Now get out.... Go on, go. *Get out!*'

He threw the book without aim at James; it struck the middle of his forehead, piercing the skin and sending a trickle of blood down the centre of his brow. James reached up to touch the wound and winced.

'That's the first cut, Munro. The next one will be deeper... and you'll need more than a Band-Aid.'

'Dude...! You're crazy... you're freakin' crazy! What the hell's wrong with you? It was just a post. Just a freakin' post!'

James shook his head, shocked that Edgar would ever lash out, let alone inflict injury upon him.

'Whatever, man... I'm out of here—over and out! Dude, get some help. Seriously... you need it!'

James moved to the door and opened the lock to the impatient crowd.

'Yo, people... listen up!' he shouted, addressing his adoring audience. But Edgar didn't count himself among them. Edgar wouldn't listen, not now, not after discovering the truth about his friend. That the showman was nothing more than a con artist who hid behind the façade of his performance; a miserable shallow actor that had sculpted a play for his own personal gain. He had nothing left to offer Edgar, and Edgar, no appreciation left to give.

This was indeed a day of firsts, and for all the belief that Edgar had in his own abilities to lie, he now realised that he knew nothing at all. He was no better than those losers out there. In fact, he was probably worse. After all, he was foolish enough to believe that James was his real friend, not just a virtual one who he shared a few interests with. Not like those moronic, laughing people in the corridor. Surely if they couldn't see that James was just using them, then they deserved everything they got? Edgar was closer to James than anyone, yet he didn't see nor suspect a thing. The truth, the real truth, was that Edgar hadn't just been played; he'd been played like a Steinway in Carnegie Hall by Beethoven himself.

He placed his hands down upon the desk, clenched his fists and pressed them hard into the wood. His knuckles turned white; skin, tight to the bone as he looked through the glass pane of the door and saw James, still talking. It had been a day of firsts, but more importantly, it had also turned into a day of lasts. Because today would be the last time that Edgar would ever allow himself to be ridiculed. The last time that he would ever allow his word to be questioned. And the last time that he would ever be so foolish as to trust—anyone— again. The people, those people laughing at him now, they would all become insignificant in time; he would see to that. And if James thought of himself as the narrative, then Edgar would become the words, the very letters that he needed to tell his stories. If James wanted to control the user, then Edgar wouldn't stop until he ruled them. And if they, the people, called him "Evil Spear," for simply believing that he had taken on a handful of criminals, then imagine how they'll fear him when he takes down hundreds more?

As the laughter continued to ring out, Edgar could hear James' mocking; his taunts for him to come and face the unsparing crowd. But the voice of his once best friend now served only to fuel his resolve. Edgar pushed his fists still farther into the desk, his knuckles bleeding as he imagined them ploughing through James' body. His rage was growing, his anger in need of release. This was, however, not the time nor place to express it.

Edgar turned his back on James once again, knowing that this time would be the last; that this time, it was for good. He opened the window and climbed out to the carpark. Swaggering across the tarmac, he told himself not to look back—that he would never go back, and why should he? There was nothing to go back to and there would never be a need anyway. California was finished; it just didn't know it yet... no one did.

2

THE MONSTER

E dgar looked up from his desk. The harsh ceiling downlights formed a silhouette around a large, overbearing man; his sparse remaining locks were gathered into a thin comb-over that did little to prevent the beams from shining through. The man's face was almost entirely in shadow, yet revealed a pair of thick, bushy eyebrows, that looked remarkably like those enormous hairy tropical caterpillars often seen in documentaries on National Geographic. These, however, were greying in colour, aged and possibly endangered; most definitely without any chance of transforming into anything of beauty.

'Do I look like I have *all* day?' boomed an irate voice.

'I… I'm sorry, sir. Sorry… h-here… I have it right here.'

Edgar fumbled around the desk trying to locate a file. The man leaned farther forward, his face now out from the shadows as the caterpillars appeared squeezed, pulled down and adjoined. He pointed at a section of the desk with manila folders stacked like overlapping pancakes.

'There boy. *There!*'

The man clicked his fingers, impatiently waiting for Edgar to hand him the file.

'What the dickens is wrong with you, Spear?' he demanded. 'Useless—you're useless…. You're the worst I've ever seen here. God knows where they found you!'

Despite his fluster and the unending flow of compliments, Edgar continued to search for the file unfazed.

'H—here, sir,' he said, grabbing a folder from the cluttered piles. 'Here it is… A—Amanda Jenkins.'

Edgar offered the folder to the man and began to grovel.

'Again… I… I'm sorry it took so long to—'

The man snatched at the folder and interrupted Edgar in order to finish his opinionated rant.

'After scraping the *bottom* of a very deep barrel, I should imagine,' he said, before he turned and walked down the corridor, muttering beneath his breath as he went

The man was still complaining about Edgar, when suddenly, he was halted by an orderly pushing a bed.

'Damn it, man! Don't you have eyes?'

The orderly froze, not expecting to meet someone on the corner.

'Well, for God's sake use them…. *Use — them!* That's what they're there for, aren't they?'

The man shoved the bed to the side as he walked past and continued down the corridor, waving the folder angrily in the air. The embarrassed orderly glanced down at the patient, offering an apologetic smile before looking up towards the desk. Edgar simpered and rolled his eyes. The orderly smiled back and nodded; their secret message had been received and understood.

As Edgar set about reorganising the files, the phone rang.

'Dr. Spear.'

'You'd better come now, Doctor,' replied the voice. 'He's shouting again.'

It was Nurse Davis; Penelope, or Penny, as Edgar often called her. The nurse with whom he performed most of his early morning rounds.

Edgar dropped the phone and flew out of his chair; the towers of files collapsing again into clutter. He raced down another corridor, towards the elevators, past a no running sign that read, *Accidents Can Happen*. The elevators were slow, as always, and his frustration obvious.

'Come on. Come on,' he whispered anxiously, stabbing repeatedly at the up button.

He coughed, quite unexpectedly; overpowered by a pungent perfume that caught his unwanted attention. Beside him, an elderly woman stood supported by an elderly man. Edgar hadn't noticed them before as his entire focus was on getting to where he needed to go, but in an effort to be polite, he smiled.

'And how are we this morning?'

His greeting was anything but sincere, the type that only doctors and customer service people can do really well; a few words said to break an otherwise awkward silence, and the kind that always starts with "And," then refers to someone as "we." It was an easy way to appear courteous without caring, and for Edgar, who was still only a resident, he had already mastered the art of hypocrisy. Sadly, the elderly lady still believed in the sincerity of all doctors and eagerly began her reply.

'Oh, good morning, Doctor. I'm fine thank you. We're just on our way—'

However, the loud *ping* of the arriving elevator, offered opportunity to save Edgar from the tortuous torment of idle chitter chatter. As the doors opened, he leapt inside and quickly pressed the number seventeen button; smirking at the couple who hadn't managed to take more than a step towards the closing doors. Watching as they shut, he felt a sudden sense of pity, after all, it wasn't their fault that they were slow. Contrary to what he had learned, he decided instead to do something kind: he pressed the Open Doors button to hold the elevator and was met with gasped surprise.

'Please hurry', he said. 'I'm late for a *very* urgent appointment—lives are at stake.'

The elderly couple dragged themselves into the elevator.

'Floor?'

'Oh... erm... oh, Doctor.... Thank you... erm—'

'Yes. Yes,' said Edgar impatiently, already regretting his decision. 'Floor?'

'Oh... sorry, Doctor. Yes... floor... now let me see....'

The elderly lady was clearly ruffled and not quite prepared to answer any questions.

'Erm... the Lunder Building.'

Edgar huffed frustratingly. 'You're in the Lunder Building. What *floor* do you want?'

'Well, you see it's our son—'

'Mel,' interrupted the elderly man.

'Yes, Mel,' agreed the elderly lady, intent of regaining control of the conversation. 'Our son, Mel. He's a physician—'

'Chief physician,' said the man, interrupting her once again.

'Yes... chief physician,' she said. 'Of the neurosurgery department. And he's a terribly busy man. We're just—'

'Mel?' asked Edgar in bewilderment.

The elderly lady took a deep breath. Interrupted yet again and unable to finish a sentence, she struggled to remain genteel.

'Yes,' she replied reluctantly. 'We're on our way to see him now.'

Edgar's mind began to race. He was a resident in the neurosurgery department, but had never heard of a Mel, and there was most definitely no chief physician who went by the name either. The chief physician was called... suddenly, like a lightning bolt, it hit Edgar, or struck him to be more exact, and he forgot why he was even in the elevator. Did the elderly lady mean Melvin? Melvin Abelman? Edgar's mouth lagged a little behind his thoughts.

'Not *Melvin the Mon*—' he said, stopping suddenly; his brain quickly catching up, silencing him before he created irreparable damage.

The elderly lady nodded, and her smile broadened in recognition of her son's name. 'Yes. That's right, dear. Our Melvin.'

'Well, isn't that a coincidence. I'm just on my way to see Mel... I mean Dr. Abelman, so it would be no trouble to escort you.'

'Oh... oh, Doctor, that's very kind of you, but we know you're awfully busy. And you said yourself—you have an urgent appointment... that lives are—'

'Nonsense, I insist. It would be my pleasure.'

Life at the hospital had taught Edgar many things: insincerity, rudeness, interruption. All of these were standard practice. But the most important part of becoming a doctor, was that whenever cornered or trapped, to always say there was an urgent appointment; rather, lives were at stake and people were dependent upon him. That being said, the chance to confront Melvin Abelman with his parents, was an opportunity that just couldn't be missed.

The doors opened.

'This way,' said Edgar, as he gestured in direction down the corridor. 'Please, allow me.'

He took the elderly lady's arm as he walked, as if out on a country stroll, and the elderly man followed alongside.

'Almost there now.'

As they rounded another corner, not more than a few metres from them was a doctor. His white coat was incredibly white; whiter than white in fact and not at all like the grubby stained one that Edgar wore. The doctor was attending a patient, and even though his back was turned to Edgar and the elderly couple, his body language was unmistakable. He paced like a caged animal, back and forth as he rolled his right hand, as if to say, 'Come on! Come on! Get on with it!'

A nurse, standing beside the bed, looked at the doctor the way an army recruit looks at a staff sergeant. Not quite in awe, but not quite in fear; eyes forward and stood to attention.

'Mel!' called the elderly lady, and the doctor's hand stopped rolling.

Whatever the doctor was saying, most probably highly informative, no longer mattered. Once he saw the elderly couple, it was not just his hand, but everything else that stopped. In fact, the only sound that followed from the doctor, leaked from his mouth; a sombre and somewhat deflated, *aah....*

This was a surprise. Dr. Melvin Abelman, now also known as, "Mel," reduced from being an odious tyrant to a small gentle boy with just three little letters. Even his large protruding caterpillar eyebrows seemed to shrink, or at least recede like a snail into its shell. Edgar was going to milk this for all that it was worth and enjoy every moment of doing so.

'Dr. Abelman!' he said enthusiastically.

Abelman's face, seeing his mother escorted on the arm of a subordinate he had not long berated, wore the look of one that had just been served an extremely large slice of humble pie.

'Can I escort your parents to your office?'

Abelman clearly struggled with the unexpected serving from Edgar because he found himself dumbstruck and unable to answer.

'Oh Melvin,' said Abelman's mother, 'this kind young doctor held the elevator for us and helped us all the way up here. He's such a lovely young man.'

'Yes... erm... quite. Very good, Spear. Please see them to my—'

'It's Doctor Spear, dear,' interrupted Abelman's mother. 'His name is Dr. Spear.'

Edgar smiled. No, it was more than a smile. It was a triumphant grin. And although he tried to conceal his delight, what else could he do? The parents of the chief physician had forced their son to recognise him as a doctor; as his equal. This was the stuff that legends were made of.

'Yes... quite,' muttered Abelman once again, now resigned to having to at least acknowledge Edgar's title. 'If you could see them to my office... *Dr. Spear.*'

'Why certainly, *Dr. Abelman*,' replied Edgar proudly, his chin held high.

Edgar walked the elderly couple into a corner office that had several large windows and provided a stunning view of the city. In the background he heard Abelman chastising the nurse, his frustrations and embarrassment of being corrected by his mother most likely being taken out on her.

'It's quite a view from up here, isn't it?' Edgar said happily.

'Oh yes. You can even see some of Mel's apartments from here. He has the penthouse there—and two apartments there,' said Abelman's mother, as she moved towards the window and pointed at a newly built complex.

Edgar's mouth dropped. 'Really?'

He knew that Abelman's salary was good but had no idea it was *that* good.

'Oh yes. I think he has twenty-three now doesn't he, dear?' she asked, as she turned to her husband.

'Twenty-four.'

'Wow!' exclaimed Edgar.

'Oh yes. Mel invested in social media didn't he, dear? Now let me think... when was it that—'

'Two years ago.'

It was obvious that Abelman had inherited his father's gift for small talk.

'Yes, that's right. Two years ago. It all seems to be going rather well. He did say that he was looking at another one now. But... do you know... for the life of me I can't remember—'

'Social media?' Edgar interrupted, before Abelman's father could speak.

She nodded. 'Yes, Doctor. Now what was that called again?'

The door opened, and in walked Abelman.

'Very good, Spear.'

Abelman's mother looked sternly at her son.

'Erm... *Dr. Spear...* that'll be all now. Thank you.'

'Mel dear, what was the name of that thing you invested in? You know that media thing?'

Abelman looked back at his mother. His cheeks were puffed, and his nostrils flared; he remained silent in defiance.

'Melvin!' she persisted sharply. 'The media thing. What's it called?'

His protest noted, Abelman looked sheepish, and the humbled child did as he was told, in part.

'Erm... Cali something or other,' replied Abelman. Hoping that in surrendering half an answer, his mother would drop her line of questioning.

'CaliChat?' asked Edgar.

'Erm... that might be it. CaliChat. Yes... sounds familiar.'

To learn that his superior had profited and done so well from CaliChat, the very online service that had once been the source of his humiliation, was a remarkable coincidence.

Edgar's eyes widened as he tried to conceal his dimpled smile. 'I went to university with the founder.'

Abelman's mouth fell agape, his face frozen for a moment. 'Do *you* know James Munro?'

He was more than intrigued, he seemed astonished that Edgar might be acquainted with someone like James. Perhaps it wasn't coincidence after all; perhaps it was fate? And if it was, then perhaps fate had also created the possibility for Edgar to profit from the Machiavellian Munro?

Edgar nodded. 'Yes, of course. We were undergrads at UCSF together for four years.'

'Swinging in the sunshine state, hey?'

In an instant, Abelman's tone and demeanour changed. He seemed warmer, friendlier, not at all like the Abelman that Edgar had come to despise these past two years. Edgar was at a loss. Was this a trap? Abelman talking to him like a human being? Another part of the secret doctor code that he hadn't been told about or picked up on yet? Uncertain, but unwilling to forego the opportunity, Edgar recalled his story.

'Well, I say together, we were best friends, actually…. The truth is that CaliChat was *my* idea. James and I worked on it together for the first years while I developed the algorithm. The basis for our machine learning. More of an A.I. really. How our servers would manipulate data from user profiles. Fill in the missing blanks and such… but I had to move on. I had to focus on my studies.'

'I never knew! Listen, why don't we take a coffee?' Abelman checked his Rolex. 'Say one-thirty? Would that work for you?'

'Sure. Why not? I'll erm… catch you at one-thirty.'

Trying to remain calm, yet confident, Edgar turned his attention to Abelman's parents.

'Well, it was a pleasure to meet you both. I'll bid you a good day and let you enjoy some time with your son.'

Edgar stepped out from the office, unsure if he had overstepped the mark. He knew how to use his charm and he now had Abelman's parents wrapped around his little finger. That might give him some degree of power, if he could use it wisely. Was this the day that he had been waiting for; the day that finally delivered a little leverage on Melvin Abelman?

From the corridor he could hear Abelman's mother speaking. 'Such a lovely young man, Mel. You must bring him over.'

Edgar smiled broadly as he walked back towards the elevator, feeling like a man who had just won the lottery. Nothing could be better than this, and nothing was going to take this away from him. He pressed the down button and waited until the doors opened, then squeezed inside the crammed elevator.

'Ground Floor, please.'

Edgar waited for the doors to close. Life was great; better than great, it was perfect. Here he was in an elevator, and everything was just wonderful. Everything except a nagging thought. His lips pursed and his brow dropped heavy as it knitted; his face falling victim to a frown. He chewed at the corner of his lip and began to backtrack in his mind. Why was he here? He had answered the phone and…. Edgar swallowed hard. Penny! Oblivious to the others, packed like sardines, he struggled to reach across and pressed the Open Doors button. He ran back out into the corridor, down the ward towards the nurse's staff room; knocked the door, then opened it. There she was. Inside and alone.

'Penny! I.,, I'm so sorry. I was—'

Edgar stopped. He could see that Penny was upset. Her mascara was smudged from the tears across her cheek. Her long blonde hair was loose, untangled, and not in its usual immaculately braided bun.

'What's wrong?'

'That man… that man's a brute. *He's a monster!*' blurted Penny, as she blew her nose with her tear-stained tissue.

'Who? Abelman?'

'Yes! Abelman.'

'Nah… he's not so bad. You just got to get to know him… understand him a bit.'

'Understand him?' she snapped. 'How can you understand a monster? I wish someone would take him away… far away…. As far away from here as they can!'

Penny sobbed inconsolably. Gathering herself for a moment, she tried to explain her reason for calling.

'I rang down because he was yelling at a patient—then he started to yell at *me*—right in front of her! He shouldn't be allowed to treat us this way, Edgar. To talk to patients like that. Someone has to take a stand. I thought if you were there... to see it—as a witness—then you could give a statement? Make a complaint with me?'

Edgar wasn't going to do anything to upset Abelman. Nor would he allow a simple nurse who held foolish romantic notions for him to do so either. Penny was a colleague; nothing more. However, knowing how she felt about him gave Edgar an advantage; an advantage meant leverage, and leverage meant a way to manipulate and get what he wanted.

'Penny, you're overreacting. Abelman's a good guy. It's just... well, you know... like all doctors he's passionate and his passion sometimes gets misunderstood—that's all.'

'*Misunderstood?* How does calling me "a pathetic woman" get misunderstood?'

Edgar struggled for a reply, for an excuse that might help, but nothing would; Penny was livid.

'Or calling the patient "an appalling actress" be excusable...? Edgar, he can't be allowed to continue like this. He thinks he's God. But he's not. He's a monster!'

Realising that Penny was not going to be swayed as easily as he hoped, Edgar decided instead to try and gain her sympathy. Sympathy always worked. Always gain the customers sympathy, that was the first rule of selling, and Penny needed to buy what Edgar had on sale. So, he began by drawing a long and overly exaggerated breath.

'Penny, his parents just arrived to tell him that his father is dying. That's why they're here—why they're in his office right now. I was in there to help break the news to him.'

'*You?* But he hates you!'

'Hate is such a strong word, don't you think? I prefer to say that we have a mutual respect for each other, even if we don't always see eye to eye.

'I've known the family for years. Abelman's parents practically raised me after my mother and father disappeared on a yacht in the Caribbean....

'Look, I know you're upset now, but think about Abelman. His whole world is falling apart. He really needs people around him you know, not against him. I know you're angry, and you have every right to be... but you don't have to do it for him. Do it for me. Do it for a friend asking another for a favour.'

'A—a friend...? I... I never knew. I never thought... I didn't know you thought of me—'

'Penny, you're so much more than just a friend. You must know how I feel about you—the effect that you have on me? I've always wanted, but never had the courage to ask you out. I mean... how could I? What would a beautiful, caring woman ever see in a lowly resident like me?'

'Oh Edgar, you're wrong I think you're amazing. I see—'

Edgar didn't need to see, what he needed was to be sure, and he interrupted Penny to make certain she understood.

'So, you'll do it? You'll do this little thing for me? Drop the complaint and support Abelman?'

Penny dried her eyes and took a deep breath to steady herself, then nodded.

'Of course, Edgar. Anything for you. I'll do anything you ask.'

Edgar smiled; the sale was made. Now, he needed to increase the incentive; a little something that would help to keep her side of the deal. Edgar got up and sat beside her. He placed his arm around her trembling shoulder, enjoying the power that he held, knowing that she was willing to do anything for him, and he spoke softly into her ear.

'Thank you, Penny.'

Believing that his feelings were true, she raised her arms in response to hold him; waiting for him to pull her close, she wanted to show, for him to see just how much she had longed for this moment and the touch of his embrace.

'Oh, Edgar,' she murmured, eyes closed in anticipation, but Edgar had already pulled away.

'Ow! My contact lens… I think it's slipped.'

Edgar pretended to gently rub at his closed eye, as if trying to find and reposition the wayward lens. With one eye closed, his other spotted the morning issue of The Boston Globe on the coffee table; the headline which read: *Senate to Investigate CaliChat.* Edgar was curious, reached down and picked up the newspaper.

The Senate is set to investigate CaliChat after allegations of data misuse, sale and collection. CaliChat's founder, James Munro, strenuously denies any wrongdoing and has previously said that CaliChat never collects, sells, or offers any user data to any third-party without the user's own expressed consent.

"CaliChat has always been focused on our user's privacy. Without user trust there simply wouldn't be a CaliChat. In fact, we only exist to serve our users," stated Munro.

Edgar smirked and read on.

CaliChat's growth has been nothing short of meteoric, and many opponents have suggested the reason for this is due to their questionable, often illicit, methods of collecting and manipulating data. Critics of CaliChat, the world's second largest social media site, have even gone as far as to say that the company is now a corporation beyond any juridical control. That data is collected without the user's consent and sold without the user's knowledge to fund company growth.

Edgar glanced away from the page and saw Penny staring, still wondering why their embrace had been broken.

'But Edgar… your lens?'

'My what?'

Enthralled by the news and the paper's main story, Edgar sat upright.

'Your contact lens?'

His interest in Penny quickly faded, and he waved her away with his hand. 'Oh... oh, that's fine.'

During the past six months, CaliChat has acquired nine competitors in the social market space and done so at a cost believed to be close to $20 billion US dollars.

'Twenty billion!' shouted Edgar.

The raising of these funds has never been explained with Munro previously stating they were the results of an earlier intensive investment program.

Munro is to appear at a congressional hearing later this month and expected to explain the origins of these funds as well as the methods used by CaliChat in harvesting, storing and using its members' data. At a request for interview, Munro gave no comment, saying only that the inquiry would end with his exoneration. The honourable members of the committee would see that CaliChat not only took privacy seriously but did more than any other platform to prevent data breaches or misuse.

Edgar put the paper down and looked at Penny; her face unable to hide the questions she so wanted to pose. But Edgar had no hankering for the emotional callings of an easily manipulated nurse, there were more important things at hand, and time was wasting; instead, he got up and went to the door.

'I'll see you soon,' he said. And like a lover that sneaks from a warm bed to leave his mistress before the dawn, Edgar turned, and left Penny longing for more.

Almost an hour passed before Abelman stood at Edgar's desk.

'Come on, Spear. Let's ditch these whites and get out of here.'

As they sat in the coffee shop beside the hospital, at the corner of North Grove Street, Edgar realised that he had never seen Abelman without his white coat on before. Sitting here now, in the outside world, Abelman looked... well... almost human.

'Great coffee isn't it, Spear? Love this place... and the waitress, did you get a good look at her? Boy, would I give her a latte—with extra cream! If you know what I mean?' said Abelman as he winked at Edgar.

Edgar was amazed at how much Abelman could say, ask, and mean with so very little.

Always looking for the angle, waiting for the sales opportunity, Edgar was happy, content to sit and listen as he gathered intel on his senior. So far, he was certain that Abelman was either a real man's man and a complete male chauvinistic pig, or, thought that Edgar was a bit slow and might have missed his comment, which was why he overly emphasised it.

'You're a strange one, Spear. You know, most of the interns that come through here go home crying or jump into the Charles.'

By "Charles," Abelman was referring to the Charles River, which meanders through Massachusetts, and had seen more than its fair share of suicides over the years.

'Either way, it's the same for me. If you can't take a punch, don't step into the ring. If you don't like the stakes, don't cry to the dealer. Go find another table—play somewhere else.

'Only suckers spin a wheel they can't control. And only chumps place a bet they know they're gonna lose.

'Now you... you I can't figure out, Spear. Are you a sucker or a hustler?'

Abelman paused and took another sip from his coffee.

'I know what they call me, "Melvin the Monster." You think a man gets a reputation like that for being a sweetheart? Or that I give a damn about what a group of deadbeats call me?

'Let me give you a piece of advice, Spear. A piece of Abelman Advice.

'There are two kinds of people in this world. The ones that get ahead and the ones that get left behind. Do I look like a guy that's trying to play catch up to you?

'I used to pull in close to five hundred grand a year playing the good doctor. Helping patients. Saving lives. Trying to make the world a better place—all that textbook baloney… and for what? A miserable five hundred grand? Come on… give me a break.

'It took me twenty goddamn years to get this far, and you think a few hundred grand is gonna cut it? Pay me back for all the hours I spent saving those pitiful, insignificant, ungrateful little ants?

'Give me a goddamn break.'

Abelman lowered his eyebrows. Almost squinting, he flicked his head in disgust as he dismissed his unworthy patients.

'There are millions of them, Spear. Millions of them just standing in line. Rolling in day after day with their problems. Stealing your life. Sucking the oxygen out of the air.

'Those people… they're the real problem in this world. It's not global warming or the nuclear threat. And it sure as hell ain't guys like me getting ahead. It's those people, Spear—*those ants*—they're the real problem. They're the real disease that's eating this earth.'

Edgar sat silently. The steam from his coffee carried the aroma continuously to his nostrils, tempting him to taste it, but he hadn't, and he wouldn't, not while Abelman spoke his mind. Like a sinner confessing to his priest, Edgar was compelled to hear everything. He needed to. How else could he pass a suitable judgement or offer penance?

Abelman paused; an invitation for Edgar to deliver his verdict. But Edgar was no "sucker." He knew exactly what he was doing. He knew that Abelman had just thrown his philosophy out there as a test, to gauge his reaction to such extreme beliefs; his mocking of the Hippocratic Oath, and everything that a physician was supposed to stand for. What Abelman didn't know—what he didn't realise—was that Edgar was no ordinary resident. He was so very much more than just a simple "hustler."

'You know, Dr. Abelman, when I was at med school, they asked me why I wanted to study medicine? I told them I wanted to become a neurosurgeon—to find new ways to cure victims of brain disorders. Discover new techniques that could one day correct the most complex organ in the human body. But that was then....

'When I moved to Mass Gen and began to attend patients myself, I wondered if I was really doing the right thing?'

Abelman was listening. Edgar had his attention and established that he was no idealist; that he was questioning his very reasons for being a surgeon. It would have been all too easy to have agreed with everything that Abelman had said, to try to impress his mentor by pretending that he mirrored his beliefs. But that was not the test. Not the real test. Abelman would never believe that Edgar was already bitter and tired of patients. He might, however, believe that a young resident was questioning his motivations for wanting to become a surgeon.

'At university, after I met Munro, I began to think that maybe there was a better way. An easier way—a way to get all the things that I deserved.'

And there it was, the reply to what Abelman was really asking. A sample of what Abelman wanted to know, which had in fact nothing to do with patients, or even being a doctor for that matter. Abelman wasn't testing Edgar's response to his extreme opinions about the sick and the infirm. It made no difference what he thought, if he approved or not. Edgar understood that, and only a sucker would allow themself to be so easily suckered. Abelman was asking if Edgar was enticed by temptation and greed? And Edgar had said, without actually saying, that perhaps he was, or at least, could be. He had set it up perfectly; it was time to move in now and close the sale.

'So, Munro and I began to develop CaliChat. We knew that if we sold user data without them knowing, then we could fund the platform to become the biggest in the world.'

Edgar spoke casually, as if nothing was morally wrong with the things that he said. There was no need to brag. No need to say anything more. He knew what he said was already enough. He had given Abelman the two other missing aspects of his personality, and now Abelman knew that Edgar was a man of intent; willing to be corrupted, easily so, if it helped him to achieve his ambition. It was the perfect storm, and Abelman was helpless to resist. *Temptation. Greed. Corruption. Ambition.* The very foundations upon which all successful business institutions are based. The four values held in highest regard by any respectless monster, and Edgar possessed them all. If ever Abelman was in search of an apprentice, then that search was surely over. Abelman reached across the table as he grabbed Edgar by the cheek, shaking him the way only a father can, to show his pride for his son at scoring the winning goal.

'Would you look at this kid! *Would — you — look — at — this — kid!*' shouted Abelman, gaining the unwanted attention of a young couple at another table.

Edgar looked at the couple who were now staring, and Abelman saw that Edgar was distracted; he turned to face them.

'What?'

It wasn't just his tone, but the way in which he spoke that made Abelman sound so threatening. The couple nervously shook their heads. They looked at each other, then looked to the floor and decided to leave. Edgar was amazed. One word was all that it took to intimidate them; to scare them into doing what he wanted. That was power. Real power. The power of fear. Something that Edgar desired but would need to learn. And as for Abelman, he was not only impressed—he was sold; signed, sealed, delivered with a cherry on the top.

'I knew it. *I — knew — it!*'

Abelman could barely contain himself in the crowded coffeeshop.

'Listen, Spear… Spear? What's your real name?'

'My real name, sir?'

'Yeah, you know, your first name.'

'It's Edgar.'

'Edgar? Jeez… I can't call you Edgar… sounds like an undertaker.'

Abelman paused.

'Look, Eddy—oh, and you, you call me Mel. Ok? From now on you call me Mel…. Do you think you can get me close to this Munro guy? Set up a meeting?'

A meeting with James Munro? That would be difficult; impossible actually, because Edgar had nothing but hate for the man. Despite the years that had passed since that day of the graduation, Edgar's animosity had not eased a bit. In fact, if anything, it had only grown. Festered, like an open wound, decaying into contempt and loathing. His hatred wasn't the kind that people often had for things like cauliflower or cabbage; for rainy days or missing a bus. It was a very different kind of hate. A purer kind. The kind of hate that tensed every fibre in the body and made teeth grind. And this hate was like a poison, an infection that was consuming him from the inside out.

Since leaving California, not a day had passed that Edgar hadn't thought about how he was going to kill James Munro. He hoped that one day he would be lying on his operating table. Edgar would stand over him, scalpel in hand, ensure there was no anaesthesia, then make sure that Munro felt nothing but torturing pain; misery like Edgar suffered on graduation day. When he last spoke to him, he warned Munro that the next cut would be deeper, and Edgar knew precisely how deep he could cut while still keeping his victim alive. It was that thought, the idea of Munro's life hanging by a thread, by the tip of Edgar's blade, that had kept him going through these first difficult years as a resident doctor. Now Abelman, Melvin the Monster, the man responsible for making his life a living hell, was asking him if he could set up a meeting with Munro? There was no need to waste time or to think about it; the answer was simple. *Never!*

He could never do it. He would never do it. He would give Abelman his reply and that would be that.

'Sure,' said Edgar, 'I could arrange a meeting. I know he's busy... but sure, I could get us together.'

Edgar's hatred wasn't going to stand in the way of his greed and ambition. It certainly wasn't going to put an end to this talk with Abelman. The game was just beginning, and Edgar about to play. This was his opportunity; his chance to get to the high stakes table and he had no intention of going home, leaving this coffeeshop, until he left with all the spoils.

'That's what I wanted to hear. You know this Munro guy... I like his style. I mean, he's made me a lot of money... a serious amount of money, Eddy. But it's nothing compared to what we could earn if we sat down and talked.'

'Talked?'

'About precision.

'You see, this social media stuff... it's just the tip of the iceberg. You've gotta look below if you wanna know—if you wanna see what's *really* going on. I mean they all sell data... they'll sell anything about anyone to anybody.

'Take a user, get their profile—what you need—then sell it.... Push it on to the companies who try to sell whatever the user says it is they're looking for. New refrigerator. Pair of sneakers. I mean, you know this—*everyone* knows it. They don't like it. They don't wanna admit it. But everyone knows it. It's easy business—no guarantees— just hit and miss.

'Now, you and me... we don't do hit and miss, Eddy. We're in the precision business.

'If you're holding a scalpel then you better be prepared to use it— to cut clean. You suture a wound you better not leave a scar. You know what I mean? It's *precision*, Eddy. It's all about precision.

'Take a look at this congressional stuff going on now—'

'Yes. It's ridiculous. The whole thing—' Edgar tried to voice his agreement. Abelman, however, was uninterested in anything that Edgar had to say at the moment and put an end to his interruption.

'—all these sites... they're all the same. One starts up, does well, buys another one out. One starts up, does bad, gets bought out. It's the name of the game—competition—survival of the fittest... the way it's always been.

'The small grow big, Eddy. The big get bigger. It's business. Who cares? Why is Congress getting involved in this?'

Edgar looked at Abelman, unsure if he was expecting a response or not.

'I tell you why... because when the big become the biggest, they get power. The power of information, Eddy. And if you have all the information then there's money to be made. It's there for the taking.

'The Senate don't care about your data. They don't care about these users. They care about the money it makes.

'If you pull some founder in front of a committee, you make an example of him. You show the world that it's ok to be an entrepreneur—make your money—as long as you don't make too much. As long as you play by their rules and give them their share, they'll leave you well alone. But the day you flip them the bird... that's the day they give you the shake down. When you see them for who they really are—a glorified mob out for a hustle.'

Edgar remained fixed on Abelman.

'It was like that with the railroads, the car industry, the pensions, the pharmaceuticals, you name it. Mark my words, wherever there's a dime to be made, there's a congressional hearing at the end of it.

'But you, me, and this Munro... we're gonna change that, Eddy. You know how?'

Edgar was again unsure if he should offer an answer, or if Abelman would continue to read out the monologue he had clearly been waiting to express for so very long. Taking a chance to remain a part of the conversation, Edgar decided to speak out.

'Yes.'

'That's right,' said Abelman. So completely focused and committed to his own thoughts; Edgar could have said anything that he wanted, and the reaction would have been the same.

'A guy walks into a lamp store. He looks at a lamp. He asks the guy in the lamp store, "How much do you want for this lamp?" The guy tells him it's four hundred bucks. "Oh," he says, "that's a bit out of my league."

'Ten years ago, all of those social media sites used the location on your phone to know where you were. They knew you were in a lamp store and the next time you went online....'

Bam! Abelman smacked his hands together; Edgar jumped.

'They hit you with an ad for a new lamp. How did people think they were able to do that? With magic? I mean come on.

'These social sites have been selling your data since the day they were made—since the day you signed up. The only difference today? The difference with CaliChat? Let me tell you.

'A guy walks into the same lamp store. He looks at a lamp. He asks the guy in the lamp store, "How much do you want for this lamp?" The guy tells him it's four hundred bucks. "Oh," he says, "that's a bit out of my league."

'Same story, right...? *Wrong!* Because now CaliChat activated the mic on the guy's phone at the minute he walked into the store. It's been recording everything. *Everything.* So now, the next time the guy goes online, he doesn't just get hit with an ad for a new lamp. He gets hit with an ad for a new lamp that costs less than the four hundred bucks he was quoted for.

'You see?

'The only thing that CaliChat has done is make the guy's data more relevant. And if you make the data more relevant, then you make it more valuable.

'If my lamps cost a thousand bucks, and I'm paying for ads but the people who see them can't afford them, then you're wasting my time. And you know the only thing that's worse than wasting my time, Eddy...? It's wasting my money.

'But if you could guarantee that the people who see my ads are not only looking for a product like mine, but looking *exactly* for a product like mine—then I'm giving you my money. All of it. Every nickel and every dime....

'This hearing business... don't listen to what anyone tells you. This is Congress after their piece of the pie—nothing more. Bunch of greedy little rats trying to steal a slice of the cake.... Munro took all the risk. He made all the money. Now he's got all the power and the government want their share.

'Don't get me wrong. Munro's a risk taker, I like risk takers, but he's not in the precision business, and his CaliChat sure as hell isn't.'

Abelman, looked around, he checked to make sure that no one was listening and that no one else was paying any unnecessary attention to them. Once satisfied, he pushed his coffee to the side and leant across the table; his caffeine-soaked breath tickling Edgar's face.

'Eddy, what if I was to tell you that I could not only give you a customer, but I could *guarantee* that they would buy a lamp from you right there and then. What do you think that would be worth? What would you be willing to pay to get that customer?'

Edgar knew that this time he had to give an answer. The sermon was nearing its end and Abelman would soon reveal the moral of the story.

'What would I pay?' asked Edgar, as he paused to buy himself a precious few seconds and conjure up an intelligent answer.

'Well, I'd see what it costs to make my lamps... I'd have to cover my costs of course. Then I'd take that away from my asking price... and I'd need a little margin—some room for profit.... Take that away... and then... I guess I'd be willing to pay you up to the amount that's left.'

'Yeah, you would think that wouldn't you. But you'd be wrong, Eddy.'

'How so?'

'You see, if it was all about cashflow, that's exactly how it would work. But business—real business—*big* business… doesn't work that way.

'You know what I'd be willing to pay for that customer? I'd be willing to pay as much as it costs to make sure my competitor doesn't get him. That's what *I'd* be willing to pay. And that's a darn sight more than a miserable thousand bucks.'

Abelman sank back into his chair and stared at Edgar. He raised his eyebrows, and the caterpillars animated back to life. He folded his arms, smugly, filled with self-satisfaction, as if having passed on some divine life-changing knowledge to Edgar. But Edgar, who understood the moral of the story—that the value of the customer was worth more than the price of the product, at least to the right seller—still didn't understand how? How could Abelman guarantee that someone would buy something there and then? How could he force someone to buy anything at all, unless he put them under some form of duress? Was this what Abelman meant? Blackmail? Was this how he would guarantee sales, through threats and intimidation? How he made so much money? Not as a monster, but as a criminal; as Melvin the Mobster?

'You're not talking about choice? You're talking about control' Edgar said, finally.

Abelman leant forward once again.

'I'm talking about precision, Eddy. I'm talking about *the price of precision.*'

Abelman leaned back and took another sip from his coffee.

'You know Munro… do you think he values the price of precision?'

Values the price of precision? thought Edgar. What was Abelman really asking him here? Was everything a cryptic challenge? A test?

He wasn't just asking for a meeting with Munro, although that in itself was impossible. What Abelman was also asking, what in fact he really was asking, was if he thought Munro was corrupt? Or could at least be corruptible?

In Edgar's mind, Abelman wanted a meeting with Munro, that much was clear. It was the basis for his interest in Edgar. And although Edgar had said yes to the meeting and managed to acquire a tenuous friendship with Abelman by doing so; the truth was that there were no lies that Edgar could spin to ever make such a meeting happen. For that, he would have to go back to James, swallow his pride, conceal his hatred, hide his contempt, plead to see him, beg him to let Abelman speak, pray that he listened, and then, after all that, hope that Munro shared the same values as Abelman. Or rather, valued "the price of precision" as he more eloquently put it. That being said, Abelman's question was only half the problem, because even if what Abelman had asked was possible, the real problem was if Edgar would be willing to do it; to crawl back to James? And to do this, or to even think about doing this for someone else, even for Abelman, was unimaginable. On the other hand, to do this for himself, for what having a friend such as Abelman might do for him, for his career? Well, that was different; that was different all together. Of course, he could. Of course, he would. Of course, he must. And without further hesitation, or leaving any doubt, Edgar replied.

'Yes. Yes, I know he does.'

3

THE FIRST PROMISE

By the fourth day, the congressional hearing was on every news network and cable channel across the country. The day's events were summarised the following morning on the front pages of every national newspaper. Such was the popularity of CaliChat, and the charisma of its enigmatic founder, that the hearing was no longer just news; it was *the* news.

The hearing had turned into a soap opera with a script of biblical proportions. It was David versus Goliath and opinions were strong and wholly divided. On the one side, there were those who saw Munro as a young upstart that had broken the law, ventured too far, and should be held to account. For those, no minimal punishment would be good enough; a lifetime behind bars was necessary in order to teach such villains a deterring lesson. On the other side, there were those who hated everything that was run or imposed by the state. Those who despised the term "federal" and the connotations of autocracy that it implied. For them, the Senate represented the epitome of a broken corrupt system; a bloated line of bureaucrats who had constantly infringed upon the rights of every citizen, and the time had come to rebel and raze the establishment to the ground. Munro was their hero, and every coarse sarcastic remark that came from his mouth served simply to reaffirm that he was also their champion.

A news reporter spoke silently from outside Capitol Hill on the muted television, as Edgar flicked through the pages of a patient's chart.

'Well, it's a complicated procedure, Mr. Clydesdale,' said Edgar. 'We've had great success with this technique, and certainly Dr. Abelman is one of the world's foremost experts in this field. You know, you really are very lucky to have him as your physician.'

Mr. Clydesdale smiled, propped up by several pillows on his hospital bed. Clydesdale was a polite elderly man, observant and in no hurry at all. Like all astute elderly men, he was very good at using questions that never actually seemed like questions as a way of steering a conversation to get the answers to things that were troubling him.

'I know, Doctor,' replied Clydesdale. 'I was wondering… is that a West Coast accent I hear? Californian perhaps?'

Edgar looked away from Clydesdale's chart; a fleeting glance as he smiled a most ingenuous smile, neither caring to answer nor offer the opportunity to engage in conversation.

'It is, Dr. Spear? Isn't it?'

But Edgar had no intention of responding. He had already acknowledged Clydesdale once, so there was no need to raise his head and do it again. Instead, Edgar continued to browse through the chart offering only an occasional, albeit disapproving tut.

'It's just… I knew a David and Olivia Spear when I lived in California… and Spear is such an unusual name.'

'Hmmm,' mumbled Edgar. His attention fixed on the notes. 'Yes. Yes. I'm sure it is, Mr. Clydesdale.'

Ignored and unable to satisfy his curiosity, Clydesdale decided that a less courteous, more direct approach, was required to gain response from the young doctor.

'Do you know when I will be seeing Dr. Abelman? I haven't actually seen him yet.'

Edgar's eyes met with Clydesdale and expressed their displeasure as he passed the uninteresting chart to Penny.

'Dr. Abelman is an especially important man, Mr. Clydesdale. He's incredibly busy and his time is *very* precious.'

'Oh, I'm sure it is... only, I was told that he would be speaking with me personally. I would so very much like to meet with him, Doctor, and hear what he thinks about my—'

'I'm sure you would. But as you can appreciate, Mr. Clydesdale, if Dr. Abelman used his time to speak with patients individually then he wouldn't have any time for surgery now, would he?'

Penny stared in disbelief. She couldn't help but notice that in recent months Edgar's bedside manner had deteriorated; his attitude had become increasingly pompous and patronizing. He was colder, more distant and less interested in those he tended to, and there were times when it felt as though she was watching a younger version of Abelman; something she neither liked nor approved of.

'He's not a good role model for you, Edgar,' said Penny, as they walked alongside each other towards the next patient's bed.

'Who?' asked Edgar, barely listening.

'Abelman. The man's a monster, and you know it.'

Edgar stopped and turned to face her. 'It's *Dr. Spear*. And the monster's name is *Dr. Abelman*.

'Nurse Davis, I would prefer that while you're in that uniform, and in this hospital, you address myself and Dr. Abelman with the titles that we're both entitled to.'

Penny was at a loss. "Entitled to," was this how Edgar was going to treat her? How he was going to speak to her; to scold the woman who adored him like a child? She had lived in hope of Edgar. A chance to prove herself to him. Consoled herself night after night with one thought; that just a few minutes alone away from here, from this hospital, was all that it would take to show him how she felt. Yet despite that one failed embrace all those months ago—a lifetime ago—Penny hadn't been given the chance. And as is so often the case, the truth was not in agreement with the hopes of the heart, because the truth was that Penny was in love with a man who didn't love her in return.

'But Ed... I... I thought that—' Penny stuttered, unable to speak.

Having delivered a knife into her heart, Edgar was now poised to tear it open.

'Thought *what*, Nurse Davis? That you and I?' Edgar looked at her with disgust, his nose upturned, and he began to laugh. 'Don't be ridiculous!'

Edgar's laugh was so false, so forced, that the very ground upon which Penny stood crumbled beneath her feet. How could he be so cruel? So heartless? Frozen in shock, at the horror of his manner, her reaction made Edgar laugh all the more. Why just the thought of it, to imagine that someone as lowly, as menial as she could ever hope to aspire to the heights and aspirations of his greatness? It was laughable, ludicrous, and Edgar burst into maniacal laughter. He roared raucously, stripping the final threads of Penny's dignity, until eventually, he was able to gain control of his hysterics.

'Not *even* if you were the last woman on this earth,' he sneered.

Penny's lips trembled, on the verge of tears. Edgar stood upright, prepared to humiliate her further. Then, as if to underline that neither Penny, nor her feelings meant anything to him, he changed the subject entirely. 'I will order an MRI for Mr. Beckett this morning.'

Her world in tatters and dreams destroyed, Penny was desperate to disguise her pain; to hide from Edgar how much he had hurt her. But her mouth continued to tremble, and her eyes began to well; nothing she could do would stop her tears from flowing.

'I... I... I'm sorry, Doctor.... Please, excuse me.'

She brushed Edgar aside to find sanctuary, fleeing hurriedly towards the haven of the nurse staff room.

'Nurse Davis!' he shouted after her. 'Davis...! I'm speaking to you!' he screamed. But Penny failed to stop or turn around; her defiance losing Edgar all authority in front of his patients.

How dare she? How dare she defy him? Who did she think she was? Edgar was furious, in no mood to be dismissed or ignored by a common nurse. The short fuse of his temper was ignited, and he stood helpless to the rage that began to burn through his veins. It spread at alarming speed, boiling his blood in an instant and searing his innards in hatred. He stormed past the patient rooms; his fury gaining momentum with every stride that he took through the corridor maze. His eye caught a glimpse of the staff room sign, and he breathed in deeply; lungs filled close to bursting as he grabbed at the handle with his jaws clenched. The door slammed against the opposite wall with such force that the frame and the hinges which held it shook.

'Edgar!'

A cold sudden shudder loosened his jaw as his lips broke apart. Unable to breathe—to vent his fury—he could not expel the anger pressed hard against his chest. There on the sofa, with his arm around Penny, sat an ogling Abelman with a lecherous grin.

'Could you give us a moment? Nurse Davis is a little upset.'

He stared; Abelman winked in reply, his comforting arm tightening further.

'Dr. Spear...? A moment... if you please.'

'Um... erm... of course, Dr. Abelman. I... I'm so s-sorry to intrude.'

He stepped back into the corridor, leaning the door ajar. Careful not to close it entirely and leave just enough of a gap for their words to flow out to his listening ears.

Despite Abelman's apparent concern, a thinly veiled attempt to show that he cared, Penny never spoke of Edgar. Instead, she told Abelman that she had received some upsetting news from an aunt and needed a moment alone. From behind the door, Edgar could hear the cheap and repeated attempts of Abelman to increase their physical contact. His relentless efforts to console her and to take advantage of her current fragile state. He was like a spider, patiently setting his trap, as he spun his web around her. His arms offered her comfort, a place to land that would be hard to escape. But Abelman was no spider, he was a lion stalking his prey; his claws were sharp, and he was ready to pounce. It was more than enough, and with no appetite for the hunt, Edgar returned to his patients.

On any given Monday morning, the only sound to echo through the sterile corridors of the hospital was that of doctors discussing their family weekends. It was always the same. Picnics, barbeques, sporting events, trivial small talk that Edgar really had no time or tolerance for. But this was no ordinary Monday, and this morning was like no other he had experienced before. The corridors were alive with energy, a buzz that spread like a wildfire across an arid grassland. As Edgar walked past an orderly pushing a patient in a wheelchair, he overheard him ask the patient if he had seen the news?

Edgar, like so many others, had become so used to the daily reports from Congress and the hearing, that it seemed as though there was no real news left in the story anymore. He checked his wristwatch; a cheap imitation of Abelman's Rolex he once bought from a guy selling on a corner downtown. The man had told Edgar not to wear it in the shower, but other than that, it was the real thing and a bargain for just thirty dollars. The watch said 9:05 a.m., meaning it was probably somewhere around 9:20 a.m., or maybe even later. Regardless, it was still a little early, far too early for any real action from the hearing, up on "The Hill." Then Edgar remembered his rounds earlier that morning, before the incident with Penny. The television volume was on mute when he spoke to Clydesdale, but the reporter was most definitely speaking from outside Capitol Hill. Edgar had to know more, and he followed behind the orderly as he continued to talk with the patient.

'The way he walked out... my oh my, did you see Senator Granson's face?' the orderly laughed. 'I thought he was going to have a tizzy fit and burst his breeches!'

Walked out? Had Munro walked out of the hearing? Edgar thought. What happened?

Edgar stopped by a sleeping patient's bed, took the remote control, and turned on the television. It was the same reporter that he had seen earlier, so he turned up the volume.

'.... And in a grandstand finale that has shocked the nation, the inquest into CaliChat and the alleged wrongdoings of its founder, James Munro, took an unexpected twist this morning.

'When asked if he had explicitly ordered the sale of data to several leading consumer brands, Munro, apparently tired and agitated at having answered the question on a number of previous occasions replied, "Only yours, Senator."

'While Munro's comments were met with laughter from the gallery, Senator Granson reminded Munro that he was under oath and the confession that he had just made was not without consequence.

'Munro replied to the senator saying, "These hearings are a farce and an insult to everyone in our great nation." A response that was met with loud applause.

'As Senator Granson called the hearing to order, Munro told Congress, "I will no longer take part in this witch hunt. We, the people, deserve more. We, the people, expect more. We, the people, demand more!" before walking out of the proceedings.

'Despite being ordered to return to his seat, Munro left the hearing, but had this to say to reporters waiting outside.

"Ladies and gentlemen, I came to these hearings to put an end to the vicious and untrue rumours that have circulated about my company. I have co-operated with the senators to the best of my ability and answered all of their questions with truth and honesty. Sadly, this hearing does not want to hear the truth... they want to make you believe that CaliChat gathers your data and sells it without your permission. This is a lie—an *absolute* lie—and nothing, I repeat nothing, could be further from the truth…. I'm just an average guy… like all of you—"

'At which point, Munro was interrupted by a voice from the crowd.

"But you're not like us, James, you have six billion dollars, and I don't have a dime!"

'As laughter rang out, Munro responded to his critic.

"Then you can have my money!"

'The crowd cheered, forcing Munro to lower his hands, as he asked for quiet and the chance to finish.

"I will give twenty dollars to every man, woman and child. That's twenty dollars to each of our three hundred million citizens. You can all have my mon—"'

Suddenly, Edgar felt a hand on his shoulder, and he turned away from the broadcast.

'Don't let me interrupt, Eddy,' said Abelman. Edgar's attention was taken, split between watching the screen and needing to listen to whatever his mentor had to say.

'He's incredible, isn't he?' continued Abelman in awe. 'He knows he can't win, so what does he do? He gives his money away to the people. Amazing… he'll become the greatest folk hero that ever lived after this stunt.

'D'you think they'll put him away now? Lock him up and make a martyr out of him as well? Never… he's not gonna spend a second behind bars. He's as free as a bird and he just made sure there's no cage big enough to hold him.

'Taking on Congress… that takes balls, Eddy. But taking them on when you know you're guilty? Well… that takes king-sized balls with a death wish.

'You know they were always gonna find him guilty, right? He knew that. So, why wait?

'He's a marketing genius…. If anyone hadn't heard about CaliChat before these hearings, they damn sure know about it now. Munro just gave every Joe in this country twenty reasons to remember the name…. Wouldn't surprise me if this was his plan all along?'

Abelman placed his other hand upon Edgar's shoulder and turned him around.

'So, Eddy, when am I gonna meet him?'

'Soon, Mel. I was thinking we should wait until this hearing business settles down?'

'It's done and dusted now, Eddy. Done and dusted. So, make it happen.'

Abelman released Edgar to head to his next appointment. He had walked less than five metres before he stopped, looked back and stared.

'Soon, Eddy…. Make it soon.'

Abelman turned once again and continued off down the corridor. Edgar looked back at the screen as the story returned to the news desk and the anchors began to discuss the developments of the hearing. He could feel his heart begin to pound. He knew that the pressure had begun to build and would not stop until he had met Abelman's demand. The congressional hearings had bought Edgar some time in which his superficial friendship had been allowed to develop these past weeks. Time now, however, was moving against him. He knew that he would have to reach out to James at some point, but he hadn't even tried yet. How could he? He hated him. He hated him with every ounce of his being. He wished Congress would have locked him up and thrown away the key. That would have been easy—for the best— but instead, it seemed Munro had bought himself a free pass. Edgar was going to need more time; he was going to have to make more time, at least until he could find a way to get to Munro.

The rest of the day was a blur between patients and writing notes. Evening fell, and Edgar readied himself to go back to his small one-room apartment in the West End. He pressed the down button, to call the elevator and make his way to the Ground Floor exit. As the elevator doors opened, there, much to his unexpected surprise, was Abelman.

'Hey, Eddy! What's happening?'

'Just heading home.'

'Home...? Little early, isn't it? You can't go home yet... the night's young and still ours for the taking. Wait for me by the entrance... I'll be there in five.'

Edgar was tired. He had been thinking about James Munro all day. The last thing he needed now was more pressure from Abelman, but Edgar was in no position to set the agenda. He took a seat on one of the hard metal benches by the entrance and rested his eyes.

'Eddy? Eddy...? *Eddy!*'

The prod from Abelman was enough to awaken Edgar; the patterned grid of the bench was impressed deeply upon his cheek.

'Sorry, buddy... things just ran on. Let's get some drinks. I'm dying to hear about the Munro meeting.'

Drinks? The Munro meeting? It was dark outside now and late for a young resident who had an early start.

'Erm... sure. Sure,' said Edgar, dazed and confused; still half asleep as he gathered his things.

They left through the entrance and made their way towards the car park. Abelman pointed at a sparkling silver Porsche that looked streamlined and fast.

'911 Turbo S Cabriolet. Beautiful, isn't it?' he asked rhetorically. 'Come on, get in! It's custom upholstery. Handmade Italian leather. The finest.'

Abelman loved his car, and he had a bulleted list of all the wonderous extras he had afforded in having it made.

'I had the engine modified as well. People should hear me before they see me. You know what I mean? They should know I'm coming!'

Abelman smiled and winked at Edgar, then turned on the ignition as the angry roar from the engine caused Edgar to flinch.

'Relax Eddy... you're in safe hands. The best,' said Abelman, as he sent the car flying forward.

'I've been thinking,' he shouted, over the sound of the engine; the top down and air screaming loud past their heads. 'That Penelope, I bet she's a tiger.... You know her, don't you? How well would you say?'

Edgar said nothing, pretending that he couldn't hear.

'Nurse Davis....' repeated Abelman, refusing the silence of Edgar as an adequate answer.

'Oh, you mean Penny?'

'Yeah. Yeah, that's her... Penny. What do you think? Can you help a friend out?'

Abelman turned a corner and brought the car to an abrupt halt. Edgar jolted forward, restrained only by the seat belt and Abelman laughed.

'I never wear them. I've got control and I keep it!'

Edgar looked up and saw a large sign that read *Domino's*, written in pale blue neon. As they walked into the bar, they were greeted almost immediately by a waiter.

'Ah, good evening, Dr. Abelman. Table for two?'

'Yeah,' said Abelman before he paused. 'No... actually, better make that three. Or... wait a minute....'
Abelman seemed uncertain and turned to Edgar.

'You know what? Let's just keep it for two. Eddy won't be here long anyway, will you, Eddy?'

'Erm... I guess not,' replied Edgar, equally uncertain, as the waiter led them to a quiet table in the corner.

The waiter seated them and asked Abelman if he would be having his usual? Abelman nodded.

'And for the gentleman?'

'I'll have a—'

'He'll have a Coke. Better make that a Zero… don't want the kid all sweet and sugary, do we?'

The waiter nodded and left to order the drinks. Abelman, as usual, got straight down to business.

'You know why I love this place, Eddy?'

But before Edgar had the chance to speak, Abelman answered for himself.

'The name… it's the name…. *Domino's.*

'You ever see those shows on the net? On YouTube?' he asked, and again before Edgar could respond, he continued. 'They're incredible. Some of them are just incredible.' Abelman paused for effect.

'You know, in many ways those little bricks are a lot like people—you stand one up, and it's easy to knock it down. Know what I mean?

'You can knock one down in the middle of bunch of dominoes and no one sees it. No one thinks about it. No one cares… it just disappears into the pile. Know why? Because they all look the same—they're *all* just little bricks.

'But… if you put them in their place. If you put them where they're supposed to be—where you need them to be—and you put enough of them together… then the whole thing goes down. You know what then?'

And again, before Edgar could speak, Abelman replied.

'Then you don't see the bricks, Eddy…. What you see is a show. A spectacle. And everyone who sees the spectacle, says *wow!'*

Abelman paused again.

'You know why they say wow, Eddy?'

And yet again, before Edgar could speak, he answered.

'Anticipation… it's all about anticipation. You see, they spend days, weeks, sometimes months setting those things up. After the first few bricks fall—you're wondering if this is gonna work? If it's gonna go all the way, or if it's gonna fail...? If all they did was waste their time....

'The longer it goes, the more bricks fall and the more excited you become. You're excited to see if it's gonna succeed—yes.... But you're just as excited to see if it's not. And that's the anticipation, Eddy. You see, you — just — don't — know.

'So, you watch knowing that all it takes is just *one* little brick, *one* tiny piece to miss its place. To stay standing when it should've gone down and the whole thing stops. The whole thing fails. There's no spectacle, no grand finale, and no one to say—*wow!*

'Just *one* tiny brick, Eddy... one tiny brick can spoil the whole show. You understand?'

Edgar realised that Abelman was not having a conversation about dominoes or describing his love for the game. He was using it as a metaphor. Perhaps to offer some more invaluable Abelman Advice? Or perhaps to describe people who got in his way; who didn't do as they were told?

'Now, the meeting with Munro. When's it gonna happen? None of us are getting any younger,' said Abelman, his rhetoric over and expecting a response.

'I was thinking in a couple of weeks,' replied Edgar, as he pretended to have given the issue some thought. 'I was thinking James would need a few days to get over this hearing and get his head straight before he'd be open to discuss anything new.'

But Abelman was not a man who liked to wait, or to be told to do so, and was obviously unhappy. He prepared to give Edgar his opinion on the suggestion as the waiter returned carrying their drinks on a tray.

'Gentlemen,' said the waiter, as he placed a bourbon with ice, in front of Abelman. The waiter then moved around to the right side of Edgar and first placed a drinks napkin on the table in front of him.

'And a Coke Zero, for sir.'

The waiter placed the bottle of Coke upon the napkin before he then moved around to the left side of Edgar and placed a glass with three ice cubes in front of him. Abelman tapped his fingers repeatedly upon the table and the waiter sensed his impatience.

'That's fine,' said Abelman, 'He can pour it himself.'

The waiter stepped back from the table and left. Abelman took a sip of his bourbon and it seemed to sooth him like a magic elixir that changed his mood.

'Yeah. Yeah, that's smart, Eddy. He has to settle this fine. Pay out on his promise so that'll take some days—a week—maybe more.... You know the shareholders will have to agree and they'll have to raise the capital from somewhere—maybe liquidate a few things—get the transfers done. So, yeah, I'm thinking a couple of weeks sounds fair.'

Settle his fine...? What fine? thought Edgar. Had there been more developments to the hearing? Had something happened while he waited for Abelman? Edgar nodded reassuringly, not wanting to appear uninformed.

'I think the fine might have knocked him back a bit,' said Edgar, hoping that Abelman would elaborate and say more.

'A *bit?* Jeez... a billion-dollar fine would rock anyone!' smiled Abelman. 'That's what I love about you, Eddy. Congress hands the largest fine in history to a CEO, and you just brush it off—like it's nothing.' He continued to smile and shook his head. 'You're a cold one, Eddy... I'll give you that.... Ice cold.'

Abelman took another sip of his bourbon and raised a finger, pointing it around the room, casually, and at no one in particular.

'You know, most of the guys here wouldn't be able to sleep at night if they got fined with anything close to that. I mean... can you imagine... if one of these little bricks got a lousy ten thousand dollars fine from the IRS—their whole world would come down. They couldn't raise that kind of capital. They'd sell their house. Their car. Hell... some of them would probably sell their wives!' Abelman sniggered, finding the idea of husbands selling their wives to pay off their debts amusing. 'But you... you see the bigger picture, Eddy. A billion dollars is peanuts compared to what we're gonna make. To what Munro is gonna make with us. Just you wait and see.'

Abelman's face seemed suddenly malign in the low lighting of the bar. It wasn't Edgar's imagination, or a trick of the light, Abelman's expression had changed. The bourbon, it seemed, no longer soothed, but fuelled his impatience, and Edgar could tell that Abelman had changed his mind about the suggestion.

'Look, Eddy... I really don't wanna wait weeks. I wanna see him now. If Munro is the kind of man that I think he is then he won't give a rat's ass about the fine or the six billion.

'It's a day of reckoning, Eddy—*A day of days!* We need to show Munro that we're not just in the game... we need to show him that we've the only hand worth playing.'

Edgar had to think fast. James had not only promised to give away all his wealth, but he had also now been handed a billion-dollar fine. The hearing must have found him guilty, yet apparently, he had also managed to avoid being sent to jail. After all, Abelman would not be pushing to meet with him if he was about to become a jailbird, so how did he achieve that? And how could Edgar possibly suggest a date to meet James when he was simply fishing for information; trying to play along.

'Absolutely, Mel, which is why I was thinking about maybe this Friday?'

Edgar was so desperate to stay in Abelman's favour, that he grabbed a day out of mid-air. His only thought was to give Abelman something that he needed now. Something that might help soothe and return him to a more pleasurable mood.

'This Friday...? The twelfth?'

'Yes. I was going to call in sick and—'

'Eddy!' interrupted Abelman, as a broad smile filled his face. He clapped his hands, happy at what he heard. 'Now *that's* what I'm talking about! There's the Eddy that I'm looking for!'

Abelman took another sip from his bourbon, and his face changed once again. He had only been happy for a few brief moments, when already, he had a look that was serious and solemn. What else could Edgar do? How else could he please him? What more could he want? Abelman leant forward.

'You know I can pull strings, Eddy? I mean *real* strings. The kind of strings that make things happen—you understand what I'm saying? Strings that are thicker than ropes... the kind of ropes you can only dream about.'

Edgar nodded.

'You set this up—make this happen—and you won't have to worry about your residency. Your seven-year stretch at the Slaughterhouse disappears.... Understand?'

Abelman clicked his fingers to show Edgar what he meant. That he could bring an end to his residency, in a flash.

'Y-yes, Mel.'

'I'll even sweeten the pot for ya, Eddy. You get him onboard— use your influence over Munro to take our deal—and I'll go one better. You'll never have to worry about licensing or board certifications. I'll take care of them.'

Abelman looked around knowing that no one could hear their conversation above the music in the darkened corner of the bar. But still, he remained cautious.

'They're in my pocket... the FSMB and NBME. All of them. I've made them so much money that I practically own them. If I say jump, they don't ask how high... they just need to know how far....

'Get Munro over onto our side and you'll never sit another exam. You'll walk out Mass Gen the best goddamn surgeon this country has ever produced—and you'll be the youngest, Eddy... with the paperwork to prove it.

'You'll be my prodigy. You'll be a god – damn – living – prodigy!'

Edgar couldn't believe his ears. Was Abelman really that powerful? Did he really have that kind of influence over the Federation of State Medical Boards and the National Board of Medical Examiners? He had no cause to doubt him, or reason to believe that he was not a man of his word. Even so, if what Abelman had said was true, then what he was also saying, was that not just one, but every medical board was corrupt; at least, the ones that mattered to Edgar. That any surgical license could be bought and sold; commodities to be traded and there for the taking, if a man was willing to go get them… willing to do whatever was necessary. To lie for them. To be as corrupt as the very system itself. And Edgar needed no convincing.

'H-he'll get onboard. He'll t-take the deal… or I'll die trying.'

Abelman smirked. 'Nasty little stutter you got there, Eddy. Just remember… Munro's the key to your future.'

Edgar was shaking. He had to settle his nerves and he lifted the bottle to finally pour his glass. His hand hovered in a quiver as the Coke splashed against the ice, crackling loudly.

'Drink up, Eddy… you've things to do.'

Abelman nodded to the waiter. Edgar wasn't stupid, he understood his cue to leave. Every meeting with Abelman had a purpose, one point to discuss; once business was done, then so was the meeting. That was how Abelman was. That was how Edgar needed to be. He had waited for Abelman for hours only to be driven to a bar and given five minutes of his time. Anyone else might have taken offence at such arrogance, but not Edgar. Abelman had given Edgar a card from his deck, and it was one that Edgar was going to play. He left the Coke—without taking a sip—and rose to his feet, as the waiter arrived with his coat. Abelman signalled for Edgar to lean down.

'And that thing with Nurse Davis…. See what you can do, will you?'

Abelman stared, as if to indicate that Edgar should know exactly what he meant. Edgar nodded in reply, knowing that as always

Abelman didn't make requests, he only gave orders; orders that Edgar should follow.

A gravelly voice, gritty like stone, came from behind as an elbow pushed Edgar aside.

'Abelman!'

It sounded neither young, nor very old for that matter, but the voice was very distinct and belonged to a man. Edgar gazed at the tall slender figure. His long, well-worn black leather overcoat had a grey fur lined collar that rode high around his neck. His face was hidden in shadow; cast from a tilted black fedora that had a black silk decorative band at the bottom of the crown. He turned his head and slowly exhaled. Edgar coughed, immersed in a thick cloud of smoke from the man's cigar. The man made a sound, like a grunt or a growl, and Abelman stood up from his chair. Edgar had never seen Abelman show respect to anyone, let alone stand for someone before. He glanced across at Edgar.

'Leave us.'

Edgar forced a thin-lipped smile and turned. From the corner of his eye, he could see that the man was carrying a briefcase with his right hand. Even in the low-lit bar, he could tell that it was old: scratched black leather, scuffed and worn, with combination locks. As the man reached down and placed the briefcase onto the floor, Edgar saw what looked like a tattoo on his wrist. Hidden ordinarily, concealed beneath the cuff of his shirt, now that it was visible, Edgar couldn't help but stare. It was hard to see what the tattoo was, although it looked like a number or some form of numerals; perhaps it was a symbol or a crest of some kind? As Edgar tried to decipher the mark, he suddenly spied something much more obvious. The man was missing a finger.

'Spear!' roared Abelman, his previous order not yet followed.

Edgar pushed through the bar and out onto the street where Abelman's Porsche had a ticket on its windshield. He paused for a moment, thinking about the stranger inside; about the finger that was missing: the second from the right—his ring finger. Then he smiled at the ticket as it fluttered in the breeze, pinned beneath the wiper awaiting to be found. Abelman had parked outside his favourite bar and would have known about the likelihood of being issued a fine. Apparently, he still didn't care, and it only confirmed to Edgar that Abelman's own sense of self-importance held no bounds. He had offered Edgar a shortcut to success, the key to a kingdom, for a price. It was a price that Edgar was more than willing to pay, if it meant that he would no longer need to play catch up; if it meant that he could become more like his mentor. Tomorrow would be the start of a new chapter in his life and the morning could not come quickly enough. Tomorrow, one way or another, he was going to reach out to James. He was going to set the wheels in motion and arrange the meeting. He was going to get it done; going to get ahead, and he was going to make sure that he stayed there.

There was no point arriving at the hospital, or the "Slaughterhouse," as Abelman called it, before 6:00 a.m. It was usually quiet, and patients hadn't really woken up yet or been served their breakfasts, so it was a good way for Edgar to start his day; slowly, and without the stress of having to answer to every beck and call. On his way to work that morning, having eventually calmed down and slept for a few short hours, Edgar was reduced by the cold light of day. It was all well and good trying to satisfy Abelman, gaining his approval with impromptu dates and plans that were offered in the heat of the moment. But the fact of the matter was it was already Wednesday; just no way for Edgar to pick up contact with James, then fly to the West Coast the day after tomorrow. Like it or not, he had little choice. Edgar would have to stall. Since Abelman never arrived until 9:00 a.m., a chief physician's privilege, that gave Edgar more than enough time to come up with a credible story. Not a lie exactly, just an alternative version of the truth that would sound both convincing and believable.

A new stack of manila folders were piled high upon Edgar's desk. Patient updates and recommendations that demanded his attention from the night shift. Urgent things. Pressing things. Things that might well be a matter of life or death. So, Edgar pushed them aside and flicked through the channels of the television instead to listen to the morning news.

Now that the congressional hearing was over, there would probably be the same old nonsensical stories. A stray dog that had travelled across three state lines to find its way home and be reunited with its owner. Or a waitress who gave some sob story about her life to a customer and got a thousand-dollar tip. There was always some feel-good story at the end of the news segment. Something designed to make viewers believe there was still kindness in the world; a reason to remain optimistic for our future. Edgar never fell for those stories, he knew better. As he settled back into his chair, the news was already coming to an end, and still no report of any lonesome canine or generous benefactor. The news this morning had a far graver tone. Dominated by a statement, it was issued just a few hours ago following an emergency general assembly at the CaliChat headquarters.

Following the unprecedented events that took place at the congressional hearing earlier today, the board chose to invoke article seven of its company charter and convened an emergency assembly of shareholders to consider the position of its founder and current executive officer, James Munro.

While we cannot accept the decision or levy of fine imposed upon our CEO without justification of conclusive proof, we would like, for the benefit of our shareholders and employees, to put this matter behind us and move forward into the next phase of our company development. To this end, CaliChat Holdings LLC has taken the decision to accept the findings of the committee, and further cease from this moment in time, all business activities which may involve audio, visual, textural or other recordings and or data collections made by CaliChat.

From tomorrow, all members of CaliChat who log into our service will be asked, once again, to confirm their permissions for data collection. We trust that through this action, our users will not only agree that CaliChat complies and operates fully within the law, but that it does more than any other social sharing service to abide by, respect, and uphold the privacy of its end-users.

At CaliChat, we are and will always remain committed to our user's privacy. If Senator Granson, or any other member of the congressional hearing, has conclusive evidence to substantiate charges that our CEO has operated outside of his mandate, then I would invite him to come forward with this now. Likewise, if the senator believes that there is sufficient evidence to indict James Munro, then as chairman of CaliChat, I would like to invite him to put an end to this speculation and to also do so now.

I would like to make things clear. No company is above its founder or leader. We will continue to support our CEO until such time as it can be proven that we are violating the confidence of public trust or best interests of our shareholders by doing so.

Thank you.

Edgar almost fell off his chair. Freyland had basically said that James was finished; that between the lines, they were trying to get rid of him.

The doors at the end of the corridor flung open and a man came rushing through. A typical and overly dramatic entrance by Abelman. Edgar checked his wristwatch, it was only 6:25 a.m., or possibly closer to 6:40 a.m., and Abelman was already here? This could *not* be good.

'Eddy!' he shouted, with a tremor in his voice from the bottom of the corridor. 'Eddy…! Eddy! Did you see the news?'

Hurtling towards him as if racing for his life, Edgar had never heard Abelman express an emotion until now. With his white coat unbuttoned, flapping around him like a cloak, he was positively dishevelled. His hair was uncombed, his face left unshaven, and his necktie not on: it was obvious that Abelman was not quite himself.

He approached Edgar's desk, panting heavily. Edgar, who should perhaps have been taken by surprise at his early arrival, was as always prepared; ready to lie.

'Yes, Mel. I was just going to call you because I spoke with James.'

'You did? Well…? What did he say…? *What – did – he – say!*'

Abelman was impatient and irate. What better way for Edgar to prove himself, than to show that he was calm and collected no matter the situation. Especially if, or when, Abelman was not.

'There's no way he could meet Friday—not with all that's going on—there's a huge backlash now and he has to calm things down. I tried to push him, Mel, I really did… he just couldn't make it…. We worked out an alternative and agreed on the nineteenth… next Friday… could that work for you?'

'You get us on that flight, Eddy!' Abelman roared. 'You saw what happened…? They've hung him out to dry… squeezing the man out from his *own* company.'

'I know.'

Abelman slammed his fist down on the counter of Edgar's desk.

'*God – damn – it!* They won't get away with this… mark my words, Spear… they will rue the day!'

'Don't—'

Edgar tried to tell him not to worry, that he had everything under control. But Abelman had stormed off, leaving Edgar bemused. Why was Munro so important to him?

Edgar was a doctor, not a businessman. He knew that Abelman had made all his money from CaliChat, yet if that were true then it didn't make sense. Surely if he had made so much money, then he would have to have been a majority shareholder? He obviously wasn't—he couldn't be—because he didn't seem to have any influence in the company; not even a way to get to James, he needed Edgar to do that. So, how did Abelman really make all that money?

Without answers, every question served only to ask more. If Abelman didn't know James, then why was he so angered by Freyland's statement? It was as much a mystery as the reason to why James, who was one of the richest men in America, would want to work with him and Abelman anyway? Abelman told Edgar to "get Munro onboard," though he failed to explain onboard what exactly? All Edgar had been told was it concerned control, some guarantee of power over decision. That wasn't much to go on, and even less to sell. So, how was he supposed to tempt James, and what was he supposed to tempt him with? There was no time to think anymore, Penny walked past Edgar's desk and he wanted to seize the moment while no one else was around.

'Penelope,' shouted Edgar. 'Pen!'

Nurse Davis stopped and turned.

'Dr. Spear. How can I help you?'

'I just wanted to apologise for my behaviour, Pen. I treated you terribly and... well... I just wanted to say sorry.'

Penny's face exploded with joy.

'Oh Edgar, I knew it must have been something—that something upset you. You know you can tell me anything. Anything. You don't have to....'

Edgar's hearing switched off. Suddenly deaf; temporarily, at least. Penny's mouth continued to move but he heard none of the words that came out. What on earth was she talking about? "I knew it must have been something..." did Edgar say there was something? Did he tell her there was anything? All he had said was sorry, when in truth, he was not. He wasn't sorry at all. He stared blankly at her lips, and they continued to move; to justify his behaviour with excuses for why he had treated her so badly. The pain she inflicted with her endless blabbering was more than Edgar could bear. He told himself that he was going to die, it would be slow—agonising—being bored to death; his only hope was to make her stop.

'Do you have a minute?' he asked, cutting her off.

'Of course!' she replied, before following him back to his desk.

'You know, Penny, I've become so very fond of you....' Edgar began, buying time as he prepared himself to pitch the sale. Knowing that what he was about to ask was perhaps his toughest sell yet.

'And I'm fond of you.'

'But I'm just a resident... a nobody,' said Edgar, aiming for sympathy to build his case. 'It will take me at least another five years to complete my residency, and even then, there's no guarantee that I will pass the board or become licensed.'

From sympathy to hardship, Edgar looked at the floor to signal the hopelessness of his position. This was good. This was really good.

'What future could I possibly offer you now?' he asked, despairingly.

'Oh Edgar, none of that matters. We'll find a way—together— we'll be able to do anything. You just have to put your trust in me, my love. You just have to—'

'I know. I want to... I really want to. But... well... what if there was another way? A better way. A shorter way. Would you help me? Would you stand by me then?'

'Edgar, I'd do anything for you. For us. You know that.'

'That's what I thought,' said Edgar. He waited a second, for a heartbeat or two; barely enough time to allow Penny to think over his words. 'What if I told you that you could help us to be together now? That you could help us to have our future—not in five years—but *now*. Would you put your trust in me then as you ask me to put my trust in you?'

'Oh Edgar. I'd do anything to gain your trust. Anything!' said Penny, without hesitation.

Edgar had built his argument, shared his hardship and spoke of his dreams. It was up to Penny to free him now; to meet him and join him. Edgar had only to tell her how.

'It's Dr. Abelman, Penny. You've caught his eye.'

Penny looked horrified. Edgar had to move quickly.

'It wouldn't be anything serious... just a few drinks... a nice meal. Nothing more. He's lonely, Penny. He just wants a little companionship.'

Penny wasn't horrified, she was mortified. How could Edgar even suggest such a thing? How could he even think such a thing?

'Edgar... what are you... Edgar? No! Edgar, I... I can't—'

Edgar interrupted, knowing that he had to convince Penny before she made up her mind.

'Penny, Abelman is willing to push me through the residency program. He's willing to help me if I help him... if we help him... if we help *us*....'

'Don't you see? We wouldn't have to wait five more years. You could help us be — together — *now*.'

There was no response from Penny. There was only silence.

'It's just an evening.... A meal and some drinks. Nothing more— I promise. What's one evening compared to a lifetime? To the lifetime we could have together?'

Penny stayed silent; she couldn't respond. She couldn't find the words and Edgar felt encouraged. The fact that she had not yet said no, meant she might just say yes. All she needed was a little more persuasion; a little extra effort to tip the balance and get her across the line.

'It's so lonely in my apartment, Pen,' said Edgar. 'So very lonely. I know if you could help us then we could be together.'

Edgar waited; he hoped that by playing the loneliness card, it would be enough to win the game. The incentive of living together, in exchange for just one evening with Abelman.

'I need to think about it,' said Penny. 'I need some time....'

Time, however, was the one thing that Edgar didn't have. He needed an answer. He wanted an answer. He had to deliver; to be able to tell Abelman that Penny had agreed. If a little push was not enough then he would have to go one step further. He would have to play the sentiment card as well.

'I don't understand.... You said that you loved me—that you wanted to be together and that I should trust you.'

'I do... you should... it's just that—'

He couldn't allow her to explain, to think or speak her thoughts out loud; to say anything that might strengthen her doubt.

'But the minute I do—the minute I try to put my trust in you—you say you need time.... You say you need to think about it.' Edgar turned and lowered his head for dramatic effect. 'I knew my heart would get broken if I let someone inside,' he said, pretending to be on the verge of tears.

His performance was outstanding, and he knew it; unable to resist a smirk as he recognised his talent for subterfuge was worthy of an Oscar award. Penny was helpless, Edgar's cards were just too strong. She reached out and took hold of his arm, and Edgar knew that he had done it. He had won.

'Oh, Edgar, you *can* trust me! I won't break your heart.... I love you. I've *always* loved you. It's only dinner and drinks... of course I will go with Abelman. I'd go anywhere for you.'

Recovering from his heartbreak at remarkable speed, Edgar looked up.

'Say, 7:00 p.m.? I mean... it's just better to get it over with... don't you think?'

'Erm... s-seven... today...? Tonight?'

Edgar's gaze stayed fixed on Penny, saying nothing.

'Oh... well... ok.... Ok.' said Penny hesitantly, as she nodded in agreement, resigning herself to the evening in front of her. 'Tonight, at seven.'

The rest of Edgar's morning rounds passed without incident. This was, of course, because Edgar now paid little heed or regard to his patients. He had far greater concerns than the benign complaints of the rich and affluent. Those from high society whose insurance premiums could cover these hospital treatments. Those who having lived the good life, were now in need of surgery to reverse the self-inflicted damage imposed upon their bodies. Those who lay here expecting sympathy for their troubles, and who Abelman would say were really nothing more than, "pitiful, insignificant, ungrateful little ants." They didn't deserve Edgar's attention, and besides, he was unable to think of anything other than James. In fact, he was drained from all of his thinking. The very thought of seeing him and having to be courteous; an idea enough to make him feel nauseated. Edgar's only consolation was the knowledge that this time it would be he who played James, the way that James had once played him. It would be he who now used James, the way that James had once used him. And it would be he who would do whatever was needed to get the prize that Abelman offered.

It was around mid-afternoon before Edgar was able to sit down for a break and catch the news again; CaliChat and James were still the lead story. The consequences for privacy, in the aftermath of the hearing, were being debated back and forth between the supposed experts and the alleged gurus. Everyone, so it seemed, had an opinion about CaliChat; everyone, apparently, had the right to express it. The conspiracists were all over the issue. They claimed that CaliChat was secretly working in collusion with the CIA, recording all user phone calls and browser movements before passing them on for government analysis. Leaders of women's rights groups claimed that CaliChat demonised women; that there was mounting evidence to prove illicit photographs were being shared and seen without permission. Members of human rights and racial equality groups, all came forward with their perspectives; how CaliChat had harmed their members and put equal rights back a hundred years. And yet, despite the claims against the company, there was still no proof of any of it. For all the media's criticisms—their attempts to incite public outrage—the truth was that no one really cared. After all, over ninety percent of all Americans over the age of thirteen had a CaliChat account, and the service was used by over two billion people worldwide. Two billion users, who before these past weeks used CaliChat without protest or objection: as much a part of their daily routine as going to bed or brushing their teeth.

Abelman walked past Edgar's desk. His coat now buttoned, hair combed and necktie smartly knotted; he appeared calmer and more dignified than earlier.

'Mel!'

He turned and spun around on one foot to look at Edgar.

'Tonight, at seven.'

His mind was on many things, and "tonight at seven" meant nothing to him.

'Penelope...? Nurse Davis?'

Abelman smiled. He pointed his finger at Edgar.

'My man! Who's — *my* — man!'

He spun back around, taking several steps before stopping and turning to Edgar once again.

'You smell that...?' he asked. 'That's the smell of fresh ink, Eddy.' He gestured as if writing with an imaginary pen in mid-air, as if asking for the cheque in a restaurant. 'Fresh ink on those papers we talked about.'

He winked and Edgar smiled back, before he turned to continue down the corridor. Edgar clenched his fist and secretly punched the air beneath his desk. Yes! he thought. He was one step closer. One step closer to ending his residency. One step closer to gaining his license. And one step closer to perhaps starting his own private practice; from living the life that he should have—the luxurious life he deserved.

Edgar had delivered on the first of his three promises. The second would be a meeting with James, and the third to persuade him to work with Abelman. But these were challenges for another day. Today was a day of victory, a moment to be savoured. Edgar left early, not wanting to meet Penny, or to have to speak with her before her evening rendezvous.

4

LEAVE THE PAST BEHIND

A woman staggered past Edgar, her sunglasses and neckerchief wrapping the majority of her face. It was an everyday sight at the hospital, especially for patients who underwent laser treatments and skin therapies. Edgar could tell by the way she walked that she was in pain. The anaesthetic gels were most probably beginning to wear off, and she was, "feeling the burn," as the cosmetic surgeons called it; the price for trying to defy nature and reverse the effects of aging. Still, any patient's problem was their problem and not Edgar's, especially if the patient wasn't even his. Edgar didn't have time to ask about the woman anyway, it was nearing 8:00 a.m. and he was late for patient rounds. He called them "The Flying Visits," because no matter the number of patients, complexity of treatments or their condition, Edgar would be finished by 9:00 a.m. sharp. One hour; that was all they were allowed of his time. One − precious − hour. And one hour was, as Edgar often reminded Penny, one hour more than they ever got from Abelman. It was after all, a whole sixty minutes, which was more than enough time for Edgar to review notes from the previous shift, meet patients, update their files with his own recommendations, and be wrapped up nicely by lunch.

'Good morning, Mr. Clydesdale,' said Edgar as he arrived beside Clydesdale's bed. 'You have the pleasure of being my first patient this morning.'

As usual, Edgar greeted his patients by voice only, avoiding eye contact and the possibility of inviting conversation. Besides, Edgar was already looking through Clydesdale's chart to spot any reported irregularities that might require some form of immediate treatment and jeopardise his schedule.

'Good morning, Doctor. I was wondering if—'

But before Clydesdale could finish, Edgar knew exactly what he was going to ask and didn't want to waste time procrastinating. It was bad enough that he had to visit him each morning without having to pretend that he cared.

'*Yes*, Mr. Clydesdale,' interrupted Edgar contemptuously. 'We're *all* aware of what you're wondering. And as I've said before, Dr. Abelman is very busy....'

Edgar stopped, suddenly, as he looked up and noticed that Penny was not beside him.

'Erm... everything's fine,' he said. His expression unable to hide his surprise having lost his train of thought. 'Nurse, erm...?' asked Edgar, as he glanced at the nurse's name badge. 'Parsons will assist you this morning and inform you of my recommendations after rounds.'

'But—'

'Very good,' interrupted Edgar once again. 'Well then... see you in the morning, Mr. Clydesdale,' as he continued nonchalantly, holding out Clydesdale's chart, waiting for Parsons to take it from him and put it back.

Edgar and the nurse moved towards the next patient's bed; Edgar's curiosity had the better of him.

'Nurse Parsons, do you have any idea where Nurse Davis is this morning?'

'No, Doctor. Nurse Catone told me that she was delayed and asked me to cover until she arrived.'

Delayed? thought Edgar. Penny could have ruined his schedule. How could she be so inconsiderate?

'Wretched woman!' he growled.

'I'm sorry, Doctor?' asked Nurse Parsons, shocked and surprised by Edgar's comment, which seemed unwarranted to say the least. Along with the changing room gossips and muted whispers that drifted between the hospital walls, she was only too aware of Abelman, but couldn't recall ever being warned about Edgar.

'Comes and goes as she pleases... who does she think she is?' Edgar turned to focus his anger on Parsons directly. '8:00 a.m.... Rounds begin at 8:00 a.m. I don't dilly—I don't dally—I'm not delayed—and I *don't* expect staff to be delayed either. Is — *that* — understood?'

Uncertain if Edgar was airing his opinion or merely venting his frustration over Penny, Nurse Parsons tried to remain cordial and replied agreeingly. 'Yes. Yes, Doctor. I understand.'

'Good!'

Despite the minor setback, the remaining rounds passed as Edgar expected and ended at 9:00 a.m. precisely. He seemed distracted, preoccupied throughout, and the young nurse aware that something was troubling him; something that he chose not to share, nor she dare to ask. After the Flying Visits, Edgar returned as usual to his desk and was busy writing up his notes when Abelman appeared unexpectedly; a broad smile stretched across his face.

'Like I told you, Eddy....' he said, his voice tinged with self-satisfaction. Edgar looked up from the files.

'A tiger!'

He stared down at Edgar, his comb over doing nothing to prevent the ceiling light from glaring off his scalp. His large bushy eyebrows, those caterpillars, were raised and cast long prickly shadows onto the bags beneath his black sunken eyes. They formed a look that was somewhere between happiness and wickedness, between deviance and delight. Abelman stared and Edgar was anxious, increasingly uncomfortable with the intimidating threat. Abelman knew it—he sensed it—but said nothing as he continued in his menace, taking pleasure as he revelled in Edgar's growing discomfort. The alpha male was the cat that had gotten the cream; he was marking his territory, and Edgar had been warned.

'A tiger,' repeated Abelman, with only darkness in his voice.

'Dr. Abelman!' called a woman from the end of the corridor. 'Excuse me... Dr. Abelman?'

Abelman's eyebrows rose higher, in acknowledgement of his name. His eyes, like black polished glass, reflected the light and pierced the shadows as they fixed firmly upon Edgar. More than threatening, they implied a twisted and sinister sense of foreboding that made Edgar feel as though he was staring at the devil himself. Abelman was relentless; then suddenly, he turned. Their eyes unlocked, the trance was broken, and he left to follow the direction of the voice that had called to him.

Edgar was paralysed, numb from the chill that coursed through his veins following the encounter. He had never experienced the true feeling of fear until now. It was that look... how it made him feel.... How that couple in the coffee shop must have felt. Abelman had done more than send a shiver down Edgar's spine; he had shaken him to his very core, but why? What had he done? The pen fell from his hand as he buried his face into his palms and shook his head. Why had he fallen out of favour? Why now? I've done nothing, he told himself. Nothing to incur the wrath of his mentor. In fact, all he had done was exactly what was asked of him, so why had Abelman.... Suddenly, he dropped his hands and raised his head. His face drained in an instant, ashen at the thought. No longer crippled by fear but gripped with panic, his eyes widened as he leapt from the chair and ran from his desk.

Racing towards the nurse staff room, he drowned in the adrenaline that surged through his body like water through the rapids. He grabbed the handle and flung the door open; his eyes darting around the room. It was empty. She wasn't there. He stood helpless, his fear multiplying, heart pounding, and the corridor began to spin around him. Disorientated, he turned, trying to oppose the rotation; to stay on his feet, as he stared into nothingness. It was that look... those eyes... the harrowing eyes of a madman, of a psychopath... and the only way to describe it; how it felt... was evil.... Pure evil.

His vision found focus and saw the large WC letters of the hanging sign. She had to be there—she must be—and he ran to the restroom, oblivious to the words upon the door: *Ladies Only.*

'Penny?' he cried.

'Doctor!' screamed a nurse. She jumped at the shock of seeing Edgar, accidentally drawing the brush of mascara across her cheek. But Edgar had no interest in what she was doing, in who she was or how she looked.

'Penny?' he called, and again she didn't answer.

He pushed open each cubicle, as his fear slipped deeper into despair. All of the booths were empty, and only one now remained. Facing the door, quivering as he took a long deep breath, he closed his eyes then reached out and pushed. He hoped for resistance from the turn of a lock, but the door surrendered to his touch. Looking up at the wall, his eyes glazed as he stared; his mind drifting into a fog of doubt. She wasn't there. She wasn't there because it must have been as Nurse Parsons had said. What else could it be? Penny was delayed. That was all. That was the truth of it.

Edgar hung his head; not quite in shame, not quite without, as he began to calm down and feel foolish. He scoffed, wondering why he allowed himself to become so easily perturbed? What was it that really scared him? Was it the eyes of Abelman, or his date with Penny; Edgar's guilt for misleading her that weighed so heavily on his mind?

Abelman preyed upon doubt, upon weakness—Edgar knew that. It was not necessarily the things that he said, but the way in which he said them that gave him power. Not so much the way that he spoke, but what he insinuated that strengthened his hold over others. That morning, the way that he looked at Edgar was enough to make him believe the worst; that Penny's absence was not only down to him, but the result of something terrible that he had done to her. This was all so typical Abelman, his mind games, and Edgar had fallen for it. How could he allow himself to be so easily suckered? He shook his head, angry at himself, forgetting for a moment where he was, until he turned to see the nurse still gaping in shock.

'You... you've....' said Edgar pointing at her cheek, not saying anything more before he stepped outside.

An immense weight had been lifted from his shoulders, and Edgar sighed as he breathed the air of relief, walking slowly back towards his desk. He was barely seated, his face hardly buried again in files, when a young woman approached him. She was clearly distressed, carrying a small child in one arm: a collection of folders and papers under the other.

'I'm so sorry to disturb you,' she said, her voice melancholic, 'but I was hoping you could tell me how to get to the Proton Therapy Centre?'

'Outside to the left,' Edgar replied. 'Just follow the signs to the Yawkey Centre. It's simple enough.'

He waited a moment, then looked up; to make sure that whoever was bothering him had left. The young woman, however, stood patiently.

'Thank you,' she said as she smiled at Edgar. Edgar smiled in return. Her face was tired and etched from the strain of tending the sick child, even so, there was a beauty about her, a kindness and radiance to which Edgar was drawn.

'I... I... I could... I m-mean, if you like, I could—'

Edgar's awkward attempt to escort the woman was interrupted by the child who began to cry. Not wanting to delay her appointment further, she rushed outside to follow his instruction. As visitors streamed past, Edgar dreamt of the day that he would be finished with his residency. When he would have some privacy, something better than being mistaken for a receptionist, or someone that you go to and ask for information.

The swing doors opened, and Edgar waited before turning to recognise a familiar figure in the distance. An outline and very particular stance that was unmistakable; albeit from behind. It was Penny, and she was chatting with a small group of nurses, undoubtedly the reason for why she was delayed. Perhaps it was the sight of seeing the woman earlier that morning, covered up and in pain, that had put the initial thought into his head? A seed of doubt that Abelman was so easily able to grow into a forest of fear. A fear that played with his mind and toyed with anxiety, all in an effort to scare him; to remind him of who was in charge, of who had—*all*—the control. Edgar could feel his anger beginning to rise, treated like a fool and acting even more so. He really was the apprentice, enslaved to his master, and his nostrils flared as his teeth began to grind.

Abelman had said, "people should hear me before they see me… they should know I'm coming," and Edgar wanted the same. To be heard. To be feared. For people to know that he was coming. To make Penny fearfully aware that he was close.

'Nurse Davis!' he yelled.

Edgar's anger and frustration manifested through his voice, and it roared like the engine of Abelman's Porsche.

'Davis!'

Not wishing a doctor's beratement, the other nurses quickly disappeared as Edgar moved to within a few metres of Penny. She remained, her back still turned, seemingly ignoring him. Edgar lowered his head and raised his eyebrows in readiness. He reached out, snatching her forearm, pulling her around to face him.

'Davis! I'm talking....'

Penny winced and cried out in pain. Edgar froze—confused—and looked down at her arm. Her wrists were bruised, covered with grazes. There were lesions and sores; blood that had dried from the cuts of fresh wounds. Edgar released her and stepped back. His face stricken by horror and unable to hide his repugnance. As cold and as hard as he wanted to be, as he tried to be, as he hoped he could be, his heart wasn't ready... not for such things.

'Penny...? Penny, what....'

Edgar looked up and was silenced. There were bruises around her neck; despite her sunglasses, he saw more around her eye and the scratches above her brow.

'P-Pen... w-what the hell... what h-happened?'

There was no reply, no words of explanation, and her lower lip quivered as she tried to produce a sound. Behind the glasses her eyes began to well, and Edgar watched as the first tear rolled down her cheek. She clenched her jaw and her lip no longer quivered, as she desperately tried to stop others from streaming. But she was helpless to hold them, and succumbed to her sobbing, as her eyes closed tight to the floods of despair. Not wanting to create a public scene, Edgar led her gently towards a nearby storage closet, where alone and with no one to follow, he tried again to get to the bottom of things.

'Penny... please... you must.... You must tell me.... What's happened?' Edgar's voice was fragile, broken and unable to mask his concern.

Penny gasped between her tears, trying to release the words that choked her.

'It... it... it was... it was Abelman,' she stammered. '*Abelman!*' she screamed.

She lashed out hysterically, yelling as her arms thrashed and flailed; as if fighting, trying to defend herself. Edgar's efforts to restrain her were to no avail. Penny was traumatised and Edgar was aghast. Why did he do this? What could have driven him to hurt her this way?

As he witnessed the trauma of Abelman's abuse, he was filled with revulsion. If this was power—the face of control—he would have nothing to do with it, no part and none of it. Deep down, lingering like forgotten and now rotten fruit, there was still some form of morality left inside Edgar: a code, or ethic, that still had the ability to prick his conscience. However small or rotten it had become, the fact remained that it was there, and its stench now filled his lungs. No longer aghast, he was livid. He stormed out of the closet incensed, a man possessed, and nothing would stand in his way. He wanted Abelman. There was blood on his hands, and he would avenge every drop that was spilt.

When he reached Abelman's office, his secretary was sitting at reception; staring into a small compact mirror, her tongue flicked across her teeth trying to remove the breadcrumbs and other remains of her breakfast. She was nothing to Edgar, invisible and inconsequent, and he charged past her as if she didn't exist.

'Dr. Spear? Dr. Spear, wait! You can't go in there... Dr. Abelman is....'

Edgar was not to be told what he could or could not do, and he did not stop, nor heed the words of Abelman's muse. He took hold of the doorknob, turned it, and barged in.

'*Get out!*' he screamed.

Abelman was sitting on his side of the desk and stared at Edgar in disbelief.

'Spear?'

Edgar ignored him.

'You heard me... I told you.... *Get – out!*'

The patient was terrified and looked up at her doctor.

'Kassandra?' Abelman called, and his secretary came running like the lap dog that she was hired to be.

'Can you please take Mrs. Stevens to the waiting room and give me a few moments?'

'Of course, Dr. Abelman.'

Edgar's rage, however, could not be contained.

'And did you hit her as well?' he yelled, as he pointed at Kassandra. 'When you had your way with her...? Did you beat her too?'

Kassandra was dumbfounded. She looked at Abelman, her eyes panicked, longing for rescue as she shook her head to deny Edgar's claim. Mrs. Stevens, still stunned by the sudden interruption of her appointment, gawped in shock at the revelations taking place.

'Doctor?' she asked nervously, as Abelman took control to calm the situation.

'It's ok, Kassandra. If you could be so kind as to take Mrs. Stevens, I do believe that Dr. Spear is upset and not feeling well.'

Abelman walked around to the patient's side of his desk. He helped Mrs. Stevens to her feet, to allow Kassandra to escort her out, before he closed the door behind them and turned to face Edgar.

'Eddy, what the—'

But nothing and no one was going to stop Edgar. Not even Abelman. Not this time.

'Dinner and drinks you said.... Dinner and drinks!' screamed Edgar, as he ran over to grab Abelman by the collars of his jacket. 'I'll kill you.... *I'll – kill – you!*'

In a state of rage, wild and seething, Edgar was still no match for Abelman. He seized Edgar by the throat before he was able to get anywhere near him and tossed him aside with ease: throwing him to the floor like a child that throws away a broken toy.

'Get a hold of yourself, Spear,' said Abelman dismissively, as he wiped the arm of his white coat. 'What's the matter with you?'

Edgar was shaken but got back on his feet; ready for round two. He made another run, undaunted as he charged at Abelman, determined to bring him down. Standing like a matador, steady in wait, Abelman opposed then raised one hand to end the advance.

Edgar slammed into a small drinks table, sending glass and bottles flying.

'I won't tell you again,' warned Abelman.

Nevertheless, his words offered no deterrent. Edgar was not to be stopped. He would rain destruction down upon his master, tear him limb from limb, and again got back on his feet to make another charge. Abelman raised his other hand and this time pushed Edgar into a wall. Edgar fell heavily to the floor, and Abelman bent down to drag him to his feet, pulling him up by his throat.

'What's this, Eddy? Sentiment? Feelings…? For *that* girl?'

Abelman threw Edgar onto the chair that Mrs. Stevens had sat on, and he landed with a thud.

'Sit down! Take a seat…. Maybe you've forgotten the rules of the game? They're simple, even for a numbskull like you. You see, you get me what I want, and you get what I give. That way, everyone wins.

'You wanna judge me—*fine*. You wanna hate me—*fine*. But you *ever* raise a hand against me again, and I'll break it off. I'll take your whole goddamn arm and throw it off the bridge.

'You're nothing, Spear. A nobody…. A shadow of a shadow on a wall that no one sees. You breathe because I let you to breathe. You live because I let you live. Interrupt me again, and I'll take away your privileges. *I'll* kill you. You and your pathetic little girlfriend.'

Abelman walked back around to his side of his desk, calmly adjusting his tie. He towered like a mountain over Edgar, still sitting on the patient's chair.

'So, things got rough… who cares? I don't. And if I don't. You don't… understand?

'You serve *me*. You do as *I* say. That's the game. They're the rules, and they're not open for discussion.

'You want out? Say the word and you're out. But before you do, look around, Eddy. Take a good — *long* — look. I don't see anyone else batting for you, do you?'

Abelman leant forward, palms down upon the desk; his callousness clear to see.

'You speak to me like that again and I'll cut your goddamn tongue out,' he said. The connotations of his words so sobering that they quelled the wind from Edgar's storm. 'I don't mind spirit, Eddy. Heck—I even admire it! But if you wanna take down the house you gotta be willing to sacrifice your hand. Throw your best cards even when you think they'll win you the game…. If that's what it takes to get the house. You understand?'

Edgar didn't understand, nor would he have time to assess this latest piece of Abelman Advice, as Abelman's patience had come to its end.

'Now get the hell out!'

Edgar rose from the chair and left without a word. He passed Kassandra, now filing her nails and smiling smugly. Edgar's head hung low, his tail tucked firmly between his legs. His humiliation made all the more complete.

Abelman may have crossed the line with Penny, but it was a line drawn only in sand. Tonight, the tide would come to wash it away, and it would leave Edgar with a choice. To forget where it was drawn, or to come back tomorrow and draw down once again. Although, what would be the point? It was clear there could be no lines with Abelman, no boundaries or place for sentiment. Was that his reason for hurting Penny, to teach Edgar this lesson?

During the hours that followed, Edgar thought it best to be alone. He gathered as many patient files as he could, and he carried them along with his tarnished pride over to the Yawkey Centre. The centre dealt with outpatient care; Edgar was able to find an empty office space to finish his notes and console himself after his degradation. He thought about Penny, about Abelman, about the position he was in and the game he now played. He thought and he thought until it was almost 4:00 p.m. and time for him to leave. Before then, he would have to return the files to his desk, for the evening and night shifts to pick up. He would have to return to the Lunder Building, which meant there was the risk of seeing either Abelman or Penny, and how could he face either of them now? After failing them both.

He had lied to Penny, which in itself was nothing new, but none of Edgar's lies had ever led to violence before. This was a first. Something very different. A new low, even by his own incredibly low standards. There was no way that Abelman would keep his promises now, not after what had happened. So, what was the point in continuing his game? In becoming a surgeon, if he wasn't even going to be around long enough to practice being one. Besides, it didn't feel like a game anymore where the prize was a title and a position. It had all become so terrifyingly real; lives were at stake, and in this new reality, Edgar had to find a way out. As he walked back towards the Lunder Building and placed the files upon his desk, Edgar's mind was made up. The stakes for becoming a surgeon were just too high. He had looked for a shortcut, a fast track and found it. He had bluffed, he had gambled, and that had got him this far, but it was the end of the line. The only way out, was to get all the way out; now, while he had the chance. On the other hand, wherever he went, Abelman would surely follow; track him down and make him pay for wasting his time, for not delivering on their deal. If Abelman was even half of what Edgar believed him to be, then it would be impossible to take Penny with him: she would only be in greater danger. And yet, he could not leave with things as they were, not after seeing her injuries that morning. She deserved something—an explanation—even if it was only another lie to make her feel better, to help Edgar feel less responsible. That would be something at least; a dishonest goodbye.

Edgar prepared himself for the performance of a lifetime, before making his way towards the nurse staff room. The door was closed, still, there was no mistaking the voice that echoed through the keyhole, as he knelt and peered through the lock; his vision obscured, unable to see inside.

'Don't toy with me, girl,' scolded Abelman. 'Everything's on camera… if you don't want your mother and the whole world to see what you were up to last night, you'll be ready at six.'

The sound of footsteps grew louder as someone came closer to the door.

'Oh, and another thing.'

Edgar swallowed hard; his heart was pounding. Abelman couldn't find him here, not trying to get to Penny. He needed to run, but there was nowhere to run to, nowhere to hide, and even if there was, his escape seemed less important than discovering the meaning of "another thing."

'Wear something nice—something smart—but chic. You'll be meeting a few friends.'

The door handle began to turn.

'If you think last night was good then you're gonna *love* tonight…. We're throwing a party!' laughed Abelman, as the door finally opened.

Edgar panicked; a split second to pretend that he was walking past innocently. He jumped to his feet and Abelman looked startled.

'Eddy? What a surprise… I was just coming to see you.'

'Really?' smiled Edgar anxiously, his voice taut and tremulous.

He peeked into the staff room. Penny was sat on the sofa, crying. Abelman's hand reached back and closed the door behind him.

'Where are we with Munro? Still on for the nineteenth?'

'The nineteenth…? Erm… oh, the nineteenth… yes. Yes, of course. The nineteenth…. Sorry… good to go, Mel.'

'Excellent,' said Abelman, as he placed his arm around Edgar's shoulder. 'Come on, walk with me a little.' And he proceeded to pull Edgar farther away from the staff room. 'You know, what happened earlier… I liked that. You showed some balls.'

His hand clutched Edgar's neck, squeezing it repeatedly, and Edgar stayed silent; he doubted the sincerity of Abelman's words. He wanted to believe, but he was beginning to understand. It was hard to accept that Abelman would have approved of his failed attempt to stand up against him. More likely than not, that he was testing his tenacity.

'We all step out of line once and a while... forget our place in the food chain, Eddy. But you know, it's then that we need to be reminded of the line... how important our place is—behind it.'

Having squeezed enough to bruise the skin, he loosened his hold and slapped Edgar hard on the back. Edgar was winded, struggling to regain his breath as Abelman turned to face him; his cold eyes, dark in their endless depths, pierced Edgar to read the pages of his suspicious mind.

'We *all* have to learn our place in this life, Eddy. I have mine, and you have yours... but remember... loyalty is my *only* vice.

'I figured after what happened you'd either run to Davis or run out. But you took it like a man—I like that. And to prove it, I'm gonna give you something... a little taste of what's to come... I'm gonna sign off on your residency—today. Call it a gesture of goodwill.'

Edgar stood gaping in disbelief. His hatred of James Munro paled in comparison to the abhorrence he held for Abelman. Even so, Abelman was going to end his residency. That would spell an end to his training and the beginning of his career as a real physician; finally, the chance to be taken seriously. A man of principle, any man of conscience, might have said no and walked away. However, Edgar was not such a man, and the conscience that drove him to confront his master only hours before, was so easily sold for the price of credence.

'Well, aren't you gonna say something?'

'N-no... I... I m-mean... yes. Thank you, Mel.'

Abelman raised his eyebrows, his face grimaced.

'Still with the stutter...? Well, anyway... congratulations, Eddy... you made it. You're a surgeon,' said Abelman as he stretched out his hand.

Edgar stretched out his hand in return, still dubious to the thought that his training was really over. The firm and determined grip of

Abelman was a little too tight, a little too strong; Edgar stared with questioning eyes. His mind wasn't filled with happiness nor the hopes of his future; just a single overwhelming fear that nothing was ever as it seemed with Abelman. There was always a purpose, some underlying motive behind everything that he did. He wasn't called *Melvin the Monster* without good reason, and that reason was not because he was famed for his generosity. What was he scheming? Why would he give Edgar his prize before the game was even played, before the meeting with James? If he was being tested to see just how difficult it was to resist temptation, how far greed could influence him, how little he cared about corruption and how much ambition he actually had, then the test was working. He might not have had the experience of a bona fide neurosurgeon, nor the papers and licenses that would allow him to practice. But with Abelman's signature, what he would have—what he was now being given—was a rite of passage.

'B-but the dates?' Edgar asked apprehensively, wanting to confirm the validity of his prize.

'Dates are like opinions—something to change and manipulate,' replied Abelman, smiling at Edgar as if to prove his point.

'It's five years, Mel.'

'Oh... then let me put your mind at rest, kid. You see you graduated... when was it... *seven* years ago...? Don't you remember? The youngest *ever* graduate from UCSF... or was it Harvard? Maybe Stanford? I don't know—I don't care. You decide.'

Edgar was speechless; could Abelman really make that happen?

'I told you, Eddy, you'll be the youngest surgeon this country has *ever* produced. You're not just a doctor... you're − *my* − prodigy.'

Edgar's plan to run was no longer dissolving, it evaporated completely.

'I... I don't know what to say....'

'Well, I believe the customary thing is to say thank you. So, say, *thank you, Mel.*'

'Yes. Yes, of course... thank you. Thank you, Mel.'

'Alright then,' said Abelman, releasing Edgar's hand. 'I guess this calls for a celebration? Meet you at the entrance…? Shall we say… 6:00 p.m.?'

'Sure. That would be great. See you at six!'

His point finished, Abelman was already on the move, before turning back to have his final word.

'Oh, and Eddy… take a shower… clean yourself up a bit. Make yourself—you know—presentable. Smart but chic.'

Abelman overemphasised his wink with a sharp clicking sound; it was loud, like the pulled trigger of a gun that had nothing in its chamber, then he turned the corner and disappeared down the corridor.

"Smart but chic?"

Words that sounded familiar, yet Edgar was unable to place them. Smart but… then, he remembered. The pieces fell into place and it all made sense. Edgar was spending so much time around Abelman that he had become suspect, sceptical of everything. It was obvious that Abelman really did like the way that Edgar stood up against him. The party that he told Penny to get ready for was obviously a surprise— his way of welcoming Edgar into the club. There were no hidden motives, there was only Edgar's paranoia, and the time had come to not only accept the will of his master, but to embrace it. Edgar pulled out his cell phone, opened his contacts and began to scroll.

'J. K. L.….' said Edgar, as his thumb flicked the screen and names flew past like credits in a film. Suddenly, he stopped. There he was: *Munro, James.*

Edgar's finger hovered above the name. It pushed back, as if repelling against it; repelling against all that it stood for and all that it represented. Edgar's anger and rage, the feelings that he struggled so hard to contain were now a hair's breadth away. He closed his eyes to focus, to breathe and remind himself of where he was; on the verge of the good life, that little bit closer to the life he so rightly deserved. Munro was his ticket, an opportunity worth more than any emotion, and he took a breath—a deep breath—before he opened his eyes and pressed the call icon.

'Yo, People! It's James,' said the voicemail.

Edgar was unimpressed; disappointed, perhaps a better description. Having contemplated this moment for so very long, dreading the thought of appealing to his sworn enemy, their conversation was not going to happen; not for now, at least. Instead, Edgar would have to listen to Munro's recording, spoken with the same tedious beach-bum-like tone that he used at university. It was the backbone of a persona that James used to make himself appear more friendly; seem less intelligent than he really was, and less of a threat than Edgar knew him to actually be. James's blathering continued until the obligatory, "leave your message after the tone." As the beep sounded, Edgar's took his cue to deliver on his promise for the meeting.

'Hey James, this is... erm... w-well... I know it's been a while, b-but it's... well... it's... it's Edgar... Edgar S-Spear. Actually, when I say Spear... it's Dr. Spear. I'm a neurosurgeon now, at Massachusetts General.... In Boston.'

Calming his nerves and proud of his achievement, Edgar found the flow of his voice.

'The truth is that I'm the youngest neurosurgeon there as well. Funny story... I completed my residency faster than—'

His mind went blank. The imaginary conversations with James, the speeches he had practiced over and over again in his head; they were all gone. His tongue was tied, rambling and talking gibberish while James had been surprisingly quiet. In fact, he hadn't spoken a word since Edgar began his monologue, and Edgar, suddenly, remembered why; it was voicemail, and that meant limited time.

'Anyway, that's not why I'm calling. I was wondering... the thing is, I'll be in LA on the nineteenth. If you're free—I mean if you have time—well, maybe we could catch up for some drinks or something? Nothing special. Just to say—'

Beep! Edgar was cut off.

It was too early; he hadn't finished his message or even suggested a place to meet. After all this time, this was how James would hear from him, sounding like some bumbling fool. Munro was one of the most influential men in the world. By far the most talked about man in America. How could he possibly have time to speak with Edgar when he was busy being hounded by his shareholders? As usual, and without hesitation, Edgar had managed to explain away the unfolding of events. Munro was busy, that was all. It couldn't have been because of anything else....

When Edgar returned to the Slaughterhouse, it was almost 6:00 p.m. Showered, shaved, and smartly dressed, he was looking forward to the evening ahead. However, after running all the way from his apartment, his clean white shirt was drenched with perspiration. An unwelcomed start for an evening of attention. Edgar checked the clock which hung above the large glass entrance doors. It was 5:57 p.m., precisely. He quickly removed his black blazer, his best and only jacket, then flapped his arms like a chicken, as he tried to circulate some air. He wiped his brow and spied the changing elevator display; there was not a moment to lose. Edgar flung his jacket back on, threw himself onto the hard metal bench, crossed his legs, and slouched. He wanted to appear calm and relaxed, as though waiting for some time, except his face was flushed. He was fooling no one.

'Eddy!' beamed Abelman, as he stepped out from the elevator and walked over to again take Edgar firmly by the hand. 'And I believe you know Penelope?' he said, as he studied Edgar's reaction, never looking back to see if she followed.

Penny emerged in a short black dress, black stockings and heels. She was wearing dark sunglasses and her hair was tied back. It was not her usual style. Not braided, nor in a bun. It was just tied back, plain and neat, as if she was going to a funeral.

'Penny!' smiled Edgar.

She ignored the reception, walking towards them looking only at the ground.

'No need to get embarrassed, Eddy.' Abelman laughed, mocking Edgar's reddened cheeks. 'Just cos a girl turns you down... so, Domino's?' he asked, or rather, informed.

Edgar felt the cold Boston breeze beginning to pick up as they walked towards Abelman's Porsche. And once again, Abelman put his arm around Edgar's shoulder, to add to the evening chill.

'What a day, huh? How you feeling?'

The support that Edgar felt from his master was comforting, and he quickly forgot any taunts about his appearance. As Abelman's hand gripped his shoulder, Edgar basked in the attention; the protection and concern that Abelman seemingly showed for his apprentice.

'Crazy,' beamed Edgar. 'Feeling good and really looking forward to tonight. Again, thanks for this Mel—thanks for everything—I won't let you down.'

'Oh, don't worry... I know you won't,' smiled Abelman.

Penny sauntered behind; still silent. Edgar walked alongside to the front passenger seat and reached down to open the door. Without warning, Abelman berated him, and ridiculed Penny in addition.

'Now, now, Eddy... where's your manners? Did your mother never teach you...? It's *ladies* first.'

Abelman walked around to the other side of the car.

'What's with the look?' he said menacingly, as he gave Edgar a nudge; the slightest of pushes, still a push, nevertheless. Edgar was forced to take a step backwards in order to regain his balance; confused as to the cause of Abelman's sudden change in demeanour. The gap created just enough space to allow Abelman to open the door. Suddenly, with all the fake and fabricated pretence of a shallow prince charming, he stretched his other hand out towards Penny, as if to say, "this way my lady." It was an act of deliberate humiliation, transforming her into his token princess while reminding Edgar of his place in the process. Penny acknowledged Abelman's hand and climbed into the front of his Porsche, while Edgar, the lowly squire, squeezed himself into the back.

The top remained down and Abelman shouted for most of the journey; yelling loudly so that Edgar could hear him speak. Edgar shouted in reply whenever prompted, always looking into the rear-view mirror: trying to gain eye contact with Penny. But Penny was out of reach, her eyes hidden behind dark glasses. Her head was tilted downwards, and always to the right; unable, or unwilling to connect. When they pulled up outside Domino's, Abelman checked the rear-view mirror, predictably spying Edgar. He smiled as Edgar tried to avert his ominous gaze, but it was too late, the little mouse was caught, and the cat's fun was just beginning. Abelman continued to stare into the mirror, and Edgar's anxiety continued to grow. He looked everywhere except back into Abelman's eyes, and only the sound of the engine broke the silence of the chase. Abelman revved again and again, goading Edgar; challenging him to make a move, to say something, to break the deadlock. Edgar shied from the contest; his eyes remaining down, his mouth closed. Abelman waited, then turned the ignition off and got out. The humbled apprentice looked up and watched as Abelman walked around to open the door for Penny. He took her by the arm—the perfect gentleman—and walked with her into the bar. The tables had turned, and not in Edgar's favour; it was he who had fallen into disregard, forced to follow and walk behind the king.

As the doors opened and the warm air escaped, Edgar coughed at the wave of body odour that immersed him. The sound of a thousand conversations competed with the loud thumping basslines of the DJ's music, drowning the voice of the doorman who recognised and welcomed Abelman. It was very different to the last time that Edgar was here; it was crowded now, heaving with people that were dancing and enjoying themselves with only the strobe lighting to guide their way. Edgar felt his heart rise as he looked inside; at the idea of his master arranging this party, doing all of this just for him.

'Good evening, Dr. Abelman. May I take—'

'There we are!' shouted Abelman, ignoring the waiter as he walked past. Pointing at an oval booth deep at the back of the bar.

Abelman forged his way through the crowd, his hand maintaining a steady hold of Penny. Edgar followed into the spaces left behind; buoyed by the rhythm, smiling broadly. So, this was why Abelman was acting so strangely, he thought. He wasn't trying to provoke him; he was trying to distract him: to keep him from asking questions that might otherwise ruin the surprise.

Nearing the booth, at a distance from the loudspeakers, the lights were raised to a soft dim glow. Edgar could see five rowdy men were already seated. A large ice bucket that held an empty, upturned magnum bottle of champagne was placed beside them. The men were laughing raucously, clearly in high spirits, and it would seem they had started the evening celebrations very early. Abelman pulled out a chair and Edgar stood silently; brimming with pride as the guest of honour awaited to be announced. However, the chair was not for Edgar, and Abelman proceeded to parade ostentatiously as he sat Penny closer to the table. Despite his efforts, Abelman's performance had largely gone unnoticed, and the men continued in their boisterous behaviour.

'Gentlemen!' said Abelman sternly, as he ordered the men to attention. 'We have a *lady* with us this evening.'

The smirk on Abelman's face was sinister, and the smile on Edgar's began to fade. Not sure why his party had started without him, Edgar was still standing, feeling out of place, when Abelman sat down beside Penny to take the only free chair that remained. Edgar glanced at the men around the table; he didn't recognise any of them. Abelman removed Penny's dark glasses and placed them down in front of her.

'That's better my dear, now we can all see your pretty smile.'

One of the men sniggered. Another, a fat, disgusting looking man who perspired profusely, whistled disrespectfully in admiration. Then another, a thinner man with a ginger moustache, curly hair and a raised scar freshly inflicted on his left cheek, spoke approvingly.

'Very nice... very nice indeed!'

And then another, a man whose nose had been broken more times than a presidential promise, stared angrily at Edgar.

'What are you looking at?' the man demanded, clearly offended by Edgar's presence.

'Boys.... Boys! Mickey, is that any way to welcome our guest? This is Eddy.'

Abelman's introduction diffused the situation, although left the men unimpressed, still weary of the stranger. Edgar felt their eyes upon him; the rhythm of his heart increasing as uncertainty began to seep deeper into his veins. He looked across to Penny, her eyes unveiled, but she seemed depressed, almost medicated. Her pupils were dilated, unresponsive to the lighters and the burning ends of the cigars around the table that all pointed in her direction. Edgar noticed another bruise. It wasn't there that morning; he was certain of it. This one went across her cheek, and even in the low-lit area, concealed by heavy foundation, he could see that it was fresh and had begun to swell. Abelman signalled for another bottle of champagne, as he told the men about a politician who had been in his office earlier that day. He mocked his patient's disabilities while everyone laughed, captivated by his story. Everyone that is, except for Edgar, who sensed that he must do something and attempted to reach out to Penny once again.

'Penny?'

There was no response.

'Penny?'

Still no response, but Edgar's voice was loud enough to gain the unwanted interest of Abelman, who paused to face him.

'Eddy...?'

The laughing around the table stopped instantly, and Edgar had the full attention of the pack.

'What are you doing?' asked Abelman, and Edgar turned pale.

'Erm... I... I was... w-well, I was—'

Abelman's face was puzzled. 'You were what?' he asked, interrupting Edgar's stuttering. He nodded to another waiter, who came running over immediately. 'Get this boy a goddamn chair!' he roared.

'Of course, Dr. Abelman,' said the waiter, who then disappeared to do as he was told.

'Sorry about that boys.... You know, maybe that's why they call it Domino's—they just wait for you to fall down.'

The men laughed, and Abelman continued with his story about the politician; his captive audience enjoying every word, enthralled by his charm as he returned to ridiculing his patient. Edgar's heart was racing, as he felt again the wet touch of his shirt. He sighed in relief, safe in the knowledge that his master was engrossed, before deciding to risk his luck one more time.

'Penny...? Penny, can you hear me?'

Luck, however, is best left to chance, and while Abelman appeared to be engaged in storytelling, nothing could have been further from the truth. His ears were pricked and homed solely on Edgar, leaving nothing to wager or whisper unheard.

'Pen?'

Penny continued to stare aimlessly as desperation filled Edgar's voice. Her eyes were wide but absent, her face frozen. She seemed so despondent, so lifeless and catatonic.

'Are you ok...? Please, just give me a—'

'Here you are, sir,' said the waiter as he arrived with a chair. 'I am terribly sorry.'

He placed the chair and waited to seat Edgar, who readied himself to sit down and join the table. Abelman paused from his story once again, looking up at the waiter: his eyes as hard as stone.

'That's ok. My friend was just leaving... weren't *you*, Eddy?'

Edgar looked at Abelman, too scared to speak.

'Seems he won't be joining the party after all.'

The game was up. Edgar tried to think quickly, to invent a reason, a believable lie for why he tried to reach Penny.

'Mel... I... I w-was only—'

But Edgar had no time, and to argue with Abelman was futile. He had heard enough, seen enough, and he was not to be interrupted.

'Seems my friend's mind is on other things—things that shouldn't concern him *any – more.*'

Edgar looked at the table, at the five cigar ends pointing at him; aimed like gun barrels, ready to fire and execute the accused.

'He needs to get some rest... maybe think about his future.... Leave the past behind.'

Edgar's eyes pleaded with Abelman, as they searched for some evidence of his earlier affection. He couldn't ask him to leave, this was his party, his celebration; the graduation that he never had. Abelman returned no warmth, he offered no cause for hope or sway. He stared coldly instead as their eyes remained locked; never flinching, never blinking, and waited for the mouse to scurry. He had issued his command and Edgar had no choice but to obey.

'As you wish, Dr. Abelman,' said the waiter.

He smiled; it did nothing to break the tension, and he bowed slightly to confirm Abelman's authority, then removed the chair. Edgar was left to stand alone, isolated once more.

'Ok,' mumbled Edgar, nodding resignedly. 'I... I'm....'

He wanted to tell Abelman that he was sorry, but the words choked in his throat as he looked at the men around the table; the men now laughing at him and not the stories of Abelman. Any doubts about the intentions of the evening were well and truly over, and Edgar stared at the men, studying their every detail; their eyes, their hair, their faces and committed them all to memory. He would know them if their paths should ever cross again, and God help them if they should, because he would make each of them pay for this night. Make each of them suffer for this humiliation. Edgar turned to leave, pushing his way through the crowd, and as he did so, he heard the men still laughing; they mocked him from behind his back. Years had passed, nothing had changed—he was back in California, trapped in the classroom on graduation day. This was the second time that Abelman had taken him to this bar and the second time he had dismissed him from it. It was going to be the last. It would never happen again. How could he have been so stupid to believe that Abelman was going to treat him as an equal? So naive to believe that Abelman was throwing a party in his honour? Had he even signed off on his residency?

Edgar reached the door and looked back one last time; one last feeble attempt to try and reach Penny. It was hopeless. She was lost. Bewitched. A mannequin positioned and posed at the side of a monster. There was no one there and there was nothing he could do to save her. He turned back to face the street, his heart heavy in his chest with the weight of regret on his shoulders. As he left the bar, he pushed past the doorman who was arguing with someone trying to sneak in. In the midst of the scuffle, Edgar spied a parking enforcement officer standing at the curb issuing a ticket.

'Excuse me, officer?' Edgar called out, as he walked over to her. 'I don't wish to intrude, but... well, I was just leaving Domino's and overheard the driver of this car talking with his friends. He was pointing at you, and they were laughing.'

The officer stopped writing and glanced up at Edgar.

'What did you say?'

'The owner... I just heard him say that he parks here because there's nothing you can do to make him park anywhere else.'

Edgar tried to force a smile, an expression to acknowledge his sympathies for the officer before he turned to begin the long walk home. As he walked back through Little Italy in Boston's North End, the air was filled with the sound of restaurants opening their shutters. They were marking the end of the working day and busily preparing to entertain their evening dinner guests. If only life was that simple, thought Edgar to himself. If only he could mark time by the opening and closing of a door. If only he had not abused Penny's feelings and asked her to meet Abelman. If only he had done what he had planned to do: disappeared and left Boston without a trace. If only he could find a door to turn back time and undo all that he had done. If only....

The longer he walked, the more he hoped to find a way to put today behind him. Be that as it may, he could never forget and would never ignore the lesson he had learned. Abelman was not a friend, and no matter what came through tomorrow's door, he would never be foolish enough to trust him again.

5

A SIMPLE PLAN

The next morning Edgar completed his rounds with Nurse Parsons. So much happened yesterday that Edgar had laid awake for most of the night. He was tired and time passed slowly with Abelman nowhere to be seen. As the day dragged on tediously, Edgar had to wait until almost 3:00 p.m. before he finally saw his master scuttling down the corridor; in no mood to stop, with no need to talk.

'Mel! Mel! Do you have a minute?'

Abelman looked unhappy; he was weary and his face drawn. Edgar ran over from his desk to greet him.

'What is it, Spear?'

'Well, I was wondering about the residency.... Now that it's over... what happens next?'

'Residency?'

'Yes. Yesterday you said that you'd signed off on my residency and I was wondering if—'

'That was yesterday.'

Abelman turned to carry on to wherever he was going. His abrupt interruption had realised Edgar's worst fears. He had failed Abelman, but he needed to try to keep focus; to get answers to the questions that had kept him awake. He reached out and took hold of Abelman's shoulder.

'Yes, I know. I know it was yesterday and we discussed that my residency was complete, but I was wondering—'

'Complete?' Abelman turned and brushed Edgar's hand away. 'Who said anything about it being complete? I told you it was over.'

'Over?'

'Look, Spear, I'll cut to the chase…. There's no place for you at the Slaughterhouse. It's time you looked for another hospital to complete your training.'

'W-what…? B-but you said… I don't understand… w-what do you mean…? Complete my training? You said—'

'I said what?' barked Abelman as he interrupted Edgar yet again. 'What *exactly* did I say to you? Huh? You can't even speak… so how the hell are you gonna tell me anything?'

Abelman's eyes blackened, squinting slightly as his lips narrowed. Edgar watched as his face paled, draining of blood, becoming ever colder. Suddenly, he grabbed Edgar by his arm and pulled him to the side.

'I told you… forget about the girl. I told you to get me on a flight— into a meeting with Munro—and get him onboard. But you… you *don't* seem to listen… do you, Spear? You don't *do* what you're told… and I don't *give* without getting…. You had your shot. Your chance to give. A onetime deal, Spear, and you blew it.'

'B-but I thought—'

'You thought what…? Whoever gave *you* permission to think? If I wanted you to think, I'd have given you a brain transplant,' scorned Abelman, as his stare froze Edgar speechless. 'Pack your things and get the hell out of my hospital—out of my city! You're through, Spear…. You're done.'

He released Edgar's arm and began to walk away. Edgar, no longer caught in the chill of hostility, tried again to speak.

'B-but Mel....'

Abelman, as always, had to have the final word. The final say was always his and he turned back to look at Edgar one last time, to offer one final piece of Abelman Advice.

'I told you, Spear, Munro was the key to your future, and now you don't have one. Now you're just a kid without a future... and a kid without a future is going nowhere.'

Edgar didn't understand. He had done what was promised. He had called Munro, left a message, and said that he was arriving on Friday. What more was he supposed to do? As far as Abelman was concerned, everything was on track and had always been on track, so this reaction made no sense. No sense at all. Not unless... of course, Abelman must have found another way to get to James? A way that made Edgar's role meaningless, his value worthless. Perhaps Abelman had spoken to Munro himself? Found out that Edgar had been lying about the arrangements of the meeting; that he had been lying about their friendship and his involvement in CaliChat. That he had, in actual fact, lied about everything.

He was devastated. Edgar knew the power of Abelman and if he said go, then you went. He had once told Edgar about the medical boards; the influence that he held over them. If he said jump, then they never asked how high, they only needed to know how far? That was the reach that Abelman had; the command that he brandished and control he maintained. If he said Edgar was out, then Edgar was out. There were no independent panels he could appeal to or claims that he could submit for unfair dismissal. His career was over, on the day it was meant to begin.

As he went back to his desk, Edgar checked through his hospital email for the last time. There was one new mail, unread and unopened from SouthWest Airlines: the subject line confirming his trip from Logan Airport to LAX on Friday. He sighed heavily, and his head dropped in dismay. With the scathing attack and dismissal, he had forgotten about the tickets purchased that very morning while waiting to see Abelman. It was another slap in the face for Edgar; one more kick in the long line of kicks to his teeth and the hardest of blows to now have to take. After all that he endured during these past two years, everything he had suffered in chasing his stupid dream of becoming a surgeon; Edgar had now thrown away the last of his allowance in trying to please his master. He closed his eyes and a tear rolled down his cheek. He had bought two tickets that would take him nowhere. Nowhere except perhaps to his knees, begging his grandfather to pay to take him back to California. It was the only way for him to end this ordeal and hammer the final nail into his Slaughterhouse coffin.

Edgar opened his eyes and another tear fell, splashing on the M of the keyboard. Munro, he thought. Damn you, Munro. How did he allow himself to get into all this? To pursue his enemy with the pretence of a renewed friendship, guided under the coercion of a tyrant whose every word was a threat. Abelman had broken him—destroyed his dreams—but he would not give him the satisfaction of seeing him cry. He would lift his head and... suddenly, the television flashed a photograph of James. Edgar turned up the volume to listen to the report.

'.... Munro said he was sad to be leaving the company, and was parting with a heavy heart,' said the news anchor.

What? What was this? What had happened? Was James dismissed; kicked out of CaliChat?

'And if you're just joining us this afternoon, our breaking story is the resignation of James Munro.'

Resignation? There was no way that James would ever....

'Addressing reporters an hour ago, Munro had this to say,' said the anchor before the feed cut to a press conference.

"When I first created CaliChat I had a dream of bringing the world together, by making it easier for everyone to find each other, to connect and share.

"These past years have been an amazing journey, but the events of recent weeks have taken a heavy toll on myself and everyone at CaliChat. As founder and CEO, I have to recognise that I am, in part, responsible for that toll.

"After meeting this morning with Martin Freyland, the chairman of our great company, we agreed by mutual consent that it was in the best interests of all parties for me to step down and allow—"

Edgar pressed the mute button on the remote. There was no need to hear anymore. He understood why Abelman had changed his mind, and it obviously wasn't because he had called or talked with James. James had simply left CaliChat, which meant Edgar's value to Abelman had ended, and with it so had Abelman's offer.

He sat down and began to delete the emails from his computer. It was time to remove the last remanence of his existence at the Slaughterhouse. As he clicked through the unending list, Edgar fell into a blind robotic trance. The realisation that this really was the end of his failed residency had begun to sink in. Edgar's mind drifted onto other things; the practical and immediate consequences of Abelman's decision. He would need to vacate the apartment, that was for residents only, and it would be better to leave before being thrown onto the street. He would have to begin work at his grandfather's company, starting off at the bottom before there would be any hope of moving into an office position. As the list was finally all but depleted, the bold font of one last unread email remained at the top of his inbox. It screamed for attention and awoke Edgar from his trance as he stared at the subject line.

Your SouthWest Airlines flight details to LAX
with Dr. M. Abelman.

Edgar looked at the cardboard box beside him; at the few paltry possessions he had packed inside: a Boston Red Sox baseball cap; an imitation Mont Blanc fountain pen; a few thank you cards, given to him by patients; and little things, forgotten items left behind that he had taken. They amounted to nothing. He was leaving without riches, and it was all because of one man. All because of Dr. Abelman... Dr. M. Abelman... Melvin Abelman.... Melvin The Monster.

Something inside Edgar clicked. Instead of deleting, he moved the mouse towards the print icon, then went to collect the pages from the printer. If I'm walking out of here today, then he'll get these before I'm gone, thought Edgar, as he tried to console himself that at least Abelman would see that he had kept his side of the arrangement. He rolled the printouts like a baton and carried them in one hand, his box with the other and made ready to leave. He wasn't coming back. He was going to Abelman's office, where Kassandra was sitting at her desk, puckering her lips after smearing them with lip gloss.

'Dr. Spear, there's no point going in because Dr. Abelman isn't there,' she said sternly.

Edgar was indifferent and handed her the sheets of rolled paper.

'I'm not going in... I came to give him this. Please see that it gets to him.'

Edgar turned and made his way out of the Lunder Building for the last time. As he walked past several nurses, he tried to stay focused on looking ahead, ignoring their gasps of surprise; the shock of a doctor who carried his possessions which meant only one thing. He offered a cursory smile, a poor attempt at maintaining his dignity. And as he passed through the glass doors, he held his head high, never looking back or turning to see who was watching him leave; whoever it was that sniggered and giggled behind his back. It didn't matter who the culprit was anyway. It was over, and Edgar no longer cared. He had no love for California, even less for Abelman, so that was at least one small consolation. He found a dumpster and threw the box away. There was no place for sentiment in Edgar's life. No need for souvenirs or mementos, and no point in remembering Boston. He was done with it, done with empty promises of a better future. Abelman was right about what he had said: it was time to "leave the past behind." It was time to look ahead.

The long walk home in the chilling wind had given Edgar time to think. Tomorrow he would have to begin the plan to return to Port Larsen, a place he had vowed to never see again, but like so many of his plans, was based on decisions that were beyond his control. The life of a manual labourer and the harbour now awaited him. It didn't seem so bad now, so beneath him as before, and nowhere near as bad as having to admit to his grandfather that he had not lived up to his mother's expectations. That after all of his boasting and all that he had done, in the end, he was no better than his father; an apple that had fallen close to the tree and failed to produce anything of value.

Edgar's melancholy was interrupted by the *Ding!* from the microwave, to inform him that his half-burned, half-uncooked TV dinner for one was ready. As he inspected the plate and compared it to the image on the packaging, the bubbling food which was supposed to resemble a lasagne, looked more like a serious nuclear accident and did nothing to improve his mood. Suddenly, there was a knock at the door. No one ever knocked Edgar's door—*ever*—they rang the buzzer from outside. Edgar dismissed it; a visitor for another tenant, as he continued to inspect the aftermath of the explosion that lay upon his plate. The door knocked again. Whoever it was, they were persistent, but they would soon realise their mistake and move along. Another knock followed. Silence clearly was not enough to deter the guest, and Edgar began to wonder if it might actually be someone for him?

A key turned in the lock, and Edgar panicked as his mouth dropped to release a silent scream. He grabbed the blunted table knife he was going to use to eat his dinner, a gut reaction, and prepared himself to meet an intruder. The door opened, and a familiar voice called out.

'Eddy...! There's my boy, is this where you've been hiding?'

Edgar was lost for words as Abelman strutted into his apartment without a care.

'What's this...? You gonna try and stick me with that?' laughed Abelman, derisively.

At that precise moment, nothing could have described Edgar's thoughts or feelings better. He would have loved to have taken the knife and with large letters—capital letters—the larger the better, carved his name into Abelman's chest.

'What do you want, Abelman?'

Abelman's head jerked backwards. Surprised to be called "Abelman" and at hearing Edgar's tone of voice.

'Eddy, is that any way to treat a friend?'

'We're not friends,' replied Edgar defiantly. 'We're not anything.'

'Now, now, Eddy—'

'This is still my apartment, at least until the morning, and there's nothing you, or your stooges, can do about it. I'll be out of here by eleven, so until then, get out and don't come back or I'll call the cops!'

'Well look at you... all pumped and ready for action,' said Abelman, sarcastically. Edgar pressed his lips firmly together; his fingers gripped tightly around the knife. Abelman softened his tone. 'Calm down, Eddy, you've got it all wrong. I haven't come here to throw you out.... I'm a man who comes bearing gifts. I've come to give you these.'

He unzipped the Hermès folder that he was carrying, and the fresh scent of expensive new leather easily overpowered the bland, tasteless aroma of Edgar's lasagne.

'You wanna drop the knife?' he said, as he produced several sheets of paper and handed them to Edgar. 'Before you hurt yourself.'

Edgar's eyes glanced across the top sheet, and he put the knife down awaiting an explanation. It was a first-class medical degree with honours from Harvard University. According to the degree, he had graduated seven years ago. Not for the first time, Edgar found himself speechless in the company of Abelman.

'Let's just call it… a little upgrade,' said Abelman with a shrug.

Edgar lifted the diploma and peered at the page beneath. It was a signed declaration from Abelman, confirming the completion of a seven-year residency at Massachusetts General hospital within the field of neurosurgery. He lifted the declaration and found a draft employment agreement; it carried his name for a position as chief physician at a company he had never heard of.

'DomiGen Labs?' asked Edgar, his brain intoxicated by all that it saw.

'It's the company we're gonna set up, Eddy. The company Munro is gonna use to get his new venture off the ground. The company you're gonna run for me.'

'For you?'

'For us.'

'I… I don't understand….'

Sensing that Edgar was calmer, more open to persuasion, Abelman put his arm around him and led him towards the window.

'You see out there…? That's a world… a world with over seven billion people. And all of them are waiting… wanting more than they have today.

'You know what we call them, Eddy…?

Edgar stared.

'Suckers… but others call them *customers.*

'You and I… we're gonna give them what they want. But we need Munro—we need his expertise. We need him to get the first bricks in place and then they'll come… all of them… wait and see. Standing in line, queuing like dominoes. But they won't see the bigger picture. They won't see the show. Not until it's too late. Because it's *our* show, Eddy. It's our world…. It's – *all* – ours.'

Edgar turned his head to Abelman, expecting to see that familiar psychotic look after such a speech. Abelman talked like a lunatic, yet his words were not of one. He sounded entrepreneurial, like an ambitious businessman with global expectations.

'Yesterday you t-told me my residency was over.... This afternoon you t-told me to get out. Now you c-come here... w-with these papers... and you say you w-want to make *me* a chief physician?'

Edgar stepped back, making room for what he needed to say, and his stammer disappeared.

'Are you insane? Why would I believe anything you say to me? Everything you say is a lie... everything you do is—'

Abelman's view turned from the street outside to the young disobedient apprentice. Edgar stopped, unable to finish or expel the words that crawled back inside his throat. The face of Abelman had dropped. His eyebrows were raised, warmth again replaced by that cold and sinister expression. Edgar braced himself for the threat and the delivery of that harrowing sense of fear that aims to strike terror into its victim's hearts, when quite unexpectedly, Abelman burst into fits of laughter.

'Because you have no choice! That's why. You can't practice as a surgeon—*you* don't have a license. I've signed your papers and ended your residency, so you're finished at the Slaughterhouse. You can stay until the end of the month but after that... without a license... you're done, Eddy.... No one else can take you and trust me... no one else will.

'So, what you gonna do? Where you gonna go? You gonna go crawling back to granddaddy and show him what a loser you are? I thought you were made of more than that... were more of a man.... A man with ambition.

'I told you... get Munro onboard—you'll get your license and board certificates.'

Edgar was listening, knowing deep down that Abelman was right. What choice did he have really? He was resigned to returning to California, working for his grandfather and accepting his fate. But it wasn't his decision, it was someone else's destiny that was being forced upon him.

'And when you get your license, what are you gonna do then? Huh?

'You gonna start your own practice? Is that what you think? Well, who's gonna fund that? I don't know if you know it, Eddy, but it takes dough—*real dough*—to buy a practice, and that's the kind of bread you just don't have.

'So, that leaves the Slaughterhouse… is that your plan? You gonna beg them for a measly hundred grand a year? Try to make it up to five, thirty years from now when you retire? Is that how far the ambitions of the great Edgar Spear are gonna take him…? Straight to Nowhereville?'

The master of manipulation took several steps closer to the now informed Edgar.

'Two kinds of people in this world, Eddy—the ones that get ahead and the ones that get left behind. The *only* question you need to answer, is are you gonna be one of the guys playing catch up, or are you gonna get ahead?'

Abelman paused.

'Check the agreement,' he said as he prodded the papers with his index finger. 'You *start* on five hundred grand a year.'

Edgar looked down at the draft contract; the words, *Five Hundred Thousand Dollars*, clearly marked and underlined. He breathed sharply, a gulp of shock, and the papers rustled in his hands for a moment. Abelman saw the wheels of Edgar's mind turning; slowly gaining speed as his taut expression morphed to forgiveness. His eyes, filling with approval and desire.

'Look—let's cut to the chase—you chose this. I gave you a hand, but you chose to play it. Now we're at the table and I've just shown my cards. You need to ask yourself if you're in...? If you're willing to go — *all* — in? Because if you're not, then it's game over my friend. There's no license. No certificates. No papers. No job. No nothing. You're out, and you're walking home empty.

'I told you, Eddy, you're in safe hands. I *always* have control. *Always.*'

Edgar knew that everything Abelman was telling him was true. Ten minutes ago, his thoughts were of packing a suitcase and preparing to fly to his grandfather; the prospect of beginning life on a minimum wage. That was the harsh reality of his world without Abelman leading the way.

Edgar nodded. 'Ok.... Ok, Mel. I'm in... I'm all in.'

'My man.... Whose — *my* — man!' said Abelman, as he patted Edgar on the shoulder. 'I gotta run, so I'll see you at the Slaughterhouse tomorrow. You keep hold of the papers... they're yours now.'

Abelman was halfway out the door when he turned, as usual, to offer one last word of advice.

'Go buy a frame or something for that degree.... First-class honours... top of your year at Harvard. A man should take care of such things,' he smirked.

But Edgar had a question that he needed to ask and to which he needed an answer.

'Mel?'

Abelman stopped again and this time waited for Edgar.

'I... I don't understand... you told me to get Munro onboard.... Munro was fired. He's out of CaliChat. So, what good is he to you now?'

Abelman smiled.

'Eddy, my boy, you gotta learn to open your eyes and see what's in front of you... stop looking behind—that's the past. This morning our deal was dead, but then I thought, Munro's a free agent... nothing to tie him down—no one to hold him up. The chances of getting him onboard just doubled, if the right guy could convince him.' He checked the time, seemingly impatient. 'We'll take this later. I need to run. Some deadbeat traffic cop impounded my car last night and I gotta get it back. Goddamn taxis in this city cost a fortune.'

Abelman left leaving the door open behind him, taking the key he had used to let himself in. Edgar placed the papers down upon the table. His name stood out in large black letters on the bachelor's degree, embossed with The Harvard Shield.

'VERITAS,' said Edgar, as he read the lettering upon the shield. Truth? he thought. Are you kidding me?

Edgar laughed to himself, amused by the irony of it all, at Abelman's mockery of the institution he once held in regard and dreamt of attending. Still hesitant to believe, he lifted the counterfeit diploma to reveal Abelman's confirmation of Edgar's completed residency. He had in his hands a new medical degree to back up a fictitious graduation from seven years ago. More than this, a signed letter by one of the chief physicians at Massachusetts General. On their own, each document was precious, but together they were priceless. He had done it. He was home and dry... almost.

The following morning, Edgar arrived at the Slaughterhouse. Nothing, and no one, was going to ruin his day. There was still no sign of Penny, so Nurse Parsons again assisted him on his rounds. It was the usual thing. Clydesdale still complaining to see Abelman and Edgar still trying to reassure him that he was busy saving lives. The day passed quietly, and more importantly, brought him closer to the nineteenth and the trip to Los Angeles.

By Thursday, the day before Edgar and Abelman were due to fly, Edgar still hadn't heard back from James. Not surprisingly, Edgar had become increasingly worried. Tomorrow was the biggest day of his life—make or break—and everything he had worked for hung in its balance. Helpless once again, without control over his destiny, Edgar was unable to prevent his frustrations from spilling out. That morning during patient rounds, after Clydesdale had asked to see Abelman,

Edgar erupted in a charged temper and ordered him to be quiet. He found himself unable to remain polite or courteous any longer and warned Clydesdale to stop with his incessant demands. He was not going to tolerate his badgering, nor answer to an overindulged, selfish old man who had already lived longer than he deserved. If he continued to persist about Abelman, Edgar would see to it that he was discharged and left to foot an overly inflated bill.

Parsons was mortified at the way in which Edgar spoke to Clydesdale and his other patients: shouting at them, bullying them, and telling them to be quiet. She decided to notify Nurse Catone, the head nurse, to lodge a formal complaint against him, but Edgar didn't care. He wasn't concerned with the grievances of Parsons, especially since she was only filling in for his regular nurse—wherever she may be.

It had been over a week since Edgar last saw Penny. He knew that Abelman had seen her several times, as he would often make lude and insinuating comments about the previous night; his time with that "little tiger," as he continued to call her, even though Penny never came to the hospital anymore. In fact, the last time that Edgar saw Penny was when he failed to reach her, that terrible night at Domino's. He had since told himself that the reason for her absence was most likely due to her drug habit. And as so often the case, the lie that he repeated so many times had now become the truth; made even more so, by the convincing concerns he expressed to others at the mention of her name, and the obvious drug problem he had witnessed first-hand.

Edgar's empathy was far from sincere. It was as superficial as the Rolex that he wore upon his wrist. Penny's problem was Penny's problem; she was not Edgar's problem. Munro was his problem, and he was about to become a very large one at that, if he did not hear from him before the end of the day. As Edgar sat with his tower of precariously balanced patient files, he filled in various details of treatment adjustments as best he could during late morning and lunch. His mind, however, was on other things, and taken almost entirely by the clock on the wall at the bottom of the corridor, opposite his desk. As he watched the minute hand move painfully slow around the face, his heavy tired eyes fought to stay open. Each hour seemed to pass like an eternity, like the final lesson of a school day. Yet instead of a bell, it was the telephone on Edgar's desk that rang out to waken him, causing him to jump and the file laden tower to fall.

'Spear,' said Edgar, as he answered confused; not quite awake.

'Dr. Spear?' said a voice on the other end. 'We have a grand mal seizure.'

It was Nurse Lopez. Edgar dropped the telephone and sprinted towards the ward. He knew a nurse would never call to report a grand mal seizure, as restraints would normally suffice until the patient's immediate risk had passed. If a doctor was needed, then it was because the seizure had lasted for more than five minutes, and the patient was still unresponsive. When Edgar arrived, he could see the commotion in the first patient room; the focus of activity on Clydesdale.

'Status?' he shouted, as he pushed a male nurse aside.

'Status epilepticus, Doctor.'

Edgar stared at Clydesdale, and the nurse continued his summary of the situation.

'Patient delirium. Breathing erratic. Movement from absence to tonic-clonic. Severe convulsions. Loss of consciousness. Erratic cardio activity. Arrhythmia, possible myocardial ischemia—'

'What!' screamed Edgar as he interrupted; surprised to hear that Clydesdale was experiencing problems with his heart. 'Who missed that?'

There was no time to point fingers or place blame. Clydesdale's condition was serious. His life was in danger; Edgar needed to act.

'Benzodiazepine?' he asked.

'Lorazepam. 5mg. Unresponsive.'

'Stats?' His eyes fixed wholly on Clydesdale. Stats!' he shouted, demanding an answer.

'127BPM. 160 over 114.'

The heart monitor sounded louder and faster; the pauses between the tones becoming shorter and shorter.

'We're losing him.... Crash cart. Now! Epinephrine 1mg. Prep.'

The monitor signalled a long, continuous tone. Clydesdale's heart had stopped.

'No! Not today, Clydesdale... you're not going *anywhere* today! Where's my cart?' Edgar screamed.

'Here, Doctor,' replied a nurse, as she forged her way through to him with the defibrillator trolley.

'Charge?' he shouted.

'Charged, Doctor.'

Edgar took the paddles. 'Clear?'

'Clear!'

He placed the paddles onto Clydesdale's chest and administered the charge. Clydesdale's body shocked. The monitor beeped loudly. Then a flicker. Then a pulse. And then the single continuous tone.... Still no heartbeat.

'Epinephrine?'

'Ready, Doctor.'

'Go!' he shouted, and the adrenaline was administered.

'Charge?'

'Charged.'

Edgar took the paddles again. 'Clear?'

'Clear!'

He placed the paddles onto Clydesdale's chest and again administered the charge. The heart monitor beeped loudly, and all eyes turned to the screen. The tone stayed continuous; Clydesdale remained unresponsive.

'Epinephrine 3mg.... Prep.' Not wanting to wait for the nurse, Edgar began to administer CPR. 'One... one thousand. Two... one thousand. Three... one thousand. Four... one thousand.... Come on, Clydesdale.... Come on!'

Edgar continued to press his hands into Clydesdale's chest, counting out the compressions, desperately trying to resuscitate his heart.

'Where's my Epinephrine?'

'Ready, Doctor,' replied the nurse, as Edgar grabbed it and administered it himself.

'Charge?' he shouted, while continuing feverously to deliver CPR.

Clydesdale's lips began to turn blue.

'Come on!' screamed Edgar. 'Charge?'

'Charged, Doctor.'

And again, Edgar took the paddles. 'Clear?'

'Clear!'

He threw the paddles onto Clydesdale's chest and administered the charge. The monitor beeped loudly, and Clydesdale's body jolted, as all eyes turned again to the screen. But the tone was still continuous and there was still no reaction.

'Damn it, Clydesdale... come on! Come on!' Edgar screamed. 'I'll drag Abelman here myself if I have to... now come – on!' And again, Edgar continued with CPR. 'Epinephrine 5mg.... Prep.... Come on... I want that Epinephrine, now!'

'Ready, Doctor,' replied the nurse, as Edgar again grabbed the syringe and administered it himself.

'Come on...! Come on...! Come on, damn it!' Edgar shouted, as he pushed down and pressed hard, desperately counting out the number of compressions. 'Charge...? I – said – *charge?*'

A hand reached over and took Edgar's arm firmly.

'He's gone.'

It was Abelman; a nurse had left to fetch him.

'He's gone, Dr. Spear.... It's over.'

Edgar wasn't listening, neither was he stopping the CPR.

'Come on, Clydesdale...! Come on!' he screamed as he pressed frantically on Clydesdale's chest.

'You have to call it, Doctor. You have to let him go.'

Edgar ignored Abelman and continued the CPR, but Abelman knew that Clydesdale was gone. He grabbed Edgar by his arm, and not to be ignored this time, pulled him off the patient. Edgar was like a caged animal—wild—eyes wide and crazed. Surrounded by nurses, his face dripping with perspiration; the monitor still sounding the continuous tone.

'Doctor,' said Abelman trying to calm Edgar and return him to his senses. 'You *have* to call it.'

Edgar was confused and disoriented; the room was spinning around him. All the training that he had learned, the practice on resuscitation manikins—on Resusci Anne—nothing had prepared him for this.

'Turn that off!' he screamed, pointing at the heart monitor. 'Turn – that – damn – machine – *off!*'

A nurse turned off the monitor, and the agonised gasps of Edgar's breath were the only sound as the room fell silent.

Abelman cleared his throat. 'Doctor?' he said, as he nodded at Edgar and checked his watch. 'Time of death: 3:17 p.m.'

The words ripped out Edgar's heart and tore through his soul. He lashed out, kicking the crash cart and sending it clattering against the wall.

'How did we miss the arrhythmia…? How in God's name did we miss it?' he cried.

His wrath scolded everyone. There was no reply, no explanation or offer of response. No one dared. He walked back to the bed and looked down at Clydesdale, laying peacefully. Filled with anger, weighed down by regret, Edgar kicked the wheel of the bed before placing his hand upon Clydesdale's arm.

'Damn you, Clydesdale…. Damn you.'

Abelman put his hand upon Edgar's shoulder, knowing that this was the first time he had experienced death; felt the responsibility for the loss of life as a doctor. Aware of the scrutiny of other staff members, at times such as these when anything said in the heat of the moment or done out of grief might be seen as improper; Abelman suggested they leave.

'Some fresh air, Dr. Spear? Some fresh air and some coffee, I think.'

Abelman spoke as if casually talking to someone about the weather; as if simply passing the time of day. Except Abelman was never casual, and he was not asking if Edgar would like to join him. 'Come on,' he said, as he led Edgar out from the room.

They were barely a foot outside of the door, when Abelman wasted no time in getting to his point.

'So, Eddy, are we all set for tomorrow?'

Edgar was unable to think or speak clearly.

'A-are... are w-we...?'

'Tomorrow.... LA. Munro. Are we set?'

'Erm... set... yes.... Yes. Set.'

'Good. Well then... let's get that coffee.'

Edgar and Abelman walked to the canteen where the coffee was always bad. Brewed early in the morning, it was left to burn in the pot all day and could hardly be called coffee by the time it reached lunchtime. By then, it had more in common with tarmac than anything that was drinkable, but there was no time to go elsewhere. Abelman was due in a meeting and Edgar needed to cope with remorse. As they sat down, Abelman seemed completely unmoved by the death of Clydesdale and remained excited about the meeting with James. He told Edgar about his last trip to LA; how he always stayed at The Peninsula Hotel in Beverley Hills whenever he was there. Sure, it was expensive, and filled with tiresome celebrities, but he liked the way they embroidered his initials onto the pillowcases. It made him feel good—made him feel special—a little like royalty. After a few minutes of talking and enjoying the sound of his own voice, Abelman noticed that Edgar was still distraught; not listening to anything that he said. To help him regain interest and focus on things of greater importance, he put his coffee down and prepared to offer his young apprentice some more invaluable Abelman Advice.

'Eddy…. I've told you before. They're pitiful, insignificant, ungrateful little ants.

'Don't beat yourself up over Clydesdale… he was a goner from the minute he came in. It's nice you strung him along with some hope and made him feel better. But don't kid yourself… he was never walking out of here again. He was never gonna make it—I promise you.'

Abelman took another sip of his coffee. Edgar continued to sit quietly, still wallowing in self-pity.

'Nice touch when you kicked the bed by the way… did you see Nurse Lopez? You could have had her right there and then.'

Edgar couldn't believe his ears. He knew that Abelman was cold—ice cold—but this… this *thing* that sat opposite him had no compassion at all. It was devoid of all feeling.

'Don't you have a heart?'

'No,' Abelman replied, without needing to think or take time to reply. 'I have no heart. I have *no* sympathy. No tears to shed for the dying and no grief for the dead. You know why…? Because they're *pitiful – insignificant – ungrateful – little – ants*… and the sooner you get that Eddy, the better.

'Get your head back in the game…. Tomorrow's a big day for you… biggest of your life. So, do what you gotta do, say what you gotta say, and get your game face on.'

Abelman's pager beeped, and he looked down to check the number.

'I gotta go, Eddy. Just remember… you can't do anything for the dead. So, do yourself a favour… forget them… cos they sure as hell don't think about you.'

As Edgar finished his coffee, he realised that as brutal as Abelman was, there was a point to what he had said. People die. More people were going to die. So, if death was going to bother him then he was in the wrong profession. To Abelman, losing a patient was like a carpenter losing a nail. They came in boxes of hundreds, and none of them mattered more than the last; had any more value than the others or the next. Edgar had only just been stung by his first touch of death. He had fought to save a life that could not be saved. He had lost a nail, and he would likely lose more. It was just something that he would have to get used to. That was all. Edgar took another sip of his coffee and told himself that it was alright to be sad. He had tried his best to save Clydesdale, that was the most important thing. It was not his fault that the patient had an undiagnosed problem. If he had known about his heart, then he could easily have saved him. He was a great doctor and would be a brilliant surgeon, but he could not be expected to read minds, could he? If only those around him had done their jobs properly then Clydesdale might still be alive. It was the doctors in x-ray, the radiographers, somebody there who should have ordered an electrocardiogram. They were the reason, the real cause of Clydesdale's death. His sadness turned to anger as the blame became obvious, and he crunched the paper coffee cup to a pulp in his hand. How could he be expected to do his job with such incompetent staff around him? Now he understood why Abelman called it the Slaughterhouse. That's exactly what it was. A place full of dead meat. Not a place for a brilliant young surgeon, for an artist like Edgar, and the sooner he left, the better. He was going to be the chief physician of DomiGen Labs; together with Abelman and Munro they were going to own the world. Munro was the key to his future, and Munro was.... Edgar stopped; his mind forgetting Clydesdale. He still hadn't heard anything from James. He checked his pocket. His cell phone wasn't there. He must have left it on his desk when he ran to respond to the call from Nurse Lopez. He hurried back and found it, hidden beneath the scattered pile of manila folders. The screen showed one missed call—one new message—and a smile filled his face as he pressed the dial button with impatience.

'You have one new message,' said the voice. 'Thursday, 3:03 p.m.'

Oh, thank heavens, thought Edgar. Finally, James had replied.

'Hello, Edgar, it's—'

It was his grandfather. What did he want...? He pressed the cancel button. Whatever it was, it didn't matter because Edgar didn't need to speak to him. He needed to speak with James, yet James clearly didn't need to speak to Edgar.

The clock at the end of the corridor showed 3:54 p.m. Edgar checked his wristwatch; it was 4:08 p.m., precisely. Splitting the difference, meant it was already 4:00 p.m., and time for him to leave.

It was an early flight in the morning and Edgar was sure that Abelman would ask for details of the meeting once they sat on the plane. He had no definitive plan to share, and no idea if James was even in LA. He slumped, downhearted, onto his chair; the pressure mounting and pounding inside his head. The price of Abelman's signature and the degree from Harvard, would have to be paid. But how? He rubbed his forehead to ease the pain and looked to the ceiling without hope. What was he doing? What on earth was he doing? This... was madness. It had never sounded difficult until now. The difficult part always seemed to be getting past his feelings; sentiments that he was willing to set aside in order to fulfil his ambitions and embrace his destiny. The rest always sounded so easy. So, when Abelman said, "get me into a meeting with Munro," Edgar had never really thought about how? How difficult getting such a meeting would genuinely prove to be. Since James had not returned Edgar's call, and Edgar had no way to reach him otherwise. All he did have, was nothing.

Edgar opened the browser on the computer and typed James' name into the search bar. There were just over two hundred and forty-seven million results. He would have to revise it, to narrow the hits.

James Munro, CaliChat.

Two hundred and forty-six million, three hundred thousand results. Edgar sighed heavily. It was no good, he was going to have to be much more specific.

James Munro, CaliChat, LA. 19th September.

Sixty-eight results. Edgar began to scroll; quickly speed reading each link. He tried to see if there was anything relevant, any connection between Munro and the date.

No... next page. No... next page. No.... No.... Wait.... Yes... yes, there it was. A closed meet and greet with James Munro at La Brasserie Parfaite. Edgar clicked the link to read more.

La Brasserie Parfaite will play host to an exclusive Meet n' Greet with CaliChat founder and former CEO, James Munro, on Friday 19th September at The Grove. Entry commences at 1:00 p.m.

That was all Edgar needed, a "where." It was a time and a place where James would be tomorrow. A way to reduce the problem to just "ifs," a few "buts," and some "maybes." Because the rest, he would have to leave to chance. Edgar read on.

Due to overwhelming demand, allocation has been reached. Valid ticket holders admitted only.

That was a problem. More than a setback. There was no way that Edgar could reserve tickets online or get any at the door. Simply put, there would be no easy way to get in. He would have to use his powers of persuasion to try to get Abelman and himself inside the venue. Having said that, it would have to be more than just inside, he would have to get them close enough to Munro to suggest to Abelman that they had agreed to meet in advance. Only that would be enough to convince his master that James and he were still friends; a friendship that Abelman was banking on to bring James onboard their venture. So, the real problem, the first real problem, was how to get them close to Munro; close enough to convince Abelman that Munro was expecting them. If Edgar could do that, then perhaps he could also persuade Munro to let Abelman speak?

It was a plan—of sorts—and it was simple... more or less.... Actually, when he thought about it, what could possibly go wrong?

_____

6

ALL IN

A s they stepped off the plane at LAX, Edgar and Abelman were greeted by the scorching Los Angeles heat. There was little that Edgar missed about California, but he did long for that warm West Coast air, which even in late autumn was still sizzling.

'I'll get us an Uber,' said Abelman. 'It's cheaper than a cab and the guys drive faster.'

Walking out towards the pick-up point, Edgar felt the sun beating down as it cut through the thick polluted air of car exhausts and fumes which filled his lungs. Abelman had been quiet on the flight and said very little. He seemed nervous, a little uneasy and more troubled than Edgar in fact, which was strange. They cut across the tarmac, and as they did, Abelman reminded Edgar of the importance of the day, looking less than impressed at the car that arrived to meet them.

'I can't get in that!' he cried. 'Jeez... we'll have to push that thing out of the car park.... I mean look at it... how the hell did it get here? Someone roll it?'

It was a Toyota Prius, which in itself was bad enough, but this car had seen better days, and it was a far cry from Abelman's Porsche. Still, there were no premium cars available and Abelman didn't care to wait another six minutes for one to arrive. Despite his misgivings, he accepted the ride, although now, looking at it, it was a decision he regretted. As they confirmed their destination and settled back into the car, Edgar thought that it was time to find out more about the company.

'Mel, we need to talk more about DomiGen Labs.'

'How so?'

'Well, if I'm supposed to convince James to join us, then I need to know more about what it is we're going to be doing—he's bound to ask—so, I need to able to tell him what it is he'll be expected to do? Just the basics, nothing more... enough to give him an idea.'

Abelman looked into the rear-view mirror and saw that the driver was looking back at them.

'You know if I were you, I'd keep my eyes on the road. You might have to stop this thing and I doubt it's got any brakes,' said Abelman, meeting his eye.

The driver averted his gaze and looked forward at the long line of traffic in front of them as he waited to exit the airport.

'DomiGen's the next generation of data collection and sharing, Eddy. It's gonna define how it's collected and dictate how it's shared.... You understand?

'We're not interested in *likes* or *clicks*—that's kids' stuff— what we're doing....'

Abelman saw that the driver was again looking in the rear-view mirror and decided not to continue.

'Hey, what did you say your name was?'

'Oh, it's Dhaneswar,' replied the driver in a thick Indian accent.

'Dans what?'

'Yes. Dhaneswar. It means God of wealth.'

Abelman raised an eyebrow.

'I am from Chengannur... you know Chengannur? Is beautiful—beautiful town in Alappuzha district.... India, you know...? Southern India... beautiful... beautiful... but not much work... very hard. So, I am coming to America six years ago and my family—' began the driver, believing in the interest for small talk. However, the driver clearly didn't know his passenger.

'Ok, Dans what,' Abelman interrupted. 'If you want a rating above one star then you keep your eyes on the road and your ears and mouth shut.'

Abelman was his usual charming self.

'Absolutely.... You are boss man... and I am only working for the boss man.'

Abelman, raised his eyebrow again and looked at Edgar.

'What a guy. I tell ya... these LA types.... They come here with their dreams... they're all either wannabe actors or working on some movie script. Either way, Eddy, they'll do anything for a dollar.'

Abelman looked again into the rear-view mirror, to check on the driver. Dhaneswar was only looking at the road ahead, and Abelman smirked, knowing that people always did as he told them. *Always.* They did it, or they suffered the consequences; even an Uber driver from wherever it was he said that he was from.

Edgar tried again to prise some information.

'What we're doing...?'

'What?'

'You said—what we're doing.'

'Oh. Oh yeah... yeah... you see, it's all in the name. The attitude starts in the name, Eddy. *Domi*, is short for dominoes—like those seven billion bricks... our customers. And *Gen*, that's short for next generation. You know those guys out at the valley, they always list companies with Gen in their name... makes them sound more high-tech.'

'I see,' said Edgar, surprised. 'I thought Domi was short for domination? Like DomiGen Labs will dominate the market sort of thing?'

Abelman laughed.

'Yeah, that's it, Eddy…. You tell that to Munro…. You tell him that we're gonna dominate the market… he'll like that.'

Abelman continued to laugh as Edgar tried to ignore it, attempting instead to dig a little deeper.

'So, what is this next generation technology we're selling? I know it has something to do with creating sales, but why do we need Munro to help us reach the market? And where do I fit in… as the chief physician?'

'Jeez… Eddy. What the hell's wrong with you? We're in a goddamn Uber!'

Abelman asked Dhaneswar how long before they reach The Grove?

'11:42 a.m…. More or less… give or take.'

'This guy,' scoffed Abelman as he checked his Rolex. 'Another ant in need of precision.'

Edgar, wishing to appear equal, checked his watch at the same time. Abelman, however, was the master; he remained king and a king's privilege is to remind his subjects of their place. Just one word was enough to put Edgar back in his.

'Fake?'

Edgar frowned. 'Sorry…?'

'Your watch, it's a fake.'

'W-well… no… actually…. I… it….' He stuttered, trying to defend his counterfeit street copy.

'Sure, it is. Look at the second hand—it's ticking. A Rolex doesn't tick, Eddy… it has automatic movement. Not like that cheap quartz stuff you're wearing.'

Edgar was rumbled. Humiliated yet again. He may have been trying to fool others into believing that he was successful, but there was no fooling Abelman.

'Don't sweat it, Eddy. Do your job today and you can pick any watch you want. Heck, I'll even give you mine—call it a bonus.'

Abelman nestled back into the seat and closed his eyes.

'Wake me when we're there. I gotta catch five. It's that girl... that Penny... she's killing me. She's a tiger!'

Edgar stared at Abelman. His eyes were closed, and head leant back into the seat next to him. Why did he have to mention Penny now? What was the point? Was Abelman still testing him? Trying to gauge his reaction? Even now? Were his eyes even closed, or was he really watching Edgar? Was everything just a game to him? A contest to have to win everything.

Some minutes had passed; Edgar was somewhere between slumber and awake. The car pulled over and Dhaneswar turned towards the back seat.

'And we are here,' he said smiling. 'As I am telling you... 11:42 a.m.'

Edgar blinked and sat up quickly, trying to show that he was alert and had been following the journey all along. 'Mel,' he said, nudging Abelman. 'Mel, we're here.' Abelman made a snorting sound as he woke.

'What...? Are we here?' he asked as he jumped up in his seat.

'Yes.'

'Then what are you doing? Let's get moving.'

Abelman opened the car door; he grunted as he struggled to get out, slamming it firmly behind him. Edgar looked sheepishly at Dhaneswar, an awkward smile on his downturned face.

'Thank you.'

'No... thank you, sir,' said Dhaneswar, as he picked up some papers from the front passenger seat and handed them back to Edgar.

'Here is publicity photo and CV of projects I am working on before…. I am in total nine Bollywood films and I—'

But now it was Edgar's turn to interrupt their driver.

'Yes. Thank you.'

Edgar took the papers as he stepped out of the car and walked around to Abelman.

'I told you,' he said, as he looked down and saw the A4 sized photograph in Edgar's hand.

He grabbed the papers and waited until Dhaneswar was watching, then threw them in a trash can.

'Dime a dozen, Eddy… no self-respect.'

Abelman gloated loudly, taking pleasure in his glare as Dhaneswar raised his window. Edgar's face hung in shame. The Prius drove off and Abelman was keen to get going.

'It's just this way,' said Edgar, as he checked the GPS on his cell phone; Abelman followed behind through the crowd of shoppers.

When they reached the Brasserie, there was a queue of around two hundred people already waiting to go inside. Abelman looked on in disgust.

'You see, Eddy…. *Dominoes.* Look at them… standing there…. Pitiful.'

Edgar wasn't interested in the queue. He had no tickets and had forgotten to inform Abelman of the fact. He knew there was no point in joining the line, he had to get around it instead; to the entrance, to where James would be… sooner or later.

A surrounding crowd had amassed, large groups of people who had stopped because others had done the same. No one really knowing what was going on, but believing that something was about to, so they stayed around, hoping to see some excitement. As they waited, attracting the curiosity of yet more people, the crowd grew in number. Edgar wondered how to navigate the horde that stood between him and the entrance; his thoughts distracted by the gossip of speculative tongues.

'It's Springsteen—*Springsteen is coming!*'

No one at the back of the crowd could see over the heads in front of them, and the noise made it difficult to hear anything clearly. Everything that was said was from someone who overheard, and anyone who overheard couldn't quite overhear before telling someone else.

'Jeffery Dean...? It's Jefferey Dean!'

'Cady?' said another voice. 'Jeffery Dean Cady?'

'OMG!' screamed another with excitement. 'The first lady... *it's the – first – lady!*'

'I heard she always eats here whenever she's in town,' said another.

'The clown?'

'Yeah, you know... the guy from that movie... the guy who played the clown....'

Edgar had heard enough. He had little choice. He would have to push through to the front and try to get close to the entrance; close enough to be able to shout out to James. He spotted a small space between two women who were busy telling others that the president was coming. He turned to Abelman, who was waiting impatiently for directions.

'Over here...! Over here!' he shouted, as he loosened his tie in the sweltering heat.

He signalled for Abelman to follow, and Abelman seemed happy not to stand in line; pleased to believe that he was being led towards a VIP entrance or other exclusive point of restricted access.

A limousine pulled into The Grove: a stretched black Mercedes-Mayback. Security began to push people aside, as it crawled its way to the front of the Brasserie, stopping behind the barricade fences. The driver's door opened, and a chauffeur emerged to meet the clamouring chaos.

'Can we have a little room here?' he hollered. 'A little more room, please!'

Several security guards began to push back sections of the crowd, trying to move barricades and create additional space. The chauffeur made his way around to the rear left passenger side and opened the door; his back to the crowd was blocking their view. Restlessness spread, as they began to surge forward to see who it was that had caused the furore. Moments later, a figure appeared. Dressed in dark blue jeans, a grey jacket and sneakers, it was impossible to miss the trademark catchphrase that was written across his red t-shirt: *Dude! Seriously?*

Like a Hollywood star he turned to the crowd; his blue tinted Pilot sunglasses protecting his eyes from the barrage of cameras that exploded into life. Echoes of screams deafened the forecourt; they crammed every side street, as the word of his presence was relayed and soon known. This was no mere celebrity or even the president. This was someone of far greater importance. The one and the only, James Munro.

He raised his hand to acknowledge the reception. It was met with hysteria and Edgar was amazed. There he was—the man of the moment—the noblest of men who had stood up to Congress, to protect user rights and "The American Dream." The most decent, kind-hearted of all human beings, who gave all of his money to all of the people and asked for nothing in return. Drowning in the waves of the crowd's adulation, worshipped like a deity giving praise to his name. To anyone and everyone, James Munro was no mortal. To the people who stood cheering, Munro was a god.

For Edgar, the experience was surreal. He knew that James was popular and well-liked, but he had never expected anything like this. Working at the hospital meant that he had little time to engage in the trappings of normal everyday life. To read about celebrities and their scandalous lifestyles; the idle hearsay reported in the columns of the tabloids. He was simply unprepared for the sheer magnitude of his stardom, and the extent of his popularity was thrilling to behold. What a feeling it must be, to be loved and admired... what a life it must be to be called James Munro. The thought intoxicated Edgar. It filled his senses with a yearning, breathing life into his imagination. The idea of such response wherever he went was only befitting for an actual prodigy. Why would he settle for anything less? How could I, he thought, when the world should know who I am.... Suddenly, a voice boomed in his ear.

'Ok, Eddy, let's go!' shouted Abelman, assuming that they were about to follow Munro.

Despite having made some progress, Edgar and Abelman were still far from the front of the crowd. Abelman had been shouting repeatedly at Edgar, who was unable to hear, although certain that his master was simply unhappy at the speed of their passage.

'We're almost there!' Edgar yelled out, every few minutes. Until their progress slowed, then ground to a halt, their path to James blocked; a wall of bodies packed tightly together. There was no way around them and no openings between them. The only way for Edgar to get closer to James, was to force himself through; to aim at the centre of the last few rows and forge his way to the front. He took a deep breath, pushed his hands between two people then prised them apart: reaching in and pressing outwards, as if swimming the breaststroke. Their open-mouthed looks of shock and bemusement were no real deterrent, as Abelman moved into the spaces that Edgar had made. The crowd cheered their hero, and Edgar ploughed onwards. Prising, pressing, pushing, slowly but surely, until finally, a few metres were all that remained.

'James!' he shouted. 'James!'

The noise from the crowd was too much to be heard, and a few metres too far to be seen. Edgar waved in the hope of gaining attention, yet his hand was lost in a sea of hundreds. Suddenly, a young woman stepped out from the limousine carrying a tablet and wearing an earpiece. She signalled to James that it was time to get inside, and Edgar knew that it was now, or it was never; time to get ahead or to spend the rest of his life playing catch up.

'James!' he cried. 'James! It's me.... It's Edgar!'

The crowd continued to drown out his voice. Desperate and helpless, his future turning against him, there was nothing else for it than for one last hurrah.

A man, standing to the right of Edgar, was slurping on the straw of an enormous soft drinks cup. He was a portly middle-aged man, and his long greasy hair was balding on top. He had a large bushy beard that made his thinning locks appear worse than they might otherwise have been, and his thick plastic glasses topped the look of someone who probably invented computers. Edgar noticed that his t-shirt was stretched to a point close to breaking, and in this compact crowd, it had also risen up over his stomach. Unfortunately for the man, he was pressed so tightly against another, that he had not been able to move his only free hand and pull it back down. Subsequently, the man's pale, hairy stomach was now sticking out against the security barrier, wedged between the bars like dough between a chef's fingers. Edgar could feel Abelman pressing closely, and the sound of the crowd faded as his mind filled with the thoughts of the promises made. Dominoes—they're *all* Dominoes—insignificant little bricks... and it was time, thought Edgar, for one more to fall.

Edgar grabbed the man's t-shirt and pulled him with all the might that he could muster. The man lost balance and took hold of the barrier to try and remain upright. But for every action, an equal and opposite reaction; the barrier gave way and was no match for the man. He stumbled and fell, his weight taking the barrier as he knocked down a guard, then another as they tried to break his fall. In the confusion, other guards scrambled to their aid, and Edgar seized his opportunity; the space now open and with nothing between them, he reached out and grabbed at an arm.

'James!'

Munro felt Edgar's grip, and his eyes followed the hand that had taken hold.

'Eddy...?' he said incredulously. 'Eddy Spear, is that you?'

'Yes! Yes, it's me, James,' shouted Edgar, as Munro's face changed from surprise to delight.

'Dude...! Seriously?'

James stepped forward to embrace his old friend, when suddenly, a security guard who had sensed the threat and been pushing through the crowd, threw Edgar to the ground.

'Dude!'

'Aargh!' screeched Edgar, as his face smashed onto the paving stones.

'Dude... what are you doing...? That's my friend!'

Munro knelt down to help Edgar to his feet while Abelman continued his surveillance of the pair.

'Dude... I'm so, *so* sorry.'

'Ow!' winced Edgar, still shaken and most definitely stirred.

'It's ok. I'll survive....'

'You're coming in, right?'

'Well—' began Edgar, before Munro turned quickly to the security guard.

'He's with *me*, dude.... Seriously... don't touch my friends!'

The chastised security guard looked down at the ground and nodded, shaking his head as he realised the magnitude of his mistake. Munro glared, and the guard eager to make amends, attempted to pat down Edgar, poorly cleaning the dust from his jacket. Munro remained unimpressed; he pushed the guard aside, then took Edgar's arm to lead him towards the entrance. Edgar reached back and grabbed Abelman.

'And *he's* with me!' shouted Edgar at the guard, who having learned his lesson said nothing to protest.

Another guard closed the door behind them and the volume of the crowd outside was almost silenced.

'That's better,' said Munro. 'I know... crazy? Right, dude?'

'It... it's incredible,' replied Edgar, still flabbergasted. 'I... I've never seen a-anything like it.'

'Still got that stutter, huh?'

Munro laughed as he slapped Edgar's shoulder. Edgar's smile was subdued.

'You get used to it... I'm used to it,' said Munro, indifferently. 'Dude... it's like *so* good to see you, bro... it's been like—like forever since uni.

'I got your message and heard you're like a neurosurgeon now? Dude...! Seriously... that's awesome! *So* pleased for you... you're like the brain man of Boston!'

Distracted for a moment by the shallow flattery, Edgar wondered why Munro had never returned his call? He had obviously listened to his voicemail, so, was complementing Edgar's success and this exaggerated display of happiness just another one of his façades? Edgar might well have been paranoid about Abelman, but when it came to James Munro, he had good reason to be. He had learned the hard way not to trust James or anything that he said, and it was enough to remind him of his purpose for the trip. James, who on the surface at least, did appear genuinely happy at seeing Edgar again, was still to notice that Abelman was standing behind them.

'There's someone I'd like you to meet,' said Edgar, as he turned to introduce Abelman. 'This is—'

Munro interrupted quickly. 'Melvin Abelman.'

Edgar was surprised. More than surprised, he was stunned. 'Oh...! Do you two know each other?'

Abelman cleared his throat.

'In a way... we met in different circumstances.'

'Different circumstances?' said James angrily. '*Different — circumstances?*' His voiced raised in disagreement. 'I'll say, dude...! You seriously—'

Suddenly, he was interrupted by his assistant.

'I'm sorry, James, we really do need to get you set up. It's showtime in t-minus five.'

Edgar looked at Abelman; Abelman offered nothing. He then turned to James, hoping for enlightenment, but he was occupied: nodding repeatedly at his assistant, as she gave instruction for the things that he was expected to say and the things that he was required to do. Edgar grew uneasy. What was happening here? A minute passed, and his assistant was finished speaking. Munro turned to break the tension.

'Dude...!' he said, returning Edgar's gaze. 'Stay for the announcement... hang out and chill... we'll catch up once I'm done— ok?'

He stared at Abelman as he continued to talk to Edgar.

'And stay away from this guy... he's bad news, Eddy—*bad* news. Been helping himself to patient meds for way too long... if you know what I mean?'

Munro circled his index finger around the side of his head while making a short whistling sound, as if to signify that Abelman was crazy.

'Ok, James, we're on,' said the assistant.

'Yo, people!' cried Munro; his way of saying that he had to go, before walking off with his assistant to get ready for the press announcement.

Edgar turned to Abelman with a thunderous scowl.

'Start talking.... What was all that about?' he demanded.

Before Abelman had the chance to reply, the security guard intervened.

'Gentlemen, you heard Mr. Munro. If you would like to follow me, I will show you to your seats. Unless of course you would prefer that I escort your associate out?' asked the guard as he turned his gaze towards Abelman.

Edgar shook his head. 'No. No. He's fine... he's supposed to be with me.'

'Then let's hope he's forgotten to take his meds this morning,' replied the guard sarcastically, as he led Edgar and Abelman to two seats inside the press area that had been set up inside the restaurant.

Abelman was belittled and furious. To have his sanity questioned and ridiculed by Munro, then mocked by a simple security guard; it was all that he could do to hold his tongue, and he pressed his lips tightly to keep it at bay.

'Why didn't you tell me that you knew Munro?' demanded Edgar.

Abelman stared for a moment or two.

'Tell you...?' he said, trying to give the impression that he was in control; unmoved by the comments of Munro and the guard. 'What's to tell, Eddy? We're all friends here.... Munro and I have a history— that's all. You know he's a clever guy, but he's not smart... not like you.'

Edgar wasn't stupid; he was wary, and Abelman's attempt to sweet-talk him was wasted.

'He's smart enough to think *you're* crazy!'

After insult and indignity, Abelman was not going to be talked to like a child or tolerate any further insubordination. He put his hand on Edgar's thigh and squeezed: tight enough for Edgar to flinch. Not wishing to draw attention in front of those now filling the restaurant, Abelman leant discreetly and whispered into Edgar's ear.

'You seem to have a memory problem, Spear.... I recall telling you that if you ever spoke to me in a way that I don't approve of, then I'd rip your goddamn tongue out.'

He leant back and released his grip on Edgar's leg, before tapping it twice to confirm his intentions; Edgar winced for a moment from the throbbing pain. It was a reality check, a little reminder. Edgar may well be the reason for why they were able to sit in front of Munro, but he was not the reason for why they were there. They were there because of Abelman. Because of what Abelman had offered and for what he expected in return. And what Abelman did not expect, and what Abelman would not abide, was for his apprentice to lecture him or insinuate that he was anything less than rational.

'I... I'm sorry,' said Edgar, pausing to remember his place. 'W-what I meant to say was, w-why doesn't Munro like you?'

'Well, let's just say we didn't agree to disagree.'

Didn't agree to disagree, thought Edgar. What did that even mean? Whatever Abelman was trying to imply was unclear, and he wouldn't find the answer now as Abelman was still reeling after the insult from James.

'These people... look at them,' said Abelman, airing his disgust. 'They love Munro.... To them he's a hero.'

Edgar looked away from the podium and turned instead to Abelman. Munro was about to be introduced.

'But he's not a visionary... I'm a visionary.' The angry stare of Abelman remained fixed upon Munro. 'You might even say a prophet... a prophet in the precision business.'

He turned towards Edgar; his eyes meeting him coldly as his voice dipped into darkness.

'The world has no need of heroes.... Remember that, Eddy... it *only* needs precision.'

Munro stood and was greeted once again by rapturous applause from an over excited audience. The sudden noise startled Edgar: his nervous eyes darting back to follow what was happening at the stage. James waved his hands, pushing them downwards as if trying to say, "Enough," while still allowing the applause to continue; milking it for all that it was worth.

'Ok.... Ok,' he said. 'Thank you,' as the applause continued, and it appeared again as though he was asking for calm. 'Ladies and gentlemen.... Dudes...! Seriously?'

Despite the impression, his words were well chosen and not calling for silence. Like those of a general that issued a battle cry; the audience jumped into action and sprang to their feet, cheering as they gave their ovation. They had just heard Munro speak his infamous catchphrase in person. This was a moment never to be forgotten, one to recall and tell their grandchildren.

'Ok, come on…. People… time is money, and I can never get enough of either!'

An explosion of laughter rang out from the audience. An acknowledgement of the fun that Munro seemingly poked at himself for having donated his wealth. The cheering continued, until eventually, after more signalling, it decreased to a level that allowed him to speak.

'Phew!' he said, wiping his brow, as if relieved the ovation he had deliberately sculpted was finally coming to an end. 'You guys… you're awesome!'

He placed both hands on the podium and stood like a priest about to address his congregation.

'You know, when I started CaliChat almost six years ago, I never expected it would grow to become the world's second largest social media site.'

The audience began to applaud again. Munro was determined.

'I've got to be honest with you guys—the stuff that happened up there on the Hill—dude…! Seriously? That was tough.'

The audience burst into laughter and their applause continued. Munro kept on all the same.

'The things that they accused me of…. Woah!

'I mean, we have billions of users worldwide. A company with over twenty thousand employees… and still… still the senators couldn't find one piece of evidence to suggest that I did anything wrong. Not one single spec of proof. Nothing to substantiate any of those claims.

'They… you guys….' Munro paused as he pointed to the members of the press, 'called it a witch-hunt…. Trust me people, it was no witch-hunt, it was a purge. They wanted me out and *they* took me out.

'Now I know, when I was pushed and left CaliChat, everyone thought that I would just go away—maybe disappear. But I didn't... I haven't... I'm still here... and guess what? I'm gonna stay... right – here!'

The audience erupted into applause once again, with Munro sounding more like a president than a general.

'And since I'm still here... I wanted to tell you guys that CaliChat was just the beginning....'

The applause grew louder, and Munro spoke over it yet again. 'I'm only getting started!'

Several wolf-whistles broke out from amongst the audience, and large wild shouts of support spread across the room. It was turning into a scene of pandemonium, and Munro allowed the cheers to continue, knowing full well that the crowd's response to his statement would look great on the evening news.

'Today, I gathered you here to make an announcement. To tell you that I'm working on something new—a whole new social sharing service.'

The audience erupted euphorically; James Munro was back. Each word that he spoke, that passed his lips, added only to the excitement.

'A service not only bigger, but beyond *anything* I was able to do at CaliChat!'

The audience were whipped to a frenzy and coaxed to a state of delirium.

'People!' he called, knowing only too well that his words were muffled by fanatic enthusiasm. 'Dudes...! Seriously? Come on—let me finish!'

But the audience had been played to perfection. They continued in their fever like a choir being led by their conductor.

'The world is changing—it's moving—and I want to move with it.... I want us *all* to move together.'

The audience screamed with no idea of how the world was moving, where it was moving to, or what Munro was even suggesting.

Besides, none of that even mattered. The fact that James Munro wanted them to move together, and he wanted to include them in his ideas; that was more than enough, more than any of them had ever dreamt of.

'I'm not talking about web sites that share posts with your friends... or communities that exchange likes and comments... I'm talking about devices that are designed to make our everyday lives better. Devices that will make *your* everyday life easier.... Hardware designed to move with you, whenever you move... to share the things you want, whenever you need to share the most. So, wherever you are and whatever you're doing, you're always online, and you're *always* connected.'

The cheering was endless, celebrating the return of the people's champion.

'I'm not talking about bracelets that count steps... and who cares about watches that mimic cell phones—that offer the same functionality you already have?

'I'm talking about a whole new range of—socially sharing— *wearable* products. Made to support the things that *you* do and keep *you* online—all of the time.'

Applause became unbroken, peaking in waves at the end of almost every sentence.

'So, whether you're out shopping. At the gym. Walking your dog. Driving your car. Watching television. Making dinner. Or even at a restaurant... like this... with your friends!'

And the cheers became deafening, as the audience acknowledged Munro's reference to them as "friends."

'My products will automate many of the tasks you have to do manually today. I mean, imagine... you're at a party.... With my devices you'll *never* have to worry about remembering the name of anyone you ever meet again. Just imagine... imagine that!'

Munro paused to create melodrama; to allow his audience the time to think and picture his vision of a brave new world.

'My A.I technology takes biometric facial recognition to a whole — *new* — level.

'So, the next time you bump into someone you once met at a party, you don't have to worry about looking embarrassed if you can't remember who they are. My devices will not only tell you their name... they'll even let *you* control *when* they should.... From a distance. As they approach. Or when they're standing beside you... pretty cool, huh?'

The audience gasped as their cheers were replaced by disbelief, quickly followed by their yearnings of desire. The stunned silence burst into rapture; screams and crying. From their reaction, it would have been easy to think that Munro had just invented water, discovered oxygen, or perhaps even fire. That he promoted something the world had needed for so very long and simply could not live without; something of such importance that its announcement had just changed the very course of human history: a ground-breaking cure to a previously incurable disease that would now benefit the lives of everyone. However, Munro never spoke of such things, nor did he need to, because to these people Munro wasn't simply a god, he was their God, and his creations more vital to their existence than any other means of survival.

James Munro, the consummate performer, continued to perform. He added drama and explanations of functionality as though they were little things; tiny things he had simply forgotten to mention.

'Oh, and by the way... while you're at the party... you'll never need to take another selfie. That's because my device will capture the optimal image of you and your friends. Then, using my latest image processing technology, it will automatically select, sharpen, and optimise your best images to share with whoever you want. That's cool, huh...? A device that can tag you and your friends and automate *everything!* Just imagine that... isn't it wild?'

The audience seemed to agree because they too were wild, voracious with a hunger. They wanted this device. They needed this device. And they needed it, now!

'So, the next time you're at a party, you can focus on enjoying yourself instead of trying to focus on remembering the names and faces of all the people that you meet. You can focus on having a great time, creating great photos, instead of needing to focus on your camera.

'And the best thing of all...? Remember, it's wearable! You'll have it on... you'll never lose it... and you'll *never* forget it!'

A concept image of the device was projected onto the screen behind him. He moved to the side, introducing the world to his art like an artist unveiling a painting. The audience was ecstatic. Now they could see it. There it was. How it looked. It was everything they'd ever wanted, and Munro was ready to give it to them.

'Let me ask you.... How many times have you lost your cell phone in a cab, on a bus, or on a train? Seriously... like how many phones have you destroyed simply because they fell out of your pocket, or slipped out of your hand?

'With my wearables, you'll *never* – need – another – cell phone.... *Ever!*

'In fact, if you want, you can just throw them away right now. Go ahead, take them out and throw them away... I mean, why should you be forced to carry around some old, dated tech to make and receive calls? That's just a function... that's why they sell phones by the number of megapixels in their cameras... it's the only other useful piece of tech inside them.'

The audience started to cheer again. Several were overwhelmed with emotion, charged by the words of the creator. Those of faith, reached for their phones and without thought of consequence, threw them towards a trash can in the aisle to the left of the podium. As they hit and many ricocheted off their target, the sound of collision echoed out like suppressed gunfire. Munro paused and made light by covering his head to encourage their actions and acknowledge that the stage was under attack. Suddenly, a lone voice from the audience made cease fire and cried out.

'What's it called, James…? What's it called?'

'Well—'

'DomiGen… it's called DomiGen… and it's the next generation of dominating tech!'

A thunderous roar rang out from the restaurant as the audience rose to their feet. No longer ecstatic, they were carried in ecstasy, as Munro stood shell-shocked; left speechless and unable to comprehend what occurred.

'No… no, wait… wait! Ladies and gentlemen. No… I want….'

He tried desperately to be heard, but it was hopeless above the din. As far as the audience was concerned, and the world that was watching the live broadcast, the new name of Munro's company had just been announced: it was DomiGen, and they loved it.

The press conference was brought to an unexpected sudden end, as Munro left the podium dazed and dumbfounded. His assistant tried to help ease his dismay; his despondency clear before leading him to perform his duties with the meet and greet. He talked briefly with several important looking members of the audience who had been promised a moment with him, shaking hands and posing for photographs without raising a customary smile. It was around forty minutes or so later, when finally free, he was able to speak at last to Edgar.

'Oh dude…!' whined a disgruntled Munro. 'I can't believe I was hijacked…. Hoodwinked at my own press conference.'

'Hoodwinked?'

'Uh…. Hello, Eddy… newsflash… some dude just shouted out "DomiGen." Like seriously… what the hell is DomiGen? This is *so* messed up… so seriously messed up!'

'Well, why not?' suggested Abelman.

'Why what?' Munro asked, irritated by his presence.

'Why not DomiGen...? The crowd loved it and it's what you're doing right—next gen tech?'

Munro was uninterested in what Abelman thought, even less interested in talking with him. He turned instead to Edgar.

'When I see through the tapes and find out who it was... I swear, dude... I'm gonna crucify them.... Seriously... like nail them to a—'

'You don't need to check your tapes. It was me.'

Munro's eyes widened and his irritation turned to fury. *'You!'*

'Yes. Me,' said Abelman. 'And that's why we're here... to talk to you about DomiGen.'

'Oh no...' Munro shook his head despairingly. 'I should have known... I should have guessed.... Not more of your mumbo jumbo? Dude... what's wrong with you? Seriously...?'

He became increasingly angry.

'I've told you like a million times... I'm — *not* — interested... ok? Like what the hell...? I don't care about your fantasy stories or the stuff you watch on Sci-Fi.

'Dude... look... I live here... on planet earth. And on planet earth it can't be done. It can never be done. So, dude... *please...* for the last time... listen — to — me. Let it go. It will never be—'

Abelman interrupted to declare his revelation.

'I've done it.'

In the corner where they stood, there was no audience listening to the conversation. There were no rounds of applause, no waves of cheers or screams of delight. There was only a gasp of shock: the sound of an uncomfortable pause. Edgar had no idea of what was happening, but whatever it was, whatever Abelman had just revealed, it had silenced James.

A moment passed.

'You've done it?' he asked, his mouth agape. Still in disbelief and apparently overcome, Munro felt the need to repeat himself.

'You... you've done it? Like... really—'

'I told you. I've done it,' interrupted Abelman in reply.

'But the chip…? I mean… the chip….'

'The chip is stable.'

Munro was baffled; more bewildered than bemused.

'You've done it…?' he repeated once again. 'Seriously… like you've *really* done it?'

Abelman said nothing.

'I… I can't believe it… I mean… dude… really…? You've *really* done it?'

His mind adrift, Munro had become vacant; a shadow of the man who was there just moments ago.

'I've done it,' repeated Abelman firmly, as he broke his code of conduct to reiterate what he had said one last time.

Munro scratched the back of his head. He paced a little. Whatever Abelman had done had more than just implications, it had profound significance. Perhaps ground-breaking significance? All the same, Munro was unconvinced; he clearly believed it impossible and had to know the truth.

'So how many died this time, Abelman…? How many survived?'

Edgar stood between them, caught in the crossfire. Whatever their history, whatever their differences, they had clashed before, and others had paid a heavy price.

Munro looked at Edgar for an explanation.

'Is it true, Eddy…? Is it stable? Is it *really* stable?'

Edgar had no idea what James was asking of him. He didn't know about any chip and had no idea if it was stable or not. But if Abelman said that it was, then Edgar would say it was too, because Abelman was saying jump, and Edgar only needed to know how far.

Edgar returned the doubting stare, with a seriousness not unlike the one a doctor must have when informing the next of kin that a loved one has passed.

'It's stable,' he said.

Munro took a second, torn between what he was hearing and what he knew; what he was being told and what he believed to be true.

Edgar wouldn't lie to him, surely? Still, what Abelman was suggesting... well, it was just... just....

'I don't believe it. It's not possible. There's no way that—'

Edgar knew his place. He knew his job. Now he knew why Abelman needed him and what he had to achieve in order to get the signature on his employment contract.

'I know, James, I couldn't believe it either. When Mel first told me about the chip, I thought it was like something out of a fantasy movie... and when I heard about the deaths, I asked him to stop.... I begged him to.'

He had absolutely no idea of what he was talking about, nevertheless, the first rule of selling was to gain the customer's sympathy; to make them feel as though they were on the same page. Edgar needed James to know that they were, even if the title of the book remained a complete mystery. Munro was obviously angry about the number of deaths in whatever he and Abelman had been involved with. So, Edgar had to tell him that he was as well. That like him, he was also angry and had asked Abelman to stop.

'But he was close, James. Close for a long time. So very close....

'When I met Mel, I had just moved to Boston. I was just getting settled in at Mass Gen... finding my feet—you know—and then he told me about the chip. He told me how it could change... revolutionise the way that we work, and I knew I had to help him. Help him find a way to crack the code.'

Edgar was in full flow. He was not just keeping Munro's confidence; he was building it. He knew that James trusted him, and that gave him an advantage: leverage. He had trusted him enough to confess how he had built CaliChat. And he knew that Edgar was top of their class back in UCSF, so he was more than capable of helping Abelman iron out whatever problems he was having.

'Then one day... one late night in the lab, we'd done it.... We'd finally cracked the code. The chip was stable.'

'Even when connected to the cerebral cortex...?'

Edgar paused. He was stunned yet tried to appear stolid. The cerebral cortex? he thought. They were talking about the brain... about a chip that connects to the brain. What on earth had Abelman been doing? What had he been experimenting with?

'All four lobes,' Edgar replied, without falter. 'Stable on all four lobes.'

'That's incredible,' said James. 'It's... well, it's—'

'The future?' Edgar interrupted, putting words into Munro's mouth.

'Yeah... yeah, dude.... It's the future!'

It had worked; Edgar had sold the dream. At least, he had convinced James that it was real, up until this point. He had managed to hook the fish, and now it was time to reel him in; to get him onboard.

'It's our future, James. Yours. Mine. Abelman's.... It's our legacy for mankind.'

Then, the fish fought back. Munro repelled and pulled away.

'Abelman's?'

His dislike at the name was evident for all to hear, including Abelman himself.

'I made that son of bitch a fortune!' he screamed, pointing at him.

But Edgar had come too far and invested too much to give up without a fight. He knew that he was close, that despite their past, and regardless of the differences between the two, James now only seemed to show resentment to the considerable wealth that Abelman had accumulated from his work. It would only need a little more persuasion, another tiny push; one more little lie to get him onboard.

'Yes... yes, you have... and now he's ready to use that fortune. To cash in the apartments, liquidate the stocks, and raise the money to fund DomiGen.... To fund you.'

Munro stopped and was obviously thinking about what Edgar had said. Edgar tried to predict his response; to prepare for what the customer might say. Because Edgar was, as always, searching for a way to make the sale and close the deal.

To Edgar, whatever had happened in their past, and whether James was driven by money or not, was irrelevant. He knew that Munro needed funding for his device. That in the presentation he hadn't even presented a finished product. He had only shown a sketch, a three-dimensional model, so he couldn't possibly have had the money that he needed to build it—not even a prototype. He hadn't even come up with a name for the company, so he was obviously not as far ahead as he pretended to be. This was probably why he did the press launch: to generate interest and appeal to potential investors to help back him. So, the very idea of Abelman using the money that he had made because of CaliChat to fund him now, well, that would feel good to Munro. Feel like some form of poetic justice. Like punishment for Abelman and just reward for James. A "win-win," as they say.

He was still thinking. Edgar knew that if he was thinking then he was not resisting, and if he was not resisting, then he had to keep on reeling him in.

'Look, James, let's be honest—you need money. You just gave away your *entire* fortune. Sure, they'll be other backers out there willing to throw money at you, but why not take the money from the man who *you* made rich...? Why not take his tech as well and make the future happen today? We can go beyond wearables... think about it... with your popularity, my surgical skills and his money, we can do *anything.*

'James... together... we could do *everything.*'

Edgar knew that he had Munro eating from the palm of his hand. He wasn't only convincing him to join them, he was convincing him that by taking Abelman's money, it was the right thing to do—the just thing to do—the only thing to do. After all, a chip that can connect to the brain was far more advanced than any wearable, and James would know this. He would know that his technology, the device that he just pitched, was already outdated; trumped by Abelman and by whatever his chip was able to affect. Soon the little fish wouldn't need to be reeled in anymore. He would be swimming to the surface as fast as he could, jumping onboard and begging to be eaten.

As he continued his charm offensive, the tiny fragments of information, the opinions and meanings that Abelman had shared, were now beginning to make sense to Edgar. When Abelman referred to people as "Dominoes," what he really meant was they were all the same and should be treated as such; led blindly like bricks, in a long line of bricks unable to see their place in the show. To him, humanity needed to conform, and freedom of choice amounted to free will; that was not precise, that was imperfection. The idea was genius, albeit barbaric: a chip that would take away choice. Was this his idea of a precision business? Where everyone would be like that man in the lamp store. Only instead of advertisements, they would purchase the lamp, he would guarantee the sale, and those insignificant little ants would be programmed for a purpose; to do what he wanted, whenever he wanted it done. Was this why he needed Munro: his influence to convince the world that the chip was harmless? It all made sense, at least to Edgar, but was so far-fetched that it couldn't possibly be true. Not even if the pieces of the puzzle were clear, and the portrait that it made was the face of Abelman. A man who would never be happy without control. The complete control of everything and everyone.

'Ok,' said James. 'I'm in... but on one condition. No, actually— two. On two conditions.'

'Name them,' said Edgar without a second thought.

'He sells everything!' he demanded, pointing again at Abelman. 'I mean *everything!* And it all goes into the company... every nickel— every cent—every dime.'

'Deal,' said Edgar, not giving Abelman the chance to speak.

'And the other?'

Munro took a moment to compose himself.

'This is my company.... DomiGen. It's my company and we do things *my — way*.'

'Deal.'

Abelman, however, was far from happy, and most definitely not willing to accept such a proposition. Edgar saw that his master was about to protest—to ruin everything—and quickly intervened.

'Partners?' he asked, as he held out his hand towards James.

Munro looked at the hand then stared fiercely at Abelman; his eyes hostile as he nodded to accept Edgar's offer.

'Partners,' he replied, and he shook Edgar's hand.

Edgar extended the invitation to Abelman.

'Partners?'

But Abelman refused. He glared back at Edgar with a coldness that expressed more than any words ever could. He was not to be bullied, not to be intimidated, and he scoffed at the idea of the company being Munro's.

'*Partners?*' stressed Edgar, repeating the invite, now pleading as his hand thrust farther forward.

Abelman stayed silent and Edgar's eyes grew anxious; they widened and begged him to accept Munro's terms.

'Fine,' he snapped, reluctantly taking Edgar's hand. Then he glanced across at James.

The two men said nothing, standing opposed in a contest of will. Munro held out his hand, and Abelman cared not to, preferring instead to watch him suffer the wait. Their eyes locked in hatred as Munro reddened with anger, or perhaps humiliation; his outstretched palm was still without reply.

'Go on', said Edgar, encouraging agreement.

When suddenly, Munro blinked, and his hostility buckled; defeated by the glower that made Abelman's feelings about him and his deal apparently clear. Abelman smirked at the loser of the contest.

'Partners then,' he sneered, and he grabbed Munro's hand for the briefest of shakes. Munro's red face grimaced with a whimpering cry.

'Good... we're agreed,' said Edgar. 'Partners.'

'In crime!' smiled James, quick with his comment to distract from his pain; a little joke he believed to be funny.

Abelman began to laugh. It was a laugh that grew louder, more raucous and cruder. He laughed so hard that the others began to feel ill at ease. Munro thought that his comment was funny—a wisecrack—but not funny enough to provoke such response. In fact, he knew that it wasn't, and the smile upon his face was soon wiped away, replaced by a more troubled expression.

Abelman eventually stopped to breathe. As he did so, he pulled three overly expensive cigars from a pocket in the inside breast of his jacket. He offered one to Munro, one to Edgar, and kept one for himself. He wet his lips, slowly and methodically around the end of the cigar; rolling it between his fingers, lighting and inhaling while his partners studied the technique. The cigar ignited and Abelman took it from his mouth. He blew the smoke, a cloud into the faces of Edgar and Munro, who both stood patiently with cigars in hand, waiting to light them in celebration of their new partnership. Edgar coughed as he choked and Abelman smiled. He raised his eyebrows, that psychotic look in his eyes once again.

'Is there any other kind?' he said, as his voice spoke smugly behind the sinister grin that hung in the thick, smoky air.

PART II

Who's laughing now?

7

COLLATERAL DAMAGE

Edgar headed back to the Slaughterhouse. His hopes were high, and his dreams filled with the promise of the future that lay in front of him. During the late flight back to Boston, Abelman had voiced his distinct dislike of Munro's conditions. In fact, at one point he became so animated that Edgar believed it was best not to argue further in front of others. Certainly, it was not the ideal time, nor place, to push for his signature. However, a deal was a deal and Edgar had done all that Abelman had asked of him. So, as he strolled through the entrance of the Lunder Building that Monday morning, there was no cause for concern, and he carried with him the only thing of any real importance: the unsigned contract. Filled with expectancy, he arrived an hour earlier than usual to prepare himself to rectify the anomaly.

As he made his way through the corridors towards his desk, the eerie sound of distant cries punctured the normally sterile air. Even at this unearthly hour, when all was usually quiet, muffled tears of grief echoed around the building and clung to the hospital walls like the very paint that covered them. It was most unusual—peculiar to say the least—and as he arrived at his desk, he was greeted by a new stack of manila folders that camouflaged the majority of it. Edgar sighed despairingly at the familiar feeling of routine; his dreams crashing into the depressing reality of the day, and the bondage of a slave that could almost taste his freedom.

The hours passed as Edgar familiarised himself with the notes of patients admitted over the weekend. Suddenly, the phone rang, and Edgar looked at the clock. There was no need to answer, it was 8:00 a.m. and time for the Flying Visits. When he arrived at the first room on the ward, he did so without thinking. The bed was empty, dressed in new linen and the room had been cleaned; ready for the next pitiful, insignificant, little ant. It was as if Clydesdale had never been there, or ever existed, and Edgar stopped for a moment to stare at the empty bed.

'Doctor?' said the trembling voice of Nurse Parsons from behind Edgar. 'Dr. Spear…? We're ready for you.'

Edgar turned and could see that Parsons had been crying. There was something special about Clydesdale, something warm and comforting. He was a kind, dignified gentleman; one of those rare patients who was instantly liked and loved by all. Despite what he had tried to portray, Edgar himself was not immune and was still greatly saddened by Clydesdale's passing. Not only because he was the first patient that he had lost under his care, but because he would genuinely miss him. Miss arguing and telling him to be quiet.

'I know,' said Edgar. 'It's difficult to lose a patient.'

Edgar walked with Parsons to the next room, to Amanda Jenkins. She was still there, still unconscious, and hadn't responded well to surgery. Edgar looked at her chart and could hear the nurse sniffling.

'Clydesdale's not the first and he won't be the last… there's no place for tears on this ward, Parsons. We *all* have to carry on.'

Edgar hadn't even looked at Nurse Parsons while he spoke. He continued instead to stare at the chart, flicking through the results of a recent blood analysis. Yes, he was hard, and yes, he was cold, yet he still felt just in the words that he said; because the truth can be harsh and brutally cold, and the sooner Parsons learned that the better.

'I… I know, Doctor…. It's… it's just….' she quivered, trying to speak.

'Well, what is it, Parsons?' demanded Edgar, still looking at the blood analysis. 'The clock is ticking, and I have patients to see. I don't have time for your blubbering so spit it out…. If you've something to say, then say it.'

'You… you don't know…? You haven't heard?'

'Heard what? Good heavens, Parsons… what are you babbling on about?'

'It's Nurse Davis.'

'Yes, yes,' said Edgar, 'let me guess… she's delayed—again? Not coming in—again? It's all beginning to get *very* boring. I'll see the Nursing Director after rounds and have her permanently transferred to another ward.'

Edgar held out the chart and waited for Parsons to take it from him; to hang it back in place so that he could move onto the next patient. He stood waiting impatiently, until finally his annoyance at her tardiness forced him to look up.

'Damn it, Parsons… I don't have time for this!' screamed Edgar, as he glared at her.

Nurse Parsons was ashen. Her watery green eyes were shrunken; surrounded by red. 'She… she's dead….'

Edgar said nothing.

'Doctor…?'

His mouth fell open in silence, as he stared at the air between them.

'Doctor, did you hear what I—'

'I… I'm sorry… you said, she….'

'She's dead, Doctor…. Penelope's dead.'

The chart fell from his hand as his legs began to weaken. His eyes flickered, then narrowed, as words fought to be released.

'W-what d-did you s-say?'

Parsons took a tissue and wiped her nose as she continued to sob into it.

'They found her yesterday... someone broke into her apartment on Friday and beat her. They beat her and... and.... Oh — my — God... they killed her!'

Parsons cries became loud; her bawling uncontrollable, as she envisaged the brutality of Penny's death. Edgar, still speechless, fell onto Jenkins' bed.

'Poor Penny... she had been lying there until yesterday... when they found her. I... I can't imagine—'

Unable to control her emotions or stop her streaming tears, Parsons began to wail.

'Then don't!' snarled Edgar. 'Get out... get out, Parsons—go to the staff room.'

He leant forward to bury his face into his hands and heard the sound of hurried footsteps as Parsons' tears grew silent. It couldn't be true... how could it be true? How could anyone...? Edgar's mind was cast into exile; unable to fathom the sense of it all. Penny was kind, so very kind and would never hurt a soul. Why would... who would...? Then, a thought: a dark and sickening feeling that brought with it a word. A name that sprang to mind. Surely, he wouldn't... he couldn't...? But disbelief was fleeting, replaced by anger as suspicion raised its ugly head. Edgar felt its power burning as it roared to engulf him, then rose, resurrected like a man possessed, prepared to do only one thing.

'Dr. Spear.... Dr. Spear!' Kassandra shouted. 'Wait! He's not in yet.... Dr. Spear!'

Kassandra had faded once again into insignificance; to Edgar, she did not exist. The only thing that did, was waiting for him on the other side of the door. He kicked it with such force that it smashed the lock as it slammed open; the splintered shards firing out across the room. It made no difference. They struck no one. Kassandra was right, the office was empty. It was far too early for a chief physician, and Edgar swept his arm across Abelman's desk to unleash his fury. Everything was cast onto the floor. Everything except for a shiny desk name plate.

Dr. M. Abelman, Chief Physician Neurosurgery.

Edgar snatched it and stormed out to Kassandra, who sat frozen in fear and aghast at the terror of his wrath. He smouldered with rage and clenched his fist. The name plate snapped like a twig.

'I'll kill him…. This time… I really will!'

He raised his arm to hurl the broken pieces into the wastepaper basket beside her desk. She cowered and screamed believing that Edgar was about to strike her, but he turned instead: his vengeance reserved for only one. Back at his desk, he glowered intently at the swing doors awaiting the arrival of the monster, ready to exact revenge for the life that he had stolen.

Time had lost its purpose. The past, the present, the future—they all blurred into one. Minutes became hours and hours became more, as Edgar sat fixed. The world passed by and around him, trapped without logic or reason; imprisoned in a vacuum, in his bubble of hate.

'Dr. Spear….' came a voice beside Edgar. 'Dr. Spear? Are you alright?'

A hand shook his shoulder, and the bubble was burst.

'Dr. Spear…? Can you hear me?'

Like a robot without sense of feeling, Edgar stared blankly at the man.

'Your phone, Dr. Spear…. Aren't you going to take the call?'

The man's mouth was moving, his finger was pointing, and Edgar slowly reached down from his daze.

'Spear,' he mumbled, as he answered.

'Edgar, I've been trying to reach you—'

It was Edgar's grandfather. Edgar cancelled the call without saying a word and his focus returned to the swing doors. He followed in earnest, until finally, a coat that was whiter than white passed through them. He glanced down at his desk, at the contract, wrinkled and scruffy, it lay half rolled—almost unfolded. Beside it the cheap imitation Mont Blanc fountain pen that Edgar had brought for Abelman to sign the papers. Be that as it may, that was then, and this was now, and it no longer served any purpose as a pen. Edgar picked it up and gripped the top tightly, a dagger in his hand. Abelman came closer, smiling as he walked, and Edgar stood, waiting, the pen grasped firmly, ready to slay the monster.

'Eddy!'

He was empty, drained of emotion. His hand was charged with a single primitive goal; to do what was necessary and discharge justice. It tightened further around the pen, ready to exact its revenge, when Abelman, nearing his mark, fortuitously spotted the contract and lent across the desk.

'Ah, good, you brought it. Well, come on then... let's sign it.'

Abelman smiled at Edgar; Edgar stared straight through him. His eyes were not crazed, not like those of a maniac, more of a man who simply didn't care anymore. A man who had lost all hope, and with it all remorse. He gripped the pen tighter still; as tight as he possibly could, in anticipation for what he had to do. But this would mean murder—murder most foul—and even when contemplated, was cause for hesitation.

'Eddy...? The pen...?'

Abelman clicked his fingers, ordering Edgar to hurry up. The sound, a reminder of his bondage, eventually woke Edgar from his stupor.

'Well come on then, what are you waiting for...? Don't you wanna give it to me?'

Edgar's eyes narrowed. Of course he did. But he handed the pen to Abelman, and Abelman seemed surprised.

'Jeez, Eddy... I don't know what's worse... that fake Rolex of yours or this plastic two-bit pen... where do you get this stuff?'

Abelman straightened the contract and proceeded to sign.

'You know it's my company,' he said. 'I don't give a damn what Munro thinks. It's my money—and it's *my* company.'

He tossed the pen into the wastepaper basket.

'Looks like the janitor's gonna be busy today, huh?' he said, smiling at Edgar. 'Anything else…? Anything you wanna say to me, Spear?' he asked sarcastically, raising his eyebrow as he taunted and dared a confrontation.

Edgar said nothing; he was overcome by Penny's death and still subdued.

'Good. Then why are you still hanging around here? We got a company to build.'

Abelman pointed at the office address on the contract, then began to walk away. As usual, he was unable to do so without having one final word, and he turned to Edgar.

'Shame about that girl… you know the one they found…. What was her name again? Heard she was in an awful mess. Pity they couldn't get to her in time.'

Edgar clenched his jaw and his teeth ground like coffee beans.

'It's the world we live in, Eddy. The world we live in…. People don't always get what they deserve… and others get *exactly* what's coming to them.'

Abelman waited; one last chance for Edgar to rise to the challenge. He didn't. So, Abelman turned then began cheerfully whistling "Only the Good Die Young" as he disappeared around the corner. Deliberately crass, his unbearable sense of self-satisfaction adding only further insult to Penny. Edgar fell back into his chair and looked at the contract, at the signature scrawled across the dotted line. It was done, his dreams had come true. He was by every means a success, the very definition of it. The prodigy that Abelman had promised. Yet he felt no joy—no happiness—he only felt forlorn and ashamed. An accomplice to a name that could just as easily be written in blood.

'Dr. Spear…?' said a voice as it delved into Edgar's sorrow.

'Excuse me, Dr. Spear...?'

Edgar blinked and his eyes opened wide at an orderly that was standing in front of him.

'This was left for you at the front desk, sir. I was just passing so I thought I'd bring it up for you and save you the trouble.'

Edgar forced a smile and nodded, a sign that he was both alive and appreciative of the orderly's efforts. He looked down at an envelope that was laid upon his desk and read the words across the front.

Edgar Spear, in the event of my death.

The orderly smiled at Edgar, happy to oblige, and nodded in reply before walking away.

Edgar's fingers moved slowly across the envelope; the tips feeling each indent of the writer's stroke. But instead of the letters, he felt the sigh of anxiety as it leapt from his mouth at the moment that it dried. His lips cracked in an instant, his pulse raised as it sped, and his breathing became rapid—shallower— as a soft sudden panic began to take hold. He dared not open it; it must be from Penny. Her words certain to push him over the edge, perhaps even further beyond. Nevertheless, if they offered an insight, gave some clue as to what happened, then how could he ignore them; how could he ever face a mirror again?

He tore open the envelope and pulled out three pieces of folded paper. It was a handwritten letter, just as he had feared. Edgar cleared his throat before he started to read.

Dear Dr. Spear,

If you are reading this, then I fear that I am no longer with you. And if I am no longer with you, then I fear that I will be unable to find peace in the next life as well, unless I first tell you of what I know from this.

Many years ago, I worked at a research laboratory in San Diego together with a young and brilliant team. We were involved in a highly classified research project for the government to investigate the neural pathways of the brain. Our work was classified, and the project kept secret. Our objective was to find a way to control and condition the behaviour of our country's undercover operatives. Our mission was to protect their safety in the field. To ensure that if ever subjected to interrogation, no agent could ever implicate the government or any other operative and would believe without question the identity they had been assigned.

We conducted experiments for many years. All of them were unsuccessful and destroyed many lives, although we also discovered many things.

Olivia Spear was a brilliant doctor. She discovered that there were neurons that could not only send information to the brain, but also from it. This information could be sent and received not only through the neurons of recognised motor functions, which was something that we thought was exclusive, but through an unknown set that were able to influence and alter the chemical function of any cell. At first, we tried to control these neurons and condition the memories of our test subjects. Until Olivia discovered, quite by accident, that this set of neurons could transmit information over distances far greater than any of us could ever have dreamed. These neurons possessed unique qualities that could control and condition the strength of muscles. Multiply their mass, create what you might call, 'superhuman strength.'

The government sought greater focus on this area of our research, and we were moved to a military installation under the supervision of Colonel Roberts. Roberts wanted a regiment, an army of super soldiers, each possessing unimaginable superhuman strength. To help us accomplish this task, he brought in a young, highly spirited doctor to join our team. His name was Groy. The son of a family who had emigrated to America after the second great war.

We were all passionate about our work, still, Groy was different from us. He was obsessed with controlling the brain. Not just the behaviour of it, but its function. Groy believed that it was possible to convince the brain of what was real and then control how the brain would respond to its new reality. A construct not based on hallucinogens but a permanently altered state of mind. Imagine, if you will, the potential to clone one super soldier and control his brain. It would mean, in theory, that an entire army of soldiers could be controlled to behave. To move, and to act as one. And all this through a keyboard, or the simple touch of a screen.

What Groy worked on was dangerous. He ignored every protocol and tested only on human subjects. Each night a lorry would arrive to transport the dead, until one day, sick of the death that she was forced to witness, Olivia could take no more. She wanted to inform the agency of what was happening, expose Groy's experiments and terminate the operation. But Groy threatened the life of her young son. So, together with her husband David, Olivia and I sabotaged Groy's work. We uploaded a virus onto the mainframe computers that corrupted all of our data and would make it impossible for him to continue. Two weeks later, Olivia and David disappeared, and I was left with Groy to resume the project.

Without Olivia, our efforts were wasted. Our results were careless and unpredictable, the death toll increased, and after three years the project was abandoned.

On the day that I left, I discovered a file that Groy had kept on Olivia and David. He had placed a test serum into their tea several months before they disappeared and had used a control phrase to condition them. He had been experimenting on them for months, trying to command them, to alter their reality and force them to continue with his work. But his experiments, like all others, had failed, and his serum had adverse effects. He destroyed their once brilliant minds before abandoning them in an asylum at Santarillo State Mental Hospital. Then staged an accident, a car crash, to cover their disappearance.

I tried to find your parents, Edgar, you must believe me, but Santarillo was closed, burned down by an inmate they said, and the records were lost in the fire. Since then, I have spent my entire life trying to track down Groy, to find out what had happened to Olivia and David. But he has always been one step ahead. Changing places, switching names, using aliases. I had almost lost hope, until by chance I saw a photograph in a newspaper. The face was older, though unmistakable. It was Groy.

When I discovered that he was here I injected a small viral infection into my bloodstream. Enough to create the impression of epilepsy, just not enough to do anything more. I knew that Groy oversaw the neurosurgery department, and that finally, he would have to face me.

Edgar turned to the last page of the letter.

For weeks I have tried to see him, yet he has refused. So, now I have taken a gamble, a calculated risk you might say. I have told Nurse Davis that I know who Melvin Abelman is. Who he really is, and the secrets of his past. Only she knows, and now you.

You cannot imagine my surprise when I saw you. I recognised you immediately. You have your mother's eyes. That you also follow in her footsteps, means that you may also have her gift. An ability which may prove to be a curse.

Fate may have brought us together, my young doctor. The very same fate that seems to have brought you to work for Groy. And if all of this is just coincidence, then you need only be wary. My death is a natural one and not due to him knowing who I am. However, if it is as I suspect, something more. If it is by design, then I believe, like me, you are in very real danger. Mortal danger. I believe that Melvin Abelman knows who you are and the loose end that you represent from his past.

He is not who you think he is, or what you think he is, he is far more dangerous than anything you can imagine. If you possess the same skill, the same brilliance as your mother, then you must be prepared for what he will do to get it. To use it to finish his work. You must be on guard, and you must remain vigilant.

I should have done more to protect your parents, Edgar. Though I fear the worst, my only hope is that this knowledge can help protect you, now that I am gone.

Always yours,

Dr. Benjamin P. Clydesdale.

Edgar dropped the letter, and the pages fell like leaves drifting slowly onto his desk. Consumed by grief yet unable to grieve, he was still filled with a raging bloodlust over Abelman... Groy... or whoever he was. Now this... this from Clydesdale.... His parents alive, and his life a lie? It was absurd. A bad joke or sick prank, and Edgar was reeling; rocked to his core.

The last page of Clydesdale's letter came to rest upon the contract. Edgar shook his head as his eyes read again: *I should have done more to protect your parents.* If this were true—if all this was arranged, prepared and staged—then there was no fate. He had no destiny. Everything was and had always been under Abelman's control.

'Didn't I tell you to get out of here?'

Edgar looked up.

'Erm....' His heart began to race, wanting to stay calm. 'W-well... I... I... well....'

Drowning in panic and the fear of discovery, his anger was forgotten as he tried to appear unperturbed; desperate to gather the pages of Clydesdale's letter without drawing attention.

'What you got there?'

'Erm... w-what... here?'

'Yeah, there. What's the deal, Eddy?' asked Abelman, as he leant forward to try and move the folder now covering the letter.

'Oh, it's n-nothing,' replied Edgar, placing his hands firmly down on the file. 'Just s-some personal stuff I was clearing up.'

'It can wait…. Get over to Beacon Hill and make sure the guys hang the sign up.'

'Oh, sure…. Ok,' said Edgar, as he stood to give the impression that he was following the order and readying to leave.

Abelman looked down at the file, a corner of the letter stuck out.

'It's just temporary, Eddy—you know—until we move everything to LA.'

'Sure, I know.'

Both stood in deadlock. Each wishing the other to go and leave what lay beneath the file.

'Ok then,' said Abelman, forced to concede as Edgar remained steadfast. He began to walk, then as always, turned to have a final word. 'Be over in an hour,' he said with a grin, and his face became cold; his eyes threatening once more. 'Oh, and don't worry about your resignation for the Slaughterhouse, Eddy. I've already accepted it. Such a shame to lose you…. I only hope wherever you're going, that whoever you work with will appreciate your special gifts.'

Abelman winked. Edgar forced an anxious half-smile. He waited until Abelman had turned the corner before lifting the file and squeezing the pages of Clydesdale's letter into his trouser pocket. He removed his white coat and was about to hang it when suddenly, his cell phone rang. Edgar answered in a hurry, not looking at the screen or aware of who it was on the other end of the line.

'Spear.'

'Edgar, it's your grandfather…. Look, I need to talk to you—'

Edgar cancelled the call. He wasn't ready to speak with his grandfather, and was afraid that if he did, then he might lose his temper. The contents of Clydesdale's letter had given him the element of surprise. He would have to use it wisely; pick the right time at which to confront him if he was ever to find out why his grandfather had lied about his parents all these years. For now, he had to get to

Beacon Hill, but he needed time. Time to think, to understand. Time to plan, before Abelman arrived.

The cab driver was talkative and eager to speak with his passenger. Edgar wasn't in the talking mood. He pulled out the crumpled pages of Clydesdale's letter and began to read through them once again. If the things that Clydesdale had written were true, then Penny hadn't suddenly caught the predatory eye of Abelman; he had targeted her. He had spun Edgar a tale about attraction, when in fact it was most likely just another test. A test to see if Edgar knew what she knew and if he did, to wait for him to slip up. The minute Clydesdale took Penny into his confidence she was already dead; a thought that would have once seemed as improbable as it now appeared certain. But why had she not tried to confide in Edgar? Had she tried to protect him? The last time he saw her, she was either drugged or medicated. Was Abelman probing her mind; trying to find out if she had shared his secret? There were too many questions and no answers between Clydesdale's lines. Even so, Edgar was certain about *one* thing. Abelman had killed Penny. So, that alone meant Clydesdale was right. He really was in danger.

When Edgar arrived at Beacon Hill, two men were hanging the DomiGen office sign outside.

'Hah-wah-ya?' asked one of the men. Edgar had lived in Boston long enough to understand that the man, with his very heavy Bostonian accent, had actually asked, 'How are you?'

'I'm fine,' he replied. 'Wow! It's a lot bigger than I expected.'

The DomiGen sign was enormous, visible from several blocks away. You could say what you want about Abelman, but he knew how to make a statement.

As Edgar stepped through the large arched doors, he was greeted by the scent of rose petals and Jasmin. A delicate blend that was light and inviting; he caught the slightest hint of orange and the faintest trace of Vetiver. It was a mile away, or a million at least, from the unsophisticated bouquet of hospital disinfectant. As he closed his eyes to fill his lungs, the cares that plagued him refused to enter. He breathed out and the world faded beneath him, setting him suddenly adrift to some remote exotic isle. He was lighter than air, overwhelmed and helpless. An instant addict to the fragrance of his future.

When he opened his eyes, he stared in wonder at the gleaming white marble floors. The air was warm, as the light shone down through the atrium. It crafted a scene like a meadow of fresh snow, touched by the rays of the early morning sun. The landscape was broken by the grand ornate pillars. They stood interspaced like vast columns of carved ice, supporting the ceiling from the unsullied glacial ground. In the distance through the foyer, the reception desk rose like an iceberg; cut with its lines of delicate golden trim. Edgar stepped forward to the sound of a dancer, as he tapped his way across the wide-open stage. To his right, the rich lustre of hand dyed Chippendale leather rested upon their sculpted beech frames. He stepped farther forward, then stopped unexpectedly; arrested to a halt as he gaped at the ceiling. Strands of glistening copper fused and intertwined, forming the semblance of a network. It was stunning—ethereal—as if standing inside the brain itself, and beyond words or like anything that Edgar had ever seen. He gazed in awe at the intricate details; humbled by the colossal sculpture that hung high above him. For a moment, he was in heaven, although he felt like a god in Olympus. This was where he was meant to be—where he needed to be—and the doubts about Abelman that he left at the door would never be able to enter here, because DomiGen Labs *was* his destiny.

Edgar ran his hand along the seamless reception counter, still unable to take his eyes off the sculpture. Suddenly, a ring tone exploded to shatter his solitude. As he reached for his cell phone, a page from Clydesdale's letter fell from his pocket, and reality returned to haunt any dream that Edgar might have had of providence.

'Spear,' he said, as he answered.

'Well, what do you think?'

'Erm… it's erm… well… what can I say…? It's… it's amazing!'

'Isn't it?' Abelman asked, rhetorically. 'Have you been out back yet?'

'No. No, I'm just in reception.'

'Well make sure you do. I'm leaving now, so—'

Edgar's cell phone made the sound that he hated most: his battery was flat and about to shut down.

'Mel...? Wait... wait... where...?'

It was too late; the phone was dead. Edgar wanted to smash it against the counter but put it back into his pocket, promising himself to buy a new one with his first month's pay cheque. He knelt down to collect the page of Clydesdale's letter, knowing that he couldn't continue to carry it around, not with Abelman arriving shortly, that was suicide. He had to get rid of it.

He looked up, and the ceiling now felt like a web; it was Abelman's web, and he was the fly invited into the parlour. As he stood, Edgar spied a white panelled door across from the reception desk. It was all but hidden except for the slender contour of a shadow that was wedged between the door and its frame. He began to walk curiously towards it, and beside the door saw a small panel. It was also made to be very discreet, barely noticeable in fact. Nevertheless, there was no mistaking what it was once Edgar was standing beside it: a small touchscreen control pad. Edgar scowled. There had to be another way in, and he reached back to lean against the door as he glanced around to find one. To his amazement, albeit mainly surprise, the door opened. Edgar stumbled backwards, landing on the floor as he fell into the room.

The contrast between the foyer and the room could not have been greater: the room was darker than night. Edgar rolled off his back and rose to his feet. As he stared into the darkness, the light from the doorway bounced off the metallic surfaces of what looked like machinery inside. Beside the door was a switch and Edgar turned to press it to no effect. Already behind him, the automatic door closer had begun its return. Its momentum increased and his urgency grew as the light from the foyer vanished completely. Edgar pressed again at the switch. Still there was nothing, only the dark.

'Help!' he cried, as he pounded his fist upon the door. 'Help… can anybody hear me? Is there anybody there…?'

With no handle or way to open the door from the inside, he turned and stepped forward.

'Ow!' he groaned, as a sharp pain struck his thigh. 'Is there anyone here…? Hello….'

He reached down and his fingers brushed the cold touch of metal: the corner of a table or a workbench perhaps? They felt across the surface, gradually with caution, in the hope of finding something he might use to force the door. There was nothing more than emptiness, and his breathing began to quicken at the silence that enclosed him.

My phone, he thought, then huffed. Abelman would be there shortly. He checked his wristwatch and sighed: the dial didn't glow in the dark. His options exhausted without an escape, he edged slowly, feeling his way around the table. There had to be something… something somewhere he could use? He blinked. Then blinked again. Was it a trick of the night or the faintest of hopes? He squinted and stared. Away in the distance and deeper into the darkness, there appeared to be a flickering blue light. It was the tiniest of flames, not unlike a low stove or the embers of a fire, and it offered the weakest of beacons as a guide. Edgar stretched out his arms and moved zombielike, banging into obstacles and knocking over most everything that stood in his way or hindered his path. The scent from the foyer was nowhere now, and the smell of gas grew stronger as he approached the flame. As he neared the source, Edgar could see it belonged to a pilot light, and though the glow that it gave lacked radiance or warmth, he was standing in front of a furnace.

He stared at the flame as it danced from his breath, and a smile that was sly curled the corner of his lip. He reached into his pocket and pulled out the letter, scrunching the pages into a tight little ball. The paper ignited, burning brightly, and the room was partially lit; even now Clydesdale was helping. The blaze was short, but enough for Edgar to see that the wall he was standing beside was in fact a palette stacked high with boxes. The flames were dying, though not yet dead, and at Edgar's feet he saw a box not yet sealed. He reached down to clasp at whatever was inside, and when he opened his palm was unsure of what he saw; what he believed to be true, or the dimness of shadows in the low failing light. They were chips—silicon chips. Hundreds of them, thousands of them, tens of thousands if not more. Behind the palette, box after box stacked high and deep, like a warehouse or storage facility.

'You're not supposed to be in here,' stretched a voice from the depths.

Edgar jumped, and the chips scattered across the floor. It was Abelman. His voice booming out from behind as he marched towards him.

'I said, out - back!'

Edgar turned to the darkness and the advancing footsteps. Suddenly, they stopped. Silence returned. Then a warm gust of air stroked his cheek. Abelman was standing directly in front of him.

'I... I d-didn't know. I saw the d-door and—'

Abelman watched as the remains of Clydesdale's letter turned to ash, and his face emerged from the darkness to the shadows of the flickering blue flame.

'Cold?'

'C-cold...? Erm... no... no,' replied Edgar, protesting his innocence. 'I... I threw some old tissues onto the flame... t-to try to see better. I couldn't find my way out and—'

'You're a long way from the door, Eddy.... You're a long way from anywhere....'

Edgar felt the familiar grip of Abelman's hand on his shoulder. 'It's this way.'

He led Edgar through the darkness, back towards a sliver of light without crashing into anything.

'Goddamn power company. They were supposed to turn it on yesterday. How the hell can we keep anything secure?'

Abelman's Hermès folder had kept the door ajar. As they returned to the brightness of the foyer, he looked angry.

'You weren't supposed to be in there—not yet—this wasn't how I planned to show it to you.'

'To show me what?'

'Look, Eddy, there are things people can't understand... because they don't wanna understand.

'People wanna see the world all sugar coated and sweet—like it is out here—all pretty and perfect. They don't wanna see underneath... they don't wanna know what's in the dark bitter centre. Not like it is back there. In the places we need to turn the flawed into the flawless.

'I mean, how do you think we got out of the caves and built houses? Got to the moon and made it to Mars? I'll tell you how—by dreaming the dreams that no one else has ever dreamed.... By working our way out of the darkness... by doing what needs to be done.'

Edgar stared back at Abelman with questioning eyes.

'Those chips... are those the chips that James talked about? That connect to the cerebral cortex...? For the wearables?'

Abelman paused.

'Implants, Eddy. They're not chips. They're implants.'

'Implants?' asked Edgar, clearly alarmed. 'We never talked about implants... you never... you said—'

'What did you think?' snapped Abelman. 'Did you think we were gonna change the world with some stupid wearable? Some piece of garbage that needs upgrading every six months? Don't kid yourself, Eddy.... Munro's a dreamer... a sugar-coated dreamer. He can talk about lollipops and candy, but he can't change the world. He won't... because the world doesn't need candy. It needs control.'

Edgar shook his head in disbelief.

'Have you lost your mind? Mel.... Are you insane? I mean just the legal—'

Despite his earlier lesson, the apprentice had still not learned to accept his master's judgement. Abelman grabbed him by his shirt and pulled him to within a few centimetres, as his nostrils flared down into the face of Edgar.

'Insane...? I'm doing what *needs* to be done, Eddy. I'm in the precision business... and in case you've forgotten—so are you!'

He threw Edgar back against the reception desk and released him, but Edgar wasn't done; apparently still in denial or unwilling to understand.

'You're crazy! I thought you wanted to put chips into Munro's wearables...? I thought you wanted to guarantee sales. To get customers...? Get customers and sell products—'

Abelman had heard enough and lashed out. Edgar fell and Abelman turned cold.

'When are you gonna get ahead, Eddy? Don't you get it...? I'm not selling some guy's product. I – *am* – the product... and every schmuck out there is *my* customer.

'Why do you think you're here...? Why do you think I brought you here...? So, you and Munro can sell lollipops to kids?

'You're here because you're gonna put *my* product into the head of *every* – single – person on this planet. You're gonna *do* what needs to be done. You're gonna do it, or you're gonna end up lying next to your girlfriend—feeding the worms.'

Abelman loomed over Edgar as he lay on the floor, no match for the man that he wanted to be. Clydesdale was wrong. Abelman wasn't dangerous, Abelman was a lunatic: a deranged lunatic.

'The world loves Munro, Eddy. He'll give them our chips in his wearables, and they'll love him for it. But when they're done... when they're done with his wearables... they'll be ready to implant... and that's when I'll be *done* with Munro.'

Edgar's heart was thumping, ready to explode. It sucked the blood from his veins and drained him like a vampire; his face turned ashen, his body anaemic. He couldn't stand or rise and his stomached churned, clenching in waves as the first beads of sweat trickled from his brow.

'Look at them,' said Abelman, as he took a chip from his pocket and threw it onto the lap of Edgar. 'Take a good look at them, Eddy.'

Edgar glanced down at the chip. Still frozen in fear, unable to move, he summoned his strength towards his hand and held the chip aloft.

'Beautiful, aren't they? My little dominoes... for *all* the little Dominoes. Except for one small problem... and that's where you come in.'

Edgar looked away from the chip and back at Abelman.

'They don't work.'

Edgar was puzzled and Abelman saw his confusion. A more direct, more graphic approach might help his apprentice to appreciate his dilemma.

'They only kill.'

'B-but... you said.... You s-said they were stable. You told Munro they w-were—'

'I told Munro what he needed to hear... just like I'm telling you what you need to hear—what you better hear, Eddy. So, stop your stuttering and listen up.

'You need to make them stable, and you better make them work.... See, you're all in now... *all – in*... and you'll make them work, or each one that fails is on you.'

Abelman's eyes narrowed to focus his madness.

'Did you think I was just gonna hand you five hundred g's a year for the pleasure of your company...? Why do you think you're the chief physician? You're the *only* physician, Eddy, and you're right to be scared,' snarled Abelman, as he smiled conceitedly and turned towards the reception counter.

'Oh, I nearly forgot, *Dr. Spear*.... I mean, a deal is a deal, right?'

He unzipped his leather folder and removed several papers. 'Fresh off the press,' he said, casting them down at Edgar.

Edgar reached out to gather the sheet closest to him, and Abelman brought his foot down hard. Edgar looked up, still clutching at the paper trapped beneath the shoe.

'You're in the precision business now, Eddy—so, make them precise.'

The fear that had paralysed Edgar now clawed around his throat, choking his voice for words or reply as Abelman stared with intent. Suddenly, his cell phone rang, and he lifted his foot to release the paper.

'What?' he screamed into the phone. 'Eleven million... not a dollar less! It's worth eleven so get me eleven or I'll get someone who can.'

Abelman cancelled the call, his face like thunder.

'Realtors... like leeches they are... they want your money, they just don't wanna work for it.'

Abelman slammed his leather folder shut and ran his hands back through his ruffled thin hair.

'Don't look so scared, Eddy, got a nice surprise coming for you and Munro—now that we're *partners* and all.' he smirked, as he snatched at his folder before making his way back towards the entrance. 'Goddamn power better be on by tomorrow.'

Edgar struggled to get back onto his feet, his tenacity weakened by the encounter, and Abelman turned for his final word.

'Remember... Munro's the key to your future. Our little secret about the chip... we don't wanna upset him now, do we?'

The door closed behind Abelman. Edgar looked at the paper in his hand and the others that lay strewn across the floor. It was as Abelman had promised. They were from the United States Medical Licensing Examination, the Federation of State Medical Boards, and the American Board of Surgery. Abelman had them all—all of them in his pocket—and all of Edgar's certificates and licenses were there. His dream had become real, but his reality had become a nightmare, and the nightmare, it seemed, was only just beginning.

Edgar looked up at the ceiling one more time and was not so impressed after all. It no longer looked like a neural network or even an intricate spider's web for that matter. It looked more like the roof of a prison; a jail from which there was no parole and no release, not by Abelman anyway. This is where he would spend his days, and who knew if he would ever earn his freedom? There was no solace in Edgar's thoughts; little comfort in what waited ahead. Today might well be the start of a life sentence, yet for now, at least, Edgar was only visiting. He gathered his certificates and collected his papers, before stepping outside into the late afternoon sun. The workmen had already finished and left. He squinted and was forced to turn his head, dazzled by the polished aluminium of the DomiGen sign as it reflected the light from between the buildings across the street. The sign was impressive. Expensive like the interior, and from a distance would have the same breath-taking effect. It was just as Abelman had wanted; perfect, so long as no one looked beyond the surface or ventured into the back room to find the truth behind the façade.

Edgar sighed; his mind filled with worry, his lungs with the fumes of exhausts driving by. Sometimes, he thought, a truth is kinder left unknown—perhaps easier not to see. Standing alone in the cold light of day, it would have been better to believe that monsters don't exist, than to have to finally accept that they really, truly do.

He awoke the next morning to get ready for the Slaughterhouse; out of habit of course, since those days were now over. Wide awake and no longer a resident, Edgar could enjoy a lazy morning in his boxer shorts. He slouched on the frayed small two-seater sofa; a spring standing free having ripped through the stains of the green paisley fabric. As he zapped through the channels of the old television, he slurped breakfast cereal with the shutters still drawn. There was nothing of interest and he looked at the walls, at their dreary dull drabness and was glad to be leaving. He would finally be able to get somewhere bigger, something better. A place that he could call and make his home.

On the news channel, a reporter was covering the problems at CaliChat. It had been several days since the company had made the news. After James' resignation, it seemed as though the media had lost interest in the story; that they followed the man and not his past. Edgar was curious and turned up the volume.

'.... And we have more on the story from our financial correspondent, Janet Cove,' said the news anchor as the image changed to a video feed.

'Janet, Freyland said "lower than expected." Can you tell us anything more about what he meant?'

'Well, David, Martin Freyland might not have gone so far as to say that the company was in trouble, but he did give a very clear indication that they simply did not have the liquidity to pay.'

'So, what implications would that have?'

'What I think Freyland is saying here, is that they need to appeal to investors to find a way to get hold of the billion dollars they still owe the government. Either that, or they need to find another solution.'

'And what type of solutions might they consider?'

'To be honest, David, I think Freyland might have to evaluate every option. Potentially, we might see an emission, and if that fails, he may consider other options such as a merger. Maybe even a takeover, if they're going to be able to pay off this debt.'

'Thank you, Janet.... Janet Cove there, reporting live from outside CaliChat's headquarters in Los Angeles.'

Edgar's jaw dropped and his spoon fell into the bowl. It was sad that CaliChat was in trouble, but it wasn't going to spoil his breakfast. After all, he wasn't the one who pushed out James, his conscience was clear. Edgar fished out the spoon and took another mouthful of cereal: chomping away at the last few pieces that were not yet soggy with milk. He nodded, mulling over the recent events; convinced that all he had done was to bluff a bit—lie a little—that was all. He had outplayed his partners and sealed the deal. Won the hand and was still in the game. He was now ahead and had to find a way to stay there. Even so, as he stirred the bowl in search of a piece still able to crunch, it was Penny's death and Clydesdale's revelations that continued to plague him.

He began his amble up towards Beacon Hill at around 9:00 a.m. There was still no power and there was nothing to do other than watch the cleaners wash down windows and doors. Some workmen, different to those who were there yesterday, were putting finishing touches to handrails. Edgar decided to look around the rest of the building. To the left of reception, two large glass doors were controlled by a sensor. Edgar could tell that they should open and close automatically; at least they would when the power was on that is. For now, they could simply be pulled open, and Edgar wondered if this was what Abelman meant with "out back"?

It was all so white and sterile inside; so clean and futuristic. There was room after room with large displays sunk into walls and touchscreens that were built into tables. Consulting rooms, laboratories, operating theatres and recovery areas. DomiGen Labs might not have been a hospital, but it was undoubtedly the next best thing. Edgar continued along the corridor, and he climbed the staircase to follow the sign that pointed to the office area. Wherever he looked, his eyes were drawn and tempted to feast on the wealth of delicate details. More than lavish or opulent by nature; the space was magnificent, and it was clear that Abelman had pumped an absolute fortune into renovating every inch of it. Wandering alone, he traversed undisturbed, relishing each second as he dared to dream once again. Suddenly, his cell phone rang. The exploration was brought to a halt.

'Spear,' he said.

'Dude…! Seriously? How you doing?'

'Oh, James…. Hi. I'm fine thanks. Actually, I'm at DomiGen now. Just looking around—you know—keeping my eye on the place.'

'Excellent! Dude, look... I'm flying in tonight. Got a prototype ready. Been working day and night since Abelman sent the funds over.'

'Really? Oh, wow,' said Edgar somewhat surprised. 'Well... that's fantastic—'

'Later, dude!'

Munro hung up, and as he did so, Edgar's phone rang again. He answered without thinking.

'Ok, so I guess I'll see you later.... Is there anything I should—'

A voice interrupted on the other end.

'Good morning. I wonder... am I speaking to, Edgar...? Edgar Spear?'

Edgar took a moment to readjust.

'Erm... yes. Yes, this is Dr. Spear. How can I help you?'

'Ah, good morning, Dr. Spear, this is Dr. Youseth at the UC Taylor Medical Centre in Sacramento.'

'Ok....'

'I apologise for the intrusion, but I'm calling with concern to a William Herbert Calhoun.'

'Yes. I know Mr. Calhoun. He's my grandfather.'

'I'm sorry to have to inform you, Dr. Spear.... William sadly passed away in the early hours of this morning.'

Edgar said nothing as each word repeated in his mind; translated into meaning and were then understood.

'W-what...? No. No you're mistaken.... M-my grandfather's not ill... he's as s-strong as an ox. He's... I was just.... Why only yesterday he called and—'

'I understand this must come as a shock, Dr. Spear. I know that William had been trying to reach you for several days, to inform you of his condition while he was admitted with us here.'

The cell phone dropped from Edgar's hand and the screen cracked like the ice of a frozen lake as it hit the floor. He was somewhere unfamiliar as the room began to blur and his body began to quiver. The lightness that filled his head now forced his hands to cover his face, as the voice of Youseth reached out to continue his message.

'Dr. Spear…? Dr. Spear, are you there…? Hello….'

The voice only stirred Edgar's stomach to a violent surge. It weakened his knees and he slumped to the floor, racked and ravaged with guilt. It was there he remained, unable to move, until the light had already begun to fade, and with it any hope of uncovering the truth of his past.

Later that evening, Munro landed at Logan Airport. The partners had agreed to meet at DomiGen Labs; it would be the first time they had met since The Grove in LA. Edgar had managed to return to his apartment and lament his grandfather's passing, but with the meeting due to start at 8:00 p.m., he began to make his way back towards Beacon Hill.

There was drizzle in the air, getting ready for a downpour, and as Edgar turned onto Lime Street—a shortcut to get over onto River Street—he noticed that traffic was backed up. He could see all the way up to Charles and all the way down to Beacon; it was bumper to bumper everywhere. The Boston Police Department had closed a large section of the Hill, rerouting tailbacks most probably because of an accident. However, as Edgar continued his journey, he realised that there were no causalities, no fire crews or ambulances on the scene. In fact, there was no scene. What there was, and what he saw, were hundreds of police officers; whatever they were doing, or whatever it was they were trying to do, didn't seem to be working.

The streets were filled, and Edgar squeezed his way through a group of journalists performing studio checks. Wherever he turned, police were busy trying to push people back in an effort to cordon off access, while others broke through barricades and the chaos resumed. The headlights of cars had little impact: crammed tightly against each other like sardines. In the frustrated confusion, drivers got out to stand on their vehicles, to try to see why they were stuck and what all the ruckus was about. Car horns tooted, lorry air horns sounded, and between the commotion the occasional *Woop Woop!* of sirens could be heard. It was bedlam, and the rain now poured, as everyone seemed to be heading in one direction. Edgar tried hopelessly to navigate through the crowds, caught in the current, he was pushed towards the steps of DomiGen.

'Step back,' an officer instructed, from behind the barriers set up in front of the building.

'What? No... no, you must let me in. I work here.'

'I'm sorry, sir. I'm going to have to ask you to step back.'

'Did you hear what I said? I work here—I'm the head of surgery.'

'I don't want to have to use force. So please, I'm asking you for the last time... *step – away!*'

Edgar reached into his pocket. Amongst the papers that Abelman had left him was a business card. He took it out and showed it to the officer.

'Look!' he screamed, trying desperately to be heard. He pointed to the card as the rain lashed down. 'I work here.... See? Now let me in!'

The officer stared at the card with his flashlight. He could see that it said *DomiGen Labs*, but it was hard to see anything else through the spray of the driving rain.

'I must get inside!'

The officer switched his flashlight between Edgar's face and the card.

'You have to let me in.... Please....'

Hesitant, the officer stepped to one side to make a gap. He grabbed Edgar's arm to pull him through.

'Get inside and stay down—riot control are on their way!'

Riot control? This was no riot, thought Edgar. There was no violence, no damage, or looting. This was a mob; a marching mob that moved in protest... but against what?

The building was dark and only the police floodlights gave ambience to the foyer from outside. Edgar tried to make sense of the madness. Was it the CaliChat story from the morning news? Had there been further developments during the day? Bankruptcy perhaps? Surely something drastic to cause such reaction and outburst. His thoughts were interrupted by a sharp stinging pain: a search light had revolved and shone directly at him. He closed his eyes to avoid the glare and heard the sound of a helicopter whirling overhead.

He had to get to the roof. He had to get a better look at what was happening outside. Besides, it was safer up there than here in the foyer with only the windows between him and the police; only the police between him and the sprawling mob. Edgar ran to the glass doors he had managed to open earlier that morning and rushed down the corridor towards the staircase. Surely there must also be a stairwell that would lead to the roof? Suddenly, Edgar was blinded again: not by the beam of a searchlight, but by darkness, and unable to see. The helicopter blades had stopped, and footsteps beat out on the corrugated roof like a rhythm section keeping time. He knew he was close as he felt his way along the walls, and the sound of muffled voices grew louder.

'Hello?' he cried. 'Is there any—'

A bright light blazed harshly in front of him. He raised his hands and looked away.

'Don't shoot. I'm unarmed…. I work here!'

The voices stopped.

'Eddy…? Like seriously… dude, what are you doing?'

'We'll need to hurry, James,' said a voice from behind the beam that was also familiar. 'We don't have much time to get things set up.'

'James…?' asked Edgar, unable to see. 'James, is that you?'

'Of course, it's me… like who else could do all this?'

'Do you think… could you maybe move the light?

'Sorry, dude!' replied James, as he pushed his assistant's flashlight away. Edgar lowered his hands. 'But seriously? No power? What is this... like the Middle Ages?'

Edgar sighed.

'Took the chopper—*way* too many people at Logan.... Crazy once we got on the PA and announced I'd arrived... and like... have you *seen* the traffic? I mean, dude...! Seriously?'

'Yeah,' said Edgar, hiding his annoyance of Munro and the turmoil he created. 'It wasn't easy getting here.'

The flashlights from the entourage turned their attentions to the floor in front of James.

'The cops are everywhere... trying to stop me from addressing the nation.... Seriously... like trying to stop *me* from talking to the world! But listen up people, cos we're gonna rise up and stick it to the man. Nothing—but nothing—stops James Munro!'

Edgar looked dumbfounded at James. "Addressing the nation," who did he think he was, the president of the United States? Was he really any better than Abelman? Both were self-obsessed: egotistical narcissists. There wasn't enough room in the world, let alone this building, for the pair and their egos.

'So, you're planning to hold a press conference...? Now?' Edgar asked.

'Fifteen minutes to air,' Munro's assistant confirmed.

'But James, we don't have any power....'

'Dude...! Seriously? Sure, we do. You've got me—and I've got the power.... I — *am* — the — power! I could light this whole city!'

The havoc outside was small in comparison to the mayhem around Edgar. He looked on in wonder at the team who created some form of a studio; as they fired up generators, connected cables, and ran about shouting with all the prowess of a well drilled military unit. He checked his Rolex. It was 7:39 p.m. So, it could have been, or was even as late as 7:54 p.m., including anything in between. The point simply, there was still no sign of Abelman.

'Eight minutes people,' shouted Munro's assistant. 'Let's make them count!'

She pulled the lapels of Munro's jacket and brushed his shoulders, then licked her thumb and seemed to wipe something from his cheek. He turned and called out to Edgar, pawing her away.

'Come on partner, you get the best seat in the house—right beside me!'

To Edgar's surprise, James led them down to the foyer. Edgar was curious; how did he know his way around?

'Because dude... if I was designing this? This is *exactly* how I would do it.'

The foyer was now lit by a chain of spotlights. Munro's assistant led him to a stand set up at the centre of reception, strategically placed beside a large DomiGen Labs sign.

'Sixty seconds, James,' she shouted, as she asked everyone else for quiet.

Munro looked at Edgar, he smiled wildly: like a small child at Christmas staring at the stack of presents wrapped beneath the tree.

'I love this part!' he cheered, as his assistant began to count down.

'And five... four... three... two... one....'

She gave the signal, and he stared into the camera.

'People!'

One word and the crowd outside fell silent. They looked up into the rain, at the enormous projection screens that Munro's team had dropped from the rooftops.

'I'm here today to welcome you to DomiGen Labs.... To bid you all welcome to James Munro's DomiGen Labs!'

The crowd broke into applause, as they watched their idol and followed his every word.

'Now, some of you might recall that the last time I spoke, I *may* have said a word or two about a little congressional hearing.... Maybe I also mentioned a certain little wearable of mine?'

Applause turned to laughter; crowds as always endeared by Munro's self-deprecating humour.

'I was thinking... maybe some of you might like to see it?'

This was so typical James. Munro the showman. Always performing. Always playing to a crowd. As their rapturous cheering increased, there was a sense that they were about to become a part of history.

'So, without further ado, it gives me great pleasure to introduce you to a little friend of mine. Something that I like to call— *The Ally*,' said Munro, as he lifted a bracelet that was similar in design to the one shown in his previous presentation.

The crowd gasped.

'The Ally is the world's first end-user device that recognises, detects, and compares facial biometrics.

'Now people, this isn't just a bracelet.... The Ally is also going to be available as a necklace... and believe it or not... a contact lens!'

The live feed cut to a video which showed The Ally in its various forms. Spruced with dazzling effects and accompanied by a catchy high-tempo soundtrack, it was a production of which any Hollywood director would have been proud. The crowd stood mesmerised as they paid their reverence to the genius of Munro, and his assistant leapt to the stage with her make-up bag; eager to take advantage while the segment played. Edgar sat quietly at the side of James, in the wings and out of the camera's view which was entirely focused upon his partner. The best seat in the house was as close as Edgar could ever hope to come, or be allowed to get, without infringing upon the spotlight. When the film had finished, Munro talked more about himself and his new company, as he played forever to the camera. The rain was unable to dampen their cheer, and as the presentation came to its end, Munro gave his exiting catchphrase, before his assistant called for a wrap.

'Amazing, huh?' said Munro, as he turned to Edgar.

Like it was with Abelman, Edgar was unsure whether James was asking his opinion or merely telling him how it was. However, he knew that when Abelman saw the news there was going to be trouble.

'You know, James.... We... we're supposed to be partners. You, Abelman, and me. We're in this together.'

Munro's entourage were busy dissembling cables and packing things down; concerned with their various duties and not at all interested in Edgar.

'I told you, Eddy... and Abelman... this is *my* company. DomiGen – is – *mine!*'

Munro's assistant interrupted. 'We're ready in ten,' she said, as she gave their departure time.

'Excellent!' continued Munro, as he turned back to Edgar. 'Then there's just enough time to show me around my ground floor. To see how Abelman has spent my money '

Edgar never ceased to be flabbergasted by the arrogance of Munro. Yet still, he was almost always unprepared for being so.

'Well... I mean... there's—'

'Woah...! Check – it – out!'

Munro was distracted as he spotted something across the foyer. Edgar panicked; not knowing what to do or how to stop him as he walked brazenly towards the secret door.

'Dude,' he called out, suddenly realising that Edgar was not beside him. 'What's the PIN?'

Edgar had no choice and hurried over towards James, afraid that he might push open the door.

'W-wait! J-James... the thing is... you see the thing is—'

'It's locked!'

Edgar stopped. He turned to the voice behind him as Munro's eyes narrowed.

'Dude...! Seriously? In *my* building?'

'Your what!' scowled Abelman, at the petulance of Munro.

He was standing in the middle of the foyer as the lights came on. The control panel beside the door lit up, and James heard the electronic lock clamp shut.

'What's my PIN?'

Abelman's eyebrows were raised. He had that cold psychotic look in his eyes once again as he brushed past Edgar and stormed across the floor. But Munro was preoccupied—not even looking—pressing the numbers at random on the keypad before noticing that Abelman was standing behind him. He sighed an overly dramatic sigh.

'You're getting old, dude... I said, *my — building.* Now, what's *my* PIN?' he demanded, his eyes still on the keypad.

Edgar expected Munro to be cut down. To be put in his place and for Abelman to bring an end to this pretence. He raced across, expecting the worst.

'There is no PIN,' smirked Abelman. 'It's a key card.'

'Oh yeah...?' scoffed Munro, as he turned to face Abelman. 'Well, where's mine?'

'Yours...? Yours is with ours. They arrive tomorrow.'

'Damn... I'm flying back to LA now.'

'Don't worry, Munro. You'll be in there soon enough... won't he, Eddy?'

Edgar looked at Abelman. Why was he not berating James, not arguing that this was his company?

'Oh... erm... yes.... For sure,' said Edgar. 'Definitely... I can even call you and let you know how it looks...?'

'Dude... don't stress. I'm sure it looks great.'

'Trust me. It's to die for,' said Abelman, as he interrupted before Edgar could speak.

Munro glanced quickly back to Edgar.

'Ok.... Anyways.... You need to focus on getting those chips into my Ally. I was thinking my next device could—'

'Like you said,' interrupted Abelman again. 'Don't stress. Enjoy the flight back to LA.'

Munro's assistant came to take him to the awaiting helicopter.

'Yo, people! James Munro. Gotta go! It's been awesome!'

Abelman looked at Edgar and Edgar at Abelman. Neither were willing to comment on Munro or his performance as he was led back towards the stairwell.

'The first truck arrives at six. Make sure you're here to greet them.'

'First truck?'

'Your guests, Eddy.'

'Guests?'

Abelman put his hand inside his pocket and handed him a key card.

'Your lab rats.... You'd better let them in... we wouldn't want them to feel like they're not welcome now, would we?' he said laughingly.

8

THE INSURANCE POLICY

'And hereby bequeath all of my property—both real and personal—to my grandson, Edgar Spear,' said the lawyer.

Edgar smiled. 'So, what am I supposed to do with his company? I don't even live in California.'

The lawyer paused and replied. 'May I suggest that you employ someone to run the company for you, Dr. Spear? Until such time, at least, that you feel you may either want to do so yourself or relinquish the asset and profit from its sale.'

'And the house?'

'Will be sold as you requested. Once you are sure that all items of personal value have been removed.'

'Very good. And the rest?'

'Will be donated to the charities as per your instructions, after we receive the keys to the property as agreed.'

'Thank you,' said Edgar as he stood to leave, shaking the lawyer's hand.

When Edgar arrived back at his grandfather's house, dust sheets lay draped and covered the majority of furniture. It was eerie, almost macabre to enter the traditionally styled residence, where six white Doric columns stood guard supporting the balcony above the door. Once inside, the ornate oak staircase rose up from the centre of the hall. It split left and right to lead upstairs, which played host to ten bedrooms and four bathrooms. His grandfather had appreciated the finer things in life; his home was luxurious, sumptuous and grand. But now that he was gone, his home was just a house, and there was time for one last look around before Edgar's flight back to Boston.

In his grandfather's bedroom, clothes had been sorted and spread out across the bed; ready to be collected for a local homeless shelter. Beside them, the belt that his grandfather used to discipline him as a child, now lay coiled like a snake. Beneath it, his money clip: the band that held his dollar bills and would make a loud, crisp, cutting sound as he pulled them out to give Edgar his allowance. None of these things would ever happen again. Like his grandfather, they lay at rest.

Edgar was filled with a mixture of emotion. He knew that despite their differences, the lies and lack of love between them, the old man was still his grandfather. Now that he was gone, all that remained were these things around the house; an inadequate compilation of life that represented his time on earth.

He lifted his grandfather's favourite suit from the pile and placed it on top, like his grandfather would have done to show off his finest clothes. He remembered each Sunday when his grandfather wore it to church; the only time that the cantankerous old man was ever happy. It was bittersweet. A reflection of the motley feelings that Edgar held towards him, and he lowered his head, a little in shame for not feeling more than he did.

He brushed his hand across the lapel to remove the dust that had gathered, and in doing so, the prickly feel of the tweed material brought back other memories: helping him to remember how it was at home each Sunday, after they arrived back from the service. That was when his grandfather would begin drinking heavily, angry over the loss of his daughter. In a way, Edgar had grown up accepting it; he understood why he did it. Only now he no longer could, not after Clydesdale's letter. Now he questioned everything, and the question that had haunted Edgar these past months, was not his parent's disappearance, or whether his grandfather knew of how or why they disappeared. It was how he could possibly remember growing up happily with them in Renfield, with memories so vivid and clear, if they vanished just two weeks after Groy had supposedly threatened the life of their young son? There was no way to explain how Edgar could have lived with his parents until he was ten years old unless Clydesdale was lying. Although everything that Clydesdale described was true, or was seemingly coming to pass, so why would he lie about this one little detail in an otherwise unbelievable story? It just didn't make sense, and with his grandfather gone, perhaps it never would.

Edgar moved his hand down the jacket, straightening it the way his grandfather would have wanted. Despite his repeated attempts, the right pocket would not lay flat, and it was not because it was creased; there was something inside it. Edgar reached in.

'Ow!' he winced, as he quickly jerked his hand out. 'What was that?'

Whatever it was, it had pierced the skin of his index finger. Edgar pinched it, trying to stem the flow of blood. He reached back inside, carefully this time, not wanting to repeat the same mistake. His finger moved over the object. It felt thin, cold to the touch, and he tried to take hold, not wanting to damage or break it. As he slowly pulled it out, he saw what looked like a small silver brooch. The emblem seemed to resemble two crossed daggers: they may have been swords, or knives perhaps, joined behind a helmet. It was a strange looking helmet, though. Not like one of those King Arthur or Knights of the Round Table type helmets, and not like a helmet that a soldier would wear either. When he examined it more closely, Edgar began to wonder if it really was a helmet at all? It might have been a mask? And yet, at the same time, it didn't look like a mask either. In fact, the only thing that he was certain of was the writing beneath the emblem. Written in capitals, were the letters: *W.A.T.C.H.*

Edgar turned the brooch over in his hand. The words: *Nomini tuo da gloriam* were engraved on the back. He wasn't an expert by any means but had learned some Latin as a child; forced to do so by his grandfather. While his translation was probably not perfect, he was confident that the core of the message meant: *Unto thy name give glory.*

Edgar was perplexed. What was this thing? It couldn't have been his grandfathers as his grandfather never wore jewellery, not even a wristwatch. So, what was he doing with this trinket? Suddenly, there was a knock at the front door. Edgar ignored it. Perhaps the pin was his grandmothers? Edgar had no memory of her at all as she had passed away when he was just a baby. She had been ill for a very long time apparently, and her death had come as a relief; put an end to all her suffering. Perhaps it had belonged to her and his grandfather carried it in her honour? That would seem to make sense, yet Edgar's face was not quite happy with the deduction; not at all convinced with his assessment. He bore a smile that was never a smile, nor a frown to be exact, and seemed a little lost. His past was an endless maze of unanswered questions, and the longer that he dwelled, the deeper the labyrinth became. It was time to go; like Abelman said, "Leave the past behind."

Able to finally straighten his grandfather's suit, he took one long last look around the room before making his way back down the creaking staircase. Outside, his driver had grown increasingly impatient.

'Dr. Spear?'

'Just a moment,' said Edgar, as he gathered himself. 'I forgot my coat.'

'It's just that your flight will be leaving....'

Edgar walked back down the hallway, past the large painting of his grandfather which was done when he was younger; when he was less weighed down by life and had darker hair. He looked up at the mountain that had raised him, at the man who had always stared down and watched over him. This was goodbye, for one last time. When he lived at the house, he was always fearful of the painting; his grandfather's eyes followed him around from the canvas, no matter where he went or wherever he stood. But as Edgar gazed, smiled and said thank you, he was drawn towards something new. Silly really, and yet it was something he had never noticed or paid attention to before. However, now that he saw it, he couldn't unsee it, because there, beneath his grandfather's jacket, a small fleck of white paint was made to look like something reflective. It was barely noticeable, and only the very top of it could be seen in the painting. All the same, it was definitely similar, in fact almost identical to the top edge of the silver brooch.

'Dr. Spear? I'm sorry, we really must—'

'Yes. Yes,' said Edgar, 'I'm coming.' He grabbed his coat and walked back to the driver, closing the door behind him, and with it, the life he once knew.

It had been almost nine months since Abelman gave Edgar his key card and he began working at DomiGen Labs. The first morning was the worst, when seven patients died within minutes of each other. Clydesdale described how a lorry would arrive each night to remove the bodies of test subjects that had failed under Groy. Despite almost thirty years since those first experiments, the truth was that nothing had changed. There had been no progress, no breakthroughs or eureka moment, and the lorries still came.

Everything that Abelman had told Munro was a lie, and everything that Abelman had told Edgar was the truth, albeit perhaps for his real identity. The chips were unstable—they had always been unstable—and who knew how many thousands of lives had been lost proving the point? There was just no way that Edgar could synchronise the frequency of any chip to the synaptic terminals: the receivers of the brain. These were the axons, or connections between the cells, and they differed greatly. So, it was impossible for a single frequency to perform a variety of functions across the varying neurons. What this meant in practice, was that Abelman's implants had been extremely limited in success. That is, if success could be defined as being able to perform one activity in an endless repeated loop; like saying a word, or moving a muscle over and over again, until the brain eventually shuts down and the subject enters a vegetative state.

While Edgar had been struggling in the laboratory, James had been thriving with his wearables and A.I. technology. Sales for DomiGen were at an all-time high, and records were broken daily. Demand had been so great in fact, that James was already working on a new wearable device: something that he called "The Scout."

Abelman had kept his word, almost, liquidating the majority of his properties and shares to fund the company. By keeping control over corporate finances, he was able to shield the real cost of Edgar's work, as well as any compensation that was paid to grieving families who threatened to expose the experiments. As far as James Munro was concerned, Edgar was still working on integrating Abelman's chip into The Ally, and the new improved version of the wearable would go into production next year. With profits surging and developments coming, Munro was back to his best; on the cover of every magazine, basking in the limelight. But the problem for James was always the same: his arrogance. He still had no idea of the real work that Abelman was actually forcing Edgar to do. That it was Abelman who pulled his strings; Abelman who controlled *all* the strings. As the puppet master often said, "Munro's nothing more than a marionette," and to him, Munro only had one purpose: to be the face of DomiGen... for the time being.

'We've bought CaliChat,' Abelman declared.

'Dude...! What? No!' replied Munro in the video call, appalled and astonished at the news.

Edgar was sat beside Abelman; as startled by the revelation as Munro, who tried to assert some form of executive authority from a distance.

'Dude...! It's not happening! Look... it's my company and it's my decision... and I say *no way*.... No — way, Jose!'

James was yet to learn that Abelman was uninterested in discussion or the subtle art of conversation. He informed people of his intentions. He issued his instructions. Made clear his expectations, and people did what they were told as a result.

'Listen,' he sneered, cold and without interest in Munro or the objections that he voiced. 'Edgar agreed with me. So, we have the majority vote.... As chairman I've made the decision... it's all legal and above board.'

'Eddy...?' asked James, as he looked at Edgar through the camera for support. Edgar had none to offer. Abelman held up a paper to show his signature along with Edgar's on the agreement. A signature that Edgar had never made.

'We're negotiating the final settlement, but the lawyers will have it tidied up today. Just thought I'd let you know... *partner*.'

'No way, dude...! You can't do anything without—'

'We can.... Or rather, I have—I did—now it's done.' Abelman cut him off with clear precision.

Munro was rocked. He fell back in his chair with a taste of real partnership.

'Dude...! What the hell? We do wearables... what about The Scout?'

'I'm not interested in sales... I'm interested in users. I want *more* users, Munro. I want *every* user. Don't you get it...? CaliChat adds value... it adds users and a bigger incentive to buy The Ally... it makes the most of both worlds.'

'No... it doesn't.... Dude, don't do this! We... we don't need CaliChat. We just need—'

'More,' interrupted Abelman, now tired of James. 'Not next month. Not next week. Not tomorrow and not today. I – need – more – *now!*'

'Eddy...? Please?' begged Munro, turning once more to his old friend.

Caught in the middle, with no choice other than to play the devil's advocate, Edgar tried to justify Abelman, while spinning a lie to show his support for James.

'It's just been going so badly.... I think they've lost around five or six hundred thousand users already this year? The timing was perfect... to get it, I mean.... To get it back for you... so you can run it again... use it with your wearable tech and give everybody what they—'

'Get it back? Dude...! Seriously? You guys are over there... you're.... The cold air must be freezing your brains cos you're both being so dumb!

'You don't have your finger on pulse like I do. I'm the one in LA. I'm here and I know—'

"Dumb" was perhaps not the best choice of words to describe Abelman, and a little yank on the strings was needed to remind his partner of his place.

'It's the finger that I pay for, Munro—on the hand I can chop off.... Just remember that.'

'What did you say...? What did you say to me? Are you threatening—'

'What's the matter, Munro...? LA affecting your hearing? Maybe all that warm air is making you deaf?'

James was furious; not only because of his threat, but because Abelman was mocking him and there was nothing that he could do. He ended the call. Unhappy and unwilling to accept the decision, he was still without a choice or a say in the vote.

'That didn't seem to go too well—' began Edgar, trying to ease the tension. Abelman turned with that all too familiar eyebrow raised and faced his apprentice.

'Munro's about to outlive his value, Eddy... make sure you don't do the same.'

'Erm... h-his—'

'So long as they keep buying his Ally, he keeps breathing. But once we get The Scout from him... once they see what I have in store... well... then that LA air becomes a precious commodity. You understand?'

Abelman's words were not meant as a warning. They were a promise of what would happen when James, or Edgar, ceased to be of value to him. There was no doubt that Abelman had planned to get rid of Munro, although it now seemed more a reality than a possibility. However, Abelman's mask had begun to slip; the pretence harder to keep up. His patience with James, his attitude and need to be centred in everything was coming to an end, that much was certain. These were dangerous times—for everyone.

'Been nine months, Eddy. I don't see any progress... I only see bodies.'

'The erm... the problem is—'

'The problem *is* there's no chip!'

Munro had riled Abelman. He had no tolerance now for anyone or anything other than what he wanted to hear.

'That's the problem... that's *your* problem.... Fix it.'

He understood and knew Abelman well enough to know that there was no point in talking now. What else was there to say? His message was deafeningly loud and transparently clear.

'I best get back to the lab,' said Edgar, sheepishly.

'You do that, Eddy.... You run along now... there's a good boy.'

By "lab," Edgar meant the room with the furnace—the factory. It was Edgar's laboratory; the "Labs" in DomiGen Labs. Back inside, he sat down despondently, beginning to believe that he too was on the verge of outliving his value. Like Abelman had said, he was going to do what needed to be done. Either that or end up lying next to his girlfriend… "feeding the worms."

He placed his elbows upon the desk, raised his forearms and lowered his face into the palms of his hands to exhale his frustrations. He was no closer to understanding why Abelman's chip was unable to adapt to the synaptic terminals, than when he first began. It was hopeless, he thought. Perhaps the real reason for why it had never been done was because it simply couldn't be done? And if it couldn't be done then how long would it take before Abelman lost patience with him as well? He was running out of ideas. He was running out of options. More importantly, he was running out of time.

The one thing that he did understand, was that Abelman never shared, and the one thing that he knew, was that Abelman never gave without receiving. Clydesdale had warned that Abelman knew who he was. So, if he could forge his signature on a contract, then how hard would it be for him to pen a suicide note from Edgar? How easy would it be for him to tidy up a "loose end" from his past if he failed to receive what he expected to get?

The following morning, Edgar arrived early. He hadn't slept well, and it showed. He had to find a breakthrough; a way to make things work.

'Good morning, Dr. Spear,' said Daphne from behind the reception desk, as Edgar entered the building.

Edgar forced a smile and tried to stretch it as best he could; to acknowledge that it was morning but was in no mood for talking.

'Messages?'

'Only from Mr. Munro, sir.'

'James?'

'Yes. There was a message to say that he was arriving this morning at ten.'

Edgar looked puzzled and checked his wristwatch, it was

7:30 a.m. In his rise to success, he had thrown away his imitation copy and decided to buy the real thing; a genuine rose gold Rolex Cosmograph Daytona. It was a tad more expensive than the thirty dollars he had paid previously, nevertheless, it was still a steal at just forty thousand. More to the point, if his Rolex said it was 7:30 a.m., then you could bet your life that it really was.

'He never phoned to say—'

'It was a message left at two this morning, sir,' replied Daphne, knowing what Edgar was about to ask. 'Between you and me... he did sound quite annoyed.'

'Oh dear,' said Edgar, as he thanked Daphne and went into the laboratory.

James had not been back to Boston since the night he unveiled The Ally; the night he basically brought Boston to a standstill. The last thing that Edgar needed now, in the middle of added pressure from Abelman, was any more of his theatrics.

More patients had been delivered that morning. Seventeen poor souls that probably wouldn't survive the next forty-eight hours: more than half, not even the next twenty-four. Edgar looked at them in the holding area behind the reinforced one-way glass. They were mainly the homeless, the drug addicts and forgotten destitute people who were now abandoned by society. Another group of pitiful, insignificant, little ants, blissfully unaware as they sat stuffing their happy faces with the free food and drinks provided to them, courtesy of Abelman. Edgar watched as the sedatives began to take their affect; a little something to help them sleep while their heads were shaved, in preparation for a craniotomy. It was this procedure, the removal of a piece of bone from their skull, that would allow Edgar access to the brain and the insertion of a test implant. One by one they drifted into unconsciousness. Edgar looked away, catching sight of himself in the mirror on the opposite wall.

It had been a long time since Edgar had been proud of his reflection; at what it was that stared back. An eternity since being able to face the truth of what he was doing. How could he continue like this? Day after day, week after week, month after month, knowing that he was essentially killing these people; that whatever he tried, this obsessive experiment of Abelman's didn't work. You could wrap it any way you wished, tie it with a bow or a pretty ribbon. Say it was in the name of science, or in the progress of mankind. It made little difference, because whichever way you saw it, and however you chose to slice it, the verdict was always the same. Edgar was a killer— a murderer—and he was executing these people. His debt to Abelman for the Harvard degree, the certificates and licenses, his wealth and position, was sold at a price: the cost of his soul. That was what Edgar paid in search of Abelman's precision and control. A burden too great to continue to bear.

He needed air; a break before attempting the first implant of the day. Edgar went to the door, to step outside. As his key card beeped, the lock turned, and the door swung open.

'Eddy.'

Munro was sombre, his forehead furrowed, and it darkened his face with a solemnness that Edgar had not seen since that morning of the graduation.

'We need to talk.'

James tried to enter the laboratory. Edgar stood in the way and blocked his path.

'Erm... ok... well... why don't we step outside?'

Edgar walked forward, forcing Munro back until the door of the laboratory closed behind them and he heard the lock clamp shut.

'What's going on in there?'

'Not now—not here....'

Edgar shouted across to Daphne.

'Mr. Munro is just going to show me some alterations he would like us to consider for the exterior... maybe we'll grab a coffee.'

He turned to Munro.

'Pull your cap down, James. We don't want an audience now.'

Edgar and James left DomiGen and turned onto Arlington Street. It was dry and sunny, cold and windy—a typical autumn morning in Boston.

'The Common,' said Edgar, as he led James towards Boston Common: a large public park and garden.

'Look, Eddy, I know we haven't always seen eye to eye—'

Time was short and Edgar knew it. Daphne would report to Abelman and there was no need for small talk. It was best for both of them if Edgar just got straight to business, like his master always did.

'What are we going to do?' he asked, interrupting Munro. 'He's got to be stopped.'

'Abelman?'

Edgar looked at James and said nothing. Was it really necessary to say his name; who else needed to be stopped?

'I'm killing them... the patients.... When I put one of Abelman's chips into them, I might as well be putting a bullet into their heads. At least that would be humane. They'd die quicker... less pain... less suffering... less—'

'What...? What are you talking about? The chips are stable... Abelman said.... You said.... You said they were stable!'

'It's a lie, James. The whole thing's a lie. I'm sorry.'

'Sorry? But....'

Munro's face emptied with confusion.

'They're not stable. They never have been. A van comes to take away the ones that are still alive... and a lorry comes to take away the ones that aren't.'

Munro shook his head, as his eyes widened—gaping at Edgar. They searched for a sign, for a tell-tale twitch: something to show that he was bluffing.

Just saying it out loud was difficult; to be able to tell someone about his work. Edgar felt his burden shared, and his eyes revealed nothing as his shoulders dropped. The sinner looked upwards, and their gaze was broken.

'You... you said.... I... I've told the world.... They think DomiGen is mine. Eddy, they'll think I'm behind....'

Munro held his hand over his bloodless face and leaned away. Edgar lowered his head and glanced at him again, then peered deeper into his eyes. A silent pact was drawn as blood began to return and redden Munro's complexion.

'We've got no choice.'

Edgar nodded, but before he could speak, he was stopped by the ringtone of his cell phone.

'It's Abelman—I'll have to take it.'

'Spear,' said Edgar as he answered.

Munro couldn't hear the conversation. Even so, it was obvious from Edgar's intermittent replies that Abelman was angry and wanted to know their whereabouts.

'We'd better go,' said Edgar, as the call ended.

'Eddy, we can't... we need a plan.'

'I know', said Edgar as he turned to begin the walk back to DomiGen.

'No, Eddy... you're not listening!' Munro grabbed Edgar's arm. 'I mean a plan. *A real plan.*'

'I heard what you said,' snapped Edgar as he pulled his arm free. 'Now come on!'

Abelman was already waiting for them at reception; his eyebrows raised and a sneering smile.

'There they are... my busy – *little* – partners!' he shouted, as they walked through the entrance. 'You're just in time.'

Abelman's tone was so insincere—so superficial—that it sounded ominous. Munro looked at Edgar, anxiety etched all over his face, as Edgar stared in reply, tightening his brow just once: a signal for James to relax. Abelman walked across and warmly embraced them both; an act of showmanship that James himself would have been proud of had he not been frozen in fear.

'You'd better come with me, boys—I've got some wonderful news for you this morning!'

Edgar and James followed cautiously behind, like two naughty children caught stealing from the pantry. Abelman led them upstairs to his spacious office and opened the top draw of his desk to take out a pile of paperwork. Their silence was not unnoticed.

'What's the matter...?' asked Abelman menacingly. 'Fresh air disagree with you?'

The faces of Edgar and James confessed their guilt, though neither were ready to speak of it.

'Take a look!' said Abelman, as he tossed eight contracts across the table to break the silence. 'We're buying them all.... FaceUp, MeetHere, Sprong, Kachow, LiveLine, ShareWithMe, PostChat, and ShareAStory.... All of them.'

Munro turned ashen. His mouth agape, his face unable to hide the shock of disbelief.

'*What!*'

Dumbfounded and stunned, he quickly returned to his theatrical self. 'Dude...! Like... no.... No, you can't do this.... Dude! There's no way... this is forgery... this is like... *so* illegal....'

Edgar and James continued to shuffle through the papers; their signatures, along with Abelman's, beside the valuations they had agreed to pay for the acquisitions. Abelman had expected them to have seen this as a good thing, as a sign of ambition and shortcut to success. To be able to buy out so many competitors in a single swoop would make DomiGen the world's largest social sharing platform overnight. It was no simple task and deserved more than ungrateful objection.

'I can't do what?' he screamed. 'Who do you think you're talking to, you imbecile?'

Abelman's patience had finally given way.

'I gave you a seat at the table when they kicked you out—brought you back into the game, Munro. You ungrateful little—'

James, however, still staggered by Edgar's confession, had also lost his patience and pulled back on the strings to defy the puppeteer.

'This is *my* company, Abelman.... We might be partners, but it's still *my – company*. I'm not—'

The master, no longer content to yank on Munro's strings, pulled them tight until they snapped.

'Partners...? *Partners!* We're not partners,' bellowed Abelman. 'You work for *me*. Look around you, boy. DomiGen's mine.... It's always been mine... it will *always* be mine....

'You do what I tell you to do—say what I tell you to say—and you goddamn better deliver what I tell you to deliver.'

Abelman slammed his fist down upon the desk and the floor shook like the tremor from an earthquake. He reached into the draw and pulled out another contract before slamming it shut and throwing the pages into the face of James

'Read it, Munro... and read it well.... Because I own you... I own you and everything you do. Everything you've got—everything you're ever gonna get—belongs to me and me alone. It's mine... everything.... *All – mine!*'

The contract slapped James in the face then fell to the floor. He knelt to pick it up but remained crouched. It was clear as day. In black and white. Abelman owned DomiGen. He owned it outright: one hundred percent. Every acquisition he had ever forged had only given him more stock—more power—taking everything away from Edgar and James.

'Did you really think I was gonna pay for all this and settle for a third...? I mean, "Seriously...? Dude!" what are you... a fool?' Abelman mocked Munro as he continued to punish him for his disobedience. 'Did you think I would take all the risk and let some California college kid tell me how to run a business? How to run *my* business...? You *stupid* boy! I told you, I always have control—*always!*'

Munro glowered, unwilling to accept humiliation, and threw the contract back at Abelman.

'You'll never get away with this.... Never!'

'Oh, I already have,' replied Abelman, his voice suddenly calm and eerily so. 'Seems you forgot...? You signed all your stock over to me.'

'I never signed a thing, and—'

'Well... that's not what the papers say... what your signature says... what the witnesses who'll testify to it will say.... Right, Eddy?'

Abelman smirked as he winked at James. He was dispassionate, the opposite of Munro, and Edgar had seen this side of him many times before. It was pointless to argue: Abelman only fed off anger, off hatred and loathing. It made him colder, darker, harder. The more you resisted or tried to fight back, the angrier you became and the stronger you made him. The only way to survive was to say nothing at all.

'You'll do what I tell you to do, Munro, or I'll feed you to Congress. A piece at a time until they beg me for your head—and I'll give it to them—on a spike.'

Munro stormed around to the other side of Abelman's desk and raised his fists, wanting to punch him. Abelman laughed hysterically.

'Go ahead... take your best shot, Munro.'

He pulled back his arm and Abelman stood still: the perfect target. Munro lunged forward with his punch and Abelman simply grabbed him by the collar, then threw him to the ground.

'Get back to the lab, Eddy. Munro and I haven't finished talking about his ideas yet.'

Edgar looked at James and James met his gaze. It was the same forlorn look, the same expression of helplessness that Penny had given him when she was trapped in the nurse staff room with Abelman. A cry for help that Edgar couldn't answer because Edgar was unable to help. He had tried to take on Abelman once before and lost. Lost badly, in fact. That time Abelman tossed him around like a ragdoll and it was a mistake he would never make again.

'You got a problem?' asked Abelman, wondering why Edgar was still there.

Edgar shook his head and turned to abandon James as he left the office.

In the lab, Edgar paced worryingly as he wondered what James might be telling Abelman. Alone, he had time. Too much time. Time to think, to imagine, and several hours had passed before Edgar's cell phone rang.

'Eddy, you in the lab?'

'Yes. I'm—'

'Good,' interrupted Abelman. 'That's good... listen, Munro is holding a press conference now and I think you should come listen.'

Edgar came out from the laboratory to see that the foyer and reception had been transformed into a press area and was already filling up with reporters. James was sitting centre stage with Abelman at his side. Edgar walked over to join them.

'What you doing, Eddy?'

Edgar glanced at James; he was uncomfortable, that much was obvious, yet it was more than that, he seemed scared.

'Erm... well... you said come and—'

'Then go take a seat.'

Abelman pointed to the rows of seats in front of the makeshift stage, and Edgar smiled nervously then turned to do as he was told. Rather than sit at the front, he decided to find a seat at the back and become invisible, as he disappeared into the myriad of journalists. Abelman nodded and the doors opened, welcoming hundreds of people from the street outside. The crowd were ushered to their seats and Abelman stood to address them, reading from an autocue nestled between a row of cameras.

'Ladies and gentlemen, my name is Dr. Abelman.... I'm the owner here at DomiGen Labs, and I'd like to thank you all for being with us at such short notice.

'Today is a new day for DomiGen and a great day for us all. Here to tell us why, is our CEO and product specialist... a man you all know and love... so please, join me and put your hands together, for Mr. James Munro!'

The audience cheered and screams rang out from around the foyer, as James rose to his feet and waved.

'Dudes...! Seriously?' said Munro, and the audience went wild.

Edgar sat silently. "Product specialist"? When did James Munro become that? The CEO, a partner, the guru, God, he was all of those things—but a product specialist? It sounded like something a teenager becomes when asked to take a cola challenge.

'After the enormous success of The Ally—' began James, before he was again interrupted by cheers.

'People... come on.... Seriously?'

The cheering continued as James, forever the showman, had the audience as always in the palm of his hand.

'As I was saying, after the enormous success of The Ally, we wanted to make sure that our next wearable would break new ground. It had to be something that everyone would want—that we all need.'

Edgar couldn't believe what he was hearing. Did James just say "we"? He was sure that he heard him say "our," he certainly never said "me," or "I."

'We wanted to make sure that we didn't just take our technology to the next level... we wanted to blow it off the chart!'

The crowd's cheering turned to excitement as anticipation grew, spreading like a wildfire around the room.

'Which is why.... Hang on... people... come on!' Munro glanced at Abelman. Abelman nodded.

'Which is why we created... The Scout!'

James stretched out his arm, then turned slightly towards a large projection screen behind him. However, instead of a high-end pulsating video production, a presentation slide with a crude wipe effect revealed what looked like a blob: a quite ugly and unexceptional black blob in the middle of a white background.

The audience cheered and screamed regardless in their expectant frenzy. Edgar really couldn't understand why. Perhaps they weren't looking; couldn't see what he saw? Because this was not like The Ally, like its bracelet, or the necklace; not smooth or attractive, nor something with beautiful lines and curves. This looked like a lump of coal and had all the visual sophistication of a brick. A brick with a strap, to be exact. It looked like something you would want to hide, something thrown together without thought or consideration to design; something made very quickly, perhaps even under pressure.

'The Scout represents the next generation in geolocation technology.... It uses precision point geometrics to track the device down to a geographical location of less than one millimetre.'

The crowd silenced to gasps of amazement. They may not have been sure as to why they would need the device, what implications, or advantage there was in being tracked to a distance of just one millimetre. But like everything that came from James Munro, in the end it made little difference. It had to be necessary, and if it had to be necessary then everyone had to have it.

'The applications for this technology are endless.

'Imagine... in automotive vehicles for collision detection. At home, trying to find lost items... and I don't just mean leaving a tablet on a shelf or a key on a dresser.... I mean on which shelf...? On what part of the dresser...? Pinpointing exact locations—precisely.

'By not having to rely on outdated GPS or maps to find your whereabouts, The Scout will take you *exactly* to where you need to be.'

The silence returned to ecstasy as the audience begged Munro for more. He glanced again at Abelman, and Abelman nodded again in reply.

'Please,' he said, as he raised his hand like a Roman emperor and appealed for quiet. 'Can you hear it?'

A sound—not unlike that of a sonar—could be heard from inside the foyer. James stepped down from the stage with a prototype of The Scout on his wrist. Edgar was curious and tried to peek between the people in front of him. They too were equally as curious and were trying to see between the people in front of them. Suddenly, the audience were swaying like a tide: each row a wave, trying to catch a glimpse of whatever it was Munro was doing.

James moved amongst them, and the sound of the pings became shorter, closer together and louder.

'Dude…! Like could I just… would you mind?' he asked, as he squeezed between the chairs of several journalists. 'Ah, there it is!'

He bent down and picked up a white credit card that was lying on the floor beneath a seat. The pinging stopped and became a single continuous tone. James raised the card aloft for all to see.

'Yay, I found it! My key card… can't get into my lab without it, dude!'

The audience laughed and clapped. He smiled at the journalist while Edgar held back his approval. It was all so clearly staged; the sound of The Scout coming from speakers and not from the wrist of James. A piece of theatre made for a point.

'The Scout is not just a tracker… it's *so* much more…. Come on… let me show you….'

Munro made his way back up onto the stage, heralded by the cheers of the audience.

'It can tell you *everything* you need to know about where you are. Now I don't just mean like…. "Hello, you're here… at DomiGen Labs…" or "dude… after one hundred metres you've reached your destination."'

The audience laughed.

'I'm taking about information... vital information. Things that you - *need* - to know.... Check this out.'

Munro showed the screen of the device to the audience.

'Can you zoom in on that?' he asked, pointing to one of the cameramen.

'Dude... read it out... nice and loud so that everyone can hear.'

The cameraman read what he filmed off the screen.

'It says, *Product launch at DomiGen Labs.*'

'Excellent! Now, keep your camera focused on it as I begin to walk... ok?'

Munro began to walk towards the cameraman.

'Dude... would you read that out for me now?'

'It says, *Warning: You are fifty centimetres from the edge of the platform.*'

The audience followed open-mouthed: awestruck.

'Excellent!' said Munro. 'And now?' as he walked even closer to the edge.

'It's red and blinking.'

'Yeah, dude... I know... it said warning before, remember?'

The audience laughed again, enjoying the banter between James and the cameraman.

'Now wait.... Dude... seriously.... What does it say?'

'It says, *Warning: You are seven centimetres from the edge of the platform and in danger of falling.*'

'Awesome! Thanks man, I owe you... I mean, you like totally saved my life!'

Sections of the audience laughed and clapped; others shed tears of joy. Those closest to the cameraman stood and hugged him, and those within distance reached out to pat him on the shoulder, expressing their gratitude for saving James Munro. Edgar was still unmoved.

'Our A.I technology not only updates your precise position... it gives you information based upon it. For example, like being in danger.... That's pretty cool, don't you think?'

The audience agreed and wolf-whistling broke out, drowned by the cheers which were louder than ever.

'People... come on...! Seriously?' Munro shouted, as he did what he always did and basked in the adulation of his audience.

'Hey...! We're not done yet... come on....'

And they cheered again.

'Like I told you, The Scout's not just a tracker. Dude...! Seriously? It's *so* much more.... Check *this* out!'

Munro pointed to the entrance, and the cameras turned towards the main doors. Abelman was stood alone; his shoulders back and head held high, as he raised his arm to show that he too was wearing a prototype. During the performance, he had left the stage and made his way discreetly to a new position. Edgar felt a chill: a coldness in his bones that sent a sudden shudder of fear at what he thought was happening. At what he hoped wasn't true.

'Dude...!' Munro shouted at the cameraman he had spoken with before. 'Can you zoom in on Dr. Abelman's screen and tell us what it says?'

Dr. Abelman, thought Edgar. Did James really just call him "Dr. Abelman"?

'It says, *Welcome to DomiGen Labs. The reception is twenty-seven metres in front of you.*'

'Ok,' said Munro, and Abelman took a step forward, then stopped.

'And now?'

'It says, *A product launch is currently underway. You may experience difficulty in reaching reception. Press here to dial for assistance.*'

The audience clapped as Munro nodded to Abelman who began to walk towards the stage.

'Now... The Scout's not just giving you information... it's giving personal information... learning from you and your surroundings.'

The cameras followed Abelman as he climbed the steps to Munro, and the cameraman who had interacted with James was asked to follow closely.

'Ok, dude...! What's it say now?'

'It says, *Dude... you've made it this far, so you better get an autograph!*'

The audience went wild. Laughing and cheering, they rose to their feet with a standing ovation for their God. Abelman put his arm around the shoulder of Munro, and Edgar felt that sudden shudder once again. James Munro was a brilliant performer, but Edgar was well acquainted with the masquerade and the look in his eyes said it all. His smile was nervous as he freed himself: as if Abelman's grip was all part of the act. Edgar knew now that his fears were real, and Munro toyed with his audience to maintain the charade.

'Now, you might be wondering why...? Why something this cool looks like this?' joked Munro, pointing to the bracelet and poking fun at it.

The crowd began to laugh in agreement.

'Well, to explain, let me hand you back to the owner of DomiGen Labs.... He's my dear friend... and people... seriously... a totally awesome dude.... Please give it up for, Dr. Melvin Abelman!'

The crowd clapped and cheered, as Edgar fell faint in his chair; his senses numbed by all that he saw, from all that he heard.

'Thank you, James,' said Abelman. 'Really, you're too kind.... Thank you. Ladies and gentlemen, please, our product specialist— James Munro.'

Abelman began to applaud Munro on stage along with the cheering and whistling from the audience. For all the world, and the cameras that broadcast it, Abelman showed genuine admiration. Edgar, however, knew better. He knew that the God was being dragged back to earth, and his place dug into a trench deep behind the line.

'When we first created The Scout,' began Abelman, 'we knew the applications for this technology were endless. All of you have helped us to get to where we are, and given us so much, that we thought, isn't it about time we gave something back?'

The crowd began to cheer Abelman, clapping with the same near intensity they had given Munro.

'Our world... your world... is more complex than we can ever imagine. With our products, we want to make it an easier world.... A more connected world.... And more importantly... a better world. A safer world for you, *and* your children.

'Today, there is crime on our streets, crime in our homes, and crime in our children's schools. When perpetrators are caught, and criminals are incarcerated, how do we know that our children are safe when these offenders re-enter society? How do we know that anyone who breaks the law will not do so again after they are released?'

The applause became muted as excitement was replaced by support. Before the audience shouted their endorsement for their newly chosen champion.

'Statistics show us that over *forty percent* of all criminals are re-arrested for a new crime within the first year of their release. Over *sixty percent* are re-arrested within three years. Over *seventy percent* within five. And over *eighty percent* within nine.'

The crowd were shocked by the numbers, at what they were hearing and Abelman moved to calm their fears.

'The figures speak for themselves, ladies and gentlemen. The majority of crime committed today, is committed by criminals who have been convicted before.... Repeat offenders... and our prisons are filled to overflowing with these individuals.'

Abelman paused; the power of his words were like Munro's— increasing with every breath.

'It's *your* taxes that are used to pay for their accommodation. *Your* hard-earned money that feeds them... that provides them with free legal aid to get them released. Allows four out of every five to return to their life of crime and reoffend again. This is the system that we live in... and the time has come for us to break it.... To break the criminal cycle.

'Incarceration does not prevent crime... it only delays it. Criminals remain criminals because our system's not working. It does not. It has not. And it – will – *not* keep our children safe!'

Abelman paused again and the audience applauded wildly. They were spurred on by everything that he was selling them. He was leading a revolt. Not only did he have them with him, but he had them all behind him.

'As a parent myself, I want to know when I send my child to school that they are coming home safely at the end of the day.'

Edgar lowered his head; he shook it in disbelief. Abelman was more than convincing, he sounded as though he was telling the truth. In fact, his voice was so calm and so steady there was never a doubt that he actually was.

'At DomiGen Labs, your safety and your children's safety are more than a concern.... They're *our* priority.... They're *my* priority.... Because your children, and my children... are *our* future.

'When we learned about the horrendous statistics of crime—this stain on our great nation—we couldn't simply commercialise our product. We had to take a stand... we had to take action... because we knew that if no one else was willing to stand up for the sake of every child... then *we* had to.'

The audience began to yell out. Cries of "Hell yeah!" and "Amen!" echoed around the foyer. Abelman had become a preacher—a politician—and was more than just a champion or the leader of the revolt; he had taken the place of Munro.

'Today, ladies and gentlemen, it gives me great pleasure to announce that DomiGen Labs has signed an agreement with the

United States Federal Government. Together, we will take the first steps to ensure our children's safety.'

The small pockets of audience not on their feet were now standing. Everyone was cheering—people were crying—holding and hugging each other.

'From December first... *every* convicted criminal, *every* law breaker, *every* felon and delinquent released back onto our streets, will be issued with The Scout.'

The cheers from the audience were deafening; as if their team had just won the Super Bowl, or an Olympic athlete representing their nation had just won gold.

'I give you *my* word... *my – oath*... that every offender will wear the device at *all* times....'

The audience cheered louder still.

'And my promise to you, is that this will not only be a provision of their parole... it will be mandatory requirement during the first decade of their release!'

Their screams were thunderous; despite his microphone, his voice was a whisper overwhelmed by acclaim. How quickly their praise moved from one false deity to another. Edgar remained seated. A dejected figure in a world of joy.

So, this is how freedom ends? he thought: on a bracelet from the offices of DomiGen.

'Ladies and gentlemen... please....' shouted Abelman, trying desperately to rise above the euphoria. 'Today, we tell every criminal in our great nation, that if you choose a life of crime then we choose to stand against you. Together, we will make sure that no criminal is ever allowed to roam our streets freely again.... Not without being monitored.... Not without being observed.... And *never* without having proven that they are no longer a threat to our way of life!'

The audience erupted, unassailable in their jubilation and Abelman was forced to yield. He waved as he left the stage with all cameras focused upon him; Munro, followed meekly from behind.

Edgar forged his way through the excited audience and made his way up to the office area. Before reaching Abelman's office, he could already hear Munro from the corridor.

'So, we work for the government now…? Everything I've fought against… you now fight for?'

He was angry. Clearly upset as he screamed, believing that they were alone. Edgar paused for a moment outside the door to eavesdrop. Abelman was aloof: he didn't care about Munro. In fact, he failed to acknowledge that Munro was even there, that he even existed, perhaps because in his mind he no longer did. Edgar knocked and entered. Abelman seemed pleased to see him.

'Ah, Eddy! What did you think?'

'W-what did I think…?' he replied in bemusement. 'I… I think you just said that we're about to throw the Bill of Rights out of the w-window, and the government has agreed to let us do it?'

'Eddy. Eddy…. Always the pessimist, never the optimist. Didn't I tell you to stop worrying? It's all under control…. I *always* have control.'

Edgar looked at James and could see that he had none.

'Over my dead body!' he roared.

Still indifferent and feeding off anger, Abelman finally acknowledged his presence.

'Whatever you say, Munro… if that's the way you want it?'

James was boiling like a kettle: a raging steam that had to be released. He kicked a chair as hard as he could and stormed out of the office, shouting with every stomp of his feet.

'First CaliChat and now this? It isn't over, Abelman—this *isn't* over!'

'I think I'd better go calm him down.'

'Let him be,' snapped Abelman. 'You're not going anywhere.'

He pulled himself up from his chair and walked around towards Edgar, who followed his every movement. Trembling as Abelman approached, unable to move or step back, the moisture soaked his palms as a cold sweat fell upon his brow.

'Can't see the wood for the trees huh, Eddy?' Abelman folded his arms and perched on the edge of his desk. He leant forward with his eyebrows raised. 'How many times do I need to tell you... we're in the precision business. I'm not interested in selfies or anything else Munro has to offer. He builds that stuff for those pitiful, insignificant, little ants.'

'But—'

'Don't interrupt me again... especially when I'm trying to educate you, boy.'

Edgar swallowed hard; not enough to colour his paled cheeks.

'Everyone trusts that schmuck. You'd do well to remember that, Eddy, because that's the only reason I need him... to build The Scout... to use that trust and get the contract.'

Edgar waited before continuing the discussion, confident that Abelman was finished. 'Y-you mean the prison contract?'

Abelman rolled his eyes.

'Maybe I was wrong about you...? Don't you listen? Almost every two-bit loser is back inside within nine years... don't you get it?'

Edgar stared at Abelman, unsure, as was so often the case, if he expected a response or not.

'It means a ten-year contract. It'll take a *minimum* of ten years to show those bureaucrats that we can bring those numbers down. Think about it.... Ten — *long* — years.'

Edgar was relieved to learn that the question was rhetorical.

'At any one time there are over seven million suckers in those cells, and you know how much that costs?'

Edgar waited, and Abelman carried on.

'A hundred — billion.... That's one — hundred — *billion* a year... each year... *every* year....

'Now, you're a smart kid, Eddy... you do the math.... Over ten years? That's a trillion. One — *trillion* — dollars. That's how much it costs—how much money goes around in the system. That's how much there is to be saved... and a large chunk of that is gonna be mine.

'With Munro's bracelet, we'll track every convict once they're released, and know where they are every second of the day. Now you combine that with CaliChat, and all the other profile sites and we'll know *everything*.... We'll know what they eat for breakfast... where they eat, when they eat, and who they're eating with. You can forget big brother—we'll know more about them than they know about themselves. The one's that stay clean and the one's that can't. Think about it... eighty percent of those suckers can't keep their fingers out of the cookie jar. So, what do you think they'd be willing to pay us to turn a blind eye...? To keep their location out of the cop's hands. I mean, if we say they weren't there then they weren't there, right? And Munro's bracelet will prove they were somewhere else. So, how much you reckon that's worth from any job that they pull? Ten percent...? Twenty? Try *ninety...!* I'll leave them with ten for their trouble. The rest is mine.

'I told you, Eddy... it's *all* about precision. We get paid by the government for saving them money and paid by the criminals for letting them work. Everyone's happy... making me rich.

'You know if you think about it, I'm a stand-up kind of guy... a regular model citizen trying to help everyone. Jeez... I'm a goddamn saint!'

'B-but the chips...? Why the chips?' stammered Edgar.

'A little safeguard, Eddy.... You and the chips—you're my insurance policy.'

Despite his explanation, Edgar was none the wiser, and Abelman decided to enlighten him... a little.

'Munro's bracelet doesn't work... how could it? He hasn't made one yet. What you saw was a show.'

Abelman lifted his wrist and pushed his finger slowly into the side of The Scout. Edgar stared and looked at the compartment that slid

open. There were no electronics, no circuits or batteries. It was empty.
It looked like... no... it was... an empty matchbox.

'A little paint and a piece of plastic,' smirked Abelman.

'But the messages...? I... I saw the warnings... I—'

'The cameraman, Eddy. He wasn't zooming in.'

'I... I—'

'It was a projector. All I needed for them to believe that The Scout
works. Now they know—or they think that it does—I'll get the
contract. But if Munro gets cold feet... I need an alternative... and
that's where you come in.'

'So, all this... all this was just—'

'A backup. Think of it as plan b.'

'But the experiments? The bodies...?'

'What about them...? You can't make an omelette without
breaking a few eggs.'

'A few eggs...? I can't... I... I've....'

Edgar felt sick to his stomach; the knots wrapping tighter than a
hangman's noose. It churned and lurched as the cold sweat chilled
further: sapping his energy and pressing him to sit before he fell onto
the chair.

'Don't look so surprised. I told you... if you wanna take down the
house you gotta be willing to sacrifice your hand. Throw your best
cards even when you think they'll win you the game.... If that's what
it takes to get the house.'

'B-but it's the government...' stuttered Edgar as he looked up at
Abelman.

Abelman scoffed. 'What my associates would call "the house."'

'And Munro?'

'A marked card... and once you know it's there, you gotta change
the deck. You understand?'

Abelman paused to stretch out his arms before holding them down
and gripping the desk. He lowered his head and raised his eyebrows
again, as Edgar felt that cold sudden shudder of fear.

'Don't wimp out on my now, Eddy. I still need you. I need you to get those implants stable... whatever the cost. Cos if the day ever comes when Munro's bracelets fail, they'd better be ready—for both our sakes....'

9

UNTIL TOMORROW

After the events of yesterday, Edgar decided to keep a low profile. If he was ever in doubt as to the stakes of the game, those doubts were now extinguished. He may have hated Abelman, for all that he was and all that he stood for; the games that he played and the lives of the loved ones that he stole. But as Clydesdale had said, "he is far more dangerous than anything you can imagine," and Edgar could imagine many things… many terrible things.

On the morning news, there were no reports of any dead bodies floating in the Charles, nor coverage of a suicide. So, Munro had either made it through the night, or they had not found him yet. Either way, it was best for everyone if Edgar just stayed out of it.

There was no cause for loyalty now that Abelman had shown his hand, and Edgar cared little for it. Still, the concerns he harboured over his survival were enough to motivate him to stay in the lab all day, determined to find a means or approach to stabilise the implants. Like every day at DomiGen, everything he tried had failed. As the weeks passed, his efforts remained futile and were taking him nowhere, only closer to the end of Abelman's patience. Today, it had been eleven. Eleven poor souls who would never be seen or be heard of again. They would simply disappear—along with the rest into nothingness. Their lives sacrificed in pursuit of a dream; the delusional fantasy of a wicked master, and his monstrous obsession to control everything.

Edgar stared at the ghostly pale face. She could have been sleeping if not for her lips: rigid blue and dry.

'I'm sorry,' he murmured, like he always said, then pulled the sheet to cover the last of the day's experiments.

He thought again of Clydesdale, of his parents, of how they had tried to stop Abelman. The price they had paid for believing that they could, and for daring to hope when all was hopeless... because that's what it was. Hopeless. Abelman could never be stopped, and even if Edgar should try or was able to expose him, what was he actually guilty of? Ownership? It was Edgar who did all the work in the lab and it was James who was the CEO. How could Abelman know what Edgar was doing? That was James' job—Munro's responsibility— and that was how it would look, how Abelman would play it if Edgar should try to force his hand or endeavour to take him down. The only thing that Edgar would achieve was a legitimate way for Abelman to get rid of both him and James, just as easily as he did Edgar's parents.

It was hard to find light in a room full of gloom, but the screen of Edgar's cell phone lit as it vibrated on the metal surface of an overbed table. Edgar wheeled the body back to the holding area and walked over to read the SMS text.

Eddy, need to clarify things. Meet me at The Round Hat in an hour. Don't be late!

This was not an invitation, just another order, and it was already 4:59 p.m. Edgar had to hurry and tidy a few things first; to remove traces of his work and cover his tracks before the lorry arrived for collection.

"The Hat," was a nearby bar. It was a quiet place, at least on weekdays. From the outside, it looked like a sports bar, the kind of place that blue-collar workers went to on a Sunday. A place to get away from the family and watch the game with friends, while enjoying a few beers and a bucket of buffalo wings.

Edgar didn't need clarity. "Things" were crystal clear. So why the meeting? What had happened that required clarifying?

He placed his operating equipment—his scalpels and knives—into the autoclave and felt a coldness: that sudden shudder of fear in his bones once again. Nothing about this felt right. Abelman never sent an SMS. He always called and told you what he wanted. In the years that Edgar had known him, Abelman had never once mentioned The Round Hat, or any other sports bar for that matter, and he certainly didn't seem the type to frequent such places.

Edgar sat down and tried to think. It was hard to rationalise, harder still to be rational. He had become as paranoid as Abelman, as suspicious as his master, and with good reason for feeling the way that he did.

Abelman said that he needed him, and that much Edgar did believe, unless of course the truth was that he had lied. After all, Abelman was a gambling man, so what if he simply gambled on the fact that as long as Munro built The Scout—and it worked—then he would never need an implant? If the performance of yesterday had won the government contract, then in reality it might also mean that both Edgar and James had already served their purpose?

Edgar closed his eyes, tired after a long day under the bright lights of the lab. He rubbed at his forehead. It pounded painfully, throbbing with the thoughts that screamed inside and banged against the walls to find their way out.

"For both our sakes." That was the last thing that Abelman said to him yesterday, which meant that it wasn't just Edgar's neck on the line. Whoever Abelman's "associates" were, they were powerful. Important enough to scare him. So, he probably did have a plan b, but it wouldn't be the implants. Getting them to work was something that was still left to Edgar, and that meant something still left to chance. It would have to be something else... something that only *he* could control; because no matter the stakes, no matter the game, Abelman was always ahead. If push came to shove and he was forced to bluff, then who could argue if The Scout did its job? In the meantime, he had ten years to take his cut from the system and the majority of loot from every criminal heist; that would be plenty, if a man ever wanted or needed to disappear....

It was 5:52 p.m. The bar was just a four-minute walk at a slow pace, two if he ran, so Edgar grabbed his coat and made his way to the street. As he pulled the heavy brown bar door open, he looked inside.

'Erm... hello...? Is anyone here?'

Edgar walked in and looked around. The fake heavy stained mahogany sucked the brightness out of the dull ceiling lights. Nevertheless, he could see that the place was deserted. There was no one there, not even behind the bar. He was alone... but not all alone, and he could feel it. The hairs which stood on the back of his neck screamed their warnings to him. He turned and faced the door, eyes darting as he stepped back until the sticky wooden counter pressed hard into his spine. He closed his eyes for a second and swallowed; a gulp so deep as to tangle his fears—his suspicions of Abelman—and twist them into panic. He stared out into the dimness: at the dingy light that passed through the dirty windows, broken by the legs walking past outside. It flashed between the chairs that were upturned on tables, sending shadows to the bar and a chill towards Edgar. Steadying himself he reached backwards, his palms whitened with dread, clammy to the touch. Then his eyes shut tight as he tried to slow his breathing, but his heart hammered hard and his throat began to tighten, stealing the words he was trying to speak.

'H-ha...'

Suddenly, a sound came from the ceiling. Edgar's eyes shot open as he looked up at the old wooden boards. His lungs reached out and grabbed the air. His throat with no choice other than to ease its grip and let it in.

'H-hello…? Hello…?'

In the far-right corner was a staircase; to the left of the door where he came in. His options were simple: to run for the door or to venture upstairs, and Edgar ran to the door as he fled for his life. When he reached the large brass handle, he yanked and pulled it open, flooding the bar with the early evening dusk. He turned quickly—making sure there was no one behind him—then looked back to the street and the safety of pedestrians passing aimlessly by. The warmth slapped his face and it brought him to his senses. What are you doing? he thought, as he shook his head feeling foolish, annoyed with himself for again allowing Abelman to get so far inside his mind. He checked his Rolex: it was 5:57 p.m. He was early. There were no mind games, there was nothing more than his own imagination; his fear of the worst when it concerned his master, and his belief that his fears were almost—always—true.

Edgar turned back inside and walked over to the staircase. He set his foot upon the first step, and it announced where he stood with a loud echoing creak.

'H-hello…. Mel…?'

He took a deep breath and decided to climb, the sound of each step revealing his progress as he spiralled up and around in the darkness. Nearing the top, he peered over the banister as the thought of an ambush again crossed his mind.

'M-Mel, are y-you up here…?'

The dark remained quiet, and Edgar decided to shout as loud as he could.

'Hello!'

Still, only silence replied.

He turned to descend the stairs, when suddenly, at the very back—in the corner—Edgar thought he saw something move. A trick of the light, perhaps a flicker from a bulb? It looked like a hat poking up from the top of a booth.

It was dark, far away, and the lamp that hung over the table had a shade that forced the light to shine downwards and not out. Like a spotlight that was dimmed and barely able to illuminate, its glimmer faded quickly as it touched the dark green leather benches that rounded the booth. It could have been a head, just as easily been shadow, a reflection or illusion, and from where Edgar stood, impossible to tell which.

'Mel...? Is that you...? Are you down there?'

Edgar's anxiety eclipsed his thoughts. His fear of the worst was no longer almost, it was overwhelming and decidedly real. Up here—out there—lurking in the shadows as far away as possible, ignoring his call with his back turned to lure him. It had to be Abelman, and it could only have been for one reason....

He stumbled, slightly. His heart not pounding, but racing, and he reached out to grab hold of the banister to avert his fall. He stared out at the booth with eyes adjusting to the darkness, fixed to follow any movement or reaction to his blunder. As he steadied his footing, Edgar's coat brushed against the panelled wall and he felt a small prod against his thigh. He reached down into his pocket, remembering that he had placed something there earlier. A little insurance policy of his own.

'M-Mel...?'

The floorboards creaked loudly and shouted each step of Edgar's position as he slowly edged his way towards the corner.

'I... I know you're there.... Mel... look... this isn't f-funny....'

It wasn't a shadow or an illusion of light. It was definitely a hat—a baseball cap—worn by a man who sat without reply.

'Mel, please,' he pleaded. 'Can't you hear me?'

Edgar held his breath. He could feel his face burning, about to explode. He dared not exhale so close to his target, so near to doing what needed to be done. When he pulled out the syringe, his hands were quivering, fumbling to remove the soft plastic cap that covered the tip. He raised his arm and placed his thumb firmly on the plunger, ready to stab Abelman in the neck.

'Eddy!'

'J-James?'

'You came,' Munro said happily, removing his earphones.

Edgar breathed with such relief that it drained him of every ounce of strength and left him completely deflated. He slumped into the booth and dropped the syringe onto the table, forgetting for a moment about who it was he was certain sat waiting.

'Of course I came,' he said. 'Boy, am I glad to see you!'

Munro looked at the syringe filled with the mysterious substance.

'Are you sure about that?'

Edgar nodded. 'Oh yeah... I'm sure. Did Abelman invite you as well?'

His relief was short-lived, and the fear that had followed him from the lab once again took hold. He jumped to his feet with Munro no time to reply.

'Listen, James... we can't stay. We have to get out of here — *now!*'

'Erm... Eddy—'

'I think we've walked into a trap.... It's Abelman... we've got to hurry—'

'Eddy! Relax... it was me. I sent the message.' Munro placed another cell phone on the table. 'Abelman doesn't own the networks... not yet anyway.... So, I cloaked his SIM while he was on stage stealing my show—to send you a message.'

'You did what? Why...?'

'I had to be sure, Eddy. That you're not siding with him.... You know I only act stupid. I know he's gonna try and get rid of me... and I needed to know that I can trust you.'

'B-but I thought it was a trap....'

'So, can I?'

'Can you...?'

'Trust — you, Eddy?'

For a moment Edgar and James were talking over each other.

'I thought Abelman brought me here to... well... I guess the point is that maybe I'm no use to him now...? You know, a loose end?'

'Then it looks like we're in the same boat, doesn't it...?' smirked Munro. 'Looks like we've no choice other than to trust each other.'

Edgar sat back down and slid further into the booth. Destiny, so it seemed, was not without a sense of humour. Edgar hated James. For years he had despised him—loathed him—and dreamt of the day when he would finally be able to destroy him. Now, here they sat, alone in a bar, knowing that the only people in the world they could trust was each other. Munro pushed the syringe aside and looked at Edgar reproachfully. He leant across the table and lowered his voice.

'We've gotta end this... you know that don't you? We've gotta end this—*today*... before it's too late. Before he puts an end to us.'

'I know,' replied Edgar, lowering his head with shame. 'But how?'

'With this!' said James, as he pulled out a pistol: a Glock 9mm handgun. 'We go back to DomiGen now... and we blow his brains out!'

Edgar jumped and pushed against the backrest as far as he could.

'Are — you — *crazy!* Where did you get that?' he demanded.

'Don't worry about the gun, Eddy.... I'll take care of him. I just need to know that when he's gone, you and I are still partners?'

'James, we can't... Abelman's not alone. Whoever he's working with, he's more scared of them than anything else. If I can't get the implant to work, they'll come for him.... If we kill him, they'll come for us too.... They'll know it was us.'

Munro took a moment to think about what Edgar was saying. He may have been hot-headed and not always in control of his anger, even so, like he said he wasn't stupid, and what Edgar told him made sense. He placed the gun down on the table.

'You're angry... I know... I know that anger, James... I live with it *every* day. But I tried to face him—and he beat me—just like he beat you....

'We can't win playing his game, and that gun won't solve the problem.... You shoot Abelman and it only gets worse. He's always a step ahead and he'll always win, so long as you try to face him—so long as you do what he expects.

'You have to stay calm. Learn which battles to win and forget about the ones that are lost....'

Munro looked down and sighed despondently. He knew that Edgar was right. It was a foolish plan, and only a fool would think about shooting Abelman.

'He just humiliated you in front of the world... made it clear that DomiGen is his after you told everyone it's yours. You don't think he's expecting a reaction...? You'll play right into his hands. Think, James. Be smart.'

'Ok. Ok, you made your point,' said Munro, tired of the lecture. He took the gun off the table and put it back into his pocket. 'Well, you tell me, Eddy, since you know *everything*.... What else can we do?'

'I don't know... but we can't just sit here and wait for him to take us away in a van.'

Edgar stopped. He raised his eyebrow, as if struck with an idea.

'Of course, that's it,' he said, 'the van!'

'What...? What van?'

'We can't kill him, James.... At least... not the way you think....'

Edgar's mind was racing as he planned; not focused on talking or finishing what he had begun to explain.

'What do you mean the way I—'

'That phone,' said Edgar, interrupting Munro as he pointed to his other cell phone. 'Can you send Abelman a message and make it look like it came from someone else?'

'Huh…? Erm… sure… of course, I just need—'

Edgar interrupted again. 'Well do it… do it now!'

'Ok… but… what do I say…? What's the message? Who's it from?'

He paused for a second then stared at Munro, with eyes as cold as his master.

'Tell him it's Freyland… make it look like it comes from Martin Freyland.

'Tell him it's urgent and that he needs to meet… here… now. Tell him that Freyland's got reason to believe that he's trying to misuse CaliChat. That Freyland's learned of his intention to monitor profiles of convicted criminals… that he suspects that it might have something to do with the contract the government just awarded DomiGen.'

'What…? Are you nuts? There's no way that—'

'Just do it,' ordered Edgar.

Munro removed a small electronic box from his pocket and connected a cable to the charger of the cell phone. He tapped the screen, entering details and updating the SIM.

'It's almost there,' he said. 'Just confirming Freyland's cell and… there it is. Ok… now… tell me again…. What should I write?'

James wrote what Edgar told him and read it back, to confirm that it was exactly as he wanted.

'Send it,' said Edgar. 'Now, give me your cap. Go to the washroom and wait till you hear from me.'

'Eddy…? What are you—'

'Just do it, James. We don't have time to argue.'

He removed his cap with some trepidation and handed it to Edgar. 'Be careful, my friend.'

Edgar cleared his throat noisily and looked up at Munro. 'Go,' he said firmly, as he put on the cap and moved round in the booth to sit where James had been sitting. With his back to the staircase, he took hold of the syringe. The fact that he could see it meant the light might show his face; a chance he might be recognised before it was too late. Loosening the lightbulb above the table, the corner become noticeably darker. Edgar began to breathe—long and deep—as he tried to relax, to slow his heart that was thumping once again to a vigorous beat. He was counting on Abelman's fear. The fear of someone like Freyland, someone he could not control. Someone who had appeared credible and incorruptible during the congressional hearings. Someone with the mettle to expose his plans. The fear of what his associates would do if his government contract collapsed. Because fear, as Edgar knew only too well, was a great motivator.

Edgar heard the front door slam. He pulled at his sleeve to check the hands of his watch that glowed in the dark. Two minutes and twenty-three seconds. That was how long it had been since James sent the message. Abelman had ran to the bar, and fear had clearly motivated him well enough.

'Freyland?' barked Abelman. 'Freyland…? I'm here!'

Edgar closed his eyes and clenched his teeth. His breaths no longer deep, but shallow and rasping. He sat motionless, waiting in the darkness as he listened to the footsteps that stomped around downstairs.

'Goddamn it, Freyland! Where are you?'

Edgar heard the clatter of chairs as they hit the floor. He was stressed, thought Edgar, not looking where he was going, and probably short of breath after running here.

Suddenly, there was silence. Then a loud echoing creak.

Edgar's breathing quickened. His lips pursed. In his trembling hand, he gripped the syringe tightly.

'Freyland!' yelled Abelman from the foot of the stairs. 'Goddamn it! Where the hell are you?'

Edgar listened and counted the sound of the creaks. Twelve… thirteen… fourteen… fifteen… sixteen…. He was there, at the top of the stairs. The lion was close, although the prey was camouflaged. Edgar whistled, like an owner that calls to their dog.

'Are – you – *deaf?*' screamed Abelman.

Edgar breathed in one more time and held his breath. He felt a trickle of sweat run down the back of his neck, and he raised his quivering hand from the table. Abelman stormed towards him, the floor vibrating so hard that Edgar could feel the weight of each step in his stride. He was a metre away, two at the most, and Edgar could hear his panting: hear how tired he was. The lion had found his prey, now ready to pounce and devour his victim.

'Freyland, I don't know what you're playing at—'

Abelman stopped, suddenly. He looked down, and there... sticking out of his leg, was a syringe. Edgar stood up and took off the cap, then turned around to face him.

'Eddy...? Eddy, what are....'

Surprised and confused, Abelman reached out to take Edgar's shoulder, but his hand fell short as he collapsed into a heap on the floor.

'James!' shouted Edgar. 'James...? Get out here!'

Munro came out from the washroom and found Edgar pulling on one of Abelman's arms, lifting it up and around his shoulder.

'Come on... hurry! Help me.... We have to get him back to DomiGen before this place starts filling up.'

Munro slung Abelman's other arm over his shoulder and they hoisted him up between them. Abelman hung unconscious—out cold and oblivious—like a drunk being helped home after a skin full. They dragged him downstairs, his shoes scuffing on each step. The front door opened, and two men entered. Edgar could hear that one was the bartender who had just gone next door to buy a sandwich. He was complaining about the service, how slow they were and how everyone in front of the queue kept ordering iced cappuccinos with drizzles of caramel. Edgar and James stood perfectly still: statuesque and safe in the shadows as they waited for the men to wander farther into the bar. When the coast was clear, they continued to drag Abelman towards the door. Then, as Edgar reached for the large brass handle, it suddenly opened outwards. Before them, a group of men—perhaps five or six—were on their way in from work for an early evening beer. They stared at Abelman as they held open the door.

'Started early,' said Edgar as he tutted. 'Couldn't hold his liquor.' One of the men smiled.

'Take it easy buddy!' he said, as he slapped Abelman on the back on their way inside.

The door closed behind them and Edgar's eyes scouted.

'There,' he said, pointing. 'Cut down Byron. It's quiet.'

Edgar and James dragged Abelman down Byron Street. It was already getting dark. The cold evening wind had picked up again, keeping people inside unless forced to venture out, while those already outside were hurrying about their business.

'We're almost there,' said Edgar, his tiny frame exhausted. 'Around back... the fire escape.... There's no cameras.'

They pulled Abelman inside. Munro was horrified.

'What...? What is this place?'

'You wanted to know what was behind the door.... Well, here it is—take a look. Take a good look.'

'Eddy...? What—'

'This is where I work, James. Where I come *every* day to kill people. To try and perfect the implant.'

Munro was agape as his eyes darted around the room.

'Eddy, I... I... you know... I had no idea... I—'

'Just help me get him onto the table.'

He helped Edgar lift Abelman up onto the operating table, then roll him onto his back. Edgar put two fingers onto Abelman's neck and checked his pulse.

'Still alive... I thought the dose might have killed him.'

'Didn't it?'

Munro appeared to be disappointed.

'There wasn't time to test it, James. It's a concentrated form of what I use on the test subjects. I knew it would knock him out... just didn't know if it was lethal.'

They both stood silently, staring at Abelman; Munro unsure of what Edgar had planned.

'What are you gonna do?' he asked.

Edgar paused as if thinking, but he wasn't. His mind was already made up, it only needed time to find the courage.

'What I should have done years ago,' he replied, and he slammed his palm onto the screen of a remote.

The motors in the table adjusted, transforming it into the shape of a chair that raised Abelman up into a seated position. Edgar glanced at his Rolex: it was almost 7:00 p.m. Two grips clasped Abelman's shoulders from behind while a restraint came out from the table and held his neck. Another two gripped his forehead from either side, as a robotic arm swivelled down from the ceiling, then came to an abrupt halt. A drill started, and the robotic arm began to move—slowly and precisely—towards a tiny red laser dot that was projected onto the upper back of his head.

'Eddy...?' asked James warily.

But Edgar was stressed, and almost was not exact. He checked his watch again: it was 6:55 p.m., precisely.

'There's no time... I'll have to do it myself.'

'Time...?'

Edgar hadn't a moment to lose, nor a second to waste explaining. The drill pierced the back of Abelman's skull and Munro recoiled; he winced at the thought and the high-pitched sound as it squealed, drilling through the bone. Edgar grabbed a chip. It was far too large to implant without removing a part of the cranium. He checked his watch again. He needed to think, yet time forbid it; he had to try to find a solution.

'Quick, James... help me.'

Edgar rushed to another machine and placed an implant into the centre of a laser grid. Several vice-like holders gripped the implant once it touched the sensitive pad, and the machine appeared to adjust the position of the implant to align within the lines of the lattice.

'That machine… over there!' urged Edgar, as he pointed to a terminal on the other side of the room. Munro looked confused.

'Hurry—get to *that* machine!'

Edgar was typing feverishly on a keyboard; his eyes locked onto the monitor while more robotic arms swung into place.

'The password,' shouted Edgar.

'It's M.E.A.E.G.O.M.E.A.E.S.T.R.U.I.N.A.M.'

'What…?' replied James, unable to hear clearly over the whir of mechanics.

Edgar looked up, away from his monitor, and saw that James was still standing by Abelman.

'Get to that terminal,' demanded Edgar, as he pointed again at the machine on the other side of the room. '*Now!*'

Munro rushed over to the machine.

'Ok, get ready… now type—meaegomeaestruinam and wait until I tell you to hit Enter.'

'Huh…? Me-age-o what?'

'James, listen to me….

'M.E.A.E.G.O.M.E.A.E.S.T.R.U.I.N.A.M.'

'Ok… Ok I got it.'

'Now wait until I tell you to hit Enter.'

The robotic arms continued to adjust to whatever Edgar was typing at his station, when suddenly, the beam of a powerful laser began cutting.

'I have to reduce the casing,' yelled Edgar. 'It'll never fit!'

The laser cut through the clear transparent container surrounding the tiny chip, and Edgar pointed at the liquid that began to drip from its side.

'That's artificial cerebrospinal fluid.'

Munro had no idea of what Edgar was screaming about.

'The chip... it's suspended in CSF—connected to millions of axons—but we have to reduce the casing... drain some fluid.'

Edgar shouted over the shrill of the laser; his explanation only partially heard and doing nothing to help demystify what was happening. As the cutting continued, Munro began to look uncomfortable: his face paled as the stench of burnt plastic filled the room. He reached for a stool as the laser powered down, and a large robotic arm lifted the implant, transporting it in a split second to where he stood.

'On my mark,' shouted Edgar.

However, James had jumped, then ducked, terrified that the arm was not going to stop and was crouched beneath the desk.

'In five, four, three, two—'

'No! Wait.... Eddy, wait!'

'—one. Now, James.... *Now!*'

'Wait!'

James leapt from beneath the desk and lunged at the keyboard: hitting the Enter key and several others besides. A large cloud of gas spewed from the ceiling, like a fire extinguisher filling the air; it quenched the smell of the smouldering plastic. Startled and taken again by surprise, he jumped, his nerves now wrecked, and he ran over to Edgar at his station.

'Get back,' ordered Edgar.

Edgar typed on the keyboard and the robotic arm reached into the fog. It emerged with the implant, less than a quarter of the size that it had been, and Edgar looked at it clasped in the grips.

'Ok... we're good to go.'

He ran over to another terminal and began typing again. With one eye on the keyboard, the other on his wristwatch: it was now 6:58 p.m.

'Come on... come on.... *Come on!*' he growled, as he repeatedly hit the Enter key.

Another machine burst into life. It moved at lightning speed towards the robotic arm that held the chip, then stopped, abruptly, and the implant was passed in the most delicate of exchanges. The arm now holding the chip then swung, suddenly, and moved around with equal speed to where Abelman was being held. Again, it stopped sharply, and Munro stared in wonder, fascinated by terror, at the grip that extended to slowly reveal a thin needle with the implant attached to its end. The needle entered the hole at the back of Abelman's head. His hands twitched in a nervous reaction; Munro turned quickly and cringed. He listened to the sound of a fine hissing spray that was ejected to seal the tiny hole. Then he looked again to watch as the needle slowly retracted, until finally, it was clear. The arm swung as before, but in return to its starting position. Munro stood waiting, not knowing what would happen next; scared of where to step in fear of being struck, and his face in search of a command or instruction.

'That's it,' said Edgar, as he sighed and closed his eyes for a second.

The sound of a winch motor, and with it, the sound of the metallic shutter doors immediately alerted Edgar's attention. Munro turned, as the motor began to spin faster, concerned that another machine had started to move his way. He looked again for an answer to his quizzical expression, but there was still no time for Edgar to explain.

'Hurry!' screamed Edgar. 'We have to move him!'

Munro helped Edgar drag Abelman towards the lab door. Behind them the sounds of the motor and shutters had stopped, and they could hear two voices chatting indistinctly.

'James, we *have* to hurry!'

Edgar pulled Abelman as hard as he could, as hard as his little body could possibly pull anything; Munro was forced to have to keep up and hard-pressed to do the same. The keypad beeped as Edgar's key card came within range: the electronic lock clicked, and the door opened. The voices behind them were clearer now, and the men getting closer.

'For God's sake, James.... *Hurry!*'

They threw Abelman out the door and he landed with a thud; behind them, the lock clicked, and the laboratory was sealed.

'It's the collection,' said Edgar, unable to hide his relief that they had made it to the foyer. 'They always collect at 7:00 p.m.'

Munro was baffled.

'Collect what?'

'The living subjects.... The van... for the one's still alive.'

He stood quietly; his face still clearly confused, then solemn, as he recalled their talk in the park.

'How many?' Munro asked.

'Today...? Just two.'

'*Two?* Well... where are they taking them?'

'I don't know. I don't want to know. An institution, I guess.... It doesn't matter, their pathways are fried.'

'What! I thought.... How many have—'

'Too many,' snapped Edgar as he interrupted Munro. He averted his eyes and his voice softened slightly. 'There's been too many, James.... Hundreds.... Maybe a thousand... maybe more....'

'*Hundreds...? A thousand?*'

Munro was in shock. Edgar was indifferent, seemingly over his guilt and focused on the job at hand.

'He can't stay here... come on... this way.'

Despite Munro's knowledge of the building, only Edgar knew where the surveillance cameras were positioned. Together, they dragged Abelman back through the corridors and up the stairwell to his office. Munro was quiet—too quiet for Munro—and unable to forget what he had seen, nor allow what he had learned to simply pass without comment.

'But you must know? The ones that are alive... I want—'

Abelman was heavy, and his weight not the only thing that weighed Edgar down. He lowered him to the floor and turned to Munro.

'You want...? *You — want?*' he scowled. 'Why are we here, James... now? Because you want everyone to love you... because you wanted DomiGen for yourself... because you wanted to shoot him... and that's the problem, isn't it? All you ever do is want... want without thinking. Well, what about me? What about what I want...?'

'Woah...! Eddy, easy.'

Edgar breathed out and tried to calm his frustration.

'I wanted all this to end... that's all. It doesn't matter where they are. They're either in PVS, or experience brain death. Either way it's too late... they're gone.'

'Too late? What do you mean too late? If they're still alive and in PVS then—'

'What's wrong with you, James? Don't you *ever* learn...? Do you even know what it means?'

Munro looked blankly.

'It means a Permanent — Vegetative — State. They never come back... get it? No one *ever* comes back... and I don't need *you* to remind me... so just leave it alone. Help me get him into the chair.'

This was a different Edgar, and Munro was well aware of who was in control; of whose bumbling stutter was nowhere to be found. He did as he was told and helped sit Abelman in his chair, then slumped him forward, as if asleep at his desk.

'There. They'll think it was a heart attack and he's collapsed.'

'But he's alive?'

'I told you... it's PVS... the brain is dead. His heart could stop at any time.'

'And if it doesn't?'

'Then they'll think it's an aneurysm. By the time they get him to a hospital they'll believe it's ruptured. Either that or the implant will leak and cause toxic encephalopathy.'

Munro stared at Edgar.

'Brain poisoning, James.... He'll die of a heart attack or brain poisoning. It's the same either way—he's dead and it won't look like murder.... No one's looking for an implant. They don't exist.'

Munro nodded. Murder was a word that he did understand, now at least.

'We need to get out of here,' said Edgar. 'Out the back... the way we came. We can't go out the front or the cameras will see us—the system will register our passes.

'Daphne saw me leave before six, and you'd already left... you must have because you were already at the bar.'

'I never came here today, not before—'

'Then it's even better.... You were never in... and we were never together. She can vouch for that... confirm that Abelman was alive and kicking when I left.'

'But the collection?'

Edgar checked his watch. It was 7:23 p.m., precisely.

'Finished. They're gone, and we'd better be too.'

As they walked back out through the lab towards the fire escape, a strange silence shrouded them. Like brothers, there was no need to talk, no point to explain. They understood how things were between them and what things were around them. Abelman was dead. The king was not king for so long after all, and they both succumbed to a feeling that felt more like salvation than happiness as they stepped outside into the bitter evening air.

'Till tomorrow then, partner,' said Munro, as he offered his hand for Edgar to shake.

Edgar was solemn and shook hands almost unwillingly. 'Yeah... tomorrow... I guess.'

Munro turned and began to walk away before he stopped.

'You know, for what it's worth... I never meant it.'

'Huh?'

'It was a joke.... When I said, "in crime." I only meant it as a joke, Eddy. I never thought we'd actually be—*partners in crime.*'

Edgar tried to raise a smile. Like the handshake, it was difficult and felt strained.

'Well, we are now, and no one's laughing, James…. Least of all Abelman.'

Munro smirked, and the two went their separate ways into the night.

10

TICK TOCK

Edgar hadn't slept. How could he? It was he who was the mastermind, the one with a plan. Munro was like a child: petulant and reckless. The one who wanted action and would solve things with a gun. The bluntest of all instruments that not only lacked sophistication, but would surely have led Abelman's associates to their door. That possibility seemed over now, as the coronary report would inevitably find that the deceased had died from natural causes. Yet Edgar's night was filled with anxiety, and it was not just the wait for the phone call: the announcement of discovering the body. It was whether or not he could trust James Munro. Whether or not he would keep their secret....

Munro's ego was the problem. It had always been a problem. Would he think twice about bragging of how he won back control of DomiGen? Even if it meant incriminating himself, or implicating Edgar? Probably not. In fact, it was only a question of time before it was sure to happen. Munro would be back to his old egotistical self, and the world would revolve around him once again. He would feel untouchable, be certain that he was safe and had gotten away with it. Then, at some party or public event, he would tell someone, and that was all that it would take: just one person to know.

Daphne smiled as Edgar entered DomiGen.

'Good morning, Dr. Spear,' she said.

'Erm....' he replied, anxiously.

Since no one had telephoned during the night, Edgar had spent the early morning perfecting a look of shock and horror, wanting to appear grief-stricken when learning about the loss of his mentor from Daphne.

'Late night?' she asked.

'I... I'm sorry...? L-late night?'

'Well, you're later than usual, Doctor.'

Edgar looked blankly.

'It's 8:30 a.m.'

He blinked repeatedly, then checked his wristwatch.

'Oh... yes.... Yes... I... I had to wait for the cable guy this morning—problems with my connection—d-didn't realise it was so late. Goodness.... Are there any m-messages?'

'None this morning.'

'*None...?*' he questioned with surprise. 'You're s-sure?'

Daphne looked at her computer to confirm, then glanced quickly at her desk phone: there was no flashing red light, so that meant no voicemail.

'Quite,' she replied. 'No messages this morning, Doctor.'

Edgar's face was a sickly pallor. He arrived at DomiGen at 5:55 a.m. every morning. He would enter through the rear fire escape, unlock the shutters, and await the delivery of the day's test subjects. Daphne always arrived at 7:10 a.m. So, Edgar would wait for twenty minutes before leaving the lab to walk around to the front entrance, where he would then enter and say good morning. This way, Daphne was under the impression that she was the first to enter each day, and her routine allowed her to settle at her desk before Edgar's arrival.

On this particular morning, however, Edgar wanted to wait. He stayed in the lab until 8:27 a.m. precisely, before making his way around to the front. The extra hour, he thought, would give Daphne more than enough time to get over the initial shock of discovering the corpse. If she was calmer, she would be more aware of his performance and of how upset he was after hearing the heart-breaking news. That way, should the police or any associate of Abelman's enquire about Edgar's reaction, she would recall it more vividly. To Edgar, this was a plan with nothing left to chance, except, apparently, for one small detail—they hadn't found the body yet.

'Oh... well... ok.... Then you know where to find me,' he said, as he bit his bottom lip and tried to smile. He turned, looking awkward as he began to walk towards the lab.

'Dr. Spear?'

Edgar stopped. His legs were shaking as he tried to stay composed.

'Y-yes?' he replied, turning back to Daphne.

'Is everything alright?'

'Sorry?'

'It's just that you look rather pale.'

Edgar blinked and gulped simultaneously. A bead of sweat that had trickled down his forehead now hung from the end of his nose. He may well have been responsible for the deaths of hundreds of test subjects, but he had never brazenly committed cold bloodied murder before.

'I... I ran,' he murmured.

'Doctor?'

'To get here... I ran.'

'Oh well, don't worry. I won't say a word to Dr. Abelman. Your secret's safe with me,' she said smiling.

Edgar's lips were pressed tightly together. Instead of a hearty chortle, a muted titter limped from his mouth; a poor attempt to compensate for his lack of response to her wit. He nodded, the best that he could offer, and swiftly headed to the lab.

The test subjects were sedated, and Edgar paced the laboratory with only his thoughts for company. How could they not have discovered the body yet? Had James done something... said something? Had he gone to the police? Had they set a trap and now lay in wait for him upstairs? Should he get out now, before Abelman's associates came looking for him? He checked his Rolex: it was 11:05 a.m., precisely, and the nerves that he wished were as cold as his master's, were anything other than numb.

He still had his grandfather's business, he could sell that, disappear down to San Diego, Mexico maybe, or somewhere farther south. At least he would have a chance—if he ran first—if he.... Suddenly, a knock on the door. Edgar froze. He clasped his hands together, holding them tightly against his nose and mouth as he took several short breaths; not sure if his mind was playing tricks, or if he was moments away from judgement. Seconds later, there was no mistaking it: another knock on the door. Edgar took a long deep breath. This was it....

His hands trembled as he hurried to fill a syringe. The same concentrated dose of the sedative he had injected into Abelman. Another knock. It was harder this time, more urgent. He walked towards the door, his mind a daze, his vision a blur, his other hand empty. He passed a table, and his eyes were drawn to a flash of light. He reached and grabbed what looked like a scalpel, filling the empty void of his palm. Another knock, and the banging became unremitting.

Each step struggled to move him. His feet dragged like quicksand, pulling him under, closer to his doom. He gripped the scalpel, his knuckles whitening from the strain. In his left hand, the syringe clasped firmly between four fingers—his thumb on the trigger—ready to fire. His heart thumped thunderously, ready to explode as the keypad beeped, the electronic lock clicked, and the door opened.

'Eddy!'

Edgar gaped at the ghost; the scalpel and syringe fell from his hands.

'Jeez, Eddy.... You wanna watch what you're doing... you could kill someone.'

Abelman breezed past Edgar. He seemed fine, albeit suffering from the effects of a severe migraine.

'A-are you.... Are you ok?'

'The strangest thing,' moaned Abelman, as he reached up and rubbed his forehead. 'Woke up at my desk with this blinding headache. You got any analgesics or triptans round here...? What about some ergotamine?'

'Erm... erm... I... I—'

'What are you... an engine?' barked Abelman. '*Erm.... Erm.... Erm....*' He parodied Edgar, likening his stutter to the sound of a revving motor car. 'Go get me some goddamn painkillers!'

Abelman's migraine was becoming progressively acute, his mood increasingly worse.

'W-why don't you sit down...? Just for minute,' said Edgar, as he pulled out a stool.

'Yeah... sit down... I think... I think I will.'

Abelman landed partially on the stool as he fell. It was obvious that he was disorientated as he struggled to recall the events of yesterday.

'So, you woke up with this headache?' asked Edgar, praying it was all that Abelman remembered.

Abelman rubbed his forehead with the palm of his hand continuously.

'I don't... I can't.... Well, I... I went to some bar... the next thing... I was at my desk... and—'

'Sounds like you had too much to drink?'

Edgar slyly reached for another scalpel and held it out of sight. If Abelman's memory should suddenly return, then he would have no choice: he would have to defend himself.

'Goddamn it, Spear! Do I have to tell you again? I need something for this migraine....'

Edgar cautiously pushed off his back foot, moving his stool a little to right; just enough to see behind Abelman. He knew exactly where to look, where the tiny pinhole was, and needed to know this wasn't just some nightmarish dream. How was he still alive? Why was he not slumped over his desk upstairs?

'I... I don't have anything here.... Let me check out back,' said Edgar. 'Just relax... I'll only be a minute.'

'Thirty seconds, Eddy, you hear me.... You got — *thirty* — seconds!'

Edgar put the scalpel down and went back to the storeroom. It was small with space for one. The shelves were filled with supplies: bandages, gauze, syringes, and not much else. He knew there were no prescription drugs there—at least not the kind that Abelman was asking for—but he needed to gather himself because by all reason and means of logic, the man sitting in the lab should be dead. His body should have rejected the implant and his brain should have shut down. If not completely, then at least diminished to a capacity that would never allow him to talk or walk again. So how on earth did he get here?

He rubbed his face, as if doing so might put an end to this sleep deprived hallucination. Nevertheless, the sound of Abelman's suffering was all that he could hear. How could Abelman not remember anything?

The thought that this was yet another test, that Abelman was simply biding his time, waiting for him to slip, caused Edgar to panic. His perfect precision plan was in tatters, and all that he had learnt from his master was worthless. The fragile ice of his nerves cracked, then collapsed like an avalanche down his spine, severing the audacity that

Abelman had afforded him. He took out his cell phone, his hand aquiver, and he called to his accomplice.

'Dude…! Seriously?'

'It's Abelman,' whispered Edgar, frantic with worry. 'He's still alive…. He's alive and he's here—in the lab!'

'What…? Eddy, what are you talking about? You said that by the time they find him—'

'I know what I said,' snapped Edgar. 'But he's alive. He's alive, James…. Abelman's alive!'

Edgar felt a weight bearing down upon his chest. His heart pumping harder and harder against it. Unable to think of any plausible explanation, only certain that Abelman was incapable of being killed: nothing less than immortal. He fell faint, then backwards—against some shelves—his head raised gasping for air, and his arm no longer able to hold his phone aloft.

'I'm on my way…. Keep him there!' screamed Munro before hanging up, although Edgar couldn't hear with the phone by his side.

'Spear! Goddamn it, Spear! Your time's up, boy… where's my pills?'

He had to focus. To calm down. To slow his breathing—if he was going to be able to face his master.

'N-nothing,' he shouted. He pushed the cell phone into his pocket and went back into the lab. 'There's n-nothing. I… I looked but—'

'Useless! You're *still* useless! Always have been—always will be… just like you were at the Slaughterhouse.'

Edgar stood over Abelman.

'And you wanted to be my partner…. *You…?* You're a joke!'

He took a deep breath as he tried to restrain himself, his eyes fixed upon the scalpel.

'Just like that girlfriend of yours… good − for − *nothing*… and good riddance.'

No longer fearful and resigned to defeat, the words of Abelman only gave him strength. He picked up the knife, only this time he was determined to use it. His master was a monster, and Edgar yearned for freedom from this creature. He had taken all that he was going to take. There would be no more humiliation, no more lies, no more tests, no more mistreatment, no more belittling, no more degradation, and no more mention of Penny.

He raised the scalpel high above his head. He wouldn't fail; not again, not this time. Because murder was not really murder when the victim did not deserve to live, and it was Abelman who had now outlived his purpose. There could only be one master, and this was his task, his alone: Edgar's final test—his destiny to take his rightful place. The place of Abelman.

A cell phone rang, breaking Edgar's concentration.

'Make it count!' Abelman roared. 'I told you... the first million ship next month. Stop wasting my time.'

He ended the call, clearly irritated by the questions being asked, and looked up to see Edgar beside him.

'What now, Spear...? You gonna try and kill me?'

Edgar's determination was shattered.

'I... I... I know... it's not.... What I mean... it's not... I was just preparing for a new subject... when you came in... and I—'

'*I... I... I....*' mocked Abelman, as he again ridiculed Edgar. 'You're a fool, Spear.... You can't speak. You can't talk.... You can't do *anything*... can't even get me a goddamn pill—'

Abelman's cell phone rang again.

'What?' he screamed. It was Daphne.

Abelman reached out to take hold of the table and struggled to his feet. Even now, in this state of decrepitude, he still towered above Edgar.

'I told you before... if you're holding a scalpel then you better be prepared to use it.'

Abelman scowled; staring down into the eyes of Edgar, deep into his soul to challenge what little was left. The silence between them was deafening, as Abelman, having goaded Edgar into testing the strength of his character, found nothing of value or substance. Edgar had failed again. He lowered his arm and his head in shame, then placed the scalpel onto the table. Abelman shoved him aside.

'God − damn − *coward*…. Get out of my way! I'll deal with you later… after I finish taking care of another sap.'

His breathing was heavy: sounding breathless as he staggered towards the door. He stepped on the syringe and the contents splattered like an egg.

'I… I can help,' said Edgar, as he scrambled to his master's aid. Yet once again, Abelman brushed Edgar aside, flinging him against the wall.

'You…? You can't even help yourself…. You're pathetic.'

His eyes glazed as he stretched out a hand and managed to break his fall against the doorframe. He fumbled in his pockets, searching for his key card. His pain was excruciating, etched fiercely upon his face.

'My car… card… wh… wh-where….' he garbled, as his speech began to slur.

Like a punished child, Edgar was desperate to please and regain favour.

'Here,' he said gently, 'let me help,' as the keypad beeped, and the electronic lock clicked.

Abelman was slumped upright against the door: his dead weight preventing it from moving. The strained grinding sound of the pneumatic opener continued, until finally, it forced him back and he stumbled as he lost his footing. Edgar lunged to intervene, grabbing at Abelman to halt his descent, but his hand slipped and Abelman hit the hard floor with a sickening thud, pulling Edgar along with him.

He blinked, as light returned to his eyes from the ceiling swirling above; then blinked again, shaking his head, and the room eventually came to rest. Suddenly, he felt a twinge in his arm and looked across to see Abelman laying lifeless at his side: Edgar's arm trapped beneath. He wrestled to free himself. Even so, the weight of Abelman was more than a match for the strength of Edgar, and as he struggled from the encumbrance, he rose stiffly to his knees to make sure that his master had finally succumbed to the fate of his implant.

Abelman's pulse, however, was incessant, and his eyes opened wide unexpectedly. The door was wedged open against him, and believing that Edgar had attacked, he instinctively fought back.

'Get... get off... get... off... me.... I'll... I'll kill you...' he ranted, lashing out.

'Daphne told me Abel....'

Edgar looked up towards the voice. Munro was standing in the doorway: startled at seeing Abelman on the floor with Edgar trying his upmost to pin him. Munro's thoughts turned quickly from whatever Daphne had said, to the opportunity that now presented itself before him.

'It has to be now!'

'Mm... Mun-roo?' slurred Abelman, incomprehensibly.

'You know it, Eddy.... We can take him... but it's gotta be now... it's now or never!'

'I know,' said Edgar, desperately trying to keep Abelman's arms under control. 'Get inside, quick—help me get him away from the door.'

Munro hurried inside and pulled Abelman away by his ankles. The lab door closed shut.

'Hold him... I'll get a sedative.'

Munro tried to restrain Abelman as Edgar had, albeit less successfully.

'I can't hold him!' he screamed. 'You gotta help me, Eddy!'

There was no time to fill a syringe; Edgar ran back to answer the cry and bolster support for Munro's tiring arms.

'We'll never hold him... we have to get him to the table.'

The two grappled to overcome Abelman and drag him towards the operating table. His endless reserves resisted the pair, contesting their paltry grip. But the longer he opposed, the more he exerted, and the more incoherent his speech became.

'It's his brain. It's shutting down,' said Edgar, as Abelman's condition visibly declined. 'I don't understand how he's managed to survive for—'

A long loud beep from a computer at the end of the lab interrupted. It was followed by a series of fast high-pitched beeps, and then a whirring hum, as a row of several computers awoke from their dormancy. Every monitor quickly jumped into life, and their displays were filled with activity. Then a sound—more an alarm than a siren—rang out and the prisoner immediately fell limp.

'What's happening?' asked Munro, his voice clearly panicked.

'I... I... I don't know,' replied Edgar. 'I've never seen anything like this before....'

His face was a mixture of bemused concern, forgetting for a moment the contest as he gazed in wonder at the frenetic computations taking place around the room.

'Eddy...?'

Munro tugged Edgar's arm. Edgar turned to face him.

'What are we doing?'

'Huh?'

'What — are — we — *doing?*' Munro asked again, rousing Edgar from his trance.

'Oh, we... we have to get him onto the table.'

'Ok... so let's do it then before he wakes up,' urged Munro. 'Give me a hand.'

'Yeah, sure,' said Edgar, lost in thought. 'Good idea... before he wakes up....'

Edgar and Munro hoisted Abelman up onto the operating table. Edgar's eyes widened as he pointed at one of the monitors.

'You ok, Eddy?'

'It... it can't be... it's the implant.... It's the implant! It's working, James.... Look... look it's working!' screamed Edgar with excitement. 'Don't you see...? It's binding with his synapses—look—hundreds of billions of connections.... Look at them... *look!*'

Edgar's delight dampened almost instantly as he fell again into thought. 'How...? How could...?'

Munro looked puzzled: he failed to understand anything or decipher the lines of code scrolling past. Edgar was silent—spellbound again—trying to understand, to find an explanation for the impossible.

'Yes... that's it.... It has to be—'

'What?' interrupted James. 'Is he dying?'

'Dying?' laughed Edgar. 'Oh no... he's not dying... he's alive. He's very much alive—and we're gaining control of his brain.'

Edgar was still thinking through theories as his thoughts became words, trying to fathom how Abelman had not only survived, but now also appeared to be the first successful test subject.

'It must have been the casing... when I reduced the casing, it drained most of the cerebrospinal fluid. That's why—why he's alive—why the implant is working. Don't you see...?'

No. Munro couldn't see, and neither did he care to. He was uninterested in the science or the logic behind it. What he wanted... all he wanted, was to see Abelman dead.

'Look, James!' Edgar shouted, still astonished by what he saw. 'It's working! *It's really working!* Don't you see...? It must have been hydrocephalus.'

Munro was still holding both of Abelman's arms, too scared to let go and too afraid to believe that anything other than brute force would ever work against him.

'We were overloading the brain—drowning it....'

Edgar was overwhelmed, not thinking of Abelman at all. He slumped onto a stool laughing, wanting to cry.

'The implants work. Don't you understand what this means?'

Munro knew precisely what it meant.

'It means they've always worked. It was never about the implant, James. All this time... all those tests... those deaths... it was only ever the vehicle—the way we delivered it—that was the problem.'

Edgar leant back and raised his hands behind his neck; his face was suddenly solemn. Munro, who had remained patient watching Edgar's excitement grow and then fall into sobriety, now wanted action.

'Ok, Eddy... what about Abelman?'

Edgar, however, rose again and was far from concerned as his mind began to fill with the endless possibilities these small domino bricks would bring; the opportunities ahead, if only he could understand why the implant had made its connection.

'Yes, of course!' he exclaimed, as he leapt off the stool. 'That's it. The sedative. That's why we thought he was dead. The sedative was far stronger than what I normally use... don't you see...? It blocked the receptors... it stopped the connection. It wasn't until it began to wear off that the implant was able to bridge. That's why he was struggling... the headache....'

Edgar continued to work through his theory and checked his wristwatch.

'Fifteen hours.... Ok, so, we have to delay the connection—reduce the chip, the level of CSF, adjust the sedative, and *then* make the bridge,' he proclaimed, as he nodded enthusiastically to himself in agreement.

'Eddy...? Eddy! What about Abelman?'

Edgar returned to reality and saw Munro still holding Abelman on the table.

'We control him.'

He sat back on the stool and spun around to press a button on the remote. The grips that had restrained Abelman the night before, restrained him once again. Munro was relieved, then his relief turned to fear, as Abelman's body returned to life. Abelman began to resist, straining at the restraints almost immediately. Munro panicked.

'Eddy...?'

Edgar stood up and calmly walked across to a touch screen that was built into a table. He swiped through various menus, tapping and clicking.

'There,' he said, pressing a green coloured square, and the resistance ended.

'Is he dead?'

'Asleep,' said Edgar as he turned and walked back towards Abelman. He leaned over the table and patted the top of his test subject's head. 'Shh!' he whispered, grinning broadly to Munro.

'He's sleeping like a baby.'

'Asleep...? Well, is he gonna wake up?'

'Of course,' Edgar replied, returning to his stool.

'What!'

Munro saw the scalpel on the other side of the operating table. The solution to the problem was out of reach. He moved towards Edgar with his hand outstretched. 'Give me the knife. I'll do it *now!'*

Edgar had other ideas.

'*We* – stick to the plan, James. Only now we don't leave it to nature... now we have leverage.'

'What do you mean?'

'I mean we don't have to wait for brain poisoning... hope for a heart attack or an aneurysm. This way's better.'

'Which way?'

Edgar rolled his eyes. 'Like I said, James, don't you get it...? Don't you understand what this means?'

'You sound like Abelman.'

Edgar smirked as Munro gave a surly look.

'Look, he's the same as he was... only now we control him. We trigger commands... put thoughts in his head and he carries them out. Like a hypnotist, except we make him do whatever *we* want... whenever *we* ask—at any time.'

'Then it's stable?'

'On all four cortexes,' replied a triumphant Edgar. 'He's all ours.'

Munro's eyes narrowed as the corner of his mouth lifted, finally beginning to grasp the magnitude of the situation.

'I don't… I mean… it's incredible, Eddy. Incredible! Think about what I can do with this…. What I can do with my products… I mean I'll be able to—'

'What — *you* — can do?'

'I… I mean us, Eddy…. You and me, just like old times… the dream team… together at last with no Abelman, huh?'

Edgar stayed silent.

'So, how do we do this…? Does he jump off the roof? In front of a train? In front of a car…? Yeah, in front of a car—that'll hurt… make him jump out in front of a car. Or maybe a truck? I mean… just to make sure….'

Edgar smirked and folded his arms in front of his chest. He leaned back on his stool and sniggered at Munro.

'Easy cowboy…. We don't need to kill him. I told you—he's *ours*. He'll do whatever we want, whenever we want. Just imagine what we can get from him…. How far we—'

'What!' screamed Munro. 'No way. He's too dangerous to leave alive. He's gotta die, Eddy. It's my company and I—'

'*Your company?*'

Munro's face soured.

'That's right… *my* company. We agreed that we're partners again.'

'Partners, James. Not employer and employee.'

Munro was impulsive and not thinking clearly; he took a moment to rephrase as he sighed.

'Look, Eddy, you and I both know that he has to die. Isn't there like a kill switch or something?'

'No!' snapped Edgar, rising from the stool. 'He has to *suffer*. There's no pain in a quick death, there's only death—then nothingness… and I want him to suffer—I *need* him to suffer!'

Edgar was unwilling to back down. Munro could see that he had no intention of killing Abelman, not yet anyway, so reluctantly conceded the point.

'Alright… calm down…. What do we do then?'

'Well, you tell me… it's *your* company,' replied Edgar, sarcastically.

Munro was unimpressed.

'You know, Eddy, you don't just sound like him… you're beginning to act like him as well. Maybe you're more like him than you want to admit?'

Edgar glared at Munro, then smiled.

'Relax, James—we stick to the plan. Since the implant didn't kill him, we can induce a vegetative state. We drop him at a hospital and get DomiGen to pay for everything. Then, as far as the world and Abelman's associates are concerned, we're taking care of him… doing all this research to try to find a way to help our friend. It's the perfect cover. And every now and then, when we need something, we just visit him—wake him up—get him to sign some papers and post-date them. We put him back and no one's the wiser. No one will ever suspect a thing.'

Munro was quiet, nodding in response. 'Yeah… yeah that's good…. That's real good, Eddy. I like it…. You're one sick dude, you know that?'

'You better go. Here… take Abelman's key card, in case you need to get in. I'll run some tests on him now and he can sleep here till later. But we have to move him back upstairs tonight—let someone discover him tomorrow—and we stick to the plan. Ok?'

Munro agreed and left without protest. Nevertheless, as far as he was concerned, he merely approved of Edgar's suggestion. He wasn't doing what Edgar had told him to do.

Edgar sat and watched as his master slept soundly on the operating table, and the irony that it should be Abelman himself who proved the implant to be stable was one that did not go unmissed. The monitors scrolled through billions of lines of code: each representing a synaptic connection to Abelman's neural network. Everything—every pathway, every route, every neuron, and every tract in Abelman's brain, were being mapped in front of Edgar.

He decided that it was time to test some basic motor functions and swiped through various controls to force Abelman to respond. Simple at first; he raised Abelman's arm, then a leg, then a smile, then a frown. He typed in several words on the keyboard and Abelman repeated them as he slept, then took a headset to test vocal commands. He spoke into the microphone and Abelman repeated his words in real-time. The test subject was in sync.

His heartbeat was normal, his blood pressure slightly elevated—of no real concern—and as Edgar continued with his examination, there was no question of who held command.

'I've got control and I keep it,' said Edgar into the microphone, and he chuckled as Abelman repeated his words.

The conflict of his emotions was obvious to see. His eyes were filled with disdain for Abelman; his mouth upturned yet crooked.

'Two kinds of people in this world, Mel—the ones that get ahead and the ones that get left behind. Now, the *only* question you need to answer, is just how far are you going to help me to get ahead?'

Edgar laughed. Melvin The Monster was not only tamed, but his mind, that cold dark twisted place, was caged. It was the puppet who now pulled the strings.

He continued with his tests and remained undisturbed, until later that afternoon, when suddenly, his cell phone rang.

'I'm sorry to bother you, Dr. Spear,' said Daphne. 'Mr. Munro has asked if you could join us in the foyer for a few minutes.'

When he came out from the laboratory, Edgar's heart sank; his eyes were wide with dismay. Munro had called for another press conference and the reception area was filled once again with reporters. The audience had gathered, as always, at a moment's notice in the hope of seeing James Munro in the flesh. At the centre of the stage was a podium, and to the right—off camera—was Munro's assistant.

'And five... four... three... two... one....'

She gave the signal and he stared into the lens. The red lights lit up: they were live and broadcasting.

'Dudes! Seriously...?'

The audience cheered, hearing his catchphrase. Munro lowered his hands to begin his address.

'When I started DomiGen, I had a dream....'

Edgar glowered at the stage; his face chiselled from stone.

'A dream that one day every person on this planet—no matter who you are, how old or young you are, the colour of your skin, or the beliefs that you hold.... Be you a dude, or a—*dudette*....'

Laughter rang out from around the audience.

'That whatever our differences and whatever our needs, there should be a DomiGen wearable that's right for you.'

The audience cheered out and applauded Munro's ambition.

'Today, I'm saddened to have to tell you that our former owner, Dr. Melvin Abelman, has suffered what seems to be a severe stroke—like seriously—he can't even speak....'

'Oh no, James,' murmured Edgar. 'Don't do this... you don't know what you're doing.'

Despite his appeal, no one was listening. Edgar stood forty metres or more from Munro, cut off from the world by a sea of admirers that sat in front of him.

'This has been such a downer for me. When I saw him this morning, I was like... dude...! Seriously?

'Luckily for us, we have one of the finest young neurosurgeons working here, and we've been doing all that we can....' Munro looked away, as if fighting back tears, before returning his gaze to the cameras. 'It's not enough... and I'm afraid to have to be the one to tell you all that Mel's condition is untreatable with today's technology.'

For the first time, the audience failed to laugh at Munro's catchphrase. Spoken with such sadness, they genuinely seemed to feel and sympathise with him.

'But don't worry, we're gonna make sure that he gets the best care possible. Actually, Mel's condition is gonna be like a major part of my research moving forward.

'Dudes! Seriously… I'm not gonna stop until I find a way to help him come back to us… and that's a promise!'

His trembling voice had suddenly found strength, and the audience stood applauding, as they celebrated his commitment and generosity.

'I give you my word!'

The cheering continued until Munro raised his hand to speak again.

'Mel isn't just my partner—he's my friend, and I know that he wouldn't want us to be here feeling sorry for him. He'd want me to take creative control and move the company forward—get us back to my original vision—which is why we're all here.'

Edgar shook his head, knowing what would follow.

'So, today, I wanted to tell you in person what Mel and I agreed…. To be the one to let you *all* know, that DomiGen will no longer remain committed to servicing the federal government.'

The audience was silenced.

'Instead, I'm going back to doing what I do best. Which we all know is…?'

Munro cupped his ear as if waiting to hear the answer from the audience, and a voice shouted out.

'Making the coolest products!'

'Ah… dude! Seriously…? Thank you. Thanks, dude.'

The audience screamed with delight. They clapped, they cheered, and Munro waved a fist in the air like a champion of the ring. He milked the adoration that was poured upon him without expense, and as the applause finally began to die down, he took a bow, before continuing once more.

'To lead from the front and show the world that it's not just me... but all of us who need to move on... I would like to invite Martin Freyland and every member of the CaliChat board to join me— here—for an exclusive private tour tomorrow.

'If Mel's condition has taught me anything, it's that we can't take life for granted.... If we wanna make this world a better place—a more tolerant place—for the truly connected, then we need to start with each other. So, dudes... I hold out my hands, in peace....'

Munro stretched out his arms. He stood like a holy statue, as if all should come and were welcome to join with him.

'Saint James!' screamed a voice from the audience.

The voice was joined by another, then another, and another, as the cry for 'Saint James' became a chorus; a chant that could be heard from every corner of the foyer.

'I say *no – hard – feelings*. Let us put the past behind us and make the most of our lives!'

Their idol had returned, and the applause became euphoric. But James Munro was more than an idol: he was the messiah, and he would lead his people into the technological future. He raised his hand again to speak.

'Dudes... I've made a totally huge breakthrough with our tech, and I want the people who supported me at CaliChat to be the first to experience it. I'm sure that when they do, they'll all agree with me when I say—it's mind blowing!

'Who knows, maybe we can move our companies forward in the same direction...? Connect our world across all platforms and devices, without leaving anyone behind.'

Munro raised his arm again with his fist clenched. No longer a champion, he was the leader of a revolution.

'That's my dream.... My DomiGen dream—*for a better world!*'

The audience cheered, except for Edgar; he stood alone, as isolated in his view of Munro as he was of the brave new world to which he promised to lead. He felt sick, sick to his stomach, and he had to step outside to escape the nausea of James and the sound of his voice which polluted the building.

It was later in the evening when the lock of the laboratory door opened. Munro walked in, as arrogant and conceited as ever.

'Guess I'll be hanging onto this then, Eddy,' he said, as he flapped the key card like a fan. 'I mean, if I'm gonna have access to *my* lab.'

If looks could have killed, then Edgar would have sliced and diced Munro into a million and one pieces.

'*Your lab?*'

'That's right, Eddy, I said *my – lab*. This is *my* show now.'

'*Your show?*'

'You know, Eddy, for someone so smart, you sure do sound dumb. What are you, an echo…? These are my wearables… *mine*. This work you're doing, it belongs to DomiGen Labs… and DomiGen belongs to *me*.'

'And how do you figure that? The last time I looked, I saw a piece of paper that said all this belongs to Abelman.'

Munro smiled. 'That was before all this, Eddy…. Before we could control him.'

Munro prodded Abelman in the face, to check that he was still asleep: to make sure that Edgar still had dominion over him.

'Now you're gonna get him to sign a new contract. One that hands DomiGen back to me—its rightful owner.'

Edgar scoffed. 'I thought we'd gone through this earlier…? I thought we agreed—'

'Yeah, you know… I was thinking, Eddy…. I mean technically you've turned Abelman into a vegetable, and let's face it, you've murdered tens… hundreds… maybe even thousands of who knows how many innocent people…. The way I see it, is it only takes a call…

one look at a paper trail… someone to dot the I's and cross a few T's, and you'll go down as the greatest serial killer in history.'

'Are you serious…? Are you trying to blackmail *me?*'

Munro laughed. It sounded empty. 'Oh, that's ugly, Eddy, real ugly…. I mean, "trying," makes me sound like such a deadbeat. Like I don't know what I'm doing. I'd prefer to say that I'm offering you an incentive.'

Edgar said nothing, his eyes chilled in their stare.

'What did you think was gonna happen here? Did you think you were just gonna cash in on all my work…? Like Abelman did? That you could just sit back and own half of everything I've created… just because you've taken him out of the equation? And what… you take one away from three… get left with two… is that it…? Well newsflash for you, Eddy boy…. There's only one. There's only *ever* been one… and that one is *me!*

'I don't, "try," anything. I do. And from now on, so do you—you do *exactly* what I tell you to do, or I'll make sure the only room you ever see again has bars on it.'

After everything that had happened, and all that they had gone through, Munro had still learned nothing. Edgar had spent three years being bullied, beaten, and manipulated by a monster; there was nothing that Munro could say or do that could ever come close to the threats or the insinuations of Abelman. Seemingly adept at controlling his anger and how to recognise which battles were worthy to take, Edgar stared in silent fury.

'Did you really think I was just gonna let Freyland and that board get away with what they did to me?' raged Munro. 'Kick me out of my own company!

'Tomorrow, you're gonna get Freyland on this table and you're gonna put a chip in his head. But I'm the one who's gonna be dishing out the orders, Eddy. I'm the one who's gonna watch his face as the implant goes in—watch him scream without a sedative. And when it's working—when all this stuff is connected—Freyland is gonna kill every member of that board. You see, they'll be locked in here with you and me—no way out without this key card—no one else to hear their screams.

'You're gonna program him… make him do it… until they're all dead. And then… and *only* then… is the door gonna unlock… and I'll be there, begging for help—blood splattered across my face—as the cameras wait for us to come out and see Freyland holding the gun.

'Then, you're gonna get him to give him a nice little confession on camera… just to make sure that he rots in jail for the rest of his miserable life.'

Edgar smiled as he listened to Munro. He had it all worked out. His plan was simple; as predictable as the gun that he brought to shoot Abelman, and just as intelligent. Same old James, the self-serving tin god who never thought ahead, who never thought beyond his own immediate narcissistic gratification.

Edgar lowered his head and shook it slowly.

'James, this isn't a game… this is—'

'Of course, it is!' he sneered, interrupting Edgar. 'It's *all* a game…. What was it Abelman said…? Oh yeah, "I gave you a seat at the table when they kicked you out—brought you back into the game, Munro."

'Well, now I wanna play, Eddy. I wanna play them *all*… I'm gonna beat them *all*…. And you see, I'm gonna do it as well. With your help, I'm gonna win it *all*.

'You're gonna help me do it or you're gonna be sharing a cell with Freyland—waiting for them to come and give you your final sedative.'

Edgar forced another smile, as superficial as the previous: a sardonic look. He nodded. Not in agreement, and not to confirm that Munro was in control; he simply hoped that the childish tantrum would end before deciding upon a suitable discipline.

'You don't know what you're doing, James. Abelman's not alone. He has associates. He told me. He was scared. He was—'

Munro interrupted again. 'Abelman's history. A footnote on the page of DomiGen. I'm the one who's writing the book now. I'm the one holding the pen. I don't care who he worked with or who they work for—they can't touch me. I'll have my own private army... every soldier willing to die for *me*. And they'll have no choice—you'll make them do it.

'This is just the start, Eddy. The beginning of the end. The end of anyone who *ever* crossed me. And when I'm done with CaliChat, I'll do the senators—everyone who sat at the congressional hearing.'

Edgar was lost for words. He had nothing to say because no words were worth voicing aloud. Growing up, he had learned the hard way that he could never tell his grandfather to stop drinking on those Sunday afternoons. That he could never convince a drunk man that he was drunk, no more than he could now try to dissuade a man who was drunk on power to relinquish it.

'You wanna know the best thing about all of this? I won't even have to lift a finger, because you work for me now. I got plans... big plans that make little Eddy Spear his own liability. And you thought you were gonna get half of everything I've ever created?' Munro began to laugh. 'School's out, Eddy boy, and the playground's mine.... *Everything's — mine.*'

Munro sat down at a computer and plugged in a USB drive that he took from his pocket. A printer began to warm up, before printing a single sheet of paper. Edgar looked on.

'Is this thing mobile or do you have to sit here to control him?' asked Munro as he pointed at Abelman.

'Sorry, James.... I can't help you... I won't.'

Munro reached back into his pocket and pulled out the handgun.

'Oh, I think you can, and I know you will.'

Yesterday, Edgar flinched at the sight of the gun. Today, he had half expected to see it: the obvious bulge in Munro's coat pocket.

'Wow!' he said, his hands raised in the air as he surrendered. 'Has it really come to this...? Are you going to shoot me now as well?'

'Only if I have to…. So, don't make me!'

'Ok, whatever you say. You're the boss,' replied Edgar, morosely. 'Can I put my hands down… or do you want me to stay like this?'

'Don't try to be funny, Eddy… humour's not your thing. Just answer the question—is this thing mobile or not?'

'I can control functions on that,' he said, tilting his head towards a tablet.

'Good, then bring it with you.'

Munro took the sheet from the printer, his gun pointed at Edgar. 'We have to get him upstairs and sign this…. I need DomiGen back before I call the ambulance.'

'Ambulance? But—'

'There's no, "but," Eddy. This all plays out. I told the world how I found him this morning—the condition he's in. Didn't you see their faces when I promised to do everything to help him?' said Munro laughingly. 'When we left this evening, he was resting comfortably in his suite…. Looks like he must have got up and went to his office… sat at his desk to write a letter—that's how much it meant to him—to give DomiGen back to me….

'And that's where they're gonna find him… slumped on his desk with this letter. Handing everything over to yours truly,' he smirked, as he cocked his head and began to laugh again.

'James, please. It's not too late… we can fix this… I can still fix this. We just have to keep the deal that Abelman made. The government contract—'

'I don't do contracts with the government,' snapped Munro. 'And I don't make federal products. I make consumer products. That's what I do—and that's what DomiGen does. Now help me get him upstairs.'

Munro waved his gun persuasively at Edgar, and Edgar placed the tablet into his pocket. He slung Abelman's arm around his shoulder—to share the weight with James—and raised him from the table.

'Don't look so worried, Eddy. You're gonna love the place I'm sending Abelman… it's real cosy…. He's gonna spend the rest of his days sucking food through a straw.'

Together, they dragged Abelman upstairs, remaining unseen as they passed through the back corridor.

'Ok, now wake him up. He needs to sign it,' demanded Munro, as he placed the paper on Abelman's desk.

'James, I… I don't know how he'll react. I think—'

Munro pulled out the pistol and pointed it again at Edgar.

'Don't think. Just do, Eddy. I need this signed, *now!*'

'Ok… ok… take it easy. Whatever you say, I just—'

'Stop stalling. Get it signed!'

Edgar swiped the screen of his tablet and tapped through the menu system. Suddenly, Abelman bolted upright. Munro held the gun behind his back, and Abelman blinked several times.

'You two? What the hell do you want?'

'Well, I was hoping—' began Munro.

'Where's my goddamn pen…? Can't you see I have to sign these papers.'

Munro sneered at Edgar and mouthed the words, 'Good boy.' He placed the gun down discreetly and turned to Abelman, obscuring it from view. 'Here… use mine,' he said, as he took a pen from his breast pocket. Munro leant across the desk to hand it to him. 'Actually, why don't you keep it…? A little souvenir of the occasion.'

'Are you two morons sharing the same brain cell? *Get the hell out of my office!*' screamed Abelman.

'Whatever you say, boss,' smiled Munro, as he sneakily returned the gun. 'After all, it's still your company, right?'

Edgar and Munro stood outside and waited. With the gun held steadily on Edgar, Munro listened carefully to the sound of the pen as it scribbled across the paper.

'You should know by now—I don't play well with others. Now shut him down.'

Edgar was holding the tablet in his left hand and using his right index finger to issue commands.

'James, please… it doesn't have to be this way. We can use him to get what we want… like we planned.'

'Plans change, Eddy. So do partners. Now shut him down— *do it!*'

Edgar hesitated. Munro pressed the gun into the back of his neck, up under the side of his jaw.

'James, wait… be smart,' pleaded Edgar, as the barrel marked his flesh. 'Do you really think the government is going to let us walk out on that contract? Have you any idea of the numbers involved…? We can use Abelman. Use him for what we want—make it look like his company. Think about it—it's perfect.'

'I have thought about it!' He grabbed the tablet from Edgar.

'There's no government in the world who can stop me…. Not now.'

Munro looked at the screen and saw a red square. Three letters: *Zzz* written in white on the button. He put the gun back into his pocket; with his hand now free, he pressed it.

'No!' screamed Edgar.

A dull thud came from Abelman's office.

'Good,' said Munro, as he saw the body on the floor. 'Now he's sleeping, you're gonna delete this code. I don't want any traces of what we've done.'

'He's not sleeping, James.'

Munro studied Edgar, then looked between him and Abelman; lines formed on his brow.

'Huh…? Sure, he is… look at him… he's sleeping like a baby…. That's what you said… down in the lab. And the button… it says—'

Edgar's eyes turned downwards. 'He's dead.'

'*What!*'

'He's braindead.'

'No, he's not… he's still breathing—I can hear him from here.'

'That's the brainstem... the delay. The cerebrum is dead. You've killed him.'

'No... I... I can't have... he....'

Munro suddenly felt anxiety: the burden of having taken a life. Threatening to kill was one thing, however, having done it, well that was another matter entirely. For Edgar, death was nothing. He was far beyond such misery and the morality of conscience. He had lost his a long time ago, under the expert guidance of his master, and his only concern now was for the associates that Abelman represented.

'Don't look so worried, James... I know just the place to send Abelman.'

Be that as it may, Munro did look worried; he looked very worried indeed.

'It's called the morgue... and you'll be joining him there... soon enough.'

'What? What are you...? Eddy...? What are we gonna do?'

'We...? I'm sorry.... *We* aren't going to do anything. Here's a "newsflash" for you, James.'

Edgar took a step closer; his satisfied smile reaping further misery upon Munro.

'This is your mess. Time to clean it up. You're the one who told the world he had a brain injury—who said that you saw him this morning, remember? You're the one that got him to sign DomiGen over to you, and now he's dead.... You know how that looks? That looks like coincidence to me. But you know what coincidence looks like to the cops...? It looks like murder.'

'No! That's not.... You've got to—' stuttered Munro, as each mistake unravelled before him.

'Got to what...? Help you...? Hmm, well let me see... maybe I can offer you "an incentive"?' said Edgar, as cold as ice.

'You can't do this, Eddy, we're in this together. We both wanted this—Abelman out of the way—you can't back out now. You'd never get away with it.'

Edgar smirked before his grin turned sour, then became vicious as he glowered at Munro.

'Oh, I already have... you see, a monster once taught me that it's all about precision. Precision and control. Two things that you'll *never* have, James.

'So, while you were busy telling the world about how great you are, I was also busy—a busy little bee—writing a document that Abelman signed and dated yesterday. And in that document, he handed DomiGen over to me. It's going to look like more than just a coincidence on the day after Abelman gives me DomiGen, he then gives it to you and dies... don't you think?

'But you know, I don't like coincidences, James. The problem is, they're just not precise, and that's the difference between you and me. I'm in the precision business.

'Now, unlike the page you just printed, my file has already been deleted. I erased it from the network and the print logs... there's no record of it. Sadly, for you, when you pressed that red button, you triggered an unauthorised security breach. You just locked the network down with a copy of your file and the time that it was printed in the system.

'When they determine Abelman's time of death and see that your document was printed around the same time... well... that's called a trace of evidence, James.... A trace that combines with coincidence and points to a strong motive.

'And speaking of traces, would you look at the time.... Why it's 8:05 p.m. already, but I don't see any vans or trucks out back do you? That's weird. They're never late. They're always here at 7:00 p.m. sharp, aren't they? So, I wonder why they're not here yet? Oh, yeah... that's right... now I remember... it's because they're not coming. You see they won't be coming here ever again. In fact, there's no trace that they've ever been here at all. And how do you suppose that is...? Maybe it's because every payment that's ever been made was made in person. Why else did you think I always had to be here...? They let themselves in to remove the bodies, I only had to be here each morning to pay them—*cash*.

'Did you really think Abelman was stupid enough to leave a paper trail? To leave himself open to blackmail... by someone like you? Someone with a mouth as big as yours? You really should have done your homework, James. At least, dug a little before trying to threaten me. Or is that just too, "ugly"? I mean, "trying," does sound so deadbeat. Makes you sound like you don't know what you're doing, right?

'See, those collection trucks... they don't exist. At least, not that you could prove anyway. There's no camera's out back—no CCTV—and there's no human DNA in the lab, because it's sterilised every night at 7:30 p.m., precisely. In fact, if you check the lab now, the only prints you'll find there are yours and Abelman's—the prints you just left. But only Abelman and I have a key. So, how did you get in, James? I never let you in... how could I? I left for the day during your press conference. Check the system log and you'll see that I left at 3:48 p.m. Although, you won't see that I sneaked around back and let myself in again. So, the only way that your prints could have gotten into the lab, was if you took Abelman's key card after you killed him, or... if Abelman let you in, and then you killed him. Either way, doesn't matter, the time that your document printed will show that Abelman had to be alive until then... how else could he have signed it? At least, it sure looks that way... doesn't it?'

'No, your prints are—'

Munro stopped and looked at Edgar's hands. In the excitement and his eagerness to dispose of Abelman, he had failed to notice that Edgar was wearing surgical gloves. A silly little insignificant detail, and something not unexpected or out of place upon a doctor.

He dropped the tablet, his world falling along with it. He understood now that Edgar had set a trap. That he had walked in willingly with eyes closed and arms open.

'Then there's my favourite part,' said Edgar. 'The handwritten letter. The one that Abelman wrote while you were busy telling the world about how you started DomiGen with a dream.'

Munro was blanched; his face stained from confusion.

'Ah, that's right, you don't know about the letter, do you? Well, since we're old friends, and it is *your* company, I guess it's my duty to have to tell you....

'For a while now, Abelman's expressed his concerns that his life might be in danger. He suspected that James Munro was trying to steal DomiGen from him. So, finally convinced it was true, he wrote a letter and addressed it to Detective Paul Bishop of the Boston PD. That's the same letter that Daphne posted on her way home tonight. The same letter that Bishop will receive tomorrow morning when he arrives at work. The same Bishop who will telephone here, insisting that Daphne check his whereabouts. And once he learns that Abelman is dead... the same Bishop who will come to sniff around and discover your prints in the lab, along with your document in the printer log. The same document you have Abelman's signature on.

'It's beautiful, isn't it? I mean, come on... you've got to love the irony of it. The proof you need to own DomiGen is the same proof that makes you Abelman's killer.

'You see, it's the details. It's *all* about the details. That's how you get precision... how I get control. And you, well, you're just sloppy. Too sloppy to trust. Too sloppy with your mouth. And let's face it... too sloppy to have as a partner.

'I... I never took Abelman's card...' Munro protested. 'You gave—'

'You of all people should know by now... "I don't play well with others," James.

'When he came in screaming and shouting, I wanted to kill him... so I took his card... I was never going to let him leave alive... that's why he couldn't' get out... I had them both... but then you came....'

Munro tried to think back. He began to panic, desperate to find a way out; a way to incriminate Edgar.

'They'll find the chip, Eddy... the implant. I'll tell them. I'll tell them everything and get a plea bargain. I'll—'

'It's gone. Dissolved actually... sixty seconds after you pressed the sleep button.... Oops! My bad, I mean a poorly designed kill switch,' said Edgar laughingly. 'I should imagine it's probably floating somewhere inside his spinal cord by now.

'I knew you would press it. I just never thought it would be that easy... I didn't even have to persuade you!'

'You set this up... you son of a—'

'You set yourself up,' snapped Edgar. 'You and your ego.'

Munro went for his gun and began to tap it against his leg. He paced in front of Edgar, trying to find a fault in his perfect plan.

'I warned you years ago, the next cut would be deeper, and this one isn't just deeper—it's fatal. In fact, you better hurry... your time's nearly up. I reckon Bishop will receive Abelman's letter in a little under sixteen hours,' said Edgar, as he calmly checked his Rolex. 'Tick tock, James. Tick tock. Because if Bishop doesn't get you, what do you think Abelman's associates will do once they find out you've killed him?'

Munro stopped; Edgar goaded him further.

'Still, you can take some satisfaction in knowing that The Scout will be used in the prison contract Abelman made. The contract that will make me one of the richest men in the world.

'I was *never* going to share it with you, James. Like you said, "There's only one. There's only ever been one... and that one is me."

'Well, you were right... almost.

'Ironic, don't you think...? That I should own DomiGen and CaliChat. That in the end, I get to tell the world whatever I want about Edgar Spear using all the things that you've made. And how does it feel—knowing that the world will believe me, James. That they'll believe everything I tell them because it's me who'll control it… *all of it…* and to think, I couldn't have done any of this without you—the easy to read, as ever predictable, James Munro.'

Edgar's laughter became raucous. Outplayed, outsmarted, and humiliated, Munro finally exploded. He aimed the gun directly at Edgar's forehead and pushed the barrel hard into the skin, jerking Edgar's head backwards against the wall.

'You planned all this…? You planned all this from the start?'

Edgar remained calm and continued to provoke his partner, pushing for the point at which the pull on his strings would snap.

'I've waited a long time, James. I could have killed Abelman a hundred times before… a thousand times… God knows I wanted to, but where's the fun in that?

'I needed a billion-dollar contract because power without money is no power at all—it's pointless. Only Abelman had the kind of pull to bring in a contract of that magnitude. When he landed the prison deal, I was sure it would rely on the implants, but then he told me it was about The Scout, and I only had to play along. Remind him every now and then that you'd already given him what he needed. That you were difficult—unnecessary—superfluous to the plan. After that, it didn't take long before he decided to get rid of you. You see, Abelman needed control. He always needed control and that was something you *never* learned. But I did… I learnt it the hard way… and I knew he would take the company… I counted on it. I knew he could never share it. It's the greed, you see… the same greed that you have. I only needed to play the victim for you to believe that we were brothers in arms—out for revenge—relying on each other because each other was all that we had.'

Edgar laughed as he taunted Munro. He wiped at his eyes as if pretending to cry, making a short whimpering sound.

'When Abelman was out of the way, I knew your greed would take over. That your ego couldn't share the spotlight with anyone. Look at how it almost killed you… having to share the stage with him. Same old James. All I had to do was wait for the right moment—create the perfect opportunity for you to kill him, and you didn't disappoint.... I have to say, I'm really impressed, you played your part... precisely.'

Edgar winked. 'Still... even now... with your gun at my head and that *stupid* look on your face, you just don't get it, do you...?

'You never understood the game. Because the game—the *real* game—was never about killing Abelman, and never about owning DomiGen. It was always about taking down the house, and you didn't just help me, you did it for me. You gave it all to me on a silver platter, and you've turned me into one of the most powerful men in the world.... I suppose I should really say thank you...? But you'll pardon me if I don't.'

The smug smirk of satisfaction was too much for Munro. He was lost for words, unable to believe that he had been so easily played, so simply tricked and readily beaten; deceived by the man who only moments ago he believed that he owned. Nevertheless, he still held an ace, and the game was not yet over.

'Sorry to disappoint, Eddy, but there seems to be a serious hole in your little plan.... I'm the one with the gun, and when I kill you, I won't need Abelman's signature. I won't need the document—they'll only be *me* left—so I'll get it all anyway.... And since I've already killed once tonight, I guess there's no harm in killing again, is there?'

Munro pulled the trigger. The gun went: *Click!* Without a shot, a bullet, or a bang. Surprised, he pulled the trigger again: *Click!* He pulled it again: *Click!* Then again: *Click!*

'Meaegomeaestruinam,' said Edgar.

Munro stared at the gun. He pulled the trigger again: *Click!*

'Meaegomeaestruinam.'

'Mea... what?' he asked, baffled by the gun; confounded by Edgar.

'You typed it on the keyboard.... *Mea ego mea est ruinam.*'

'What about it?'

'*My ego is my undoing.* You really should have paid more attention to Latin in class... and while you were at it, the weight of your gun. I emptied the magazine when you turned your back to give Abelman your pen.'

Munro looked again at the gun and checked the magazine: it was missing.

'Tick tock, James. Tick tock. Time's a wasting... you better start running, before it runs out.'

'I'll kill you!'

Edgar smirked as he pulled out a syringe from his pocket filled with sedative; his thumb placed above the plunger.

'Not if I kill you first... and you know what'll happen if I get this into you....'

He tapped the back of his head.

'Maybe I'll just let Abelman's associates do it for me? Or the prison inmates fight over who gets to take the famous James Munro for his bride?

'Tick tock, James. Tick tock. There goes another minute of freedom. Time to run, and you better hide.'

Edgar was cold, ice cold. He played with Munro; toyed with him without remorse. He had to run, there was no choice, Edgar was right.

'I swear to God.... I'll come back, and I *will* kill you.'

'And I'll be here... waiting. But until then, you're going to spend every second of what's left of your life looking over your shoulder... and I'm going to enjoy every one of them, knowing that you're running.... Running scared. That every minute you're still breathing, you'll know it was me who took everything from you. Left you with *nothing*. With nowhere to hide and nowhere to run.

'I told you, James, there's no pain in death, there's only death— then nothingness, and you have to suffer. You're going to feel pain. You're going to *beg* to die. You're going to welcome death just to escape the life you're trapped in... the hell that I've made for you.'

James dropped the gun; his breath in short spurts as he ran towards the stairs. His arms swinging—flung forward with even greater abandonment—as they aided his desperate attempt to disappear into the night. Edgar, like Abelman before, was unable to resist the final word.

'Tick tock, James,' he shouted. 'Tick tock.'

11

SEAL OF APPROVAL

Munro was all over the news again. He was wanted around the globe for questioning with regards to the disappearance of a certain Dr. Melvin Abelman, his name on top of the FBI's, Interpol's and every international police agency's list. He was an icon, the most famous and arguably well-known person on the planet. So, how could he still remain at large after almost a year?

Abelman's body had never been found. The police, as usual, had put two and two together and come up with nine. In fact, it was only when Edgar showed the bumbling detective Bishop the file that James had printed, that they began to suspect foul play. Even so, without a body it was still—legally at least—a case of missing persons.

The letter that Edgar had Abelman write and sign, that said he was backing down, ready to retire and hand the company over to him, remained in a safe place; an ace card in the deck just in case Munro should ever reappear and try to claim the rights to DomiGen. In the meantime, and with no one to say otherwise, Abelman still owned the company on paper. It removed any suspicions about Edgar and kept Abelman's associates at bay. That being said, make no mistake, the apprentice was the apprentice no more. With his partners, enemies, and friends destroyed, Edgar had finally become the master.

It had been quite a remarkable twelve months. Under Edgar's reign, the first five million bracelets had shipped to prisons across the country. Moreover, almost two million former prisoners were now walking the streets with The Scout strapped to their wrists. To Edgar, The Scout always seemed like such a strange name to call the bracelet. It reminded him of old cowboy movies where some poor recruit was sent to keep a lookout, and more often than not never returned. Most likely, Munro had the idea of giving the product a catchy, memorable name for consumers. But with Edgar choosing to honour the federal contracts of Abelman, The Scout was most definitely not intended for general use. Edgar decided to redesign and rebrand the wearable, calling it the DomiGen Freedom of Release Trial. Not exactly catchy or easy to remember, and perhaps why the clever people in marketing came up with, "DomiGen FORT," as it became better known. Consequently, the government policy of releasing criminals with the device was called, "The FORT Program," and it had become a huge success. Crime was down by over twenty-nine percent, and the number of released convicts who committed crime during their first year of parole was now down by over sixty-two percent.

As the country had grown in acceptance of The FORT Program, little was still known about the new CEO of DomiGen itself. Unlike Munro, Edgar preferred to stay out of the limelight and never gave a press conference. He never addressed the media and the little information that did surface about him online was almost entirely fabricated and planted by Edgar himself. There were never any great revelations, only details—tiny snippets of fallacious facts—such as Edgar having an IQ of two hundred and seventy-seven: the highest ever recorded. Together, these fragments created an impression that were deliberately used to increase and enhance a mystery. A mystery that was Edgar Spear: Edgar the enigma.

He was famous, yet anonymous—a notoriety that he wanted. A public figure without social contact; a mystical recluse that everyone knew, but no one understood. He was the youngest graduate of Harvard. Youngest doctor in the history of surgical medicine. A prodigy who lecturers would claim to have taught, and a fellow who students would allege to have studied alongside. He was larger than life, and in every sense of it, a riddle; a conundrum for all, and the subject for those who sought their attention by recalling their contrary accounts of their time with him in the media.

In honouring the contracts with the criminal justice system, the revenue for Edgar and his DomiGen Labs was better than good: it was phenomenal. Abelman had automated payments to a series of changing bank accounts. So, while his associates still remained unknown, their absence did at least indicate that they appeared satisfied with their share of the deal. In fact, as far as Edgar could see, there was only one potential problem. A little obstacle that might need to be overcome.

Munro's technology was nothing more than a vision. Despite his claims—the media boasts—he had only sold a dream, and Abelman had sold it up the chain; planning an empire around it, staging the product launch, fooling the world that it was ready and winning the contract for his efforts. But the idea for the future was not feasible in the present. After his disappearance, when Edgar discovered how little progress Munro had actually made, it was hard to hide the fact that the empire was built upon sand, and it was already too late....

He was forced to lie, to continue the bluff, and the only way to maintain the illusion was to sell the government an empty shell. To deliver the dream, the prison inmates were issued a bracelet that was made to look legitimate enough, yet Munro's wearable, with its blinking LED's and printed circuit boards, was more useless than the fake Rolex wristwatch that Edgar used to own.

The last million units were about to ship when Edgar was summoned to another meeting in Washington. Since The FORT Program began, Edgar would be called from time to time by the chief of staff. Usually, he would be asked to talk to officials from the Department of Justice or the Office of the Attorney General: to reassure them that the program was meeting its goals. It was a long trip for just a few minutes of quoting various facts and figures; Edgar found the whole thing tiresome and rather inconvenient. To make the journey, he had to fly to Reagan Airport first in the company jet, before being collected by a helicopter which would then fly him directly to the White House. It was either that or face the long eight-hour drive from Boston, and Edgar cared for neither.

'It's the low pressure,' said the pilot through the headset. 'We can't get above or around it.'

He signalled to Edgar that they had no choice other than to push on through the miserable weather. The clouds were thick, dark grey and flat like saturated blankets, covering much of the roof tops and trees. It was not so much rain, as it was drizzle, and the large droplets didn't pour, so much as hang around in the air; suspended in their haze as each awaited their turn to fall. They clattered against the windscreen like bullets: hitting hard as they collided with no brakes or means of slowing their impact. The helicopter jumped again with turbulence, and Edgar gripped his seat tightly as he felt his breakfast bounce from side to side like a pinball scoring points in a machine. Minutes later, the sight of a drenched flag which clung to its pole caught Edgar's eye, and the pilot pointed to a large aluminium disc on the south lawn of the White House.

'Should have you on the ground in three, Dr. Spear.'

The helicopter touched down, and Edgar was met by two medium height—yet very well-built—secret service agents. They ushered him across the lawn, then led him through the West Wing.

'Where are we going?' Edgar asked, who despite his many trips to the White House, had never previously been inside the Oval Office.

'If you could just follow us, Dr. Spear,' said the taller of the agents. 'It'll all be explained to you.'

Edgar hurried between them. The agents moved quickly and determined through the hallways, stopping suddenly outside a door that was guarded by an agent on either side. The agent to the left of the door raised his arm and whispered into the cuff of his shirt, while the shorter of the agents who had escorted Edgar from the helicopter, finally spoke.

'Please wait there. Against the wall.'

Edgar looked at the agent, uncertain of what he meant: did he mean the wall to his left, or should he physically press himself up against the wall behind? The agent's eyes certainly gave no clue, and his dull monotone voice no indication whatsoever.

'The wall, Dr. Spear,' repeated the agent, sternly. 'Step – back – *now!*'

Before he could obey the agent's command, Edgar was pressed back against the opposite wall, as the agents who had escorted him then turned to face those still on guard outside the door. Edgar was nervous, caught between two agents and facing the other two. He was not appreciative of being manhandled, and certainly not used to obeying commands since the demise of Abelman. He forced a smile, a grimace of sorts, and attempted to make eye contact with the agents who stood opposite. However, they chose instead to ignore his existence, and stared aimlessly beyond him without blinking for an impossibly long time. Edgar's discomfort increased until the sound of high heels came running around the corner, accompanied by a voice that cried out in urgency.

'Just a moment!' shouted the White House Press Secretary, panting as she caught her breath. 'I'm afraid that we *must* take a minor precaution, Dr. Spear.'

She nodded towards the agents who were standing on either side of Edgar.

'If you would be so kind as to raise your arms, then we can minimise any further delay.'

Confused, Edgar's face was unable to conceal his bemusement. He had never been searched before at the White House, and this was not a request.

'I assure you, there's no cause for alarm. It will all be returned to you once your meeting is over.'

Edgar raised his arms reluctantly and one of the agents began to pat him down. He removed Edgar's cell phone, his wallet, and keys, which was all that he had. The agent placed them into an empty bowl on a small accent table, then turned to the press secretary and nodded.

'Very good,' she said. 'They're waiting for you inside.'

The door opened inwards, slightly, allowing light to escape. One of the agents guarding it glanced at Edgar and nodded: his signal to enter. Edgar stepped forward from between the agents that flanked him, emerging unscathed, albeit apprehensively from their long shadows. He tried to remain confident, still aggrieved at his treatment, and glared at the press secretary as he raised his chin before strutting towards the door. Shoulders back and chest puffed out, he boldly pushed it open.

'Ah, Edgar!' said the president, with his familiar, thick, deep southern drawl. 'Heard so much about you, son.... It's so good to finally meet you in person.'

The president stood behind his desk facing three large bay windows, and the light made it difficult for Edgar to see anything other than his outline. In a brave attempt to convey a false sense of humility, Edgar responded and conversed with the silhouette accordingly.

'The pleasure is all mine, sir.'

'Oh please... there's no need for, *sir*, Edgar. We're all friends here in this little old room.... You can just call me Mr. President.'

Edgar's eyes darted around the elliptic salon: it was smaller than he had imagined. The heavy fabrics seemed to absorb most of the light that shone through the windows and the Rose Garden door. The dreary off-white walls were barren and bleak without sheen; their monotony enclosing the room but for a few scattered paintings in their golden ostentatious frames, which begged Edgar to pause and study the artworks inside. Another time, perhaps, and in the split of a second, Edgar recognised only the Washington portrait that hung above the mantel. Two inordinate cream sofas slumped like sleeping dogs in front of the open fire on opposite sides of a small coffee table: it was decked with an elaborate floral arrangement that seemed to enjoy the warmth as its scent trickled between the crackling logs to create a less formal, more comfortable air.

The president turned away from the window. 'Why them clouds look meaner than a skillet full of rattlesnakes,' he said, as he stepped towards his desk.

No longer a contour, the president was a robust man. Not too tall, although not exactly short. His chin and neck blurred into one, and his face showed his age: fast approaching his sixtieth birthday. The years of fine dining and generous hospitality had added some extra centimetres around his waistline; the buttons of his shirt, especially those around his mid-rift, now paying the price as they bore the strain of his overindulgence. His silver-white hair caught the light suddenly, reflecting it like a mirror, and his warm southern smile felt as welcoming as the fireplace on a cold winters evening.

'Now tell me, son… how was your trip? Bumpy I imagine…? Like a bedpost in a honeymoon hotel!'

The president laughed, amused with his own analogy as Edgar forced the thinnest of smiles that his face could conjure. The west door to the president's private study opened, and the attorney general emerged carrying a closed laptop under his arm.

'I believe you know Bill…?' asked the president, as his eyes turned towards the attorney general.

Edgar nodded, the smile falling from his face. 'Yes… we've met before.'

'Well then… come on, Edgar, sit down son!' said the president enthusiastically, waving with his arm and pointing Edgar towards a chair in front of his desk.

The attorney general took a step forward, reached back to close the door behind him, then walked over and quietly took a seat beside Edgar. Edgar glanced across, prepared to offer a smile in armistice, but unlike the president, the attorney general was a lanky man who lacked courtesy, charm, or any obvious personality. He had no time for small talk, even less for frivolity, and preferred it best to get straight to business.

'Can I offer you some refreshment, Edgar? A lemonade? Some iced tea perhaps?'

He shook his head. 'No thank you, sir… I mean, Mr. President.'

'Bill?'

'I'm good thank you, Mr. President.'

The president sat down behind his desk and leaned back in his chair. It squeaked painfully, in need of oil and perhaps a slightly slimmer, less heavy occupant.

'Well then, gentlemen… let us commence with the order of our business on this glorious day!'

The president clapped his hands and leant forward, his chair continuing to squeak with his every movement.

'Now, Edgar… a little birdie has brought a somewhat sensitive and delicate matter to my attention… and Bill and I have asked you here today to discuss this little… problem… in private.'

'Problem?' asked Edgar.

'This program of yours, son… this erm—'

'The FORT Program,' interrupted the attorney general.

'Yes, that's it… this here FORT Program of yours… now I hear you've been doing rather well, Edgar…? Financially speaking that is.'

'Seven hundred and eighty-four million dollars so far this year, Mr. President,' the attorney general replied, before Edgar could even open his mouth.

'Hooey!' The president slapped his desk. 'Hell, you could eat fried chicken all week long…! Point is… you've been taken well care of, Edgar. And if we've been taking care of you… then *why* haven't you been taking care of business?'

The president's eyes began to narrow. Edgar stayed silent. He could feel his heart begin to beat and the noose tighten around his neck. The heat from the fire did nothing to stem the chill that crept from his toes and clawed itself up to his cheeks. He swallowed hard. His damp sticky palms stuck like glue on his trousers, as he pulled a hand free from his lap to adjust his collar and loosened his tie: more than a fraction. The president smiled—poised and relaxed—as he took a sip on his ice-cold lemonade, in no hurry to explain as he wet every corner of his lips.

'You see, son—here's my problem… Bill, if you would be so kind.'

The attorney general opened his laptop and showed Edgar a number of photographs in a slideshow.

'These images were taken yesterday in Bowie, just outside Arizona.'

'I… I've never h-heard of it,' replied Edgar, as he shook his head.

'Well, you should have!' barked the attorney general. 'Because yesterday at approximately 13:32 p.m., a twenty-eight-year-old white Caucasian male walked into a local convenience store and shot fourteen people at point-blank range. Included in his victims were two children—aged three and four.

'Approximately fifty-six minutes after the incident, a local off-duty state trooper shot and fatally wounded a suspect while he was attempting to rob a gas station off Interstate 10. A ballistics match to the AGM-1 Carbine semi-automatic rifle confirmed the victim as the assailant of the convenience store. His name was Jake Kowlaski, and he was released from Salinas Valley State Prison three days ago… wearing *your* DomiGen FORT bracelet.

'No details of Kowlaski were received by the Department of Justice or any other law enforcement agency. We have no geolocation data from DomiGen concerning his whereabouts leading up to the shootings, or from the time it took place that can confirm his involvement.... In short, there was *nothing* to link Kowlaski to, or confirm him as the killer—other than the ballistics report and the heroic efforts of the trooper.'

The attorney general slammed the laptop shut and stood up in front of Edgar.

'I've *never* liked you, Spear, but that's by the by... because here's our problem....'

He bent down and pointed his finger close to Edgar's face. Whatever their history, it was obvious that the attorney general was a man who was used to getting the answers to the questions that he asked.

'Why have we paid you *eight − hundred − million − dollars* for a tech that tracks nothing and traces no one?' he raged.

The president raised his hands from his desk to intervene.

'Now, now, Bill—let's just all calm down... ain't no point in running your mouth with a tongue enough for ten rows of teeth.' He gestured to the attorney general to sit down. 'You see, Edgar... you've put us in a bit of a pickle here, son.... Crime is at the lowest it's been since the Clinton Administration. Our ratings are through the roof, and everything seems to be going rather swell—nice and dandy with the program. Now I don't have to tell you what will happen if this information gets out, do I?

'Why, every criminal from here to New Mexico—who believes that The FORT is watching over them—would be back out there on our streets. Out there, putting lives in danger. Violating their paroles, committing crime and filling our prisons again.... Folks would be as scared as a cat in a dog pound. You understand me, son?

'It would be the end of your program, Edgar—the end of *your* contract....'

Edgar continued in his silence as his timorous eyes betrayed him to the president. He felt the perspiration soaking through his shirt; a bead of sweat rolling down beneath his arm, tickling as it trickled. The tie that he loosened, nowhere near enough to allow his body to breathe.

'The FORT Program is a deterrent, Spear,' screamed the attorney general as his finger waved profusely. 'It's the fact that everyone believes it works—that every step and movement is recorded then sent to our law enforcement agencies.... That's *why* we're winning.... How we're tackling crime—'

'I think he understands that, Bill,' interrupted the president; his eyes again meeting Edgar's. 'It's propaganda at its best, son. The power of fear proving to be stronger than the truth itself.'

Despite the president's sympathetic tone and bid to lure response, Edgar maintained his silence as the attorney general bolstered his attack.

'And in this case, we can all agree... your – bracelet – transmits – *nothing!*'

'Bill, didn't I ask to keep a civil tongue? Now, we can fix things in Bowie, Edgar... make a donation... keep things hush. But I cannot risk another incident... one that we cannot control—you understand...? Sympathise with my predicament?

'You see, I *need* to know... I *need* your reassurance, Edgar... that The FORT Program is back on track, doing what it's meant to do—what it's *paid* to do—and I need to know that before you leave this here room today.'

The attorney general stood upright. His blue eyes combusting into flames as they burned through Edgar without remorse. The president stared: his eyes blank, as cold as the walls of his office, without radiance or ability for Edgar to read. This was the high-stakes table he had dreamt of, and Edgar knew the stakes all too well. It was the game he was destined to win if only he had gotten out sooner—had controlled his greed for more. If only it had taken a little longer before they discovered his bluff; before the power of a criminal's fear gave way to temptation and murder. But that was the gamble and now he was called. His cards were exposed, and the bank threatened his funding. The associates of Abelman would be absent no more.

'I... I... I—' rasped Edgar, his throat parched and coarse.

'A little dry...?' asked the president. 'I do recall inviting you to partake in refreshment, Edgar... and as I recall you declined my invitation,' he said scathingly, no longer sympathetic to his guest. 'Now, perhaps I was unclear as to the significance of my solicitation...? So, allow me to clarify.... I want to know what *you* are going to do to make sure that nothing like Bowie *will ever* happen again!'

The president leaned farther forward across his desk, and his chair gave another long, painful squeak. Each second passed slowly as he awaited response. Edgar's thoughts raced wildly as he contemplated a plan—a means of escape. Not from the president or his snarling mongrel, since he could tell them whatever they wanted to hear. He had to find a way to evade those who scared Abelman, because the transfers that had kept them at bay until now would stop. Once they did, the truth about The FORT would be known, and then they would come; Edgar was sure of it. They would come because they would need to find Munro, and when they couldn't, when they wondered why he had never been found, then they would wonder if the real reason was not because he was a fugitive, but because he had met the same fate as his partner. No letter, not even one in Abelman's own hand would ever be enough to convince them otherwise, and they would take their payments by a different kind.

The thought tightened around Edgar's throat like a vice, choking him as it gripped. He could feel the air being squeezed from his lungs as his pulse drummed hard in the veins of his neck. He was suffocating in a trap of his own making, and there was nothing that he could do; nothing that he could say to stop the inevitable, because there was no FORT. All there was, and all that he had was....

'I... I... I can make it work,' he sputtered.

The president looked unconvinced.

'I... I can... the program... I... I can make it work.... But not with the bracelet—not with Munro's technology.'

'Munro's?'

'Yes, Mr. President, it was James Munro who created the bracelet and called it "The Scout,"' explained the attorney general.

'Ah, yes... Munro.... Nasty business—nasty business indeed. Born on the wrong side of the blanket that boy. Still haven't found him, I presume?'

The attorney general shook his head. 'No. Not yet, Mr. President, I'm afraid he's still missing.'

The president rolled his eyes. Edgar saw an opportunity to save himself.

'James Munro lied to us all! Since he disappeared, I've been working on an upgrade—an upgrade that can be controlled. I can give you my word—'

'Your word...?' interrupted the president. 'I don't need your word, son.... Your word doesn't mean diddly.... This ain't my first rodeo. What I need is a guarantee. I need to know that what happened in Bowie can *never* happen again—*ever!*'

'It won't, Mr. President.'

'Then how—pray tell—can you assure me that it won't?'

'Because it's not a bracelet, Mr. President.'

'I'm sorry, son... perhaps you can humour an old man—such as myself... as I do believe that I missed the part where you told me what it was?'

The president leaned back slowly in his chair. It gave another long, painful squeak: the kind that becomes annoying.

'W-well... Mr. President,' stuttered Edgar, as he cleared his throat and his eyes flittered around the room. 'The thing is... it's... rather, what it's based upon... if you try to keep an open mind.... I... I mean, if it's a guarantee that you need... then—'

Tired of waiting, no longer relying on his southern charm, the president decided to cut in. 'Spit it out, son. I ain't getting any younger.'

Edgar took a deep breath. 'It... it's an implant.'

The room fell silent. Time stood still; frozen for what seemed an eternity as Edgar's words were heard, reheard, digested, dissected and finally interpreted into consequence.

'*A — what?*' screamed the attorney general. 'You have no license to—'

'Bill! Must I remind you again...? Now, Edgar, you were saying.... An in what exactly?'

'An implant, sir.'

The president was confused, but the attorney general certainly wasn't.

'How in God's name...? What have you been doing, Spear...? What in — *God's* — name — have you been doing...? I'll throw the book at you!

'Mr. President, this meeting's over. We need to call in your security detail now and escort this man to a detention cell. I'll arrange a warrant to search DomiGen Labs and sit with the director of national intelligence to discuss what we—'

'Now, Bill!' interrupted the president. Leaning forward again, his agitation was decidedly clear. 'Tell me... what part of a civil tongue is hard for you to understand? Why, if I didn't know any better, I might be inclined to believe that you are trying to make our young doctor here feel as welcome as a tornado on a trail drive....'

The president turned back to Edgar.

'Edgar, I'm looking for solutions... you hear me, son.... I'm not trying to put socks on a rooster, if you understand my meaning?'

'Yes, Mr. President.'

'Then tell me... this, *"inplant"* of yours—'

'Mr. President!' begged the attorney general. 'I strongly advise you to end this conversation immediately. We have to protect you from accountability.'

He glowered at Edgar. His face furious: red from anger and getting redder by the second.

'That's enough, Spear! Not a word. Not another word, do you hear me...? Mr. President—'

'Well, I am... aren't I?' interrupted the president, yet again. 'I mean... last time we checked.... Still the president? And I do believe that the president asked the doctor a question, Bill. A question he intends to have answered.'

The president leaned back in his chair, and Edgar tried valiantly to ignore it.

'So, tell me, son... about this *inplant* of yours....'

'Well, sir... erm... I mean, Mr. President.... I was resident at Massachusetts General in Boston, and while I was there, I was assigned under Dr. Abelman.... My senior—'

'Abelman?'

'Yes. Melvin Abelman.... He disappeared at the same time as Munro, Mr. President,' replied the attorney general, trying to do as his commander in chief had ordered.

The president nodded. 'Ah yes, I do recall.... The surgeon? They never recovered a body, did they?'

'No, Mr. President. He's still missing.... Presumed dead.'

'Still missing...? So that's two you've lost... been unable to recover? Tell me, Bill, are there any more people in that company I need to be concerned about...? Should I write a letter to their mommas—just in case you lose them as well?'

The attorney general's cheeks lightened to a shameful pinkish flush. He lowered his head.

'Glass houses, Edgar. Seems someone here ought to keep his hands in his pockets... instead of casting stones. Now, if you'd be so kind... please, do continue.'

Edgar took a short breath, to try to calm his nerves. More importantly, to show that he was not to be intimidated; at least, not by the threats of powerful men or the power of which they held.

'As my senior physician, I was forced to assist Dr. Abelman with his experiments.'

'Experiments?'

'Mr. President, I really must insist—'

'Now, Bill, hush!' demanded the president, and he slammed his fist upon the desk. 'I will not tell you again.... You wash that war paint off your face, and let my learned friend here continue.'

The president looked to Edgar, and the attorney general sat like a sulking child.

'I do apologise, Edgar.... He will *not* interrupt you again—not if he wishes to remain in this room. Now please, do proceed with your account.... I do believe that you were forced... or may I take the liberty of saying, "coerced," into observing the activities of your senior?'

'Yes, Mr. President. That's exactly what happened. I was *coerced* to follow Dr. Abelman as he performed a number of activities on....'

Edgar paused. He realised the word "patients" was incriminating; admits to the fact that he had experimented on the living. The president, as the attorney general, would be only too aware of the illicit nature of such wrongful undertaking.

'My apologies again, Edgar.... Sadly, my hearing is not as it once was... but I do believe that I heard you say, "covertly." That you covertly monitored the actions of your senior in developing this, *inplant* of his...? Is that correct?'

'Yes, Mr. President. That's correct. I watched, unbeknown, as Dr. Abelman engaged in a number of trials that were based upon the implant of a small silicon chip.'

'And this chip...?'

'A neural implant, Mr. President, that attaches to the cortexes of the brain.'

The president's expression changed. He seemed troubled; his face twisted, difficult to read as he raised his hand and rubbed his chin. Edgar began to worry that he may have said too much—too quickly.

'I see....'

He slowly leaned forward in his chair once again. Edgar tried to contain his annoyance, but he cringed: his nose wrinkled, baring his teeth as his eyes narrowed to the sound.

'So, tell me, son.... This little "upgrade" of yours... this replacement for the bracelet... would this be somehow related to the "neural inplant" that you speak of?'

Edgar paused for a moment; the president sitting comfortably.

'Yes, Mr. President. It is.'

'I see... then if you would be so kind as to help my understanding of what it is these *inplants* do... exactly?'

The attorney general shook his head in disbelief. That the president would allow himself to be this compromised—open to such liability—was too much for the man who represented the Department of Justice to take.

'I'm sorry, Mr. President. I really cannot listen to any more of this conversation—'

'Then I'll look forward to your letter of resignation after you leave this office. Make sure you close the door on your way out, Bill.... Like your mouth, I like it kept shut.'

For all his charm, the president was ruthless when necessary. His will, as his power, was absolute. The attorney general was no longer a sulking child, he had been chastised and put in his place. He should speak only when spoken to or accept the fragility of his position.

'Now... under normal circumstances I would not be inclined to repeat myself, Edgar... but since we were so *rudely* interrupted... tell me... these *inplants*... do they work?'

'They connect to each cortex of the brain and forge with the subject's neural pathways, Mr. President.'

'Hmm…. Well, that is *very* interesting, Edgar, I'm sure…. But tell me… in layman's terms… what does it mean—*exactly?*'

Edgar took another deep breath. There was no going back now.

'We can issue controls to the subject, Mr. President. Tell the host what to do. Or what not to do.'

The president leaned farther forward, and the chair squeaked hard, reaching its breaking point. He raised his eyebrows, and Edgar felt his cold stare, as if Abelman had been reborn.

'Are we talking about mind control here, Doctor?'

'Yes, Mr. President. That's exactly what we're talking about.'

'And it's an *inplant,* not a drug…? Not something that wears off… in time?'

'No, Mr. President. We have control for as long as we need it. For as long as the patient…. I'm sorry, I meant subject… for as long as the subject has the implant.'

The president leaned back and sat silently. He placed an elbow on each arm rest and joined his hands together beneath his chin. Back and forth he rocked, gently in his chair, as the loud squeaking reduced to a fainter creak, like a door whose hinges needed oiling. Edgar and the attorney general sat patiently, waiting for the cruelty to end. Eventually, the chair stopped, and the president spoke.

'I see…. So, tell me, Doctor, are there any side effects… any cause for my concern? Is there anything that would make this, *inplant,* as worthless as a teat on a bull?'

'No, sir… I mean… Mr. President.'

'And this, Abelman…. It was his experiment? He was behind all this you say?'

'Yes, Mr. President.'

The president lowered his hands and glanced at the attorney general.

'And he's still missing…? Presumed dead?'

'Eleven months, Mr. President,' replied the attorney general, calmer and finally understanding his role in the conversation.

'Good... then let's keep it that way—keep him missing. We'll need someone to place this on if it all goes south.'

Despite his apparent countenance, the man of law *was* a man of law, and he knew which side of it they were now standing upon. The attorney general tried one last time, attempting a more cordial approach to plead with his president in the hope that common sense would prevail.

'Mr. President, I strongly advise—'

But the president didn't seek advice, and he held up his hand.

'Bill! Stop whistling up the wind.... Now like it or not, there's a hole in the fence that needs fixing.... The way I see it, Edgar here is riding a gravy train with biscuit wheels, and we got to get on board. If we don't, the damn Soviets or the Chinese will, and we'll still be standing at the station looking through the hole in our fence.

'Now I hear you... and God knows I've had to... but we've got to be reasonable here—look at our options....

'Tomorrow some lunatic, a pickle short of a barrel, might mosey on down to his nearest mall and decide to shoot up the place.... We'd be looking at dozens, hundreds dead.... We could never hope to contain such a catastrophe—to come close to covering that up, Bill.... Why, it'd be all over that social media and that would be the end of this administration. You and I, we approved FORT... and you know what that means...? So, stop your whining and put your pants on. We got us a job to do.'

The president turned his attention back to Edgar, and Edgar now understood that the president was willing to do whatever was necessary.

'You say you've been upgrading these, *inplants...?* That you can assure me that no one who has one of these... *neural chips*—will commit a crime?'

'Yes, Mr. President. I can guarantee it.'

'There's no question—no doubt in your mind?'

'No, Mr. President. Not a sliver of doubt.'

The president put an elbow on his desk and rubbed his chin again. He took his index finger and tapped his lips, deep in thought, before reaching out to take a candy from a glass jar in front of him on his desk. The jar was placed just out of reach, a hindrance of sorts and test to his discipline. His willpower, however, was no match for the jar, and he overstretched: pushing the limits of the chair. He took a red hard boiled sweet and placed it into his mouth, then made a long, wet sucking sound, like squelching through mud, as he leaned back once again to enjoy the treat; his guilty pleasure and reason why his chair squeaked so much. He rolled the sweet around and around in his mouth, like a washing machine rinsing laundry, until finally, he eyed Edgar once again.

'Do you see that seal, son?'

Edgar looked up at the ceiling.

'Yes, Mr. President.'

'Did you know that seal represents the symbol of this office? Of the presidency itself.... Matter of fact, President Dwight D. Eisenhower issued an executive order to create that seal on the fifth day of February in the year of our lord, nineteen sixty. It's been used by every president who has sat in this office ever since. Now, that's a fact... and of that there is no question nor doubt. Not even a *sliver*....

'Look closely... can see those stripes on the shield there?'

'Yes, Mr. President, the thirteen original states?'

'That's right. The thirteen original states... and the motto? Can you read it, son? Can you read what it says?'

'E PLURIBUS UNUM, Mr. President. *Out of many come one.*'

The president smiled. 'You see, Bill, our learned friend here *is* an educated man.

'One nation, Edgar—one diverse nation of many... full of flaws... full of faults... but one nation, nonetheless.... That's who we are—that's what we are... and you see the branch there...? The olive branch and the arrows in the talons of the eagle?'

'Yes, Mr. President.'

'Would I be right to surmise that you are also aware of what they represent?'

Edgar remained silent.

'Well then, allow me to elucidate. They represent my power. The powers that are entrusted to me for use in peace and war.

'Out there, on our streets…. In our nation's homes, our schools, our grocery stores and neighbourhoods—we're at war, Edgar. We're fighting a war in this country, and it's a war that our nation believes us to be winning. A war that criminals believe themselves to be losing.'

The president looked down from the ceiling, leant forward again, and stared intensely at Edgar.

'Now I am not prepared to give away our position, son. To hand the initiative back to our enemy.

'The powers entrusted to me will be used to make sure that we prevail. And they *will* be executed to the fullest extent of this office. Executed without tolerance and without mercy. Because I will – *not* – lose this war, Edgar. I will *not* surrender to our adversary.

'It's a bitter truth, son, but the fact remains—this world has no need of a hero.'

'I was told that once before,' said Edgar, nodding agreeingly.

The president smiled. 'By a wise, intelligent man, I would imagine.

'You see, what it needs is a monster, because you cannot fight a monster unless you are willing to become one yourself… and if you intend to be victorious—as I do—then you must first understand your enemy. Become the face of their fears and unleash the fires of their hell—if required to assure that victory.'

The president returned to the attorney general.

'You get this in place with Homeland. You get the FDA, Science and Tech, and the Intel Advisory Board, Bill. You tell them it's a matter of national priority—*national security*. I want this in place today. I don't want to hear of any ifs, or any buts…. No delays. No excuses.

The president's gaze narrowed further. 'This time tomorrow I want to see them *inplants,* not bracelets... you hear?'

'But, Mr. President, we can't... the legislation alone.... Just to get approval from the Senate... it will take—'

'We're not cruising in the sky here, Bill. We're flying under the radar....

'Ain't nobody changing any laws—we're just greasing them, is all. Now correct me if I'm wrong, but an *inplant* or a bracelet—they're both designed to gather information, are they not? To provide intelligence for our agencies. Protect our countries security interests.'

'Sir, I cannot in all good conscience—'

'Then don't!' interrupted the president sharply. 'Just get it done.' His eyes darted to Edgar: his face remained unmoved. 'Whatever it costs... you hear me, son—whatever it takes.... I want an *inplant* in every convict before he or she ever steps foot on our soil again.'

'Yes. Yes, Mr. President.'

'Good. We're agreed then.'

'No, Mr. President, we – are – not – *agreed!* We need to convene the Executive Office.... For Christ's sake, Sam, think about what you're asking here... what you're telling him to do.... At least talk this through with NSA. A bracelet is one thing, but implants?

'Samuel, please, I'm begging you... don't do this. Wait until you've—'

The president pressed a button on his desk, ignoring the outburst and the pleas of the attorney general. He spoke dispassionately instead, keeping focus on Edgar.

'They'll see you back safely.'

Edgar nodded, his face like stone, his joy and relief concealed behind the calm facade.

'Thank you, Mr. President,' he said, as he stood and turned to leave.

'Oh, and Edgar... one more thing, so we understand each other.... If DomiGen Labs ever lies to me again or makes me regret my investment, you'll spend the rest of your days in Leavenworth—are we clear?'

'Crystal,' replied Edgar.

'Good... well then, just remember.... Pigs get fat and hogs get slaughtered.'

'Mr. President?'

'Something to keep in mind, son. Just something to keep in mind....'

The clouds had cleared for the return flight to Boston and Edgar smiled during the entire journey. His delight was self-evident, and not because he had finally met with the president of the United States, although that in itself was a great achievement. Neither was it because of the blank check that he had just been given; securing his own, as well as DomiGen's financial future. Edgar smiled because of something far more satisfying. Years ago, he would have had to lie, create a story, and then worked hard to sell it. Munro would have had to wear a mask to get what he wanted; Abelman, to resort to threats of violence. Now, Edgar didn't need to sell anything. He didn't have to lie or rely on others with masks or intimidation to convince anyone. He was simply given an opportunity and took it, seizing the position that came along with it: a position of power that made himself and DomiGen invaluable. A position that freed him from the shackles of his former partners; from Abelman's contract and Munro's wearables. Now it was Edgar's contract, his agreement and his implants. Abelman and Munro may have helped him climb the mountain, but it was Edgar who stood alone at the summit, and the world beneath lay completely at his feet.

He never begged the president to use implants. In fact, Edgar had done nothing except answer the questions that were put to him. It was the president himself—the most powerful leader in the western world—who chose to abandon the principles he had sworn to uphold in accepting office. The president who chose to willingly ignore the advice of his administration, and by doing so, Edgar had discovered something far more valuable than a contract....

He had never shown his cards; never confessed nor admitted to any wrongdoing. If anything, Edgar had merely exposed his weakness, or perhaps as the president saw it, his strength: the same desperate determination to survive—no matter the implications. Yet he now found himself in the unique position of owning leverage. The type of leverage that in the right hands doesn't just bring down a house; it flattens the entire block. He was standing on the verge of history, and his smile was not one of smugness, but of triumph. Once he could show that implants had the ability to reduce, perhaps even prevent crime altogether, then his plan for DomiGen would be unstoppable. If anyone, even the president himself should try to interfere, then Washington itself would fall.

As the flight attendant informed Edgar that they expected turbulence up ahead, Edgar placed a call to DomiGen.

'Operation S.H.R.O.U.D is in effect,' he said before hanging up. Five simple words that alone meant nothing but would change the lives of everyone—forever.

PART III

The lies of deceit

12

SEMANTICS

The day would come when a criminal would be desperate enough to willingly ignore the advertising campaigns of DomiGen; the messages of continuous surveillance and scrutiny that were repeated until their lies became the truth. A time when fear, the only thing that had kept criminality in check until now, would no longer be enough to maintain the balance between right and wrong. At the hour of reckoning, Edgar knew that The FORT Program would be exposed for what it was: a fabricated smokescreen designed to fool and scare criminals into leading better lives. It was nothing more than a scam, and it would spell the end of DomiGen unless DomiGen was ready to rebalance the scales.

After Munro's disappearance, Edgar began to funnel monies from the program. His future was explicitly linked to the implant, and as far as he could see, the only option for survival. That being said, to perform the procedure from Boston would be difficult; the idea of bringing truckloads of soon to be released convicts to the city—a challenge in itself. But to bring them up to DomiGen Labs at Beacon

Hill, through the narrow gaslit streets and bricked sidewalks, well that would be next to impossible. Edgar's response to the problem was simple. If he was not going to be able to bring the criminals to the lab, then he was going to have to bring the lab to the criminals. The first trial was to take place at FMC Saven: a small federal medical centre ran by the Federal Bureau of Prisons, just west of Boston. Saven housed over three hundred male inmates who had been convicted of everything from white-collar crimes to gangland killings. In the words of the president, the "hush-hush" trial would be a private test, and the warden was informed that his detail would be visiting, along with DomiGen Labs, no more than fifteen minutes before their expected time of arrival.

It was a warm midsummers day. Away from the city and the shadowy sanctuary of its skyscrapers, the land lost cover from the hot midday sun. Without a cloud to dampen or furnish shade, the earth was baked and forced to concede its moisture. In the distance, the whirring sound of rotating blades compelled a squad of smartly dressed men to come to attention. They stood aside a line of Cadillac Escalades that were parked inside the perimeter of a tall, barbed wire topped iron fence. As the helicopter began to descend, the blades sucked the dry dusty earth into the air like a vacuum, spitting it out across the men and their tailored black suits as they stood at the heart of the sandstorm. The president emerged from Marine One, flanked either side by agents from the secret service, and was rushed inside by the waiting squad. A man in a dark overcoat followed closely behind.

Several minutes later, a long, eighteen-wheeled MACK truck pulled up to the compound and a guard ushered the driver through in haste. The truck raced into the facility, adding to the dust cloud, as another agent spoke into the cuff of his sleeve to inform the detail of its arrival. The agent signalled and brought the truck to a standstill. Edgar climbed down as the driver was then ordered out.

'This way,' said the agent, leading them both into the facility, where another was stood inside the door.

'Please raise your arms.'

The driver turned to Edgar, and Edgar nodded, as the agents quickly removed all personal items from them both.

'Follow me.'

Edgar and the driver followed the agent down a long dark corridor. It was dank and the air stale. The fluorescent bulbs flickered continually, igniting the darkness to the echoes of a rumbling hum. As they scuttled on their heels, the driver turned repeatedly to Edgar, like a prisoner nervously led towards the electrocutioners chair. At the end of the corridor, they reached a door, and the agent rapped his knuckles against it twice.

'Just you,' he said, as he opened the door staring at Edgar, who stepped promptly inside.

It was a large room, not unlike a hospital ward; white and sterile with space for at least twenty beds. But the room was empty except for three men, and for two agents at opposite ends, each standing beneath an exit sign. Edgar instantly recognised a voice.

'Now calm down, Thomas.... You know as well as I, if I'd have given you more time, you'd have called them TV friends of yours... and why, this place would be busier than a moth in a mitten!'

The president's back was turned as he stood talking to a man. The man was wearing a dated olive-coloured suit that looked as though it had swallowed him whole. Beneath it, a striped shirt with a dark green tie to match, and although the top button was fastened, it was obviously far too wide around his pale thin neck. His brown hair—like his moustache—was streaked with white, and behind them standing alone, was a man in a dark overcoat. Edgar edged closer, and in doing so could see that the man's coat was actually black. It was leather, grey fox fur around the collar and very distinctive, vaguely familiar in fact. His face was chiselled and hard; his chin, pointed like the tip of an axe. His skin was dark brown, leathery and cooked to a crisp; the deep lines etched, like perforations that allowed it to move. He was taller than the president, much taller than Edgar, yet without the physique to be threatening or fearsome; still intimidating and creepy, if truth were to be told. There was just something off-putting, unnerving about his eyes, as if having witnessed something terrible and now scarred on the inside.

'Well, looky here!' said the president, alerted to Edgar's presence. 'Would you look at what the cat dragged in.'

'Mr. President,' replied Edgar, straightening his white coat.

'Come on in, son… don't be shy… you're right on time. I do believe that we are ready to proceed.'

The president glanced to his left, to the agent beneath the exit sign, who responded by opening the door. An armed officer holding a rifle entered, leading nine patients under the escort of twelve guards into the room. The first patient was wheeled inside strapped to a chair. He looked older than forty, yet younger than fifty: he was angry and restless with a muzzle to keep him quiet. The second patient walked in freely: his head hung, making it difficult to see his face as he sniffled and sobbed unconvincingly. The third patient wore ankle restraints and waddled like a penguin. His wrists were cuffed from behind. He was prodded repeatedly to move forward and stay in time with the other patients.

'I keep telling you… she wanted me to do it,' he protested. 'She begged me to do it… what was I supposed to do?'

The fourth patient, a tall spindly man, ambled as if out for a leisurely afternoon stroll. After several steps his pace quickened, and Edgar wondered if he was about to make a run for the other exit. Suddenly, the guard behind pressed his truncheon hard into the man's back.

'Spacey!' screamed the guard. 'I *won't* tell you again.'

A small taser charge fired and the patient slowed his walk. The president turned to the man in the olive suit.

'Tell me, warden, is that Jimmy Spacey?'

The warden nodded.

'My goodness… the man looks like ten miles of bad road.'

The fifth patient was pushed in a wheelchair. He was around thirty—thirty-five at the most—and appeared overly happy as he smiled blankly into space. Believing that he was sedated, the president jumped when the patient pointed at him unexpectedly, then waved his finger erratically at the ceiling.

'There!' he shouted. 'You see them? You see them...? The fishes? We're swimming with the fishes now boys... we're swimming with the fishes!'

The patient laughed uncontrollably as the guard wheeled him past, and Edgar assumed the cause was not medication, rather a delusional disorder that explained his torment. The sixth patient walked in dressed as a woman, wearing thick lipstick and mascara.

'Take your hands off me!' he persisted. 'I told you, I want to leave. It's way past my bedtime—and honey—I *need* my beauty sleep.... Now, what's a girl got to do to get a cab around here?'

'My oh my,' the president chuckled. 'Isn't she a pretty one...? Pretty as a pie supper.'

'That's Roger Ingleman,' said the warden.

'Ingleman...?' asked the president, surprised. 'You mean, *the* Roger Ingleman... the congressman?'

'The very same.'

The president shook his head, grinning broadly. The doors then swung open, and the seventh patient entered. He was a giant of a man, accompanied by two guards on either side. His chest was heavily tattooed, even heavier built, and his head was shaved to reveal yet more ink. His wrists were bound in front, and he tested their strength, along with those of his shackles as he shuffled past, muttering something in Russian.

'Sergei Lazovsky,' whispered the warden. 'Avtoritet for the New England Bratva.'

His contrast to the eighth patient could not have been greater: a small, frail looking man whose thick spectacles sat precariously on the end of his nose; enlarging his eyes to such a degree that they looked disproportionate to the rest of his head.

'Harold Goldberg,' said the warden.

'The drug lord?'

The warden nodded. 'And finally—'

'Donny DeMarco,' interrupted the president.

The warden appeared startled. DeMarco was a medium-sized man, not strapping or sturdy, nor skinny or slight. His thick black hair was greasy but well groomed, greying at the sides like his goatee beard. He pushed an intravenous stand; something which attracted the president's attention.

'What, may I ask, is that?'

'It's an IV, Mr. President.'

Unimpressed, he stared at the warden awaiting an improvement of his explanation.

'Psychotropic Thorazine.'

The president continued in his stare.

'A liquid straitjacket, Mr. President.... What you might call, incarceration of the mind. It's the only way we've been able to restrain him.'

'Uh-huh... I see.'

The nine men were brought to a halt in the centre of the room and turned to face the president, like a regiment of soldiers ready for his inspection.

'Well, Edgar, tell me, son... what do you think? Will they suffice for our purpose?'

Edgar stood quietly as his eyes darted back and forth, scanning the collection of prisoners in front of him. The ragged band of ragged men.

'What's the matter, son...? Not quite what you were expecting?'

'Not exactly, Mr. President.... To be honest I... I was expecting to see convicts.'

'And they are, Edgar... they surely are—the worst kind. Why these minds are so twisted, so ugly and vile that they cannot be housed with the other prisoners. Truth be told, these men belong in an asylum... legally speaking of course. But their crimes are so heinous that the law can no longer apply, which is why they must reside here—in an institution like this.

'Now you can call them patients—call them crazy if it helps—but every one of these men is more slippery than a pocketful of pudding... more crooked than a dog's hind leg. They're the worst of a bad bunch, son. Criminals by nature. What you might call, *natural — born...* a product of their upbringing, and the only place they belong, is here.'

Edgar nodded in understanding. The president tilted his head to the officer, and the patients were ordered out into the courtyard while he dawdled deliberately, keeping Edgar behind as he reaffirmed his expectations for the trial. Outside, Edgar asked the officer to move the patients to the rear of the DomiGen truck.

'A little more,' he shouted, his hands indicating to the guards where they should stand as they struggled to follow; their eyes blinded by the lustrous shine of the chrome from the silver and green truck which dazzled in the sun's blazing glare.

The driver had returned to the cabin, and Edgar signalled to lower the rear door towards the men. It slowed to a stop when it touched the ground, and the patients appeared impervious to the sight: staring up into the ominous darkness of the trailer. In front of them, at the foot of the ramp, was a turnstile and a red light which displayed the shape of a large letter: *X.*

'We'll be good to go when it's green,' shouted Edgar, as he smiled at the officer.

From the left centre of the trailer, a panel containing several steps descended to create an entrance.

'Mr. President, if you'd like to follow me.'

Mounting the steps, the man in the overcoat followed. Edgar, still unacquainted, decided to wait for a more opportune moment to resolve the mystery of his uninvited guest.

A sensor activated the lighting inside the trailer and the president stood agape in the control booth as the equipment began to power up.

'And where would I stand inside this marvel of technological accomplishment?'

Edgar pulled a stool from beneath the desk. 'Please, Mr. President, take a seat.'

Edgar sat in the controller's high-back swivel chair. He leant forward to press several buttons on the panel in front, before looking up at the man in the overcoat.

'I'm sorry… I wasn't expecting—'

'Don't you fret none, Edgar,' interrupted the president. 'He's just fine.'

Disappointed to not uncover his identity, Edgar continued as the man with the overcoat remained aloof.

'Now, why don't we get to the matter in hand and take a look at these, *inplant*s of yours….'

Edgar lifted a flap on the control panel. 'Would you care to do the honours?'

'I guess that would depend on the honour itself…. Do I need to call Brad, over in defence?' asked the president, laughingly.

Edgar smiled, out of courtesy.

'Well then, don't mind if I do!'

The president reached across and pressed the large red button. As he did so, the sound of motors began to grind, and the floor of the ramp began to move like a conveyor belt; slowly gaining speed. The red light of the turnstile outside turned green and displayed an arrow. Edgar followed the external cameras through the monitor, clearing his throat before speaking into the microphone.

'Could you wheel the first prisoner onto the conveyor, then step back please.'

Acknowledging Edgar's command, the guard pushed the angry muzzled man through the turnstile and onto the ramp. It immediately began to transport the first patient up into the trailer.

'Of course, when we designed the mobile lab, we weren't thinking about patients—we were thinking about inmates waiting in line for release.'

'Son, I find thinking to be a highly overrated pastime... I did warn you this would be a test.'

'It's no problem, Mr. President. We can adjust the runway to grip mobility chairs. That way no guards would be needed in an operational environment.'

'You see, Edgar—solutions.... That hole in my fence ain't going to fix itself.'

Edgar continued to type on the keyboard as he spoke with the president, oblivious to the patient trying desperately to free himself from the chair; to flee from whatever horrors awaited him at the end of his ride.

'And now, everything's automated,' beamed Edgar proudly.

The patient entered the trailer. Struggling in the chair and unable to free his wrists, he shook his head violently from side to side, as Edgar and the president could hear his panic through muffled cries.

'Don't be alarmed... there's really nothing to fear.'

Edgar's efforts to calm the patient were less than half-hearted, failing to ease his anguish, or distract him from the robotic arm; its motors buzzing like the high-pitched sound of a mosquito, moving swiftly and precisely in controlled short bursts, before a hypodermic needle extended. The patient screamed in stifled terror, as the president winced and covered his eyes. Moments later, the angry man slumped in his chair; the president recovering to watch as three more robotic arms awoke and moved into position.

'It's all sensor detection,' explained Edgar. 'Lenses map the head and neck of the subject, so it doesn't matter whether they're standing or sitting—or even if they move. Once mapping is complete, the arms deploy their claws which recalibrate to firmly hold the subject in place.'

Edgar pointed to a red laser grid projected onto the head and neck of the patient. After several seconds, a red dot in the centre of the grid turned green.

'It's a scan… it correlates with the map…. When it's ready, we'll drill through the neurocranium—to gain entry to the brain.'

Another robotic arm moved into position behind the patient's head. The tip of a small drill emerged and began to rotate. As it spun, it lengthened and accelerated, moving slowly towards the green dot. The president seemed uneasy, uncomfortable in anticipation of what was to happen, and reached for a white handkerchief. He pressed it firmly to cover his nose and mouth.

'It's the bone, Mr President… the burning smell—it's just bone. Doesn't last long.'

The drill stopped suddenly and retracted, as another arm swung into view; in its grip was a tiny implant.

'The domino….'

'Do what?' asked the president. His mouth still soured by the burnt taste; his voice muted behind the cloth.

'I call them "Dominoes" because they look like domino bricks!' shouted Edgar, above the sound of the arm and the others returning to their points of origin. 'The tiny black chips… they look like dominoes.'

'I see. Yes… amusing, I'm sure,' mumbled the president queasily.

'They're held in translucent casing, if you look closely, you can see the chip inside.'

The president decided to take Edgar's word for it as his face began to pale, while the arm extended to insert the implant, before retracting at great speed. Another swung behind the patient and a nozzle ejected a fine spray, sealing the tiny hole at the back of his head.

'And that's it!' boasted Edgar. 'All done.'

The president looked astonished—astounded to put it mildly—and his hand moved away from his face.

'I'm sorry, son.... Now I was born at night, but not *last* night.... I believe you implied that you were finished with this here patient?'

'Yes, Mr. President. It takes exactly twenty-eight seconds.'

'Tw-twenty…?'

The trailer fell silent. Not a sound except for the president's deep pondering sigh. He was lost for words, suddenly reinvigorated; the colour returning to his cheeks.

'Why… why, Edgar.... Why, son… why that's—that's…. I do declare!'

'We just need to run some diagnostics then prepare the chip for imprinting.'

'Diagnostics?'

Edgar nodded. 'To ensure the cerebrospinal fluid is active and creating neural pathways once the implant has coupled.'

The baffled president, still amazed and unable to comprehend what he had just seen, despite having borne witness with his own eyes, looked at Edgar in search of explanation.

'To all four cortexes.'

The president stared blankly, hoping that Edgar would enlighten him further.

'To make sure that we have control over the brain.'

'Ah….' nodded the president. 'So—'

Edgar checked the control booth display once again. 'I'm sorry, Mr. President, but the sedative will be wearing off now. I need to….'

The patient convulsed with pain, and his face contorted in agony; his jaws were clenched, fighting to suppress his torture.

'It's ok… don't be alarmed, it's just the coupling. You have to be conscious for it to take place.'

But the patient was barely conscious; his energy reserved for suffering, not for listening to justification, and Edgar looked to the display.

'It should all be over in five… four… three… two… one.'

The trailer went dark, as if losing all power; the president jerked from the shock. Suddenly, a wall of monitors at the front of the trailer lit up and lines upon lines of code began to scroll.

'It's his brain,' said Edgar. 'You're looking at his brain.'

Another robotic arm turned to inject a syringe into the man's neck. He relaxed in an instant, no longer twisted in pain.

'It's just aspirin with a shot of Acetaminophen,' said Edgar, smiling. 'Helps with the migraine.'

'I see…. So, tell me, Edgar, if I may come to my point… our friend in the chair, is he relieved of his symptoms…? Suffice to say… cured?'

'Cured?'

'From his life of crime, son. Has he been absolved of his affliction?'

'Mr. President, you cannot cure crime. We're providing a control, not creating a cure.'

'Semantics, Edgar…. Semantics. Don't let yourself get hung up now, you hear…. If I say crime is a disease, then this here *inplant* is the cure. It's the cure because I say it is. And whatever I say it is—*it* — *is*… you follow me, son?'

Edgar ignored the urge to protest against another would-be master and nodded in agreement. There were other more pressing issues to deal with.

'Alright then. Now… tell me again… are we good here?'

'We just need to imprint, Mr. President. It's a sequence—an algorithm—that runs through the neural pathways to determine which receptors are responsible for the criminal aspects of his behaviour. The number and location of receptors differ from subject to subject, depending upon their personality and psychological makeup. It'll probably take a few seconds—for the implant to find them all and shut them down—after that, he'll be… well… cured, I guess—from his life of crime.'

The algorithm was already complete before Edgar had finished providing his explanation. Several alerts were displayed sequentially on the monitor inside the booth, each stating: *Success*. The final alert confirming: *Procedural Success: 100%.*

'You can go ahead and remove his muzzle if you wish,' said Edgar. 'He won't hurt you—he can't. He can't hurt anyone... there's not a criminal thought in his mind.'

The president glanced at the man in the overcoat.

'Now, Edgar,' the president said anxiously, 'there's no need for....' He glanced again at the man; the man nodded. 'I... I see no reason why I....'

He glanced again. The man locked eyes and nodded as before; the president unable to avert the intensity of his gaze. He shifted weight upon the stool, exhaling heavily, but his breath was shallow, as if resigned to no alternative.

'Well, I... I suppose I... I mean... I don't suppose it would do any harm...?'

The president stood, begrudgingly, and stepped out between the man in the overcoat and the control booth. Each step towards the patient was slower than the previous, prolonged by repeatedly looking back to the man who remained silent. He raised his hands as he reached for the buckle that held the muzzle in place, trying to steady them as beads of sweat began to form along his forehead. He turned one last time, and the man nodded once again. The president swallowed hard, as he stared down and slowly pulled at the strap until it eased free. A bead of sweat dripped onto the shoulders of the patient, and the muzzle loosened, slipping through the president's clammy fingers as it fell to the floor. He flinched, and his panicked scream was strangled by a sudden gasp for air.

'Wh-what happened...? Where am I?' asked the bewildered patient. His eyes were drowsy as he tried to turn, then looked to see his wrists still bound to the chair. 'What...? Why am I...?' He stared up at the man beside him. 'Who are you...? How... how did I get here?'

The president's face, anxious and apprehensive, transformed to relief. He turned excitedly and shouted to the booth. 'Well, what are you waiting for, Edgar? Time's a wasting, son. Get the next one in here!'

Edgar pressed a flashing orange button, and the chair carried forward as the rolling floor began to move. The patient peered at the control booth, staring through the Perspex as he passed: struggling continually to free his wrists.

'No... wait... please... please help me.... Somebody, please help me!'

'It's over now. You're going to be fine,' said Edgar reassuringly.

The track of the floor split, transporting the patient towards a smaller conveyor belt at the front right side of the trailer. Edgar spoke into the microphone with instruction of where to expect the patient, who descended gently and exited out into the courtyard; the guard avidly awaiting his arrival. One by one they entered, and one by one they left: cured. Three minutes was all that it took for rehabilitation, for a convict to be free from transgression and a life of crime. After a little more than half an hour, the final patient was returned. Edgar, the man in the overcoat, and an elated president, were alone.

'I do believe that I am speechless... unable to articulate myself in a fashion that is becoming for a man of my disposition,' exclaimed the president, unable to stay seated or contain his enthusiasm. 'You do realise, son, what has happened? Here.... Today?

'We are sitting on the greatest discovery since mankind first created fire!

'Why, just imagine, a world without crime—without criminality—where criminals and culprits can no longer exist.... A world without murder, Edgar. Where the law is absolute, and crime is obsolete.'

Edgar remained calm, watching as the president spoke compulsively.

'My boy, I find myself confounded—thunderstruck, no less. For I see before me now a vision... a prophecy... and behold... the greatest president this country has *ever* known.... The president who took our great nation back from the hands of our oppressors. Who said crime is a disease and we have found its cure! And for that—you mark my words—they won't ask me... they'll *beg* me to remain as president until the day that I die....

'By golly you've done it, son—*we've* – done – it!'

'People are going to remember us for generations to come. Why, they'll change the Constitution—rip up the amendments—and you know why? Because we won't need them, that's why!'

It was clear that the president had ambitions.

'So,' he said, as he slapped his hands together and rubbed his palms, 'tell me now, Edgar—man to man—how fast can we move on this?'

'Well, Mr. President, this mobile laboratory was designed for the trial... but I have one hundred trucks that are almost—'

The president was not interested in what Edgar had or did not have and interrupted to make his ambitions more explicitly clear.

'We'll need a thousand—and we'll need them on the road tomorrow. You understand?

'I want them in Tucson... I want them in Kansas. I want them in Beaumont. I want them in Atlanta. In Chicago. Loretto. Miami. Houston. Phoenix. Philadelphia. Cumberland. Oklahoma. California. I want them everywhere.... You hear me, Edgar?

'I want them in every prison, penitentiary, detention centre, and correctional institution across this country... and I don't care what it takes or what you have to do.... This thing's hotter than a preacher's knee and I intend to free these men from their sin!

'Now you get me a thousand of these trucks on the road, Edgar. I won't hear no excuses. You'll get everything you need—anything you want—but I want to see those trucks on the road.

'This time next year, I mean to address the good people of these here United States and tell them that this land is our land—that crime is a concept we no longer recognise. That I have eradicated its existence.'

'But, Mr. President... it will cost billions....'

The president smirked.

'*Cost...?* My dear boy, you may be some kind of a genius—to be sure—but you only got one oar in the water.... You see your little old dominoes there are never going to cost a dime—they're going to *save* billions... trillions, in point of fact—for the American taxpayer.

'Semantics, son... like I told you... don't go getting yourself all hung up in semantics.'

He walked over to one of the robotic arms, before cautiously touching the end of one of the grips. Still apprehensive, he was very much in awe. 'Incredible, Edgar... it's just incredible... I truly am impressed, son.... Now you're sure we can track them...? Do all the things that you promised with The FORT Program?'

'Of course, Mr. President. Please, allow me.'

Edgar squeezed past the man in the overcoat, who refused to move. He went to another terminal outside the control booth and began typing on the keyboard. The monitor awoke and displayed nine blinking red dots clustered together on a map. To the right of them, a list.

'Serial numbers,' said Edgar, pointing at the list. 'We can follow any implant from here in real-time.... I can zoom in on any location and get its exact geographical co-ordinates. Or I can pull up the profile of the host subject and cross reference this with any criminal files if needed.'

'And if a crime is committed...?'

'There's a failsafe. If a crime is reported, the system traces any implants in the vicinity and plots them so we can map any potential suspects.'

'Uh-huh... and how do we observe these "suspects" of yours?'

'We don't.'

The president paused; he frowned with displeasure. 'Seems I'm deaf in one ear and can't hear out of the other, because I specifically recall asking you *how* we observe these suspects... not *if*, Doctor.'

'We don't observe anything, Mr. President—the system does... everything's automated. Files and logs update dynamically so that in the event of crime, the system alerts us. That way we don't have to use resources in monitoring.'

'I see... I apologise for my ineptitude.... And security...? How are we on security?'

'End-to-end. Montgomery countermeasures to circumvent any side-channel threat.'

Edgar looked to the president; he had that same confused expression of ignorance that showed no real understanding of his work—his brilliance. He tried again, this time to explain simply.

'Every terminal is both hard and software encrypted.'

The president remained blank. That he should make light when he understood nothing; when things had to be explained to him like a child was exasperating for Edgar. He tired of the tedious questions. He knew that the trial was a resounding success and was safe in the knowledge that he was now irreplaceable. It was time to underline that fact and put an end to this tarrying.

'Basically, nothing gets through—not even air.... So, should we go back inside and examine our subjects?'

The president glanced nervously at the man in the overcoat, who was in no apparent hurry to move.

'Connections?' he asked. His voice like gravel, like the feel of a shingle beach: coarse and harsh.

Edgar was taken aback.

'Connections?' repeated the man; his ice-cold glare unsettling Edgar.

'Erm... c-connections...? Well... there... there are none... no externals... except for one—from the mobile unit to the servers at DomiGen Labs of course, but that's ECC and hardware—'

'I wasn't asking about your truck.'

'Sorry...?'

'How many external connections at DomiGen Labs?'

'Excuse me?' asked Edgar, round-eyed in amazement.

'Connections?'

'That's none of your—'

'Now, Edgar.... We're all on the same side here. Just answer the question,' said the president.

Edgar was displeased and unwilling to be forthcoming. He glanced at the man whose eyes remained upon him, then glared at the president. 'And what side is that?' he asked.

'Why the only side that matters, of course,' replied the president with a smile. His southern charm no longer warm, but decidedly chilled and unnerving.

Edgar looked away, pouting with annoyance as his eyes considered the trailer. No choice other than to confess. 'None...' he said as the word dragged from his lips. 'We're a private enterprise and we secure our—'

'Not anymore.'

'Not anymore what...?'

Angry at being snubbed; his attempt to be amicable already assumed. Edgar turned again to the president. 'I'm sorry, but if you think I'm going to allow—'

'Now, now, Edgar... let's not get all het up about this.... What I believe my esteemed friend here is trying to say... is that no one is asking for access to your data.'

The president raised his eyebrow and lowered his head slightly. Edgar's animosity towards the changing terms of their agreement was ever more obvious. His face said it all.

'This wasn't part of any deal! The contract for The DomiGen FORT Program was to provide information—*not* to give real-time access to it.... If the federal bureau needs a secure connection, then I suggest—'

'The bureau is not involved in this project,' interrupted the man.

'Then *who* are you...? CIA? NSA?'

The man stayed silent. The question, unanswered. The air uneasy, as the president intervened once again. 'Who he is, is of no importance, Edgar. What is, is where we find ourselves... at the edge of the precipice—on the verge, so to speak. So, allow me to cut through the red tape... avoid a nasty fall.'

Edgar shook his head. 'I won't give—'

'Edgar, son,' interrupted the president, as he took a step forward and placed his hand upon Edgar's shoulder. 'Try to understand. This discovery of yours, why it's too great a burden for any one man to bear. As your president and commander in chief, it would be ill advised—irresponsible even—of me to allow you to keep this kind of power to yourself.

'Now, take some time, but don't take it to heart. This here ain't personal, it's business... how we get things done. And we'll be needing access to your data. In the *real-time*, of course.'

Edgar shrugged and freed his shoulder from the president's hand. The grip, an unpleasant reminder of his former master, the monster who once warned him to be wary of the politicians; that glorified mob out for a hustle. Resentment raged beyond control, and control was all that Edgar had: it was everything to him and all that he was unwilling to lose. The man in the coat pulled out a tablet and placed it onto the desktop.

'Passwords?'

His voice—what he asked for, what he wanted—was gasoline to Edgar, and the flames of rage ignited by the president's demands, were fanned as Edgar erupted like lava from a volcano.

'*What* – did – you – say?'

Untouched by his heat, untroubled by his tone, the man was unthreatened by Edgar.

'Firewall and network.'

Edgar looked at the tablet, at the hand that held it and the tattoo that was partially concealed by the cuff of the man's shirt. A tattoo that looked strangely familiar; a sequence of numbers or symbol perhaps, not unlike one he once saw long ago. Awaiting his answer, the man could see that Edgar was absent, his eyes locked elsewhere, and he pulled his sleeve to cover the distraction.

'Firewall access and network codes.'

Edgar said nothing; defiant and unwilling to surrender.

'Now, son,' implored the president. 'I can appreciate that this is not easy, but you are doing your country a great service…. No one is taking anything away from you here. On the contrary, why, this will allow us to work more closely—strength in numbers, and so forth.'

Edgar, however, was unable to see, "strength in numbers," what he saw was an ambush. The loss of control.

'Last chance—firewall access and network codes.'

He gritted his teeth. He would never relinquish control of DomiGen, not after everything he had gone through to gain it. Nothing could force the codes from him, and nobody was going to, because no one would dictate the terms of his work. Those that had tried, had failed. The president was right. They were at the edge of the precipice, but there was room only for one, and Edgar had not climbed this far to come in second or to share in the rewards. His palms clenched into fists at the thought; the whites of his knuckles shining through the skin, as the urge to unleash them grew stronger with each second that passed. His teeth ground harder, and he raised his eyes slightly from the floor, to be sure of his standing before attempting his lunge. He took a breath, it was deep, but he would use it, then raised his fist. Suddenly, he froze. Not willingly. Something was wrong….

The man's coat was amiss: it was shorter on the right. Not by much, just enough to notice. Edgar glanced upwards and spied a bulge; a holster, for all that he knew. Any thoughts of resistance or hopes of reprisal were dashed. How could he withhold anything now? He was stood in a trailer filled with equipment that should not exist. Parked on federal land, in a prison he was not supposed to be in. Conducting experiments, using technology that was illegal in every sense of the word. He had no cell phone or personal items with him; they were still inside. So, if the president wanted him to disappear, this was the perfect time. No one would ever know how, or why, or where he was, because the driver sitting upfront in the cabin—his only witness—was even more dispensable.

Edgar stepped forward and tapped a sequence of numbers into the tablet. He looked up, his eyes the colour of indignation, and stared at the man. Who was he…?

The man tapped the enter key, and the screen flashed as a script executed to confirm connection. 'It's done,' he said.

Edgar's head dropped. Control was lost.

'Now that's what I wanted to see, Edgar—the spirit of cooperation. I knew I could rely on you, son…. A true patriot, such as yourself.' The president smiled smugly. 'My office will confirm the first hundred destinations by this evening. You just send them trucks out, soon as they're ready, you hear…? And place an order for more— for nine hundred more. Don't you worry none about them funds. You'll have all that you need.

'It's time, Edgar. Time to make a change. You and I, why, we're blowing them winds of change, son.'

The man lifted the tablet and placed it inside his overcoat. He nodded to the president, who turned one last time to Edgar.

'You know, what we have achieved here is magnificent. Truly. A wonderment you might say. Apropos, just remember, once we let the cat out the bag, ain't no putting it back. You need to understand that—what that entails… the consequences of our actions. You follow me, son?'

Edgar stared at the president. He didn't follow, he didn't follow at all, and the man in the overcoat left the trailer just as he had entered: surreptitiously.

'You might not feel like it now, but you're the man of the hour, Edgar. Mark my words... why, there's a Presidential Medal of Freedom just waiting for you. Name's all shiny and new.'

A secret service agent entered the trailer. 'Mr. President, we need to get you in the air, sir.'

While Edgar stood confused, the president took his leave.

'Be keeping tabs on you, son—watching your progress. So, don't go letting me down now... now that I'm counting on you. Now that we all are—you and your... DomiGen Mobile Labs....'

The president shook Edgar's hand to bid farewell and slapped him on the shoulder; a final reminder that he would watch over it, always.

'Carry on,' he said, before following the agent down the steps.

Edgar slumped onto the stool and listened as the sound of rotor blades warmed up outside. Sand and grit were whipped almost immediately into the air; they began to fill the open trailer. He raced to the override switch inside the panel; slamming it hard, as he tried to quickly raise the steps and rear to minimise any damage from the flying debris. He looked out: the dust formed thick clouds, forcing him to cover his eyes. As he squinted at the cyclone that encircled the helicopter, he saw the bright orange prison uniforms of what he believed were the nine test subjects being loaded into the back of Marine One.

Once in the air, the dust began to settle, and Edgar watched with wider eyes as the helicopter faded into the horizon. He stood alone and glowered at the sky, thinking about the man; how men with things to hide never have much to say, only secrets to be told. The trial was the start, and this was far from the end. They would meet again. He brushed the sand from his hair and the dust from his coat, then made his way back to collect his belongings and those of his driver. As he neared the entrance of the facility, a hand reached out and grasped his forearm. He stopped, surprised, to see who was hurting him.

'Beware....' the warden said grimly.

'Excuse me?'

'Beware, Edgar.'

'Look, I really do need to get going—and it's Dr. Spear. So, if you don't mind....'

Not wanting to waste time listening to whatever the warden had to say, Edgar tried unsuccessfully to pull his arm away.

'Now look... I don't know if the sun has got to you, but—'

'War is coming.'

'What...? Let me go! I'll call the president when I—'

'Beware, Edgar.... Soon the time will come when you must face your fears... embrace your destiny, for a war is coming. A war you cannot escape.'

Edgar stared in bemusement at the warden who spoke with such conviction. The warden said nothing more, releasing his grip before he turned to walk away in the opposite direction. Edgar was free but continued to gape.

'You're on the wrong side of the bars,' he shouted, as the warden disappeared around the corner of a detainment block. 'You should be in there—with them!'

Edgar brushed his sleeve. His arm was sore from the touch, and he went inside to collect his things.

The short forty-minute drive back to Boston gave little time to digest the extraordinary events of the day. Perplexed more than provoked, he decided to return home rather than to DomiGen, and locked himself in his apartment; with the lights off, the darkness seemed to suit his mood.

Since the only objective was to prove that his implants worked, Edgar was unwilling to complicate matters back at Saven. Nevertheless, nothing about the trial felt right, even the inmate selection struck him as peculiar. Fifteen minutes he was told. That was all the warning the warden would receive in advance. Just fifteen minutes to pluck out nine test subjects and prepare them for the trial. If I were the warden, thought Edgar, and learned that the president was to arrive shortly—to observe a top-secret experiment—would I really have time, much less be able to not only select, but assemble such a motley and high maintenance group of criminals? Fifteen minutes was not long to prepare nine individual patients and transport them from their cells; especially those who required restraints, muzzles, medication, and chairs. Wouldn't it have made more sense for the warden to have simply chosen the most straightforward, least troublesome prisoners? Why a congressman, a drug lord, a lieutenant in the Russian mafia, a mobster from the Giamatti crime family, and Donny DeMarco: *The Italian Bullet,* as he was better known?

When Edgar arrived, the warden was clearly unhappy and complaining about the time that he had been given before the start of the trial. Yet the president almost seemed to expect DeMarco in the line-up. How was that possible? Had he interfered, perhaps even controlled the selection process? Why…? DeMarco was perhaps the most infamous hitman who had ever lived. No one knew exactly how many people he had killed, although estimates ranged from a few hundred to numbers not unlike the population of a small Mediterranean island. These were not your average everyday criminals; these were all serious offenders. They were heavy hitters within the gangster underworlds, each serving multiple concurrent life sentences. As the president said, "the worst of a bad bunch." But they were also perpetrators who would never gain parole, which meant they were never actual candidates for an implant. So, perhaps the real question was not who picked them, but rather why were they handpicked specifically, and why were they picked at all?

Stranger still was the location. Why were the test subjects chosen from a federal medical centre and not a penitentiary, when inmates requiring specialised health care represent less than one percent of the incarcerated population? Was this why the president asked if they were "cured"? What he meant, or implied when he said, "consequences of our actions"? Because it sounded more like a warning, rather than the acclaim usually given to someone of outstanding achievement, such as a doctor curing the world of crime.

Then there was the warden; his premonition of the "war" that was coming, surely the ravings of a lunatic? Though nothing was more disconcerting than the man in the overcoat. The man who clearly pulled the president's strings and now tugged at Edgar's.

Edgar had tried to trace the location of the test subjects; curious to see where they were being taken. Despite his search, their implants were not transmitting any signal. It was as if they had simply vanished into thin air. Of course, that would have been impossible. Even so, they were gone. Those men were either dead, or someone had removed them from the DomiGen system. Was it the man in the overcoat? What was he hiding; was it more than just his tattoo? The design was so distinctive, that it had to be the same as the man from Domino's bar, the man with the missing finger, whose face Edgar never saw. Yet the man with the president seemed younger, and all of his fingers were intact. So, if it wasn't him, who was it? And what did the tattoo symbolise? Was it an emblem of sorts? An insignia from "the only side that matters"?

Edgar thought back to that night, to when the man spoke, the only time he ever saw fear in Abelman. It was the same look that the president had today. He realised now, however, that he was wrong. It wasn't fear, it was something else, something more. Like the timid look a mistreated dog gives its master—easy to mistake as obedience, when in reality, it is the sufferance of dominion.

There was something very strange about this whole affair, too many questions for Edgar to resolve, and wherever there was smoke, there was usually a fire. He would find its flame and extinguish his concerns, if that's what it took to avoid getting burned; to prevent losing more to the mysterious scourge and the presidential puppet constrained at his side.

13

JACKPOT

When the president announced that The DomiGen FORT Program was to be abandoned, the last remaining protests that saw the program as an infringement of human rights, subsided. However, anything new or challenging to existing norms is usually first met with scepticism. So, when the president then announced a new bill, for the Declaration of Organised Geographical Monitoring and Assurance, or "DOGMA," as it was to be called, a fresh wave of opposition unsurprisingly exploded across the country. The very idea of using implants in human beings to monitor their location was a frightening thought, and as many of the protesters argued, the first step towards totalitarianism: a dictatorial state. Having said that, the rioting served only to reinforce the president's point. Crime escalated, and drastic measures were needed to curb the violence that was now commonplace.

Lobbying throughout Congress was accelerated by the president's impending threat to resort to the use of military action. Time was of the essence. If Congress was unwilling to act, then he would have no choice other than to deploy army personnel, in order to "safeguard, support and defend the nation." Such rhetoric was of course a sly use of language, a selection of carefully chosen words that allowed the president to bypass various obstacles—legislation such as the Posse Comitatus Act—that would grant him powers to place soldiers on the streets of every city, town, and suburb in America. The House of Representatives and the Senate were paralysed, torn between endangering the lives of their own citizens, and the need to stem the ongoing anarchy that continued through increased rioting. Despite every advice, the president refused to drop his bill. With no option or viable alternative, both the House and the Senate were bullied into submission. Less than four months after the trial at Saven, the DOGMA bill was passed: the DOGMA Act had become law.

During the turbulent uprising, Edgar's fleet of trucks had continued with their work and travelled across the country. Undeterred, merely slowed by the turmoil and the armed escorts that were deemed necessary, the DomiGen Mobile Labs had processed close to two hundred thousand convicted criminals, with not a single crime reported by their hosts. The implants were very much a success, but then their strengths were never the issue, only the morality of using them. In a bid to counter the critics, a flood of national addresses by the president had centred upon providing statistics to ease the fears of the American people. Each address made it harder for opponents to argue against the facts: figures that conclusively showed crime was decreasing rapidly by the day. With released convicts committing fewer crimes than ever, it became easy for the president to manipulate the moralist argument. He pointed the finger of recent crime waves squarely towards the protesters themselves; that unruly segment of society who played upon civil rights and liberties. Those who in truth were solely committed to rebellion and insurgence. At least, that was how it looked, because with the power of the media behind him, that was how the president made it look.

In the months that followed, the DomiGen fleet expanded its reach with over eight hundred vehicles, and as the numbers of paroled convicts with implants could only increase, there was simply no way to stop DOGMA. Rioters lost support, and any sympathies they once had were replaced by public outrage; anger that this group of individuals sought only to disrupt the lives and livelihoods of good honest hard-working people. The fickle nature of politics was exposed, and the president, the man once hated with such profusion, was now proclaimed a saviour. He was the man who kept faith while the many lost theirs. The one who saw hope when all others saw none. And the hand whose steely determination was the only thing that carried them through. He was the shepherd—the leader of his flock—and like a shepherd, the president cared only for the well-being of his sheep, even when they could not see it for themselves. He was more liked, more loved, more popular, and more powerful than ever. After all, the DOGMA Act had the most honourable of intentions and was championed by the most honourable of men. It was for the benefit of all, the improvement of public safety, and as much for the children of today, as it was for their children of tomorrow. With such self-less motivation, how could any objection realistically persist?

The rioting subsided and loyalties dwindled in ranks; the few hardliners that remained appeared to abandon their cause, as they retreated and went underground. Crime not only declined, it literally stopped overnight. Petty crimes vanished almost entirely, and the numbers of more serious, more violent crimes, had plummeted to an all-time low. Public spending was down, because police investigations, prosecutions, court cases and appeals were down. There were fewer inmates as increasing numbers of convicts were released, and new incarcerations had become less frequent. Prisons began to close. Police departments reduced in size, and the role of the detective became symbolic rather than significant in any investigative capacity. It was no understatement that apart from all but eradicating wrongdoing, the DOGMA Act had seemingly changed law and order forever.

In a bid to capitalise on his monumental popularity, the president decided to run for re-election. "Four more years.... Four more years," came the chant and successful cry of his supporters once the result was announced. The majority went further, questioning how four more years could possibly be enough; that changes needed to be made to the Constitution, just as they had been made to law, in order to keep him in the White House. For now, the boastful sentiments of the president—once shared with Edgar—were echoed in reality. The United States of America was as close to utopia as mankind had ever come; from the outside, at least. Nobel Prizes and humanitarian awards succeeded only in drawing further attention to the DOGMA Act, causing nations around the world to take greater notice. A consensus had begun to form, the technology needed to be shared; the reason being, that only after reducing crime on a global scale, would children everywhere have a brighter, safer future.

It was almost five years since Edgar's first successful implant: that evening when he managed to gain control over Abelman. To Edgar, it felt like a lifetime ago, and in light of everything that had happened since then, it was. So much had changed. DomiGen Labs had grown from a start-up to becoming the biggest and most successful private company in America, arguably the world. It had launched The Ally, The Scout, and then moved on to implants. It was now worth hundreds of billions of dollars, just as Abelman once said it would be. Yet there was no Abelman, no sign of Munro. Behind it all was Edgar, the mysterious young recluse who was called by many names: *"The tail that wagged the dog.... The hand behind the wheel.... The seed that grew the tree."* There were hundreds of metaphors that were used to describe him and the influence that DomiGen Labs had on modern culture. Perhaps because crime influences everything—in some way touches everyone—so when crime began to wither and communities began to flourish, DomiGen Labs became synonymous with it all. Edgar, however, paid little interest to the media. He paid no mind to hearsay and saw no need to respond to claims or furnish them further with gossip or fodder. The fact was, that crime in America was all but abolished, and that was all that mattered to Edgar's commander in chief.

Initial fears that hosts might come to suffer side effects or succumb to neurological disorders were adjudged to be unfounded. Implants were safe, stable, and if DomiGen continued on schedule, then in two days' time there would be five million hosts in the United States. Five million was an incredible achievement, a landmark that the president wanted to toast and exploit further for his own popularity. He demanded a media event. A chance to blow his own horn. An opportunity to exaggerate his contribution to DOGMA and continue to take all of the honour for its success. It would be an event more akin to a rally than a stereotypical presidential address. More about generating enthusiasm and excitement, rather than committing to any realistic promises; the usual pledges for greatness or change. In other words, the kind of thing that Edgar hated and tried to avoid at all costs. Nevertheless, he was summoned to Washington once again; the president wanting to discuss his ideas on how to maximise the opportunity as a way to take his presidency forward. Edgar was sceptical. The president had never sought his advice before, and he suspected pretence—an ulterior motive behind the request.

Hannah's cheeks flushed as Edgar entered the lobby. He winked.

'Good morning, Dr. Spear. He's waiting for you in the Oval Office.'

It was easy to see why Hannah was the West Wing receptionist. Her broad infectious smile lit the dark and heavy furniture. It whitened the walls that owed their dreary shade of beige to the drab yellow glow of the incandescent table lamps. She was always there, behind her desk. Her fingers playfully tucking the right side of her flowing brown hair back behind her ear, revealing more of the welcome that warmed and awaited visitors whenever the doors opened.

Edgar smiled wryly. 'Then I suppose I'd better hurry. Wouldn't do to keep him waiting... would it?'

He made his way towards the room, flanked by a secret service agent who apologised once they reached the doors. 'I'm sorry, Edgar, you know the drill.'

'I know,' he replied, as he raised his arms, holding out his cell phone and keys. 'So, did Billy make the team?'

The agent began to pat down Edgar. 'Nah, some kid from upstate got in.'

'Shame... maybe next year then?'

'I don't know. Might be time to call it quits—find something he's good at.'

'It'll work out, George.... You'll see... one of these days.'

'Sure, one of these days. Now you sound like Brenda!'

George placed the items into the bowl on the small accent table. 'Right here for you when you're done, Edgar.'

Edgar smiled. George whispered into a microphone attached to the cuff of his sleeve before tapping the door twice. The door opened from the inside, and George nodded to Edgar who stepped into the open doorway.

'Why, Edgar.... Good to see you, son.'

'Mr. President.'

'Well come on in now and sit yourself down... draught's creeping in like a vine on a barnyard wall.'

Edgar took another step forward, and the door closed as he entered the room.

'You're looking well, Mr. President,' said Edgar, trying to engage in the formal pleasantries.

'Thank you, gentlemen. That'll be all.'

The president flicked his hand to dismiss three men engaged in discussion; they sat either side of the small coffee table, their folders open to show pages of scribblings and jotted notes. As they scrambled to collect their effects, Edgar walked towards the president who was stood behind the Resolute desk, and he sat down opposite. The president continued to stand. His arms were folded, shirt sleeves rolled above his elbows, and he smiled broadly, waiting until they were alone.

'Ok, Edgar…. Now, what say we cut the crap, and save the smiles for the cameras? I know the British and the Canadians both want our—'

His suspicions confirmed, Edgar had no need to listen to the belligerent bellyaching of the president looming over him, and he interrupted to break news that would add further to his misery.

'The French and Australians as well… just this morning my secretary received a call from President Xao Lee.'

'The Koreans…? Now you looky here, Edgar, I will not….'

The president paused in his ranting for a moment, as he considered the South Korean interest. He tapped the desk, his fingertips loud, then suddenly, and quite unexpectedly, his face scowled as he swept his hand across it in a blinding fit of rage. The back of his palm struck a pen, and it flew like an arrow across the room with such force that the tip became lodged in the door. In less than a second it opened, and an agent stood with her weapon already drawn.

'Mr. President. Is everything alright, sir?'

The startled president, well-trained in the art of Machiavellianism, looked up with a forced smile already in place. 'What seems to be troubling you, my dear?'

'I heard the door, sir, and—'

'Just a draught… old rooms, is all… ain't no cause for alarm.'

'Very good, sir.'

The agent nodded as she noticed the pen embedded in the door. She glanced at Edgar and closed it anyway. Alone again, the president quickly lost his smile and found his forked tongue.

'Seems I remain unclear…? Obtuse in the explanation of certain details, Edgar…. What you might call, the *understanding* of our relationship. You see, you need to understand, DOGMA is *mine* and it belongs to the people of these here United States. You don't negotiate for the people, Edgar... I do... and if any country wants to use *my* – *inplants*.... Well, then they have to negotiate with me—it's as simple as that, son.'

Edgar raised his eyebrow. *'Your* implants?'

'Mine. And don't you *ever* forget it!' scolded the president. 'Bought and paid for by the taxpayers of our great nation.'

Edgar remained silent. The president, aware that it was he who had raised his voice, took a deep breath and tried to appear more presidential. 'Now, Edgar... come on, son,' he said, slathering Edgar with his southern charm. 'We're old friends you and I... ain't got cause for no quarrelling.... We rely on each other—need one another—to do our upmost.... To do what needs to be done—to do what's right.'

'And what is, "right," Mr. President?'

The president sat down and leaned back in his chair; it squeaked loudly, muffling his troubled sigh, as his face turned solemn.

'The United States is the greatest country in the world, Edgar—point of fact—ask anyone. But we're not the land of hopes and dreams... we're the land of ambition and achievement. And what we've achieved here, is nothing short of a miracle. Now, nothing starts as a miracle, son, and just because a chicken has wings, don't mean it can fly.

'Make no mistake, Doctor, what started here was belief—the wisdom of foresight.... Why, it was nothing less than intervention from the divine... credence, when all around me had none. When even my own administration cast doubt on my ability to lead this country. But I kept my faith—believed in the Lord... though more in myself I must confess.... Closed my ears to the naysayers, because that's what achievers do. I showed them ambition and rewarded them with triumph. Now, look at my creation... go on, Edgar, look around you... for it is I who have created a miracle!

'No one is laughing at me now... no sir. To the contrary, the world looks upon our nation with their beady eyes of envy and greed. They see what we have, and they want it too—believe they have the right. But they are wrong. They have not earned that right. It is I who have earned that right... and that right is *mine—mine* alone, you understand?'

The president leaned slowly forward. Edgar's eyes narrowed; his brow knitted as his face screamed for an end to the misery. When the chair stopped moving, the president placed his elbows upon the desk.

'What I am trying to impart, is that we need to gain a little perspective—is all. Now, I've made you a very wealthy man... one of the richest I dare say... I imagine in all actuality, that you can damn near buy anything you want. But the fact of the matter remains, Edgar.... You may own that little old laboratory of yours, but you seem to forget who owns you? That privilege... why, that belongs to *me, son.*'

The president clasped his hands and glared fiercely at Edgar.

'We got us a good thing going, and I don't see no reason to spoil that.... You need to remember that almost eighty percent of all criminals in this country have a DomiGen *inplant*... and they have that *inplant* because I say they can.... You get your orders from me, son. That's the chain of command.... You might be my loaded gun, Edgar, but don't you *ever* forget who pulls the trigger around here.

'If the Koreans, or even the Queen of England herself want my *inplants,* then I will require something in return... quid pro quo... you understand?'

Edgar remained calm, unprovoked by the president's narcissism; his feeble attempts to intimidate while reminding him about the facts of life.

'In return?'

The president paused to clear his throat. His stare, like his voice, deepened. 'A little outside your area of expertise, Edgar.... Not exactly your field of knowledge—in a manner of speaking.' He paused again before raising his head, and their eyes unlocked. 'What I will tell you—out of respect for our friendship—is that a new bill will soon be drafted for Congress to vote upon. One that will... extend the reach of my powers.... Provide me with the mandate that I need to be able to carry on my work. You might even say—fulfil my destiny.'

'*Your destiny?*' gasped Edgar in astonishment.

'To become the greatest president this country has ever known. The greatest leader this world has ever seen.... I assure you, Edgar, I *will* go down in history as the man who saved mankind!'

The president paused again before lowering his hands and rising from his chair. He turned and stepped towards the centre bay window with his back towards Edgar.

'We've strived in earnest, you and I... endured the hardship of our endeavours... but everything in this life comes to its end... and everything must end—eventually. Why, it's inevitable... as sure as the sun will set and rise over them lawns out yonder. The only question that remains—that we must *all* ask ourselves—is not what we will do when it does, but what can we do before it is...?

'Life and business... well, they're not so different, are they...? Every life ends when our time is done, and every partnership ends when the deal is done. You see, it's all the same—in the end, only the end *is* inevitable.

'Now... we've achieved great things, Edgar. More than most men could ever dream of. Makes this all the more... troublesome... painful no less... seeing as there's just no easy way to say what needs to be said.'

The president appeared to heave a sigh. 'The time has come for the sun to set on our partnership. For DOGMA to enter its second phase.'

'S-sorry... second...?'

He turned to face Edgar who was still sat in his chair, aghast and appalled at what he was hearing. His head was spinning—face ashen—unable to disguise his shock.

'Well... aren't you precious?' said the president, as he smirked and looked down disparagingly at him. 'Five million, Edgar... I am days away from five million *inplants*.... By the end of the year, it'll be six. The inmates that linger, are those who will *never* be allowed to walk freely amongst us again—I'll see to that. Those poor souls, so consumed by their dreadful disease that no matter our certainty... no matter our belief... we should not cure them—we must not, and I *will* not. Why, they are evil incarnate. The scum of our society. Even their own mothers can't recognise them....

'You may not like who I am, or what I represent, but can't – never – could, never got no one nowhere.

'Lest we forget, Edgar, it is I who have brought peace, and I who have brought order to our great nation.... I have brought these things as far as any man could possibly bring them... further than any mortal man before me has even dared try—ever been able to achieve or come close to accomplish. The only logical step forward, is to secure the safety of our patriots wherever they may be.... To offer the world my gift of peace, so there may be order, everywhere. But it is I who will offer this gift... I who will decide who is worthy to receive this miracle of a crime-free society. And no leader of any land—or pretender to my throne—will ever dictate the terms of the freedom that I will grant upon their people.

'Now, these foreign interests in my program... you're little... confabulations.... Well, they've forced my hand... applied certain pressures, in a manner of speaking.

'You see, when my predecessor allowed your friend—James Munro—to grow his business unsupervised, the United States government learnt an invaluable lesson. We can *never* allow a private interest to become so big, that it becomes bigger than the government itself. After all, free enterprise without restriction... why, that's the American Dream right there! But we don't live in dreams, Edgar. You and I, we live in the real world, and in the real world, how could I ever keep someone such as yourself on a leash...?

'Fact remains... when Munro was dragged before Congress, it was already too late.... The boy made fools of us all. He made a mockery of this office, and I will not be made a fool of, son.... My authority will *not* be undermined.'

The president turned back towards the bay windows and stared out to the lawn.

'Edgar, I say with all certitude, that DomiGen cannot be allowed to provide *inplants* to the world as a private company. It must, and it *will*, become a part of my administration.... It has a higher purpose and one far beyond your understanding of dollars and dimes. DomiGen will be owned by the American people, and as the duly elected leader of those people, it will be controlled and governed by *this* office.'

The president stood, listening carefully. He spied Edgar's reflection in the glass and watched as he awaited response. There was nothing: no attack from behind following his ruthless provocation, and Edgar sat quietly, to the president's bemusement.

'I know what you're thinking,' he said, first to break the lengthy silence. 'Don't you worry none, Edgar. I guarantee you'll be well taken care of.... Make sure you have all the money you could ever want... after all... fortune should favour the brave.'

However, the president was mistaken. Edgar wasn't worried, he was speechless. He listened to every word, every pathetic excuse and justification for why DomiGen was being taken from him. He knew the game and the rules to play by; that the glorified mob would take their share. He just never imagined they had planned to take it all.

'You have done your country a great service, son. I will not forget that. But from here on in your services will no longer be required....'

Edgar continued to sit in silence, and the president continued to study his reflection; certain that his latest remark would push him over the edge. He could no longer stand with his back turned—not under the threat of retaliation—and he pivoted to look Edgar directly in the eye. Like a gunslinger expecting his rival's twitch, their stare stayed locked as the president slammed both hands—palms down—upon the table, stooping him forward. Still, there was nothing, not a blink from Edgar; the attempt to intimidate so easily foiled. Silence grew to discomfort and focused the president's failure. He was anxious, that was obvious, and becoming ever more so.

'I know you got your tail up,' he said, trying to deflect from his defeat. Yet his voice was taut, quavering as he spoke, and his pride choked further with every word. Suddenly, he blinked, and their stare was broken. The contest was lost. No place for second or the loser of a gunfight; his anxiety was slain and all that was left became incensed.

'Don't you *rile* me, son!' he screamed. 'Now I have tried to accommodate the sensitivity of your circumstance... your feelings on the matter... but I will *not* tolerate your insolence any further!'

The president yanked his chair and sat down, scowling at Edgar as he banged his fist hard upon the desk. A door opened, and another agent stood, weapon drawn once again.

'Get out!' he raged; his southern temperament gone astray. The agent stepped back and closed the door. The president's wrath returned to Edgar.

'Let me paint you a clear picture—something that's guaranteed to hold your attention.... By the time I order my security detail to drag you out of this office, your computers won't have a folder or a file... let alone an operating system to run them. Every bit and byte of data at DomiGen is being transferred to a secure federal facility, as we speak. I have authorised the use of several satellites to assist in the transfer—to ensure that *every* line of code is copied and stored on *our* network... before it is removed from the hard drives on *yours.*'

The president glared at Edgar; his nostrils flaring, expecting response. There was none.

'Hmm... cat still got your tongue...? Well, let's see if I can help with your impediment.' He reached for a remote control, and a large painting on the wall beside Edgar changed to display eight different camera views.

'Live body cams,' he snapped, as he threw the remote across the desk, not intending to strike Edgar. 'Those gentlemen are from Delta

Force… removing all the storage devices and backup copies from your residence…. We already have those from your office…. You see that thermal imaging…? Why, that detects even those little memory sticks that you've stowed away and tried to hide.'

Edgar continued to remain calm, like a coiled rattlesnake: dangerous at the best of times. The president had poked and provoked him for so long that he was likely to lash out at any unsuspecting moment. With emotions buried deep until now, the invasion of his home was a step too far; it was the cowardly act of a cowardly man. Edgar's face, chiselled in stone, finally cracked, as the first signs of displeasure crept into his eyes. It was a dangerous game that the president played. All the same, assured of control and the vanquish of Edgar, he lowered his guard with his confidence restored.

'Now, I tried to play nice—to do right by you, Edgar—but you've grown too big for your breeches…. You're not a team player, son… conversing with leaders about things that are none of your concern…. And I will not run the risk of you taking my *inplants* to other nations—interfering with our access to those machines. You see, I need everything… the whole kit and caboodle.'

Edgar coiled ever tighter, still silent as he stared blankly at the president.

'I understand this must come as somewhat of a shock, but the second phase of DOGMA—'

Suddenly, the coil unwound; finally, a reaction from Edgar, and the president was taken by surprise. It was not as he expected, not an act of aggression, nor attack for his treachery. Edgar began to smile, then chuckled as he lowered his head and laughed as he shook it.

'You find something funny?' the president asked perplexed.

Edgar tried hard to suppress his laughter and raised his head. 'Yes…. Yes, actually, I do,' he replied, forced to look away to find a straight face.

'Really? Then tell me… what is it that you find so amusing?'

He tried again to compose himself; to wipe the grin that would not leave.

'Well, a man once told me that people are a lot like dominoes... you know... those little bricks—like your *inplants*,' mocked Edgar. 'That if you stand them up, they're oh so easy to knock down.'

The president seemed dazed, and his head tilted with a furrowed brow.

'Have you ever seen those shows, Mr. President? The one's where they stand thousands of those little bricks beside each other...? They're incredible... really... and after the first one falls, there's a chain reaction—'

'What on earth are you jabbering about?'

Edgar shook his head and tutted; comically expressing his disapproval for the interruption. The president's brow tightened further as his fingernail scraped upon the desk. He was no longer quizzical, and Edgar no longer cared.

'Every brick in that show may seem small—maybe insignificant—even so, every brick has a role to play.... But then, that's the problem isn't it... I mean, the problem with being a brick, Mr. President....'

Far from enthralled, the president glared as his lips thinned.

'Nothing to say...? Well, let's see if I can help... "with your impediment."

'The only problem, being a brick, is that you don't get to see any of it.... You don't get to see the show—the bigger picture. All you get to do is your job. To know your place and fall behind the brick in front of you.... To fall *flat*, Mr. President. That's the chain reaction—that's the domino effect.'

Ambivalent to the analogy, the fact that it insinuated he was as clueless as a brick, turned annoyance into ire; the president was livid, and he sprang from his chair.

'I suggest you learn to control that mouth of yours, son, before I squat you like the bug that you are!'

Edgar smiled, unmoved by theatrics. 'You know, the same man also told me that if you want to take down the house, then you have to be willing to sacrifice your hand…. To throw your best cards even when you think they'll win you the game…. If that's what it takes… to get the house.'

His patience exhausted with anecdotes and analogies; the president's hand moved beneath the desk to trigger the alarm.

'I've just about had—'

'Tyrant,' interrupted Edgar.

The president froze. 'What…? What did you call me?'

'Seven down… on your crossword: *Any person in a position of authority who exercises power oppressively.* It's tyrant…. T.Y.R.A.N.T. Tyrant.'

'W-wh—' the president stammered, confused more than ever.

'Your crossword. Seven down…. Tyrant.'

The president glanced at the coffee table and saw his copy of The New York Times lay open. He looked at Edgar, sitting directly in front of him, a little to his right. The coffee table was at least eight metres behind, and Edgar could not have had more than the faintest of glimpses of it from his peripheral vision; certainly not enough to be able to read any print. He moved his hand away from the alarm as he began to think back and retrace Edgar's steps. Edgar had entered from the West Wing: nowhere near the table or the workgroup from the House Committee on Appropriations when he entered.

'You can't possibly… why, I myself can't….'

The president's curiosity got the better of him; his eyes fixed upon Edgar as he walked towards the coffee table. 'Someday you'll go far,' he sneered, 'and I'll make sure that you stay there!'

Edgar sat with his disingenuous smile and turned to the side. 'My best card,' he said. 'An ace in the hole… so to speak.' He tapped the back of his head with his right index and middle fingers. 'What you might call, my insurance policy.'

The president stopped before reaching the table. 'Still wet behind your ears, Edgar…? You forget yourself, son, if you had an *inplant* then I'd know…. I know *everything*. I have access to—'

'Really? Do you?'

Edgar began to laugh again, finding the president's self-assurance not only amusing but highly entertaining. The president picked up the newspaper and folded it in half as he looked for the clue. He followed the list with his finger until he came to seven down. His face turned pale; the paper falling from his hand. Edgar, finally rose to his feet.

'Oh, Mr. President, "Aren't — *you* — precious!"'

'Did you really think I was going to give you access to *my* servers…? Allow you to steal *my* work…? I gave you access to a copy—a mirror server—that's all. The data on there—everything you see—is just the data I chose to give you…. The data that you needed to make you believe you had access to everything…. And when I *walk* out of this office today, you'll be left with nothing!'

The president stumbled; he grasped at the coffee table.

'But I… I… if… then—'

'What's the matter… "cat got your tongue"?'

'Edgar, you… you don't—'

Edgar began to walk towards the president; his face bowed, his eyes forward, his voice darkened.

'Oh, but I do Mr. President, and I have. You see, before you there was Abelman. Before Abelman there was Munro. Before Munro there was my grandfather. There's always been someone—someone bigger. Someone smarter. Someone wiser. Someone who thinks they know more. You sit here and profit from my work… think that *you* can tell *me* what to do? Believe in your own greatness and bask in your own glory…. You think you're a prophet? You think you can control DomiGen—'

'Edgar, please… please listen—'

The president's voice was stained with genuine worry.

'I have listened... and I have watched.... And while I've listened and while I've watched I've recorded—*everything*. My implant doesn't stop me from being what I am... it makes me more of what I will become! It doesn't inhibit my neural pathways—it enhances them.... Increases my senses. Improves my sight. Broadens the range of my hearing. It's made me... well, how should I put it...? A superman... and one that doesn't need a cape, or tights, to use his powers.'

Edgar began to laugh. 'You know, Mr. President, you might find it hard to believe that I once had to wear spectacles. I was blind— couldn't see more than two metres in front of me.... Now I can see the colour of a man's eyes twenty miles away... and it's just the beginning. When I'm finished, I'll be able to see the craters on the moon. Hear the sound of an insect—breathing.'

'Edgar... I... I implore you... I beg you—'

'It's a little late to start begging, don't you think? So, unbecoming for a president....

'DOGMA is yours, remember...? *All* − *yours*. They're *your* implants. It's *your* legacy. That's what *you* said.... That's what I recorded—what I filmed,' said Edgar callously, as he tapped his index finger twice on his lower eyelid. 'And it's all ready to be uploaded— broadcast and shared with the world... but not yet.... You see, you have five million timebombs... each one walking around—waiting— ready to receive a line of code.... One little sequence of numbers that will turn them back into who they are... into what they *really* are....

'You shut down DomiGen FORT because one man killed fourteen people... and you... you did everything to cover it up— didn't you...? Just to − keep − things − *hush*.'

Edgar smiled again. 'Well, what are you going to do now, Mr. President...? Or more importantly, what are the people of this great nation going to do—when the five million convicts you released commit spontaneous murder? When millions of innocent lives will be lost because of a malfunction in *your* implant? Will you worry what will happen when the people find out then? What will happen to DOGMA...? To you...?'

'Edgar, now I know we've had our differences... but son, you must listen to me—'

He was tired of listening, tired of doing what he was told and tired of living in the shadows of others. He was filled with resentment and rage; with all the transgressions and lies of his former partners. Their threats and broken promises all amplified, heightened and exaggerated by this: sedition from the highest level—from the president himself. The man who claimed to represent the people, yet like so many before him, was only concerned with his own personal gain. Edgar had toyed with him long enough.

'You dare.... You *dare* to try and take DomiGen away from me...? *From me!*

'Did you think I wouldn't plan on your betrayal? On the treachery of a man as corrupt as you.... That I haven't met men like *you* before? Greedy ambitious men not satisfied with their share... who can't live with a piece—so they die wanting it all.

'You're just another brick.... An insignificant – pitiful – little – brick that's been waiting to fall. And when you fall, you will be forgotten. The show will go on without you because it's *my* show. And all this... all that you know... is just beginning....

'You're no prophet—you're nothing. When history is written, they won't even remember your name. They'll only know you as a follower—a servant of my bidding.'

Edgar's wrath knew no end, no pause until his lungs, empty of the fuel that had fired his rage, gasped for air and he breathed.

'Your arrogance has made you blind.... You think you know what power is? Ordering men to salute... you have no idea.... You can't imagine how it feels—how it really feels... to control... to really know command.... And to think, it was you, Mr. President, you who set the wheels in motion... who pushed Operation S.H.R.O.U.D into effect.'

The president's brow was furrowed once more. 'SHR... SHROUD?'

'Strategic. Human. Recruits. Obeying. Ultimate. Dominion.'

'R-recruits...? B-but I... I've never—'

'Every implant. Every inmate. Every convict.... All those criminals that you were curing, you were simply recruiting. I gave each of them an implant and in return made each of them a slave—my slave. You see, you were wrong.... The world doesn't need another monster. I – am – the – *monster*. The *real* monster. And you gave me an army—the first step to achieving S.H.R.O.U.D.... You even paid the bill.'

Edgar began to laugh again at the president struggling to comprehend, his brow ever deeper, as his face fell ever paler.

'Edgar, please... son, you don't know what you're doing—'

'The world leaders never forced your hand, it was you who forced *mine*,' snapped Edgar, as he walked around the desk. He trailed his fingers upon the timbers of the oak surface, like a comb through hair, or a dog that marks its territory and makes clear of what he owns. When he reached the president's chair, he placed his hand along the back of the old worn leather headrest.

'You know, I would have waited.... Waited until every convict had a DomiGen chip. If only you had the courage—the resolve to see DOGMA through to its end. But you lack conviction—the strength to do what it takes—to give *every* convict an implant without exception. You don't get to decide who has one and who doesn't, no more than you get to call yourself a saviour.... Mankind doesn't need to be saved, Mr. President. It needs to submit. And it will. Because in the end, they – *all* – will.'

The roles reversed, it was the president who could not believe what he was hearing, who now shook his head in denial. He was afraid of something, but it wasn't Edgar.

'Edgar, son.... These people... they'll come and—'

'Let them come.... Let them *all* come!'

The president looked wistfully to the doors as he took a step backwards under Edgar's advance; the agents had learned their lesson for the day.

'I've waited in the shadows of men for my time… and now there's an army of five million waiting for me…. Soon, it will be six. Then, the "*scum of society*," those you refused to release—will all be implanted. They will all join me… they will lead my armies and vote for me.'

'Vote…? For you?'

'Of course,' sneered Edgar. 'I don't want money… I want power—real power. And real power isn't in money, it's in this chair… in the hands of the one who sits here.'

'So, that's what this is?' interrupted the president, as he stared spiritedly at Edgar. 'A coup? A coup d'état?'

Edgar's face stiffened; his jaw clenched. 'Even now, you still understand nothing…. I'm not trying to overthrow this administration. I'm delivering it to justice. What's the point in bringing down the house when the casino is corrupt? I'm not going to level Washington—I'm going to level it all—drag you and everyone else to their knees!'

'You're as crazy as a bullbat,' scoffed the president impudently. 'You'll never get out of this office….'

He lunged forwards—trying to duck past Edgar—to reach the panic button. Edgar grabbed his arm.

'Get your darn hands off me!'

Edgar held firm, then closed his eyes.

'HR seven… nine seventeen.'

The east door opened; an agent entered and closed it behind him. The president looked up, relieved that he had successfully raised the alarm.

'Thank God, Jim…. Hurry! Help me get—'

'I'm sorry, Mr. President,' interrupted the agent, as he handed Edgar a syringe.

'Jim…? What in tarnation? Call the others, I want this man in—'

'His brother was arrested for grand larceny.'

'That's impossible,' said the president, as he looked at the agent who lowered his head. 'Why, he'd have lost this detail. There's no record of any....'

'It was his third offence, Mr. President.... If there had been any other way—'

'Third? Jim, what are you talking about...?'

The agent helped Edgar to restrain the president and pinned him down upon the desk.

'You should have come to me, son... I could have—'

'Helped?' interrupted Edgar, as he held the needle against the president's neck. 'Tell me, *son*.... How...? When all you see are mirrors.'

Edgar pushed his thumb down hard on the plunger and injected the president with the contents of the syringe. He pulled it free and handed it back to the agent. 'I told you... you only see the things I let you see.'

'No... son, wait....'

'You know, you really shouldn't call me, son... I have a father.'

'There's s-something you n-need to know.' The president's voice began to slur. 'Edgar, the test... Saven... it's not w-what you think.... They... they....'

The president lost consciousness. He slumped to the floor and Jim shouted into his cuff.

'Samaritan is down... I repeat, Samaritan is down. Code red! I repeat... code red! Request immediate WHMU response.'

The doors of the Oval Office burst open; agents flooded the room, their weapons drawn and pointed on Edgar as they closed in around him.

'Step away from the president! Put your hands in the air and step away from the president!'

Edgar had no time to move or step away. Before he could raise his arms, he was pulled from the desk and flung against a painting of the president that hung on the wall; pressed so hard, that it tore.

'Stand down!' shouted Jim, as he tried to intervene and get between Edgar and the agent suppressing him. 'Release the civilian. He is not a threat…. There is no civilian threat!'

In the turmoil, another agent repeated the initial call. 'This is the Oval Office requesting immediate WHMU response. Samaritan is down… I repeat… Samaritan – is – *down!'*

Another agent, who was knelt by the president, examined his vital signs and commanded the attention of the majority of the men. Having checked his pulse, the agent ripped open the president's shirt and finally spoke into his cuff. 'Samaritan is in arrest… I repeat… Samaritan is in cardiac arrest, WHMU respond immediately.'

'Out,' screamed the agent holding Edgar, as he nudged and then began to frogmarch him towards the door. Edgar glanced at Jim and nodded inconspicuously. Jim returned the sign in reply.

Suddenly, the White House Medical Unit burst through the doors with their apparatus. They raced to the president, where the kneeling agent was now administering chest compressions. Edgar looked down at the floor, at the president and the medics that were waiting for the defibrillator to charge. The last time he had seen one of those was at the Slaughterhouse: when he had tried to save Clydesdale. The same Clydesdale who once worked with his parents and had written to tell Edgar about the danger that he was in. The same Clydesdale who had told him how the government had turned his parents research into a military project. The same Clydesdale, the same Dr. Benjamin P. Clydesdale, who told him that a Colonel Roberts had brought in Abelman and moved them to a military base, where they were forced to work until they got rid of them.

Edgar watched the medical team working frantically on the president. The agent, unhappy with Edgar's pace, nudged him again—harder this time—to hurry him along. Edgar's head jerked and his eyes focused upon the president's desk…. The desk that he would soon be sitting behind, and the engraving on the name plate that was easy to read: even without his implant.

President S. Roberts.

Edgar smiled. 'Jackpot,' he murmured.

'You said?' asked the agent, finally pushing him out of the room.

'Blood clot…. It's probably a blood clot… pulmonary embolism.'

Edgar sat on a chair outside the office. The door was closed in front of him with two agents opposite either side. The chair was hard and uncomfortable, the cushion as thin as paper; worn down by all those who had been made to wait. Edgar sighed and folded his arms, seemingly unhappy at being detained. He looked at the floor, biting at the inside of his cheek as the sound of footsteps came running around the corner. The door opened to allow more medical personnel inside. He tried to spy a glimpse, but the door closed quickly; the agent that had marched him out, glared suspiciously as he released the knob.

'Don't worry,' said the other agent. 'It's just protocol. They'll be someone along to take your statement shortly.'

Edgar looked up and smiled. 'Thank you, George. I never have to worry for the president when I know you're here. Keeping watch… keeping him safe. I don't know what we'd do without you.'

He was like a silent assassin. He had planned and he had plotted; he had bided his time and waited for the perfect opportunity. As he sat staring at the door, Edgar remembered his first meeting with the man inside. It had always been a gamble that the president might suspect who he was. Nevertheless, Edgar knew how to play the president and he knew that his cards were good. He bet on the fact that his parent's project was three decades ago, and a lot can happen to a man's memory over thirty years…. You forget things—you forget names—you fail to remember the details. Little details like the fact that two people you once placed in a mental institution had a young son. A young son that would one day grow into a man: a man around Edgar's age. Anyone else might recall such things, but when your life had changed as much as the colonel's; when you move into politics and rise to the Oval Office, the chances of remembering such details are small. Small enough to bet against, with odds enough to win.

Edgar's thoughts were interrupted by the arrival of the vice president.

'Edgar!'

'Nathan,' replied Edgar with feigned enthusiasm. He stopped his wriggling; the attempt to ease his suffering on the cushion and rose gratefully to receive a very much staged embrace.

'Terrible news… Isn't it?'

'I know. I was with him. He just keeled over.'

'They tell me they're working with him now… although… it doesn't look good.'

The corridor was jammed and filling with more people. In the confusion, the arrival of yet more members of the administration had gathered as they congregated in hope of better news. Voices were raised—in conflict with conversations already taking place—as they shouted over each other to be heard; their numbers spreading like a swarming plague of locusts throughout the West Wing. Amid the crowd, the speaker of the House jostled forward and asked the vice president to accompany him. There was no time to lose, they had to discuss the implications of the Twenty-fifth Amendment: the powers and duties of the office. The vice president needed no convincing, following eagerly after the speaker, and the corridor cleared as the administration followed on from behind: their concerns for transition far greater than their leader's recovery. The agent raised his eyebrows; Edgar needed to sit back down. Much to his dismay and continued discomfort, he had little other choice. He sat and listened to their arguing—their disagreements about various aspects of law—until a door slammed and their bickering ceased. An hour passed, and Edgar was still sat on the chair: his restless fidgeting now unbearable. Suddenly, George touched his earpiece and both he and the other agent stepped aside. The door opened and a wave of sorrow swept out to drown the face of Edgar. He edged to the side of his chair, balancing to try and gain a better view, as the sound of sobbing and mournful tears grew ever more lucid. A stretcher emerged, pushed by a doctor— escorted by agents—and on it, a long black zipped bag. Edgar's right cheek began to rise as he struggled to stop the corner of his mouth from stretching. Samaritan was down, and from the shape of the bag, Samaritan was going to be staying down.

Edgar sat and watched as the stretcher rolled past, his hands clean and innocent of any wrongdoing. He glanced into the office and saw the defibrillator still on the floor; it had not saved Clydesdale, so there was a justice. His mind began to drift, staring at the pitiful little ants running back and forth inside; none of them knowing what to do or where to go, like the way he used to stare at those patients in the holding cell at DomiGen. The death of a person in a laboratory—in the name of science—might be considered regrettable. The murder of a partner in crime, even considered necessary under specific circumstances. But the assassination of a president, inside the Oval Office... in the White House itself... surrounded by his security detail—even aided by a member of it... well, that was nothing short of astounding. A shockingly wonderous accomplishment; a secret best kept between the devil and the dead.

'If you'd like to step inside now, they'll take your statement, Edgar.... Edgar...? Dr. Spear...? Is everything alright, sir?'

He replied with an absent cursory smile. He was already inside, already behind the desk, leaning back and forth on the chair, listening to it squeak like a mouse having stolen the cheese from a trap.

'Oh, sorry... it-it must be the shock.... The shock of it all.'

'I understand, Doctor. But they're waiting for you... inside...? For your statement...?'

'Yes. Yes of course,' replied Edgar, as he checked his Rolex. Eight hours and twenty-seven minutes. That was how long it would take until the toxin that he laced on the glass of the syringe would stop Jim's heart. Like Abelman said, "no loose ends," and Edgar offered a more convincing smile before going inside to give his account of the president's demise.

In the days and weeks that followed, Vice President Nathan Barnes made numerous appearances across the country, aimed at reassuring the American people of his commitment to continue with the work of Roberts. He would strive for better healthcare, for greater gun control, and reaffirmed his commitment to upholding the DOGMA Act. In his efforts to win support and public opinion, Barnes promised that he would fulfil the pledge of his friend and former president. That the baton had now been passed to him—reluctantly of course—to eliminate all crime from society. It was now his job to cure every inmate and continue to fight the good fight of President Roberts. His message was simple, powerful just the same; he would cure them all, free them all, and do it all before the end of the year.

By early December, almost all of the last remaining million convicts had received their implants and were released back into society. It was all too easy for Edgar with Barnes as president. He was so predictable, so easy to manipulate, and it was less complicated—for now at least—to continue with things as they were; to simply carry out the orders of his commander in chief and move ever closer to achieving the first step of S.H.R.O.U.D. Besides, the people loved Barnes, he was a hero, the natural successor to Roberts, and to destroy their hero would first require disdain. That would take time if Edgar was to avoid arousing suspicion, especially if it led to the wake of another dead president.

A much younger, more vibrant man, Barnes swam in the fountain of youth. He was always smartly dressed, relying more upon his natural boyish good looks, than his modest intellect. If Roberts was a wise old owl, then Barnes was the sly young fox; he was slicker than oil and as deep as shallow water. He adored the limelight, had hoped and most probably prayed for his moment to come. Now that it had, he accepted the merits and accolades that were bestowed upon him without hesitation or qualm. Still, the fox was clever: he knew politics was a matter of popularity and a question of seemingly keeping his word. Roberts had done that, and to maintain the people's high regard, Barnes remained true to his, closing all the remaining prisons, penitentiaries, and correctional facilities in the country. All, that is, with the exception of one: ADX Adeline in Kentucky.

The trial subjects from Saven may well have been "the worst of a bad bunch," with their tortured minds that were highly unstable making them extremely dangerous. Be that as it may, they were far from the worst of the cruellest bunch, and the evil that was housed at ADX Adeline was far beyond any depravity that could ever be made: such malevolence can only be born and nurtured. Adeline was the only supermax prison; a stronghold that contained the last remaining three hundred and twelve prisoners being held on American soil. These were terrorists, bombers, the murderers of mass murderers, the highest of all ranked organised crime figures, cult leaders, and the most violent of all serial killers. Their crimes against humanity were so foul—so sadistic—that many had also become celebrities: known throughout the world for their diabolical acts of appalling cruelty. What greater test for DOGMA, or stronger way to cement Barnes' presidency, than to put an implant into each of these last remaining inmates?

In many ways, Barnes was even more insufferable than his predecessor. Always trying to step out from the shadow of Roberts, Barnes yearned to be seen as the man that the nation would have voted for—if only given the chance. He never saw himself as the prince in waiting, more of a king in his own right, and the prisoners at Adeline would be his coronation: an opportunity not to be missed. It came then as no surprise when he announced a media event to mark the occasion. News agencies from around the world would be gathered for a global broadcast: to witness the pinnacle of two presidents' efforts to finally put an end to crime. Barnes had ordered three hundred and twelve DomiGen Mobile Labs to be parked side by side; each ready to take one prisoner and transform a life of debauchery into one of decency. This would be the president's finest hour—a spectacle to behold—and nothing less than the greatest show on earth.

The helicopters filmed overhead, as the hype exceeded every expectation. It was truly spectacular. Even from the air, the gleaming silver and green trucks stretched further than any camera could possibly see. Everything about the event was huge—larger than life—like a carnival that could only be imagined at a Las Vegas show.

Three million spectators had gathered. Families and friends prepared with their picnics; watching as the artists performed, cheering as the bands marched by, and applauding each fanfare as the moment of truth drew near. Thousands of flags flew: the colours of red, white, and blue, draped over everything. If ever there was doubt, that doubt was removed, because whoever was watching and from wherever they watched, there was never a question that this was America: the nation without crime.

As the school choirs finished, and the final verse of *The Star-Spangled Banner* was sung, the bandstands erupted with confetti and streamers. The president took to the enormous steel framed stage as the sun began to set, like a rock star about to perform at a sold-out concert. A solitary figure, alone in the light, he looked out across an ocean of arms that held cell phones and lighters aloft.

'My fellow Americans.... Citizens of the world,' began Barnes, his strong Philadelphian accent a stark contrast to the southern timbre of Roberts. 'Today is a historic day... not only for every man, woman, and child in our great nation. But for every man, woman, and child around the globe.

'Today, we put an end to crime. We choose to put a stop to the pain and the suffering that crime has inflicted upon us for as long as we can remember.... Today, we show the world that crime no longer has a place within society.... Today, we show you—the people—that crime is no more.

'The days of the criminal represent a bygone age—they are prehistoric—like the dinosaurs that once roamed these lands. And like the dinosaurs... criminals will no longer exist in the United States of America, because today... we – declare – crime – *extinct!*'

The crowd cheered and applauded, as if the rock star had returned for an encore to sing his most beloved song.

'How fitting it is, that on the third day of the twelfth month, the last remaining criminals that are registered in our country will finally be cured of their disease.... Tonight, we can rest—safe in the knowledge that none of us will be forced to endure the hardship of injustice ever again. And as we rest, we can dream—knowing that when we wake, crime will never again rear its ugly head!'

The crowd clapped and whistled as the president's voice echoed for miles. He happily took their praise, then raised his hand as if swearing to an oath. His lips mimed for the cameras: "So help me God," or something to the effect, and the crowd continued to pay tribute as he lowered his hand to press a buzzer. On the ground below, a parade of criminals in their orange jumpsuits were accompanied by guards to either side; they left the Adeline compound at the sound of the siren and marched simultaneously to the DomiGen Mobile Labs. Two large digital boards, twenty metres or more in height, lit up behind the president. The board to the left displayed the number: *312*. The board to the right: *180*. As each convict reached their trailer, a pyrotechnic rocket shot into the sky and a starburst exploded.

'My fellow Americans.... Citizens of the world... I give you... *freedom!*'

Barnes pressed a second buzzer, and a dozen more rockets fired into the air. The rolling floors at the rear of the DomiGen trailers began to power up, and one by one, the prisoners moved slowly up the ramps. When the final prisoner had entered his trailer, the guards turned to salute the podium. The board that read: *180*, suddenly began to countdown. It was a timer, and the crowd shouted out the seconds in unison.

'Thirty.... Twenty.... Ten... nine... eight... seven... six... five... four... three... two... one.'

Then, there was nothing: only silence. The rumblings of displeasure slowly began to grow, as confusion spread. A short time passed, and the rumblings became jeers, peppered with heckling catcalls. Unseen by the cameras, the first convict emerged from the side of a trailer and descended down a smaller rolling stair; the number on the other display changed: *311*. Another appeared, and the number changed again: *310*. Then another... then another... and the booing turned to cheers as each set foot upon the tarmac; the number counting down at speed.

309   274   237   187   149

The crowd roared ecstatically as the numbers of remaining criminals fell like lightning.

132.... 77.... 39.... 12.... 1....

Then, it stopped. The crowd became unsettled; the atmosphere was anxious and tense once again.

'You didn't think I was going to miss out on all the fun now, did you?' said the president jokingly.

Laughter rang out from the amused crowd, as Edgar moved into position and waited at the foot of the stage.

'Ladies and gentlemen.... Allow me to introduce a man who really needs no introduction at all. A man whose company has single-handedly pioneered the use of implant technology. I am of course talking about my dear friend, Dr. Edgar Spear.'

Edgar smiled nervously and remained where he was.

'Come on, Edgar,' coached the president. 'Come on up here!'

Reluctantly, Edgar walked up the steps and was met with thunderous applause. Munro once introduced Abelman as a, "dear friend," but the crowd's adulation reminded Edgar of another time. Of the time when he saw James again at The Grove; when he wished that he could have been loved and admired in the way that Munro was. That was a long time ago, and love was for fools who believed that good guys can sometimes win. When the feeble thoughts of a naïve resident were only to try and get ahead. Now Edgar was ahead, and he didn't need love, admiration, or any other childish sentiment. All he needed—all he wanted—was the only thing that mattered.... Power.

At the top of the podium, Barnes shook his hand and placed the other around his shoulder, embracing him like a brother. They turned and waved to the cameras. A rehearsed show of collaboration from Barnes; another partnership for Edgar to endure.

'Ladies and gentlemen,' said the president, as he raised his hands to speak. 'Dr. Spear has kindly agreed to allow me to initiate the final implant. Now, while we cannot allow cameras inside the vehicles, we can reset the countdown. When the clock reaches zero, then this number behind me *will* disappear.'

The crowd erupted euphorically.

'And we all know what that means…?'

The country had waited with bated breath as it stood on the brink of deliverance. The crowd, wild with excitement, teased by the president and the day long festivities, could barely contain their exhausted emotions.

'After you, Mr. President.'

Edgar signalled to Barnes and they began to descend the steps. *Hail to the Chief,* played from the bandstand, and the president waved as he went, making his way with Edgar towards the nearest DomiGen trailer. Waiting at the rear, at the base of the ramp, stood the last remaining convict beside another ceremonial buzzer. The prisoner was huge in comparison to Barnes. He was a giant of a man. The stitches of his jumpsuit were stretched to breaking, and the unreserved anger in his eyes was evident to all. Barnes looked at Edgar, terrified with fear; the same look that Roberts had at Saven, removing the patient's muzzle.

'We're quite safe,' said Edgar reassuringly, as he pointed to the ankle chains and hand restraints.

'But it's Richard Reams,' muttered Barnes; his lips like a ventriloquist.

'Yes, I know, Mr. President, and soon to be model citizen.'

Edgar smiled. Barnes couldn't; his face was paralysed.

'The cameras, Mr. President…. Remember… they're on you.'

Barnes took a moment and Edgar heard the deepest of breaths. 'On my mark!' shouted the president. 'Three… two… one!' Before he slammed his hand down upon the buzzer and the countdown on the large display reset to one hundred and eighty. The rolling staircase began to move, and Reams went up inside.

'Mr. President,' said Edgar, his open palm pointing towards the middle of the trailer.

Barnes climbed the series of small steps into the control booth, and Edgar followed behind. With the cameras unable to film inside, and the president's security detail outside—on guard at each entrance to the truck—the president was finally able to drop his charade.

'Ok, Edgar, let's get this thing over with. Do what you gotta do so I can get the hell out of here.' He pulled out the stool and sat down, then stared up at Edgar. 'Well…? Get on with it!'

Before a reply, Barnes felt a sudden sharp sting in his left hand.

'Ow!' he cried. 'Edgar, what are you—'

The president slumped: he lost consciousness. Edgar checked his Rolex, there was exactly one hundred and four seconds before the timer on the display outside would reach zero. Reams had already moved into the implant position, and a robotic arm had swivelled to grip his neck, as another two secured his head from either side. He struggled, as the sedative was administered, then suddenly, relaxed.

Edgar hoisted Barnes off the stool and dragged him into the operator's chair. He spun it around; the back now facing the Perspex control booth wall that looked out onto Reams on the other side. He typed frantically on the keyboard—the Perspex retracted. The robotic arms that held Reams released him, then swung around and gripped the president instead.

'Come on. Come on....' whispered Edgar impatiently, as he continued to type at frantic speed.

The red laser grid projected onto the head and neck of Barnes. Edgar waited for the dot in the centre to turn green. Another robotic arm swung into position, then stopped, and began to drill a small hole into the back of the president's skull. Edgar checked his Rolex again: eighty-two seconds.

'Come on!'

Another robotic arm swung into position behind Barnes. It slowly extended with a small implant in its grasp. Edgar checked his Rolex again: sixty-three seconds... precisely. The robotic arm retracted from the president's skull; his sedative already beginning to wear off. Reams was still unconscious—slouched and relaxed.

'Spear...? What's happening...? Get me the—'

Another robotic arm moved into position, ejecting a fine spray from the needle to seal the pinhole at the back of the president's skull. Edgar continued to type, ignoring Barnes; checking his Rolex again and again: forty seconds.

'No. No. No!' he screamed beneath his breath. 'Come on.... Come - on!'

Barnes winced in pain and Edgar checked his watch again. Twenty-eight... twenty-seven... twenty-six.... He ran around to another terminal and began to type. The chip was imprinting, and the face of Barnes scrunched, contorting in agony.

'Almost there... almost there....'

Edgar's focus was broken as he heard the excited crowd outside.

'Ten... nine... eight... seven... six... five... four... three... two... one.'

Then, the silence. Reams shook his head and began to regain consciousness; he rose, unsteadily, to his feet.

'Just relax,' said Edgar. 'You do as I told you and you'll be fine.'

Reams nodded. He looked across, his vision blurred, and became angry at the sight of Barnes.

'Take it easy... I needed him awake... for the imprinting. Your dosage was heavier. You're feeling it now.'

Reams took a deep breath. He held onto the corner of the desk, weak-kneed, his head spinning wildly.

'Drink this... it'll help.'

He struggled to hold the plastic cup, so Edgar helped pour the contents down his throat.

'Reams...? Reams?' Edgar slapped him across the face. 'Hey! Stick to the plan... what I told you... nothing else. This only works if you stick to the plan.'

Reams was queasy, his eyes heavy as they floated without purpose. The rolling floor began to move, and he jolted as it carried him towards the front right of the trailer. He turned to Edgar one last time. Edgar nodded, and the staircase took him outside; out to the cheering crowds that awaited his arrival. The number on the display board disappeared, and the crowd was euphoric as the pyrotechnics exploded: shooting rockets that showered red, white and blue glitter everywhere. Edgar could hear their screams and looked one last time at his Rolex: zero seconds... precisely. He raced back to the control booth and stared at the monitor.

Procedural Success: 100%.

The imprinting was complete, and the final robotic arm had retracted. Out of time, Edgar reached for the chair and spun it around; it stopped just as Barnes opened his eyes to look out through the Perspex.

'Wh-what happened? I felt a—'

'You fainted, Mr. President... I think it was the craniotomy.'

'The cranio—'

'You turned pale and fell off the stool....'

Barnes rubbed the back of his head, surprised to be in the operator's chair. 'Yes,' he said, nodding gently. 'Yes... I... I think I did. I... I remember—'

'The implant, Mr. President.'

Barnes could hear the cheering crowds.

'Yes... Reams... I... I remember the drill and then I....'

A member of the security detail entered the truck, wondering why the president was still inside.

'Mr. President, is everything ok?'

Barnes was muddled and confused.

'Mr. President?'

He looked up. His eyes roaming somewhere towards the voice of the agent.

'Mr. President, is everything ok...? Can you hear me?'

'Yes,' slurred Barnes. 'I... I can hear you.'

'The president fainted,' said Edgar. 'He just needs a—'

The agent rushed into the trailer. 'Here, let me help you, sir.'

Barnes shook his head. His eyes closed tightly. 'No,' he mumbled, struggling to his feet; unable to look up or settle his dizziness.

'But sir....' insisted the agent, reaching out to offer support.

"I'm fine. Don't touch me.... You want me to look like an invalid... in front of the world? In my moment of triumph?'

Clearly annoyed at the suggestion, Barnes tottered towards the opening at the side of trailer. He braced himself against the wall; shaking his head as he blinked, trying to regain his focus. The cheering was relentless. The crowds wanted their hero, and he moved out onto the top step to drown in great rapturous applause. Like an emperor receiving the adulation of Rome, he stood majestically acknowledging his greatness. Edgar remained inside, permitting Barnes his moment of glory. The agent—caught between the two—kept his suspicious eyes solely on Edgar.

Barnes walked back to the stage, stopping constantly to shake the hands of well-wishers, as his security detail tried hopelessly to offer protection. They urged him along, but he ignored their efforts as he reached into the crowds at every opportunity. He relished his success; he bathed in it and wanted everyone there and everyone watching to do the same. Progress was slow, deliberately so, and when he finally reached the podium steps, he climbed them as though his legs were made of lead. The fanfare proclaimed his victorious return to the peak; celebrating with yet more rockets that fired their glitter and confetti as he turned to wave—his head in his hand, overwhelmed by it all. It was an act the great showman James Munro would have been proud to deliver, and like Munro, Barnes shared many traits....

As the music came to an end, the coloured smoke cleared. He walked to the third and final buzzer at the centre of the podium, then turned to face the cameras.

'My fellow Americans... Citizens of the world... The light of crime will never again shine in our great nation.'

He slammed the buzzer and the supermax prison fell dark. The crowd gasped as the other lights and illuminations turned off for effect. For a moment, the world had slipped into darkness and an eerie silence descended upon the crowd. Suddenly, a spotlight shone down to light the president from above.

'I give you my pledge, that I will remain a beacon of light for you all to trust... always.'

Edgar smirked as he stood at the opening of the trailer, looking up at the angel and the promise that he made. That's a good boy, he thought, chuckling to himself.

'And they say you're the tail that wags the dog, huh?' said the agent sarcastically.

He looked away from the spectacle and smiled at the agent, remembering the names that they called him in the media; knowing he was no longer the hand behind the wheel... not even the seed that grew the tree. What Edgar was—what he now had—was so very much more....

14

PITY THE ENEMY

Tuesday marked the four-year anniversary since the closing of ADX Adeline. True to his word, Barnes had put an end to crime. There had been, and would probably always be, minor isolated instances of petty crime. Sadly, such things were unavoidable and always made the headlines. The occasional shoplifter, a drunken man breaking into a liquor store in the middle of the night; hardly the sort of thing that was typical of serious organised crime, but then crime wasn't organised anymore. In fact, it was unquestionably a thing of the past.

The president may have taken the credit, yet he was smart enough to always include praise for his much-loved predecessor. It was a tactic that paid off as he won the last presidential election by a landslide, not only securing the Republican nomination, but the votes of every released convict across the country. However, it seemed that the president remained oblivious to whatever Roberts had discovered in his trial at Saven; either that, or he was determined to overturn the decisions made, releasing every convict and closing every prison by doing so. After winning the election, the first order of business for

Barnes was to transform and expand the DOGMA Act. The DOGMA Program was applauded by the United Nations, and it had become the sole focus of his presidency. By the second year of his first term in office, Barnes had granted over one hundred and twenty-two governments access to implant technology; nearly half of the world's recognised countries were now tracking their own criminals. Behind it all, was DomiGen Labs, the largest and most profitable company in the world: an annual turnover estimated to be between six and seven trillion dollars.

Worldwide demand placed huge pressures on the manufacturers of silicon chips for DomiGen, and implants were prioritised over the production of other processors. As a result, sales of items such as new computers, home entertainment consoles and smart devices were forced into decline. Ironically, creating a crime-free world, came at the cost of furthering technological advancement. With the makers of hardware and home electronics struggling to survive in a market of reduced revenue; high-profile bankruptcies made easy pickings and cheap acquisitions for DomiGen. The company expanded into areas such as security, surveillance, and engineering. DomiGen was no longer just the creator of implants, it was fast becoming a brand that was recognised by everyone, everywhere, in every corner throughout the world. If Roberts believed that Edgar was his loaded gun, the roles under Barnes had surely been reversed. It was Edgar who now held power over the trigger, and the hand that rocked the cradle had moved one step closer to ruling the world.

National policing and intelligence agencies kept track of their own offenders. That was a requirement of The DOGMA Program; one of four directives set in place to ensure that the American government did not become a self-appointed global police force. The other directives covered areas such as implant protocols, system security, and criminal justice infrastructure. All were designed to provide reassurance and the belief that every country maintained their own levels of self-control. For Edgar, whose DomiGen had grown so far and infiltrated so much, belief was easy to give to those who were only too willing to believe.

While governments lauded the success of their individual programs—paroling their convicts as they closed their prisons and penitentiaries—no one thought to question who kept track of the company that kept track of the criminals? The company whose implants, whose systems and technology, recorded, stored, and analysed everything. Any lessons apparently learned from CaliChat were already forgotten. Munro's ridiculing of Congress and the lecture once given by Roberts to Edgar, were memories long since lost. History, so it seemed, was only all too eager to repeat itself.

The networks of mirror servers that Edgar had put into place under Roberts were now global. DomiGen provided governments with selective information that was delayed, altered, and of no real value. Nevertheless, it created the illusion of implant data and tracking abilities appearing in real-time. The system itself was so advanced that it was impossible to detect or determine otherwise, and with the consequences of DOGMA's international success seeing law enforcement agencies progressively close, the probability of anyone ever being able to detect the deception was inconceivable. In fact, it had become—in no uncertain terms—a precision business, and the business of precision suited Edgar.

Less than six years after the DOGMA Act had become law, the entire criminal justice system in the United States had essentially been disbanded. The Department of Justice, the Federal Bureau of Investigation, the Drug Enforcement Administration, the United States Marshalls Service, and the Federal Bureau of Prisons were all gone. All had been dissolved, and all had been dismantled. Of the eighteen thousand police agencies that once existed, there now stood only one: a single tactical unit. A special force that consisted of around one hundred agents; a handful of dedicated men and women whose job it was to monitor every state across the country. To lead such a force and bear the role of responsibility required someone of the highest moral character. Someone exemplary and incorruptible: someone honest and true. Who else then was better positioned, more able to understand the intricacies of the criminal mind, than the man once considered to be the most dangerous in America? What better way to showcase The DOGMA Program, than to have the world's once most dangerous criminal lead the world's most advanced force on crime? Richard Reams, or Commissioner Reams, as was his official title, the only real contender for the appointment and the president's preference for the post.

Strange as it seemed, Roberts could just as easily have stayed in the chair instead of Barnes. Despite the fact that Roberts was ultimately responsible for his parent's disappearance and their probable deaths, that was not the motivation for Edgar to remove him as president. The problem was Roberts' history with Abelman: the pair were obviously involved with some form of organised crime syndicate. Both men always gave the impression of being so fearful of it, and fear makes men act the way scared men usually do—they did what they were told—which meant Roberts was always being influenced and was never really in control. There is no courage without fear, although Roberts lacked even that conviction, which made him a threat to everything Edgar had planned. An implant in Roberts would never have resolved that threat, it would only have taken him to the next step up the ladder. So, whether Roberts had his own ideas, or simply carried out the orders given to him, the fact of the matter was that his views conflicted with Edgar's ambitions. He wanted to take DomiGen but was unwilling to free every criminal. That meant convicts in prisons: some form of detention. Prisons meant the need for law enforcement: some form of deterrent. Law enforcement would require either a fully staffed or semi-functional judicial system: some form of due process. These things were all obstacles—barriers that stood in the way of precision, and why Roberts ultimately had to go. America had to prove it possible: to transform the country with the highest number of criminals into a peaceful, crime-free nation. Simply reducing serious crime was not enough to call the program a success. It had to be eliminated, entirely. It had to be flawless, to show the world that the program was perfect. The only man with that kind of leverage and persuasion—capable of getting the job done—was the president of the United States. If he stood in front of the world and said that it was so, then the world would believe it, and now that he had, they did thanks to Barnes. America was the blueprint, and The DOGMA Program was the roadmap for every nation to follow. The United States may well have had a firm head start in converting to a crimeless society; nevertheless, countries from around the world were already beginning to catch up.

As algorithms and research improved, DomiGen was not only able to inhibit the behaviour of former criminals, or "Dominoes," as they were still referred to inside the company; they were also able to test out new forms of influence and mind control. During recent months, Edgar had been present at almost every photocall from the White House, where the president thanked him in one way or another for all that he had done to bring peace and prosperity to the nation. It was quite uncharacteristic for a man who had hated the attentions of the public for so long—the focus of the media—to now flirt with them on a near weekly basis as he stepped ever further into the limelight. It was not only America, but the world who watched with awe at the meteoric rise of the young Dr. Spear. Yet still there were others, those who looked less in wonder and more in suspicion. Those who began to question Edgar and his ever-increasing influence over the administration.

Despite such concern, no one was willing to speak publicly, not least because DomiGen's public security and surveillance devices were everywhere; inside every government building and mounted on every street corner. They were as popular in London as they were in New York. As accepted in Tokyo as they were in Minsk. As in demand in Seoul as they were in Abu Dhabi. And while no one dared say or admit to the thought, the idea of being monitored—much like the implant hosts themselves—was not as absurd as it first might have seemed.

What started as a whisper, a murmur in certain quarters, had steadily grown into faint beliefs. Amongst those whispers came a rumour—hope—in the form of a group that called itself, "Cerebus."

Named after the Greek mythological creature, whose three heads were said to represent the past, the present, and the future; Cerebus was a secret society, with members united through their common cause: *The protection of the innocents*. Little was known about the group, and the stories that spread, were precisely that. In fact, no member had ever stepped forward to confirm their existence, and in the absence of proof, Cerebus had remained another urban legend; nothing more than just another modern-day myth.

As most cautionary tales begin, the story of Cerebus began with a warning:

> *Those of no moral, those wicked or mean,*
> *will soon find Cerebus, then never be seen.*

The society had supposedly evolved over centuries, from a group of mythical warriors known as the Rytterne. The Rytterne were ferocious, without mercy, and formed to fight in Europe's northern lands. As they moved south uniting clans, a skilled huntress called Fianna joined their ranks. Reider, the leader of the Rytterne, saw the strengths of Fianna in battle: her speed, her agility, and not least her courage. Following the mighty war at Polonia, where Reider was slain and the Rytterne were all but lost, Fianna fled to the mountains of Sudetes, where she gave birth to a son, Marcellus. Without the Rytterne, the lands of Europe began to divide once more. Emperors and tyrants returned to power, as men fell to the hands of their masters. From the ruins, abandoned young children were hand-picked and recruited to train under Fianna's guidance. The story tells how orphans—mostly—were of a quite specific age.

No parents no ties nor grieving goodbyes.
Young life free of sin is where we begin.
No younger than nine, hearts pure and divine.
No older than ten, not women nor men.

The children were purportedly raised in the ancient ways of armed combat. They learned to read and write; versed in the classics and the language of Latium. Courage, passion, and humility were the attributes they aspired to achieve. They were taught logic: the art of arguing. Rhetoric: the art of public speaking. And decisiveness: the art of leadership. Those who were ready, were put through the trials of the body and soul: *Corpore Tribulationes*. Those who passed, were selected to fight alongside Marcellus. Those who failed, were soon forgotten. In time, as their numbers rose, the Rytterne were reborn, and their oath was renewed.

While the story says that Cerebus stands vigilant, remains hidden at the ready, it is at this point that different versions of the myth have been created to tell a tale more relevant for a modern generation. The most popular version describes the Rytterne as the past of Cerebus; their prime objective evolving throughout the ages to offer protection to the victims of war. At present, their fight is said to be with the enemy who seeks to pollute the pure; with those who abuse technology and hold power to corrupt the minds of the innocent. In the future, that one day a force will come, so powerful that it no longer concerns itself with innocence or guilt; its only intention will be to rule over mankind.

The internet played host to countless conspiracy theories, with blogs that claimed to know the truth about Cerebus and the identity of its members. Outrageously absurd, there were those who alleged it was comprised of celebrities; popular figures from popular culture who could never be suspected of such an involvement. Others believed that its members were wealthy athletes; high achievers from the fields of various contact sports, now using their vast wealth to prepare for a very different form of combat. Then there were groups, convinced that Cerebus was comprised of business leaders from around the world. Prominent figures that had felt the impact of conglomerates like DomiGen, who shared the same concerns for corporate leaders never held to account.

While the stories of mythical knights and hidden heroes are best kept in the fantasy section of the bookshelf, the march of DomiGen Labs as it continued onwards was no fable or story of fiction. There were now over ten million convicts around the world with a DomiGen implant. Ten million former criminals who were cured and free of their erroneous pasts. Ten million people busy about their daily lives, like a dormant army that walked the streets, unaware that at any time they could be ordered to perform any action if Edgar so commanded. Ten million: a number twenty times the size of the United States armed forces. Ten times the size of the combined military might of Europe. Five times the size of the entire Chinese army. All under the control of one company—one man—and of one potentially supreme leader....

President Barnes stood on the steps of the White House. The forecast had said light showers. As usual, the forecast was wrong. He was flanked from behind by two Marine Security Guards, as he braved the elements beneath a black doorman umbrella. It blew like a kite in the strong crosswind, as one of the sentries tried hard to maintain his discipline and fought hopelessly to hold it under control. Tradition dictates that the president should never wait for a civilian; such an honour was reserved for foreign dignitaries and the members of royal households. However, this was no ordinary private citizen, and as the rain lashed down, it sounded like gravel as it bounced off the bonnet of the shiny black Escalade. Edgar stepped out, and Barnes raised a welcoming hand. He knew his place, and fortunately, should he ever forget, a single tap of a button would help the implant to jog his memory.

'Edgar! Good to see you,' said Barnes as they embraced at the steps. 'Let's get out of this weather.'

Edgar stared at Hannah until her cheeks reddened; something that did not escape Barnes.

'What was that?' he asked, turning to Edgar.

Edgar smirked. He said nothing, then walked with Barnes down the West Wing—chatting like old friends at a high school reunion. It was a far cry from the days of Roberts' presidency, when Edgar was forced to relinquish any personal items before stepping into the Oval Office. As the two sat alone, Barnes was first to speak.

'Vanilla or chocolate?'

'Mr. President?'

'With your cake... I think I'll have vanilla. It's why you're here isn't it... to celebrate our anniversary?'

Edgar stared blankly.

'Adeline.'

'Is it...? Four years already?'

'To the day, Edgar.'

'Sorry. I... erm... forgot.'

Barnes laughed, believing the unscheduled meeting would be a light-hearted social affair.

'Oh, my friend... we really need to get your mind off business for a while.... You know, it's about time we got you settled... a good woman... someone to lean on. Someone who can push back a bit... put a smile on that face of yours. Look at me. Eighteen years. Still married to Cordelia and—'

'Well, Mr. President,' interrupted Edgar, not there to listen to relationship advice. 'Since you asked, the reason I'm here is because I've been thinking about DOGMA... about the success of our program.'

Quick to forget his wife at the mention of the words "DOGMA" and "success," Barnes leaned back into his chair. He raised his arms, placing the palms of his hands upon the back of his head, as a broad smile filled his narrow face.

'Yes, it's phenomenal. The American people finally have a society they can feel safe in—be proud of... and you must be proud too, Edgar...? Of your work? I know I am. When I think about our legacy—what we've achieved.... We've given freedom to so much of the world. A chance to start over.... Now, I know there's a long way to go, but freedom takes time—'

Edgar's face appeared to disagree with Barnes as he interrupted once again.

'Well, that's just it, Mr. President. You see, I think freedom is a relative term, or what I mean to say is, perhaps your idea of freedom is different to mine.... Different to others?'

'Really? How so?'

'To you, freedom is the right for the nation to choose for itself. Abide by a Constitution that was made by the people, for the people '

'Edgar, the role of any president—'

'But to your voters—to the guy on the street—freedom is the ability to change the channel. To watch what they want to watch... to go to the mall and eat what they want to eat.'

Barnes may not have been astute, however, after his third interruption, he was certainly aware of Edgar's impertinence. Nevertheless, he was in agreement with the sentiment and nodded before lowering his arms.

'So, what is freedom, if not the ability to do what we want...? To be able to choose... freely?'

'Edgar, I see your point, but we can't all just do what we—'

Edgar interrupted yet again. 'So, I choose freedom. The freedom of all. Which is why I want—'

His patience lost, Barnes was no longer tolerant of his friend's aggressive mood.

'You want?' he barked, bolting upright in his chair. 'Edgar, you forget yourself! You forget *who* you are talking to... you forget where you are. You are in the office of the president of the United States. My—'

Edgar's memory was not the problem.

'Don't interrupt me when I'm speaking. I'm trying to tell you something—something important. Something you *should* listen to.'

Barnes was furious. Chastised like a naughty schoolboy; he was equally puzzled by the sudden audacity of Edgar.

'I'm taking DOGMA to the third phase.'

'What…? Edgar, there is no third phase…. We started the second phase the moment we opened The DOGMA Program to international collaboration. Now, we are doing well, but we're not even half—'

'Then it's not just freedom that we see differently is it, Mr. President…?'

Barnes was perplexed: more concerned than angry and worried for his friend's fragile state of mind.

'Edgar, what's gotten into you today? This is not like you. I don't follow—'

'That's the problem, isn't it? I'm not sure you ever have.'

The president rose from his chair and slammed his fist down upon the desk. Abelman and Roberts slammed their fists down upon desks, and both were bigger, more intimidating men. Edgar leaned back and crossed his legs, then placed his hands onto his lap as he made himself more comfortable. Barnes grimaced. His face scrunched and turned red, as a large vein began to protrude down the centre of his forehead. Edgar watched its pulsating rhythm beat faster and faster, pumping blood around the president's body like a race car around Indianapolis. He stared up at Barnes looming over the desk and it was hard not to smile. Try as he could, Barnes was no mountain—nor barely a man.

'What is going on!'

'The thing about freedom, is it's just a matter of perspective…. You call it legacy. Someone else calls it channel surfing. Someone else, shopping. But do you know what I call it…? What I think freedom really means?'

'Edgar, I demand—'

'I think freedom is something you don't understand—until it's lost. Until it's been taken away from you and you no longer remember how it feels....

'You see, unless you've experienced freedom and know that you're no longer free to choose—to do what you want—to decide for yourself—then you never really understand what freedom is. Because you never understood what you lost.'

'You're not well, I really don't—'

'No, you don't, do you Mr. President? You never have. So, let me simplify things a little... make it easy... even for you.... The only way for me to reach my full potential is for DomiGen to grow, and the only way for DomiGen to grow, is to give it to the people.'

'*Your* potential...?' the president asked incredulously; his voice raged with annoyance and tempered with unease. 'Edgar, listen to yourself.... What on earth are you—'

'What I am, is what the world needs.... You see, most men never get to do anything.... Most men never get to change the world.'

The president fell into dismay. 'Most men never need to, Edgar. But we have—together—we've already given half the world what it needs... what it wants most of all.'

Edgar scoffed at the reply of Barnes, uninterested in his pathetic attempt to reason with him.

'What it needs? What do you know about people's needs...?

'What I *need*.... No... what − I − *want*... is to give an implant to everyone. To put a chip into the head of every person, in every house, in every home, in every town, in every city, in every country around the world.... To connect *everyone—everywhere* to the DomiGen Grid.'

'The DomiGen Grid...? There's no... Edgar, you can't be serious...? Look... you'll never... I'll never....'

Shocked by what he heard, unable to articulate an argument, the president fell back into his chair. Edgar smiled and uncrossed his legs as he leaned forward and placed his hands upon the desk.

'Oh, I am... and you will... whether you want to or not.... Actually, the only thing we do agree on, is that freedom is about choice... and that's just something you don't have.'

'Edgar, what are you talking about...?' The president's voice became urgent. 'You're beginning to scare me.... The implants... they're a cure... a cure for—'

'Freedom, Mr. President. A cure for freedom. Not crime. The next phase of DOGMA is the end of DOGMA... and the end of freedom... for everyone... everywhere.'

Edgar took his cell phone. He swiped the screen several times, before his finger hovered over a button.

'You know, you may be many things, but you were *never* my friend.'

Edgar held a barbed smile. Removed of emotion; he was a surgeon whose cuts were deep, exact and precise. Barnes sat bewildered, as his disillusioned eyes spoke on his behalf.

'In the rainforests of Brazil, there's a parasitic fungus that's called "Ophiocordyceps unilateralis." You won't have heard of it, Mr. President... but its spores are miniscule—invisible to the naked eye—and they lay on the floor of the forest, patiently waiting. When an ant comes foraging, a spore infects it and spends the next few days incubating inside its host. Then... only when it's ready... does it begin to manipulate the ant. It starts by taking control of the ant's brain, and makes it walk blindly away from the safety of the colony—like a zombie. When it's out of range, the ant climbs up a tree. Not far... just enough to find a spot with the right amount of light and humidity—the perfect conditions for the fungus to grow. Then the ant clamps down on a leaf and dies, never knowing why. Why it wanted to leave the nest...? Why it decided to climb the tree...? Or why it had chosen to die...?'

Edgar's smile stretched farther. 'You and that ant have a lot in common. More than you know, in fact. The difference is that I'm going to tell you how you got up this tree. How you found your place in the sun. And after I do, I'm going to tell you to clamp down and make your sacrifice. But don't worry... I'm not going to kill you. I need you. I just want to enjoy the satisfaction of knowing that you know what I've taken from you.'

'Edgar—'

'Your freedom. That's the price you pay for sitting in that chair.... How do you think you got this far? Released all these criminals? Everything you've done in your presidency... the decisions that you've made... they were never by choice—not by free will. They were by command... by *my* command. And ten million people under my control is *nothing* compared to eight billion.'

'Edgar you're insane... I'm calling—'

'Reams? The man you made commissioner? The convict who covers up mishaps, so that nothing can stand in my way?'

Barnes reached across the desk.

'A, a, ah...! Touch that telephone and I'll touch this screen... then you'll never get to hear the best part....'

'Ok, Edgar.... Ok,' he said, as he slowly pulled his hand away. 'Let's all just calm down now and try to figure this thing out.'

'Figure this out...? Mr. President, you're not listening.

'Freedom—your ability to choose—well that just leaves too much to chance. It's just not... what's the word...? Precise. And I don't know if you know it, but I'm in the business of precision.

'Now I know what you're thinking... that you've heard enough about me and what I want. But you know, you really ought to lighten up. After all, none of this would have been possible without you— without the power of the president. I mean, who in their right mind would give me control over all those criminals? Or even make the most dangerous one the head of his task force? That guy... why, he'd have to be out of his mind.... But then, you haven't been in yours lately, have you?'

Barnes sat transfixed; the words of Edgar fading behind the pounding of his deafening heartbeat.

'What's wrong, Mr. President? Nothing you'd like to say...? No one you want to call...? To lean on...? Come on... humour me... I'll give you sixty seconds before I tap the screen and wipe your memory.'

Edgar teased and tormented Barnes, waving his finger precariously above the screen.

'Edgar, please... whatever you're trying to do... whatever this is—'

'This...? This is the truth... and everybody wants the truth, Mr. President. The problem is that nobody wants to be honest... so, let me give it to you straight.'

'You're unwell... I see that.... Edgar, we'll get you help—'

'I have all the help that I need. You see, Reams never got an implant at Adeline. You did. You were convict implant number three one two. And on that day—the day of your greatest triumph—I achieved mine. Control over the most powerful man in the world.... The perfect programmable puppet.'

Barnes shook his head; his eyes widened as the pieces began to fit together.

'No... that's impossible. If you... then I....'

Edgar's smile deepened. He tapped the back of his head with his right index and middle fingers, before raising his eyebrows, then nodded. Barnes reached up behind his head and began to feel.

'A tiny scar... like a ridge.... In the upper third of the left Parietal bone.'

Barnes searched frantically, his desperate face showed it; his fingers ploughing through the hair at the back of his scalp. Edgar was patient—smiling constantly—he could see the position of Barnes' arm and could tell where he was probing. Edgar pointed upwards and Barnes moved his hand. Suddenly, he stopped. His mouth agape and trembling. His eyes aghast with terror. His face, a ghostly pale.

'You're shaking, Mr. President.... Don't worry, you know the night always feels coldest before the dawn. But the dawn *is* coming, I promise you. Because DOGMA is over, and from its ashes, a new order will rise…. A new dawn… the dawn of DomiNation.

'So, now that you know the truth—you will *never* know truth again.'

His smile grew ominous. His eyes on the president as he tapped the button on the screen of his cell phone. Barnes twitched. He shivered, as if a cold chill ran down his spine before wincing for a moment in pain. The hand that was raised—searching for the implant—shook violently for a second, then fell to his side.

'Now then, Edgar. Let's look at how we'll set up this DomiGen Grid of yours.'

Back inside the Cadillac, the rain continued to pelt like pebbles off the roof. Edgar nestled into the soft black leather and breathed deeply. The chauffeur glanced into the rear-view mirror.

'A successful meeting, Dr. Spear?'

Edgar smirked. 'Liberating, Piers. Thank you.'

As they made their way towards Reagan Airport, Edgar stared out of the tinted windows. It was done. There was no storming of the White House, deposing of the president, or armed insurrection. Such an assault would have been easier to deal with—simpler to strike against than a single selfish act of overindulgence. It had been a long day coming, and Edgar's shoulders sank as the weight of anticipation was finally lifted. The timing of his attack, carried out so inconspicuously, was no accident. Six million was a milestone for Roberts, when the glorified mob had aimed and failed to gain control of DomiGen. Ten million marked the milestone for Edgar, when he no longer needed to hide his cards. Nevertheless, the stakes at the table were still meagre: not enough to win it all and take down the house. It was Barnes' devotion to The DOGMA Program that had finally brought an end to traditional law enforcement in the United States. With it, the benefits of a crime-free society were there for all to see, as long as no one looked beyond what Edgar wanted them to. Enrolment in the program and international adoption, was enough to increase the size of population that could be placed under his control. But even if every criminal in the world carried a DomiGen implant it would never be enough—not for dominion.

They pulled up to a red light. Edgar smiled at a young woman driving a Prius in the next lane. She looked drawn and was busy adjusting her scattered hair while her young child lay asleep in a baby seat. He had come a long way since travelling with Abelman to meet Munro in LA, even so, it was not far enough, and his journey was by no means over. The lights changed and he was on the move once again, even if progress required the president to continue. He smiled contentedly as he rested his eyes, knowing that the power of the president was a powerful ally. The most powerful ally of all.

"*For the Truly Connected,*" was how the advertising and marketing material described DomiGen's first implant for the mass market. A chip that was painlessly inserted through a pinhole in the back of the skull, providing the host with the unique ability to join the DomiGen Grid. The Grid gave access to the internet; even in areas where traditional Wi-Fi, GSM, and other outdated technologies were unable to work. Users could stay online—all of the time—and remain connected no matter where they were. With information delivered directly to the senses, the ability to call and talk with anyone meant never needing a device again. Consumers were like lemmings, so eager to follow each other, and the technology was safe: it had to be, there were ten million hosts in the world with an implant, and not one fatality or reported side effect. Pressure from peers, from family and friends, saw a growth in sales far beyond anything experienced before. It was one of those things that came around once in a lifetime, like the invention of the wheel or the creation of the light bulb. Except, it was so much more, because they were just things and a DomiGen implant was you. A more improved, more informed, and more connected *you.*

The advantages spoke for themselves. They were so well prepared that it was difficult to argue or oppose them. Easy to understand and pitched to perfection, the power of persuasion was no longer necessary once the lure of the implant outweighed any disadvantage of concern. Backed by President Barnes—even giving his seal of approval— DomiGen began to put implants into ordinary, everyday people. Yet unlike the condemnation, attracted after those first given to the criminals, the DomiGen Grid was not met with resistance. There was only the promise of a new, better world, and another cheap cliché that was bought by the masses in their desperate desire for more.

It was fair to say that the DomiGen Grid did not disrupt existing technology: it obliterated it. The large international telecoms, computing electronics and mobile manufacturers, were all in imminent danger of becoming obsolete. Initially launched in a handful of states before rolling out across the continent, how long would it take before every country wanted to join America…? Before every nation demanded its own access to the Grid. Before everyone saw themselves: *For the Truly Connected.*

The world's largest technology companies had little choice, and little option; they were forced to abandon their iconic products with their clever logos and carefully designed badges. Because now, if they wanted to survive, then they would have to scramble whatever they could to create their own implants and enter a marketspace in which there was only DomiGen.

Although Edgar was no businessman, business was just as his former partner had said. His Abelman Advice and analogy of the lamp store owner had never been more relevant: "What would you be willing to pay to get that customer?" The answer was not the cost of producing a lamp, but the price of stopping the customer buying one from a competitor. The master had taught his apprentice well and his apprentice had listened. However, the apprentice was now the master and more determined than the former. He was more ambitious, more corrupt and more ruthless than Abelman ever was. Edgar decided that instead of trying to stop the customer buying from a competitor, it was just easier to take the competitors away. That was how to build a *real* precision business; it was how monopolies were made and empires were built. So, every implant was given away, and Edgar's price to get the customer, was everything. The DomiGen implant was free, and no company could ever compete with that. It was free to all, and free for all, financed and paid for by the monies from The DOGMA Program: the hundreds of billions of dollars that Edgar had earned in alleviating the world from crime. His resources were endless and if any obstacle arose, he simply rocked the cradle and instructed President Barnes.

As many of the world's largest telecoms and technology companies closed, the few that survived gambled on the creation of their own implants. None were a threat to DomiGen, and those that tried, succeeded only in creating novelty products; specialised implants for niche markets that they hoped to be able to control. One of the first, a replacement for baby monitors, used micro implants that could be injected into infants at birth. They were designed to provide peace of mind for parents and dissolve twenty-four months after insertion. Unfortunately, there had been many issues during the rushed development; corners were cut, tests neglected, and results falsified to get the implants to market. The first deaths were blamed on vaccinations and weaker immune systems, but a pattern soon emerged. Control of the consumer was not to be shared, and Edgar was ruthless as he chose to stomp on the poor fortune of others. He cited the rigorous testing and exemplary safety records of DomiGen in the media, to remove any doubts that remained about the Grid while condemning his stricken competitor. As the deaths continued, lawsuits crippled the company, and like the others, they soon disappeared. Desperate to reinvent themselves, many tried to improve on existing technology. Smart spectacles that combined with contact lenses to create digital retina implants. They offered an always on and "Heads-Up Display," or "HUD," as they were called, displaying internet services and GPS navigation over the user's vision. With limited appeal and means of generating sales, there was never a hope of covering costs. One by one, famous brands became forgotten words as all eventually ran out of money. The familiar names that once filled product shelves, vanished and were gone forever.

Once the DomiGen Booths were launched, cubicles not unlike the photo booths that once issued passport and identity photographs, the Grid became a snowball. Small at first, rolling down the high street past the shops that now offered easy access for anyone to join. It quickly gained momentum—increasing in size—until it became unstoppable. Less than three years after the first DomiGen Mobile Lab had parked in New York's Times Square, opening its doors to the public and the media circus, almost every American now carried an implant. The land of the free, was in matter of fact the land of the DomiGen Grid.

Temptation and the power to influence is a test for even the strongest of characters that proves difficult to resist. Fortunately, Edgar had no such character, and this was no test. This was a plan. His fanatical lust for control—his ravenous hunger fuelled by greed—had always been insatiable. Such craving would never be satisfied by the implants of a few hundred million Dominoes. Nevertheless, the pieces were falling precisely into place. With Barnes having served, close to fulfilling his requirements, an opportunity had presented itself that might see Edgar take another step towards satisfying his appetite. The president had carried out Edgar's wishes, performed as Edgar had needed, and delivered as Edgar had commanded. All in all, it had been a highly successful term for Barnes; at least, in Edgar's opinion, which was the only opinion that mattered. At the same time, as former President Roberts had once said, "everything must end—eventually…. The only question that remains… is not what we will do when it does, but what can we do before it is?"

The James S. Brady Press Briefing Room in the West Wing was packed, and the White House buzzing with curiosity. At a time when the president should have been busy in preparation for the election, to increase his hopes of winning a second term in office, it was most irregular that he chose instead to deliver an unscheduled announcement.

Not even Kiera Calderbank, the president's press secretary, knew why Barnes had called for the press conference. She entered the room, as always smartly dressed and ready for the lens of a camera; smiling an approving smile, after spying all seven seats in all seven rows filled with journalists. She flicked her shimmering, shoulder length copper hair and made her way towards the podium. To the left, the aisle was crammed with photographers awaiting the statement, and she stood on her toes to lean into the microphone.

'Good afternoon,' she said, smiling graciously and acknowledging their patience.

A faulty air conditioning unit hummed like a rainmaking ritual at a tribal gathering, beating out a faint and constant rhythm in the background. The air was dry and thin; the room stifling with so many people in such a small space. Lights added only to the heat. Whatever the president had to say, everyone hoped it would be brief and to the point. As Calderbank tried to bring calm and decorum to the proceedings, hands from the journalists waved wildly in the air, with each one desperate to gain her attention. The problem was she had nothing to say, no answers for questions of their readers or viewers, and she called once again for quiet. Suddenly, a message in her earpiece informed her that the president was ready.

'Ladies and gentlemen... your attention, please,' she said to no avail. 'Ladies and gentlemen... if I could have your attention.... The president of the United States.'

The door opened and Barnes entered with the first lady. Cordelia was a former Miss Idaho winner who finished second in the Miss America pageant. Twenty years had passed since then and she worked hard every day to ensure that no one noticed. Stylish and impeccably dressed, her blonde bobbed hair, like her makeup, was perfect. It was never too much and never too little. Enough to make her look younger than her years, still not enough to make her look desperately young.

Wyatt Lewis followed them from behind. The vice president was like a shadow: he was always there and hanging around. He never seemed as if he actually did anything, nothing except lurk. Lewis wore sharp dark navy suits and had a smile that looked like it was stuck on with adhesive. His wife was a dental surgeon and had obviously fixed all his teeth. Although, in her goal to make them perfect, she may have squeezed in too many because his lips never seemed to close properly. Whenever he spoke, they made a sort of lisping spitting sound, which meant that words like, 'president', actually sounded like *'prezzzident.'* It was unfortunate for a man who was forced to have to say the word all the time, since he was the *'vizzzeth prezzzident'* after all. As they took the few short steps to the stage platform, Calderbank moved to the side. Cordelia and Lewis joined her as Barnes held centre stage behind the podium. The president looked nervous as he stared at the floor, surprisingly anxious for the normally overconfident Barnes. He cleared his throat and took a sip from the glass that was placed beside the microphone, before looking up at the journalists now silent and attentive.

'My fellow Americans,' began Barnes as he stared into the live broadcast camera at the back of the room; his face solemn, lips drawn and tighter than usual. 'I speak to you this evening, not only as your president, but as a fellow countryman... a father... a husband... and a friend.

'For several months now, my health has been in decline.... While I know this will come as a surprise... perhaps a shock to you all, I am prepared for the outcome of what will be.'

Gasps rang out from around the room, as the bombshell of unexpected news caused the first lady to faint dramatically. Lewis glanced down, pretending not to notice and ignored her, before several aides ran onto the stage to ensure that she was alright. Unwavering and steadfast, the president continued his speech.

'In my term as president, I have had the honour—the privilege—of completing former President Robert's vision of a crime-free society.

Nothing would give me greater pleasure than to continue to help shape the future of our great nation.... However, in light of my health, I cannot, and could not, campaign with all sincerity, or seek your support for another term in office. Neither can I choose, nor ask you to vote for a man who I believe is the only real choice—my preferred candidate—for taking our country forward. A man with whom I share the same values. With whom I have had the great privilege and pleasure of working beside most every day during my time in office.'

Lewis ran his tongue discreetly across his teeth: ready for when the cameras would turn. He lowered his head and straightened his tie to accept his endorsement in front of the world. Breathing deeply, he tried to decide how best to react. He would have to accept yet try to pretend that he did not want to. He would beg the president to reconsider and reject his decision, then finally accept the nomination; only out of the love and respect that he held for his commander in chief... blah, blah, blah and so forth. He raised his hand, as if scratching his neck, though tried instead to pat his hair without drawing attention. He brushed his fingers across his fringe, to keep it to the right and out of his eyes. He was ready, and he exhaled, taking only shorter breaths. This was most unexpected, but then history has been made by the men who have risen to the unanticipated challenges of life, and who was Lewis to deny history her newest champion?

'Now we all know that protocol—that standard protocol— would ordinarily turn to each state to select a nominee to run for each party. We all know that eventually each party will choose from one of the nominees to support and stand behind.... This is how it's done—how it's always been done—since we invoked the two-party system almost two hundred years ago. And yet, if my presidency has taught me anything, it's that things change... times change... and we must all be willing to change with them.

'If you had asked me ten years ago, would we be able to close every correctional facility in the western world...? I would have said, *"No."*

'If you had asked me five years ago, could we improve the lives of every citizen of this great nation and connect them to the DomiGen Grid...? I would have said, *"Never."*

'And if you had told me, that we can—we will—and what's more, we will do it for free, then I would have said, "Oh – come – *on!*"'

Laughter rang out around the room at the president's sly humour, as he nodded and raised his hand to appeal for quiet.

'So, here we are... we find ourselves in Neverland... in the world of science fiction, and we're here because things change... because times *have* changed. Which is why today, I wanted to take this opportunity—this moment—in the event that my time is indeed much shorter than any of us would hope. To offer to you, my friends, my vote and endorsement for the man I hope will become the next president of the United States.'

Lewis dragged his hands down the sides of his trousers, attempting to dry the sweat from his palms unnoticed.

'Ladies and gentlemen, I would like... no.... Please, allow me to rephrase if I may... I would hope... that you will all—as I have—put your vote and confidence behind the *only* man that I believe has the credentials to govern this country.'

Lewis stopped his fidgeting and bared his stunning white teeth. He nodded confidently, then took a step towards the podium.

'I am of course talking about none other than Dr. Edgar Spear.'

He was not alone as the room fell into stunned silence. He froze, like a mannequin in a window; paralysed by the sting of betrayal, as the delay between what Barnes had said, and what he expected Barnes to say was dwelt upon. The superficial smile made ready for the cameras slid from his face, replaced by confusion, then the shock of disbelief. Lewis was speechless. Finally, unable to contain his surprise any longer, his mouth opened wide and accidentally blurted out.

'What!'

His sentiment was echoed by everyone in the room. Everyone, that is, except the president, who was not open to taking questions.

'May God bless you, and may God bless the United States of America.'

The red light on the camera dimmed and the broadcast was over. The room exploded with panic, and the first to sound the alarm was Lewis.

'*Mr. President! Mr. President...!* If I could just have a moment of your time...?'

Barnes turned from the audience of screaming hands that begged for his consideration. Lewis, now in his path, stood to confront him. The president was vacant, unwitting as he brushed past—as if Lewis really were a shadow. He walked slowly: awkward and methodically towards the medical staff who had joined the aides treating his wife. Lewis, however, would not be ignored—not again—and he grabbed the shoulder of Barnes to jump in front of the president. He demanded an audience, his right to be heard, as Barnes stared blankly ignoring his request before continuing on to his wife. The cameras captured everything, and the journalists grew louder as they leapt to their feet, each yelling in the hope of gaining the scoop: a formal response to the vice president's humiliation. Calderbank took to the podium to try to restore some level of order and diffuse the fever pitch. Lewis spun in circles, holding his forehead and tugging at his hair. His career was in ruins. Amid the chaos and the heart of the uproar, he spied a face in the middle of the back row. It was a face in a chair reserved for a journalist from a financial newspaper. A face that should not be there, in a chair whose occupant was the only one seated: the only one without their hands in the air. A face in a crowd of faces that was alone and tried to remain anonymous. Withdrawn from the pack that was baying for blood, it was the only one that managed to attract his attention.

'*You!*' screamed Lewis. 'What are *you* doing here...?'

The focus of the cameras left the president and took aim at the angry virulent man; at the image of a vice president who was as far from presidential as a man could possibly be. Every camera followed closely, eager to capture this historic day, but even they were surprised as Lewis leapt from the stage.

'Out of my way…! *Get – out – of – my – way!*' he roared, as he forced his way through the journalists, lashing out as he stormed towards the seated figure.

He loomed menacingly over the seated man, oblivious to his surroundings and the flashes of camera lights recording the end of his candidacy.

'I don't know *what* you have on him… but I'll find out… and when I do, you'll *never* set foot in here again…! You hear me…? *Never!*'

Edgar sat smiling, ignoring the taunts of Lewis. He knew what would fill the evening and morning news segments. There was nothing that he needed to say and nothing that he needed to do, because even in a world of free will, Lewis was finished. The master, like his master before him, could never leave without the final word, and Edgar rose from his chair.

'There are two kinds of people in this world…' said Edgar, as he leaned forward and whispered up to Lewis. 'The ones that get ahead and the ones that get left behind.'

'*What…?* What did you say?'

'Do I look like a guy that's playing catch up to you?'

Edgar leaned back to stand upright. Filled with contempt, he stared up at his opponent, who despite his height was nothing except pitiful. Nothing more nor anything other than unworthy.

'You won't steal the presidency from me!'

'Stealing implies ownership,' said Edgar, as he winked.

Lewis could barely contain himself as he quivered with anger. 'You'll *never* run… I promise you… I'll make sure of it!'

'I don't need to,' whispered Edgar. 'I've already won... the house has fallen.'

'What...? What house?'

Lewis shook his head, dismissing the wild ramblings of the doctor. He aimed to push Edgar but missed, managing to remain on his feet as he stumbled, losing balance.

'Whoops!' smirked Edgar.

Lewis would have to do better than that if the king was to fall, and Edgar's broad grin made it more to the point. It burned through Lewis as his simmering rage boiled into fury; exploding violently as he reached and took Edgar by the throat.

'You'll regret the day you made *me* your enemy!'

Edgar said nothing, smiling only in reply. He glanced to his right, to a parting in the press. A member of the administration had forged her way through to insist that Lewis follow her, immediately. But Lewis was toe-to-toe with his adversary, one-on-one and unwilling to back down. This was, however, not a request. A man grabbed hold of his fist, while another removed his grip, before they dragged him away like a disgruntled prize fighter.

'Pity,' murmured Edgar.

Lewis should have been grateful and conceded the contest. He was saved by the bell, from himself and from doing more harm. All the same, he lacked decency or the sense to see either, glaring instead; transfixed on the winner of round one.

'It's *not* over! I know what you are... I'm going to show the world—'

As they pulled him back, it was clear that his eyes sought righteousness, even though it was obvious to Edgar they would settle for revenge. His words faded to noise and his threat stayed unfinished, as the journalists surged forwards with their questions for Edgar. Unmoved and indifferent at the heart of it all, he shied away from the cameras as they screamed for an answer.

'Dr. Spear.... Dr. Spear, will you run for the presidency?'

Edgar glanced at the journalist with her microphone pressed further at his lips. He tried to move as another pushed forward, blocking his escape.

'Dr. Spear, would you care to make a comment about the president's health?'

Edgar paused, then turned to look into the lens. 'It's at moments like these, that we're all reminded about the hands of time—'

'Dr. Spear,' yelled another voice. 'Would you mind speaking up?'

'Because whoever we are, and wherever we may be, we all know that our time is running out....'

'Dr. Spear?'

'Tick tock.... Tick... tock—'

'And the behaviour of Vice President Lewis...?' interrupted another journalist. 'Would you care to comment on the vice president, Dr. Spear?'

A flash of cameras blinded his view.

'Any comment on the extraordinary behaviour of the vice president?'

'Precisely,' he replied, suppressing his smile.

15

GETTING AWAY WITH MURDER

President Barnes stepped back from public view. In the weeks and months following his announcement, the media, television, and internet were filled with endorsements for Edgar. Celebrities, musicians, stars of the stage and the silver screen, all paid for billboards. Leading officials, well known business leaders and entrepreneurs, had taken full-page advertisements in national newspapers. All carried the same message, and the mass media was flooded with one proposition: *Vote for Dr. Edgar Spear.* It was all highly irregular and most definitely not within the boundaries of normal nomination convention. Most specially since Edgar was wholly independent and neither represented the Republican, nor the Democratic Party. He kept his own council, and as always, refused to be drawn into the spotlight to discuss himself or anything other than the tragic condition of his friend, President Barnes. Endorsements were one thing, but Edgar's silence had neither confirmed nor denied his entry into the presidential race. Speculation continued to grow, as pundits claimed the ploy was a tactic to concentrate press coverage; to keep Edgar's name in the media, and the Grid within focus of the public eye. After all, the question itself was so very straightforward, yet dominated the headlines. Was Edgar going to run for president: yes, or no?

Lewis was never particularly well liked, and the court of public opinion was often harsh in its judgement. Nevertheless, the fact that he was the "vizzzeth prezzzident," with one foot already inside the White House door, made him the natural choice for succession. He had worked hard to increase political support, yet despite his greatest efforts, not least personal expenses, Lewis still lacked that "*man of the people*" feeling. He was simply too stiff, without any real personality or appeal. He came from money and represented money, which is perhaps why he often came across as being overly privileged. The incident at President Barnes' last press conference, when he showed the world that he clearly didn't have the temperament expected of a leader, had not helped either. Then of course, there were his teeth. Those blindingly bleached white teeth. After analysing footage from the incident, the stylists of Lewis had decided that more contrast was needed to make them appear less garish. Sadly, the heavy orange spray tan that Lewis now sported only made matters worse. His teeth were just impossible to escape and had become something of a continual joke. In short, Lewis could never be an election winning candidate for the Republican Party. In fact, it was only thanks to the efforts of his public relations team that he was able to continue his political career at all, and succeeded in becoming the running mate to Jeffery Montanas.

Montanas was a middle-aged, straight-talking senator from New Jersey. A man who rose from impoverished humble beginnings, and who unlike Lewis wasn't born with a silver spoon. He was a hard man who never took no for an answer and stood with the blue collars for the rights of every worker. Now, he also stood as the man with whom the Republican Party pinned their hopes, if they were to gain another four more years in office.

The Democrats began their search for an opposing candidate, finally nominating Claudia Miller, a former Wisconsin state senator who ran together with Elijah Williams. They called themselves, *"The Dream Team,"* and in the run up to the election, they fought it out against Montanas and Lewis through a series of various televised debates. As their arguments swung back and forth, it felt like a never-ending game on a tennis court. Each side sent volley after volley, desperately trying to score points with the public over who was best suited to lead the country. Consensus was fairly clear, and a winner looked to have emerged, when just a week before the election, much to the shock of everyone, news broke that Montanas had taken his own life. In a handwritten letter, he had said that the pressures of running for office were simply too great and the burden too heavy to bear. He could no longer contend with the expectations of being the Republican nominee, nor face the possibility—or humiliation—of letting so many people down if he should fail to be elected. It was a terrible blow for the party, and with little time left to promote a new candidate capable of gaining public trust, Lewis was left to lead. The Republicans seemed destined for defeat; hand delivering the game, set, and match to The Dream Team. Washington was already decked with blue banners, in preparation for Miller's inevitable victory. Her slogan throughout the campaign, *"Dare to Dream the Impossible,"* was about to come true. This was not only a win for the Democrats, but a triumph for equality. Miller would be the first female president and history was about to be made. History, however, waits for no man, or woman for that matter, and on the eve of claiming glory, just two days before the election, an unexpected public announcement was picked up and shared by every major news network.

'Good morning. My name is Dr. Edgar Spear. You will have heard of me through my company, DomiGen Labs.'

Edgar sat calmly in his office. It once belonged to Abelman, but like everything else, it now belonged to him. His hands were clasped on the desk in front of him, and his direct address failed to conform to the usual pleasantries. There was no question that everyone had or should at least have heard of him.

'During these past months, there has been a great deal of conjecture regarding my participation in this election. In light of Senator Montanas' death, and the ailing condition of my dear friend President Barnes, I feel that the time has come to put an end to these speculations. I wish, therefore, to take this opportunity to inform you that I will be running for the Office of President of the United States.

'Let me be precise. I represent neither the Republican, nor Democratic Party... I represent change... and in doing so reject the requirements of the past. Consequently, I do not endorse the role of vice president, and have no need of one. Your vote for me, will be a vote for me—a vote for change. Thank you.'

When the broadcast ended, the scrutiny of Edgar's speech began. By simply announcing he had joined the race, was running alone without giving more, saw him brutally savaged by political commentators and parties alike. He offered no agenda, no clear position or presentation of proposed policies. He had come with nothing: no manifesto or political experience. With so little time before the election, what hopes could he have except the indignity of defeat?

The media were relentless as they begged for response to his statement. Every news network and agency solicited promises of an exclusive: the chance to tell his side of the story before it was too late. Yet Edgar cared little for stories or platforms for public support. He chose instead to ignore the claims, the things being said, and the invitations that were offered. In his absence, came the ridicule of his opponents. Each took turns to lambaste his decision to run. Gone were their arguments of policies and improvements, replaced instead by cheap vicious blows as the man they attacked refused to appear. Without a defence, there was no one more damning, more unstatesmanlike than Lewis. Persistent with insults that were aimed to discredit, nothing was off limits in his sordid attempt to win any vote.

His pitiful efforts lasted only a day. A measly twenty-four hours was all that Lewis had to destroy Edgar. In next to no time, the sound of marching bands and street parades began to drown out his, as well as every other insult. It was a great day for America, and for every American. For everyone who ever valued independence, and for anyone who ever valued the price of freedom. It had been a long hard race for Miller, Williams, and Lewis. For their families, their supporters, and the volunteers who had worked tirelessly to get them to this point. For their parties, their generous benefactors, and for those who had hedged their bets in the hope of the benefits their support might one day bring. Now it was over, the end of uncertainty would come for all, and the end of the road would arrive for some. The day slipped into darkness and the long wait of the night, as votes were counted, tallied, and delivered. Hours passed, as slowly, but surely, results began to surface. There was now no question, no doubt or need to recount. With over ninety-three-point-eight percent of the entire electoral vote, there was only one winner: a landslide of unprecedented proportion.

The people had spoken, yet their words made no sense. Almost every eligible voter had cast their ballot for Edgar. As a result, the Republican bastions of the south and the Democratic strongholds in the east were all gone. All had surrendered to him. Once the shock had subsided and the president-elect was declared, without representatives in Congress, in the Senate, or even a vice president, how could Dr. Spear—or rather—President E. Spear, legally be sworn into office? Laws would have to be challenged, and the Constitution itself thrown into difficulty; because if Edgar should be president, then everything would have to change, whether it chose to freely, or not.

The formal process of inauguration had begun. Change was inevitable. It started with the ceremony itself, which Edgar refused to hold in front of the Capitol Building. There were no concerts or gatherings, no cameras or parades, and Edgar refused to allow the event to be televised. He was the president, not the defender of worthless tradition, and the formalities would be held in Boston, in the lobby of DomiGen. There was no need for pomp and circumstance, or even a ceremony itself. Although the irony of the oath was one of which Edgar approved, and for that alone demanded some form of commemoration.

The midday sun lit the foyer, igniting the familiar scent of rose petals and Jasmin. Edgar placed his left hand on the Bible and raised his right.

'Please repeat after me,' said the chief justice.

Edgar stared at the old man. He looked him up and down disparagingly.

'No,' he replied. 'I think we should start how we mean to go on.'

An anxious smile crept onto the face of the chief justice. His silver-white beard parting to the sides to make room for his bewilderment.

'I… I'm sorry—'

'Don't be,' interrupted Edgar. 'I'll make this simple. I'll speak. You'll listen.'

'B-but… you—'

'I do solemnly swear that I will faithfully execute the Office of President of the United States, and will to the best of my ability, preserve, protect and defend the Constitution of the United States…. So help me God,' said Edgar, laughingly.

He lowered his hand. The chief justice, still in shock, offered his to congratulate the new president.

'You can go,' said Edgar, as he turned and began to walk towards the sliding doors; the hand of the chief justice, still left waiting. Edgar stopped, suddenly, then turned around. 'Take that book with you… and the others. We don't need them here.'

His inauguration was the start of how he intended to lead: unequivocally. That being said, President Spear controlled many things but not everything, not yet, and a cell phone had filmed the ceremony before the footage was posted online. It drew widespread criticism, and in the time that followed, there were many who asked how a man of such ill-breeding had managed to become president? Many more who wondered how he was able to secure such a monumental amount of the vote? Edgar had won—for better or worse—and that much was indisputable. Still, no one quite understood how, at least, not for certain. As the weeks passed and people went about their everyday lives, no one claimed to have voted for him at all, yet apparently almost everyone had. The names on ballot papers and their numbers added up, so why was there a problem?

Had it been only one or two, a few who complained, then their grievances might well have been dismissed; the gripes of defeated sore losers who backed the wrong horse in the electoral race. But the chatrooms and forums overflowed with opinion, with the misgivings of those who had claimed to have never tendered their vote. There was a problem—a nagging problem—and in that grey zone where questions linger, meanings are formed while uncertainty persists. Conspiracies spread as stories are born, and one such conspiracy gave life to a group long since seen. The rioters, those anarchists who once plagued DomiGen in the early days of implant technology, raised their ugly heads once more. However, unlike before, they now had a radical, motivated young leader who went by the name of Gabriel Grey, and they called themselves: *The Remnants.*

The Remnants were a legion of free-thinking people unwilling to connect to Edgar's brave new implanted world. Like a tribe, or a clan of sorts, they had nothing in common accept the total rejection of the Grid and the use of implants in human beings. They were the missing six-point-two percent, remaining invisible with their allegiance hidden from families and friends. Through planned strategic attacks, they mobilised cells to take aim against the government, against Edgar, against DomiGen, and all they believed was a threat to their freedom. Their assaults were conspicuous—highly audacious—and to the bystanders who watched or viewed from afar, the president was not losing, he had lost his control.

The rise of the Remnants now meant that extremism, not crime, threatened the livelihoods of the American people. As their attacks grew in size, ever worse in severity, the agents who oversaw the monitoring of former criminals, were unable to contain or combat the violence. Unwillingly forced, or so made to seem, Edgar announced the disbandment of the unit in order to make way for one more able to tackle these threats; more capable of infiltrating the faction to bring Grey and his followers to justice. It would be a force to be reckoned with, and one to restore peace... once and for all.

As the last of the agents left their post, the final traces of traditional law enforcement disappeared with them. Change was no longer inevitable: change was assured. Commissioner Reams was promoted to Commander Reams, taking control of the new agency; an elite troop of armed guards and rangers known only as the DomiForce. Within twelve months there were over a million recruits: each of them a convict from The DOGMA Program, now paid and trusted to protect the lives of every American citizen. They were soldiers of an army more menacing than heartening, more militant than modest, and their imposing black uniforms were designed to emphasise such facts precisely.

Despite the promises made by Edgar and the threat from Reams of unparalleled reprisal, Grey remained an outlaw. He was more than a rebel or fighter of freedom. He was all that opposed a world of precision. A symbol to others. A brick out of place.

Times had changed. The Remnants were everywhere: spread throughout the world and across every land. Wherever a protest erupted, every march saw a step of defiance, and every skirmish the act of rebellion. Gaining attention was no longer the aim, and concerns over safety no longer the problem. The issue that Grey and his followers had was one of morality. Their mission to end selective conformity; to free all those being forcibly reformed.

When statistics first showed that crime was decreasing, the objections to implants in convicts declined. The public lost interest as the benefits of controlling anti-social behaviour outweighed any risk to the criminal mind. Just as it had under Roberts, this new form of sedition, albeit more organised, had also failed to gain public support. Each act of aggression brought sympathy for Edgar and kinship from other world leaders. Grey was a criminal of international repute, and not one driven by simple financial gain. His political ambition, the mistaken presumption that he was aiding liberation and the rights of others, made him harder to understand—for people to accept—and something that The DOGMA Program was never designed to defeat. All but a few countries now remained outside the program, and the message from Grey and his Remnants was clear. If DomiGen could alter the minds of a group in society, then who was to stop them from doing it to others? Who was to say they had not done so already…?

A world summit of leaders was due to be held in New York at the General Assembly Hall of the United Nations. Edgar had been asked to speak about the successes of DOGMA, and the end of crime in countries that had used DomiGen's implants. He would appeal to the last two member states who had not yet implemented the program, and more importantly, use the platform to discuss the very real and growing threat of political activism.

As Edgar's motorcade entered First Avenue, the shadow from the United Nations Secretariat blocked the sun like an eclipse. It towered over the world below, and the convoy continued, undaunted through darkness as they sped towards the entrance of the Plaza. Returning to the light, Edgar stared out through the window; his face surprisingly pleased and brightened in awe. There was just something majestic about the flags, of seeing all hundred and ninety-three fly in unison along the length of the building. Alone they were symbols, representing their homelands and carrying their colours. In contrast, together, in a line like this, suspended in mid-air over the perfectly cut and deepest of green hedges, they were something else, and more than just a symbol of unity. There was a power to them, a sense of greatness and nobility. A feeling that Edgar very much liked. Driving past, he felt again the sensation that he found each time that he came here. The sound from the flags as they flapped in the wind gave chorus like the clapping of hands. They were not there to welcome, but to herald and announce him; to proclaim his arrival so that others may prepare for the entrance of a god.

His chariot came to a halt as they rounded the fountain. The door opened and Edgar stepped out into the brilliant sunshine. Be that as it may, this was not Olympus, and he was met instead by the icy chill that blew across the East River. He shivered as he stood, pulling his navy-blue cashmere coat ever tighter, raising the collar to break from the cold that froze against his neck. Two DomiForce Guards appeared from the car that had followed behind and ushered him quickly across the tarmac towards the entrance. As Edgar climbed the grey concrete steps, an echo rang out from around the forecourt. It was loud and it boomed like the sound of explosives; like the bang of a building that was being demolished. Then it rumbled like a tremor, like the aftershock of the building as it collapsed into dust. The echo came from afar, miles away in fact, travelling across the East River like a ripple upon its surface. Edgar turned to the sound, stopping short; his face suddenly surprised as it paled and stiffened. He glanced at the guard, the one closest beside him, his eyes searching for something his lips could not express.

'Mr. President?'

He looked down at his chest, then back at the guard, seemingly poised to reply.

'Mr. Pres—'

His eyes rolled up as his head fell back, and Edgar collapsed in a heap.

Blood seeped onto the cold concrete as it pooled and dripped from the step. The two DomiForce Guards scrambled around him. They drew their weapons, gripping them tightly with both hands; eyes and gun barrels darting quickly as they scouted their lines of sight. Another four guards, quick to react, raced from the convoy and charged up the steps to create a shield around Edgar.

'The lair is compromised… I repeat the lair — *is* — compromised!' shouted one of the guards as he touched the lobe of his ear. 'We need extraction.… We need immediate—'

Suddenly, the doors opened, and a woman oblivious to what was happening looked up from her cell phone. She jolted, then screamed, her coffee spewing from the paper cup as it crashed onto the hard ground. Reaching to cover her mouth, her hand was unable to hide the horror. She recoiled, piercing the air with another scream. It was muffled this time, still managing to escape through her fingers.

'Get down! *Get — down!*'

She froze instead in the panic and confusion, as the shrill of terrified voices cried out from inside.

'Find cover… *now!*'

The doors jammed as she crouched, caught like a deer in the headlights. A hand grabbed at her arm and pulled back to the side, dragging her in to safety.

'Stay inside! Keep low… *stay — down!*'

Members of the United Nations security team rushed out. They lifted Edgar into the building under cover of the guards who stood firm in formation—shielding their chief—backing towards the entrance once the imminent danger was over. Within minutes, armoured trucks and vehicles had poured into the forecourt as DomiForce flooded every inch of the Plaza. Nothing was going to get in, and no one was going to get out. Unbeknown and unprepared, the cameras that had gathered to film the arrival of world leaders, had broadcast instead an attempt on the life, or the successful assassination of the American president.

It was almost an hour before the sound of whirring blades filled the air; driving the desperate efforts of those on the ground to create space, as Marine One attempted to land as close to the entrance as possible. Two DomiForce Rangers emerged, frantically signalling to hurry. Every second counted, the possible difference between a life and a death. A company of guards—five hundred at least—separated into two columns, forming a sentry from the door to the helicopter. They surrounded a stretcher that emerged from the entrance and was carried in all haste through the centre. Pushing on, their heads stayed bowed against the vortex that tried to force them back in retreat. Behind them a trail of bloodied footsteps, and the blood not yet dry walked through like a path. The cameras stayed fixed as his pale lifeless body was lifted onboard. Those crammed at the windows and squeezed at the doorway, lamented their loss as Marine One lifted, then sped up and away.

The world fell silent, and the thoughts of every leader from around the globe were expressed. There had been no official word and no formal statement made; nevertheless, the president's blood had been spilled. Everyone saw it, and within minutes every news channel had screened it. The unthinkable had happened. The inconceivable had been conceived. The unimaginable was now a reality, as incredible as it may have seemed.

In the hours that followed, it was not just America, but the whole world that stopped. Crowds had begun to converge, and candlelight vigils lit up the Secretariat. The thirty-nine-storey skyscraper, so often symbolised as the headquarters of the United Nations, was now the closest that anyone could get to the cordoned off scene; the closest thing that the crowds were going to have to an altar. At first, people came in their hundreds, then not before long in their hundreds of thousands. They prayed and they sang as they hoped for news. Yet despite their devotion, there was still no word of their president. Where had they taken him? Was he alive, or were their prayers left forsaken…?

Eleven hours had passed since the shooting, before a man appeared shortly after midnight. Escorted through the crowds, he arrived at the doors to address the nation and to speak to the world.

The man was short, slim in build and closer to sixty than fifty. His greying hair was parted at the side, and he wore a white jacket, like a doctor or surgeon. As he approached the microphones set up outside the entrance, he was clearly nervous, appearing overly so, with the cameras pointing at him from behind the barricade at the bottom of the steps.

'Good evening ladies and gentlemen,' said the man as he cleared his throat. His accent wasn't local; it was possibly Canadian, perhaps even French. 'My name is Dr. Kylian Chapon, and I am the Head Physician in the Department of Surgery at Mount Sinai Hospital.

'I have... erm... prepared a statement that I would like to offer to you at this time.

'A short while ago, President Spear was airlifted to our facility. He was admitted with what was believed to be physical trauma, sustained as a result from a single gunshot wound.'

The crowd gasped; their fears confirmed.

'The projectile entered through the lower third of the sternum, where the right atrium of the president's heart, the ventricle, and the inferior vena cava, subsequently succumbed to injury.'

Such incidents were commonplace, a part of the daily routine for Dr. Chapon, especially in New York. However, he now seemed unnerved and needed to steady himself. The attentive crowd, profoundly silent, followed his every echoing word.

'X-rays revealed that the projectile had become lodged in the right paravertebral muscle mass at the lower thoracic level. I erm... I attempted to remove it....' Chapon swallowed hard, struggling to continue. 'However, the president had suffered severe blood loss, and profuse bleeding as a result of the GSW.'

Averting his gaze from the cameras, he looked to the ground as he spoke.

'Approximately nine minutes into surgery, the president's breathing became extremely laboured... before experiencing both respiratory and circulatory failure as he entered into sudden arrest.'

Chapon paused. He was interrupted by another wave of loud involuntary gasps, by those unable to suppress their shock or stop themselves from crying out. A deep breath was picked up by the microphone, and it rang out over the crowd.

'The president's heart stopped for approximately four minutes, until we were able to successfully resuscitate him at 9:27 p.m. It was also after this time, that we were able to stem the bleed and the loss of the president's blood....'

He cleared his throat once again.

'The placement and location of the projectile gave no alternative... I was forced to try again to remove it if the president's life was to be saved. On the third attempt, at approximately 10:18 p.m. I was able to successfully do so, and the bullet retrieved would appear to be consistent with that of a point-four-one-six Barrett cartridge—such as those that are typically used in bolt action single-shot precision rifles. These are long-range high velocity projectiles, designed for only one purpose.... It would seem that tonight, we have prevented that purpose, and the president is now in a stable, albeit critical condition.'

Chapon lowered his head and removed his spectacles, as the crowd listened to his heavy drawn breath.

'I am afraid that the next twenty-four hours will be critical.... I... I cannot give you more details at this time.'

His voice trembled as his eyes began to water, looking up and directly to the cameras.

'I can only say that whatever your faith—no matter your conviction or background—if you believe in God, then whatever God may be to you, please pray for our president... for he is no longer in our hands.'

The doctor turned, wiping his eyes as he quickly walked away from the microphone. The crowd, like the world, fell to a stunned silence. Edgar was alive, but for how much longer?

Commander Reams announced that DomiForce would do whatever was necessary to bring the assailant to justice. There should be no doubt or ambiguity, all agents were now focused on one mission, and one mission alone. No stone would be left unturned, no person exempt or immune, they were on the hunt and they would find whoever was responsible.

Days passed, with no update on the president's condition. Life went on, still far from normal, until it stopped again on the morning of the seventh day. An insurgence of thousands of DomiForce Rangers unexpectedly arrived in the city. Every street—every alleyway—was overrun, and those who protested against the disruption were dealt with quickly. Within the space of a few hours, New York was overwhelmed, looking more like an occupied territory under martial law than the shopping capital for which it was better known. A motorcade made its way through the blockades towards the hospital, surrounded by DomiForce Guards. From the crowd, few were able to catch a glimpse of a dishevelled frail man being helped into a heavily armoured car; whisked away in the blink of an eye.

The days turned to weeks, during which time the White House was flooded with cards and flowers. Even the most ardent of Edgar's critics came to offer their best wishes for his recovery, and today was no exception. Wyatt Lewis had asked for an audience with the president, and Edgar had granted one.

'Mr. President,' said the DomiForce Guard.

Edgar heard a door behind him open as he looked out of the bay windows across the White House lawns.

'Edgar! It's so good to see you on your feet again. How are you feeling?'

Edgar stood without reply, and the summer air felt chilled without logs burning at the fire.

'Look, I know that we haven't spoken since before the elect—'

'It's Mr. President.'

'Sorry?'

'The way to address me... how *you* will address me.... It's Mr. President.'

Lewis gritted his teeth. Edgar waited to hear a hint of humility; an acknowledgement that he had earned his title.

'Fine... whatever you like.... I think I speak for everyone when I—'

His tone was only hostile, so Edgar interrupted again.

'You speak for no one, Wyatt. For no one and for nothing. In fact, whenever you speak my ears hurt and I'd prefer it if you didn't.'

Edgar turned to face Lewis. He met his eyes with that cold, blank, sadistic stare that he had learned from his former master and perfected so very well.

'Actually, I'd prefer it if you did nothing... nothing except answer the question.'

'Question...? Edgar, I'm not here to answer your—'

'That's right, Wyatt. I only have one question for you.'

Lewis paused. His face troubled by the president's apparent confusion; his struggle to express himself clearly. Edgar was far from reticent.

'How?'

'How...? How what? I'm sorry, Edgar, you—'

'That's the second time you've apologised, and you still haven't answered the question.'

'Edgar, what the Devil—'

'Oh, we'll get to the Devil... don't you worry... but first, I want to know how you could hope to ever get away with it?'

'A-away...? Away with what...? What is it that I am supposed to be getting away with?' demanded Lewis, tired of Edgar's ambiguity.

Edgar smiled and looked up at the ceiling. 'Do you see that seal?'

'Seal...? Edgar, you're not well—'

'The seal,' interrupted Edgar; repeating himself decisively.

Lewis scowled then glanced upwards. 'Of course, I see it!' he snapped. 'What about it?'

'E PLURIBUS UNUM…. Do you know what it means?'

'What the hell is this?'

'It means, out of many come one.'

Edgar looked down, forbiddingly at Lewis, then walked around the desk towards him.

'You know, Wyatt, I am one… and from me there are many.'

'What's going on here…? I mean… I come here to see how you are and—'

Lewis stopped, unable to make sense of Edgar, rambling again like he did the last time they met. Edgar leaned back, perched on the edge of his desk, as he folded his arms and glared.

'And if you object to the one—you object to the many…. Cause outrage to the one—you'll find outrage from the many…. Oppose the one… and *you* oppose the many.'

Lewis put his tongue in his cheek. He shook his head, deriding the president. '*Really…?* Oppose the many…? The many what? Are you listening to yourself…? I don't know if you banged your head when you hit the concrete, but you don't make sense—you've never made sense—and you've *never* been fit for this office.'

Lewis was brazen. He was scathing and felt untouchable, especially in the White House: his second home for many years. He narrowed his eyes believing that he finally had Edgar's attention.

'I told you once, and I'm telling you again… I'll find out what you had on Barnes and—'

Edgar's voice, still calm and detached, spoke at will and interrupted at leisure. 'Barnes can't help you, Wyatt… he's convalescing…. In fact, I doubt he'll ever be able to speak to you again.'

'What's that supposed to mean?'

'It means Barnes served his purpose,' replied Edgar with a smirk. 'He did what he was told to do, and for that, I allow him to live.'

'You – allow – him – to – *live?*' Lewis began to laugh jeeringly. 'My God, even *you* can't believe something so ridiculous?'

'Everyone has a purpose, Wyatt. Barnes served his and now he'll spend the rest of his days in an armchair—talking to fairies and Leprechauns.... But you're missing the point... asking all the wrong questions... it's not Barnes you need to worry about, is it?' Edgar raised an eyebrow, his stare still fierce and cold. 'Like I said, how could you hope to ever get away with it?'

'Away with *what?*'

Lewis was exasperated at being ignored. He pinched his lips as he breathed out and lowered his head, shaking it slightly to the side. He paused again, a poor effort to gain composure, then looked up.

'Listen... I don't have time for your games, Spear.'

'Purpose, Wyatt,' said Edgar as he smiled. 'Not games... I'm talking about purpose.'

Irate and incensed, Lewis was no longer interested in Edgar's rambling, or whatever point he was using so long to make.

'What's wrong with you...? Nothing you say makes sense. I'm going to call the medical examiner and have you removed immediately!'

'Well, why don't you? Here, go ahead.'

Edgar pointed to the phone on his desk. Lewis hesitated; his face beginning to scrunch.

'Go on... call him.'

He watched as the brow of Lewis deepened, then tugged a little harder on his strings.

'Go on....'

Annoyed by the taunting, the eyes of Lewis seemed to cloud over, and his cheeks began to flame.

'Well...? What are you waiting for, Wyatt? Go on... do it.'

Edgar's smile stretched to a very wry grin. Lewis snapped. He grabbed the phone and dialled the direct line to the White House Medical Unit.

'Dr. Rowly?' he asked, his eyes locked with Edgar's. 'It's Wyatt.... Wyatt Lewis...? The former vice president? Yes... that's right.... Yes, the Oval Office... I'm with him now... I think he's having trouble speaking. You'd better come immediately.'

Lewis put the phone down, and a smugness wrapped around his face.

'You think I'm scared of you...? You're finished, Spear. I warned you—you should have listened. I told you I'd find a way to make sure you never set foot in here again... you'll be locked up and medicated before nightfall.'

Edgar continued to lean on the edge of his desk, saying nothing. Nevertheless, Edgar's silence was an admission to Lewis: a confession of Edgar's failure to intimidate his adversary. Lewis felt roused, as ungracious in victory as he was in defeat. He found a sudden strength of nerve.

'Call yourself the president...? I'd call you an embarrassment... a disgrace to this office. So, look around you, Spear... because this is the last time you'll ever be in it... in *my* office,' he scoffed gloatingly, as he slumped into a chair opposite the Resolute desk. Brimming with confidence, he crossed his legs and clasped his hands. He tapped his thumbs as he tilted his head to the side, looking curiously at Edgar. 'That chair belongs to me,' he said nodding at the president's chair. 'Shame I won't get to see you thrown off it.'

Edgar stood upright, silent and defiant, looking down upon Lewis as he took a step towards him. Suddenly, the northwest door knocked and opened, as Dr. Rowly entered, breathing heavily.

'Mr. President...? Is everything alright, sir?'

Edgar turned casually to Rowly, and the tension broke.

'Everything's fine, Dom. Actually, I'm glad you're here. Come in and take a seat.'

Lewis looked at Rowly who stayed in the doorway, not wanting to disturb further if his services were not required.

'Well come on... I won't ask again.'

Rowly obeyed and closed the door behind him. He hurried over and took a seat beside Lewis.

For a physician, Rowly was a peculiar man, quite unconventional and most definitely eccentric. He always wore a thick woollen chequered V-neck sweater vest and trousers that were only in fashion for a few months every few years. His tangled auburn locks were always unkept, thick and curly, split by an occasional white strand; natural highlights, he called them. His tortoise-shell spectacles were wrapped with brown parcel tape across the bridge, and they perfected a look that was not unlike a retired mathematics teacher from the 1970s. He tended to perspire quite heavily, and as a result, the tape that held his spectacles together more often than not lost its adhesion. As he took out a handkerchief and loudly blew his nose, his glasses began to slide apart. He reached quickly to hold them, squeezing the tape in the hope that it glued, then mumbled something about an errand, before looking up at the president.

Edgar removed his jacket, then hung it methodically over the back of his chair. He took a moment to dust it with his hand: to emphasise the point further. Lewis scoffed again as Edgar loosened, then removed his tie. He laid it over his jacket, as he unbuttoned his collar and winked.

'For God's sake man! Rowly, can't you give him something? A sedative? Anything…? There must be something…? He's clearly lost his mind… I mean, look at him!'

Edgar continued, casually unbuttoning his shirt.

'Yes, please do… take a look, Wyatt. Take a good — *long* — look.'

The doctor stood to help the president.

'Where you were, Rowly. Don't get up. There's no need… I think I got this.'

Edgar signalled to Rowly to stay seated as he removed his shirt and placed it on top of his tie.

'Now, Dom…. Now that we can all see… why don't you tell us what you see—precisely?'

'Of course, sir. Your bandage.'

'My…? I'm sorry, Dom, didn't quite catch that… my what?'

'Your bandage, sir... to protect your wound dressing.'

Rowly blew his nose again.

'Yes, that's right. Thank you, Doctor.'

Edgar looked to Lewis, open-mouthed but lost for words, without complaint or condemnation of the president. His wide eyes gawked disconcertingly at Edgar. His teeth, so blindingly white, now dulled as the blood drained from his hollowed face. Edgar stared without remorse, like a wolf at a lamb instilling terror; his lips curving to a grin, unable to reach his heartless eyes.

'B-but it's not... there's—'

'Nothing there?' Edgar asked, as his eyes wrenched his grin into a broadened smile.

'H-how...? How is—'

'No dressing...? No wound...? No scar...?'

'It... it can't be—'

'Why...? Because that would mean no gunshot?' Edgar turned to Rowly. 'Seems our guest remains unconvinced about the extent of my injuries, Doctor.... Maybe you can help put his mind at ease...? I wonder, could you tell us, just how big is the scar on my chest?'

'Oh, it's substantial, sir.'

Rowly wiped at his nose again with the handkerchief, talking as he did so. 'Quite large to be exact. We're all so very lucky to have you with us. For a while, I thought we had—'

Edgar nodded. 'That's fine, Dom, but please... if you could be so kind as to tell us what type of dressing you used on my wound?'

'Erm... a non-vented chest seal, of course,' replied Rowly, surprised by the question. 'Occlusive dressings are the most reliable bandages for this type of wound, sir. You see, when a bullet penetrates the chest wall—'

'Ok, Dom... I think we understand... and if it's not too much to ask, I was wondering, when did you last change my dressing?'

Rowly looked at the president. 'Sir...? Are you sure you're feeling alright?'

'Just answer the question… we don't want Wyatt to feel like we're hiding anything from him now, do we?'

Rowly checked his wristwatch.

'Well, that would be a little under an hour ago, sir… at 8:00 a.m. As I have done every third morning since we got you back from New York.'

'Thank you, Doctor.'

Edgar put his shirt back on and began to button it up. Lewis gaped at Rowly, then at Edgar, then back at Rowly. His troubled face in search of answers.

'What is this…? Is this some kind of a joke…? I don't know what's going on here, but you'll never get away with this… do you have any idea who I am? What I can do—'

'You see, that's your problem, isn't it Wyatt?' said Edgar, knotting his tie. 'You're always so busy telling people what they'll never get away with, that you never actually see with all that they can…. And you still haven't answered my question.'

Edgar picked up his jacket and slipped his arms into the sleeves. He straightened it and adjusted the knot of his tie as he raised his chin and sneered down at Lewis.

'How could you hope to ever get away with it?' he asked again, pretending to wipe any dust from the headrest of his chair.

'Away with what?'

'Why, the attempt on my life of course…. Your attempt to assassinate the president of the United States.'

Lewis bolted upright in his chair. 'The — *what!*'

Pointing wildly, he was out of control. A stark contrast to Edgar, who as always remained calm and in full control of everything.

'Are — you — *insane…?* You haven't even been shot! What the hell are you playing at, Spear?'

'Don't you know that sanity is a state of mind? I should know, after all, I control the mind… I control *every* mind.'

Edgar took his right index and middle fingers, tapping the back of his head. He raised his eyebrows and nodded at Rowly while staring directly at Lewis. Lewis felt the wickedness of Edgar's smile, and his clammy palms gripped the arm rests, as he pressed himself harder into the chair in horror at the beast before him. His eyes still fixed on Lewis, Edgar sat down and relaxed; reclining as if to listen to music. But music was not what Edgar had chosen to enjoy, it was the sound of his own voice. The symphony of his own orchestrated plan, and a fitting requiem for an unsuspecting enemy who had falsely assumed that victory was within his grasp.

'You know, Wyatt... I think I'm getting used to your chair... I might even keep it.'

Lewis was scared, unable to argue or protest while Edgar toyed with his prey, watching as he made him suffer—as he would have to suffer. The little lamb was trapped, cornered by the wolf as he rocked back and forth on his squeaking chair. Suddenly, it stopped, and the wolf licked his lips.

'All this... everything... it could have all been different... so very different for you, Wyatt. If you had only learned your place in this world. It's a pity that some people just don't know where they should stand... they're just... stubborn.

'Take Rowly here, he knows his place—he found his place—because I gave it to him. But you.... You plague the living pretending to be a man, and there's nothing worse than a man of ambition, Wyatt. An unenlightened man who doesn't want to play the game.'

Edgar leaned back once more.

'So, what else could I do? You gave me no choice... the hand of fate had to be forced.

'You see it all started with triggers... tiny triggers that could alter the user's state of mind. Easy at first... just enough to release the smallest of doses—a drop of dopamine—to relax and give pleasure... make sure the host wouldn't reject the implant. Get them addicted to the feeling of being, *"Truly Connected."*

'But why stop there when I could do *so* much more? When I could promote the production of adrenaline and even change the state of mind....

'Changing algorithms allowed me to program memories... create realities that would remain, or moments to take away. I mean, can you imagine, I could even convince a president that his health was failing and force him to step aside.' Edgar howled raucously. 'Ah, the tricks the mind can play....'

He leaned forward again; his voice enthused, as he placed his elbows upon the desk.

'And then it occurred to me... if you can believe in death, then why not accept it...? Why not make someone believe their depression is coming from the very thought of becoming president? That their presidency is assured. It only takes a little push... just enough to upset the chemical imbalance, and there's no way out.... Or actually, there was none... not until I gave him one.'

He smiled, savouring each second, watching as his words imprinted their meaning on the expression of Lewis.

'So, making a doctor like Rowly here truly believe that he changes my dressings, is nothing compared to say... making an entire hospital staff believe that I have a gunshot wound... or convincing a nation that I am their only real choice for president. Why else do you think that I waited so long...? Tolerated Roberts and Barnes for all those years? I had to... don't you see? Until the men that people trusted most, betrayed them the hardest... legalised implants and gave me power—the absolute power to control—I could never become what my destiny demands.'

Lewis looked at Rowly. His eyes pleaded for help, his world crumbling around him; his ambitions dying before him. Rowly was oblivious. He was there, yet somewhere else. Somewhere distant. Another space and time.

'Don't worry, Wyatt.... He won't even remember being here after they've taken you away.'

Sensing conclusion, Lewis was ready to beg for mercy. Edgar, however, was not ready to listen. After all, there was no pain in death. There was only death and Lewis had to suffer some more.

'Look, Edgar, let's be reasonable....'

'Reasonable...? You mean like *fair*, or *decent*...?' Edgar sniggered. 'I might be many things... I get called many names... I don't remember "reasonable" ever being one of them.... Anyway, this isn't about me or Rowly, is it? It's about you, Wyatt. You and your association with Gabriel Grey... didn't you know? I must admit, I had my suspicions... the same suspicions that ninety-three-point-eight percent of all Americans will have in let's say....' Edgar checked his Rolex. 'Ten minutes from now...?

'It's just too bad that I couldn't convince more. You know I tried? I thought I could get the last two and half million implanted... I really did... but you know, some people just want to hang onto this notion of free will.... People like you, Wyatt. People who believe they can think for themselves—who just don't seem to get it.

'You see, I don't care what people think... I do that for them... and besides, you still haven't answered my question.... So, come on... tell me... how could you hope to ever get away with it?'

Lewis looked back again at Rowly, his face a vacuum to everything and everyone; his vacant smile passing through Lewis like air through an open door. Lewis choked with unease.

'A threat only works when you execute it, Wyatt. And you've been threatening me for a long time... far too long. Now personally, I don't waste time threatening people... I remove them.'

'Now wait... wait a minute, Edgar!'

Lewis rose from his chair, his hands out in front, in anticipation of stopping Edgar moving towards him; to fend off the wolf.

'I... I can help you.... I can help you get what you want. I—'

Lewis wasn't scared, Lewis was petrified; perspiration dripping from his brow. Edgar rose from his chair, still calm—not quite ready to bite—despite the overwhelming stench of fear. He stepped around the desk, closer to his cowering adversary.

'But I already have what I want... I have everything that I need thanks to you, Wyatt.'

'T-to me?'

'Of course. Every hero needs a villain... and I needed one for the world to see. I needed someone to help me... and now that you have... you're just... well, a loose end....'

'I... I haven't helped you. I would never help you... I hate—'

Edgar placed a finger upon his dry lips. 'Shh!' he whispered. 'I know... and I needed your hate. I counted on it. Don't you understand...? I don't care about being the president. I needed to be. It's the only way that I can get to rule it all....

'I didn't cure ten million criminals, Wyatt. I created an army of ten million convicts... and what good is an army without a war?'

'War...? Y-you're going to war...? To war with the world?'

Edgar laughed again at the pitiful, insignificant, little ant shrinking before him. Still unable to comprehend his plan; too weak-minded to understand his ingenuity.

'Oh, Wyatt.... That's why you could *never* be president. You still don't see the bigger picture, do you? We are at war... but what kind of lunatic goes to war with a few million convicts? What chance would ten million criminals have against eight billion people...?'

'Y-you want an army... an army of eight – billion – people?'
'*What!*'

Edgar roared with laughter, genuinely startled and surprised as he perched again on the edge of his desk, needing both hands at his side to grip and steady himself. Lewis stood in frozen panic.

'What would I do with an army of eight billion? And you called me insane...? No, Wyatt, all I need is for everyone to have an implant... that what's I need... and that's what I'll get now, thanks to you.'

Lewis shook his head. 'I... I haven't helped you. I haven't—'

'Of course, you have. You were the missing piece. Without you, Wyatt, they'd be no more Dominoes.'

'Dominoes?'

Edgar sighed.

'You know the problem being divine, is that no one appreciates divinity.

'I offered everyone the path to find freedom, and most accepted their future... most, but not all... because there are still those... those who reject progress... those who try to stand in its way rather than give in and submit to it.

'The Remnants. The Gabriel Greys of this world... those who believe that their pathetic demonstrations... their meaningless acts of aggression against DomiGen can disrupt my plan... prevent *me* from fulfilling *my – destiny!*'

Edgar raised himself from the desk again and walked back towards the bay windows; his back turned to Lewis.

'DOGMA was the first step in dissolving the old world, only Roberts hadn't the guts to complete it. That was his undoing... I knew Barnes wouldn't be able to resist the honour of implanting the last criminal himself... and that was an opportunity too good to be missed.'

'I... I don't understand....'

'I needed control of the chair long before I could sit in it.'

His legs aquiver; Lewis sat down again, trying to make sense of things.

'B-Barnes was your friend... you said so yourself... he said—'

'I despised Barnes,' snapped Edgar, as he spied the reflection of Lewis. 'He was greasy and slick. He stood for everything but stood for nothing... a chancer who took advantage of Roberts' death... or his murder—to be precise.'

'Y-you murdered Roberts...? I... I don't believe—'

'That's your problem, Wyatt. Your lack of faith. You see I don't pray to God... I am God. The one true God. And in my world, there's no place for Grey or his Remnants.... So how do I swat an invisible fly? How do I put an end to that pestilence that spreads across my world? Those who fail to learn—who never learn—who still believe that it's better to think than to be told....

'I needed an army. A legitimate army for a legitimate cause. How else could I ever gain the approval for one if it wasn't a matter of life and death?

'If I created DomiForce without a threat, then the world would have tried to stop me. Taken sanctions against me.'

Edgar turned back to face Lewis.

'Nobody likes a dictator, Wyatt... history has never understood them... its pages turn gods into men, and I have no intention of being mortal.'

'So, the U.N... the gunshot. The—'

'Stage, Wyatt. The perfect stage. A gun fires a blank across the river, and a bag of blood bursts when I hit the ground. There had to be an attack on the president's life. It's not enough that Grey is a rebel. He has to be a terrorist. It's the *only* way to take down the house... don't you see?'

No. Lewis could not see, nor understand, and that was a fact written clearly across his face.

'The Remnants are no longer a threat to me or DomiGen. They're a threat to everyone now... to all mankind. But I needed to make that threat real, to get the approval from the leaders of the world to hunt them down. After the assassination attempt, I didn't even have to ask... they all offered to hunt Grey. Committed their convicts from The DOGMA Program to DomiForce, so we're everywhere. Nowhere is safe for him now—because you can't justify suppression without some proof of a terrorist intention.'

'And all this... all this... just to fight Grey?'

'Not just Grey... aren't you listening? Grey and his Neanderthals... I never chose to fight them—I chose to use them. Without them the world would *never* have committed to a common cause. And without that cause, the world would never have seen a legitimate reason for my army. Now every country understands why it *must* have its own DomiForce. To make sure that those who protest against implants—who try to fight them—will be hunted down and destroyed.'

'Grey's no terrorist... he just sees through DomiGen—like I do.'

'And you don't think that makes him a threat—a terrorist to all that I have planned?'

'That's why he doesn't have an implant. Because he can think... like me!'

'Yes. Yes, he can... and like you, Grey has served his purpose. I had to show the world that DomiForce is the deterrent that it was missing. If Grey is allowed to continue, he'll inspire others and the Remnant numbers will grow. That's just something I cannot accept.

'Now, on the other hand... if he's captured... with an implant I'll make him renounce the Remnants. The rebels will lose their symbol—they'll lose their leader—they'll lose their faith... and trust me, a faithless rabble is easier to squash than an organised faithful one.

'Leaders will follow my lead and use their armies to round up their own rebels. And those armies... *all* those armies... are – *mine!*

'One global implanted army... a global DomiForce, all ready for my control... ready to stop all those foolish enough to cling to that faint ideal of hope.'

'So, that's it? You think you can control the world?'

'I don't control, Wyatt. I command.'

'And what...? Get rid of anyone who refuses to kneel before you...? You really are insane!' Lewis became stern; fuelled with anger at the depths of Edgar's treachery. 'You're a monster! The world has seen better men than you try to rule it... and all of those who tried before, failed before... just like you will.

'You plan all this... deceive our country... deceive everyone... yet still... still you say you needed me to do it? But I've done *nothing*. Nothing to help you... I'm not even on the Grid!'

Edgar smiled again.

'The tallest walls are still made from bricks, Wyatt. And every brick has a part to play... I could never allow someone without an implant—someone who thought for himself—to gain the popular vote. That someone might get in my way.... So, instead of thinking for you, I did the next best thing... I thought for those whose support you needed.

'Making Montanas the candidate would keep you close to power, but always short of it. So, I kept your political career in the spotlight... as the bitter bridesmaid... without any hope of a happy ever after or becoming president. When I made Barnes endorse me, I knew you would resent it—hate me for it.... You would have to watch me rise, you would have to see me succeed, and you would hate me all the more.'

Edgar walked back towards the desk.

'Hate, Wyatt, is powerful... don't you think? And you, so predictable in your hatred of me, would use every opportunity to try to discredit me. I would need to do nothing. I would have to say nothing... just sit, and watch... and wait. Because with each ounce of hate you would lose another ounce of hope, until all your hope was lost—and only hate remained.

'You *dare* to call me a monster, but you're wrong. I'm not *a* monster.... I'm *the* monster.... The monster who creates monsters, and I created one in you. An enemy so driven by hate, that in every interview—with every comment—you chose only to smear me and make the world a witness to that hatred. Your hate is so strong that you incriminate yourself, creating your own motive to kill me. And your need for revenge, your lust for my power, it's so very simple... so very basic... and murder *is* so very primitive, Wyatt. So easy to comprehend, that even people in countries who know nothing about us, can believe it.'

The beads of sweat on Lewis' forehead had run down to leave streaks, discolouring his spray tan.

'I... I'm not trying to kill you, Edgar, you're the president... I know there are times when I wish... when I could kill you myself... but you're the president... I would never want to see you dead....'

Edgar was distracted; his mind drifted at the sight of the frightened tiger that sat in the chair. His thoughts turned to someone he had tried to forget. To someone he had blocked from his mind for many years. His face turned cold. Fierce. More determined, as the voice of Lewis returned to his ears.

'If I'm guilty of anything, then I'm guilty of—'

'Conspiracy—of conspiring to bring down my government.... Espionage—of leaking information to your comrade Grey.... Treason—of plotting and colluding to murder the president of the United States with a known terrorist. You're guilty as charged, Wyatt, and your punishment will meet the verdict.

'You were always just another little brick that was waiting to fall.... Waiting for your time—for the bricks behind you to fall first. And it's your time now, Wyatt... it's your time to fall.'

Lewis shook his head. He was afraid of Edgar, of what he showed he could do with Rowly. Yet despite the threats and accusations, he had committed no crime. Without a crime there could be no evidence, and the world would surely see the truth? His only wrongdoing was to insult a political opponent during a presidential campaign, and that was par for the course; it was far from illegal and most always expected. If Lewis had showed the world anything, he had showed that he was good at nothing: keeping his mouth closed included. He could certainly never plot to bring down a government and keep such a thing a secret. So, the allegations, wild as they were, were without grounds and served only to insult his pride.

'I'm a patriot! I'm not a killer.... Yes, I'm guilty of hating you... so what? You still have nothing. Only hearsay... only *your* say. That's no evidence. That's not proof, and I won't confess to a crime that I haven't committed!'

'But you already have....'

Edgar sat and touched a button that powered up a screen. Ironically, the same screen that Roberts had once used to show Edgar the raid on his home as he sought to take DomiGen away from him. The tables turned; it was Edgar who now sat in the chair, about to use it to not only reaffirm, but to secure his ownership of DomiGen, forever. Edgar tapped the monitor, and a video from inside the Oval Office began to play.

"It's Wyatt Lewis... the former vice president.... Listen... I don't have time for games, Spear. I speak for Grey... we're going to war with the world. I warned you—you should have listened. I told you I'd find a way to make sure you never set foot in here again.... Take a good look around you, Edgar... this is the last time you'll ever be in my office.... That chair's mine."

"Wyatt, I don't understand.... Is your need for revenge, your lust for my presidency so great? I know you're a man of ambition, but you're consumed... I must admit I had my suspicions... you've been threatening me for a long time... but I didn't know about your association with Gabriel Grey.... Now you're guilty of plotting and colluding to murder the president of the United States with a known terrorist."

"I'm not trying to kill you, Edgar... I'm going to. I murdered Roberts and I will kill you.... When you hit the concrete—"

"Wyatt, stop, this is treason. Don't you understand?"

"So what? I want to see you dead... I'm guilty. I confess."

"Wyatt...."

"You think I'm scared of you...? I'll get rid of anyone who refuses to kneel before me, and the world will do nothing...."

"Wyatt, you're insane!"

"Those who tried before, failed before... but I will see you dead."

"Assassinate the president of the United States.... You'll never get away with it, Wyatt. How could you hope to ever get away with it?"

"Do you have any idea who I am? I'm a patriot! No one will know I'm a killer because I'm not on the Grid. Grey's a terrorist... and like me... he doesn't have an implant... he sees through DomiGen—like I do. So, I'll help Grey kill you... and I'll get away with it."

Lewis sat agape at the screen, at the incriminating evidence.

'Th-that's not... I... I didn't.... You... you've just....'

'Captured the confession of a traitor? A traitor who just told the world that without an implant he believes it's possible to get away with murder?'

It was Edgar who now scoffed at Lewis.

'You know, Wyatt, you're such a disappointment to me... I had hoped that you were more... more of everything, really... like that tan and those unbearable teeth of yours. But you allowed yourself to be so easily lured—baited—and all I had to do was reel you in, like the squirming little fish that you are.... Didn't you know that I have a retinal implant? That it can edit everything I can see and hear in my mind—then send it to every chip or save the footage and broadcast it to the world.

'Like I said, I'd give you ten minutes... and the only reason I did, was for your confession—the betrayal of a traitor who once shared the responsibility of this office... who once owned its respect then disowned its integrity. A dissident. A radical. Someone who proves that anyone can be corrupted... that any government can be infiltrated, as long as the threat of Grey and his Remnants exist. At least, that's what I hoped for—an admission for the fear of possibility. Until you, you and your oh so predictable hatred did so much more... you turned the possibility into probability, and just gave me the keys to my kingdom!'

Edgar laughed, sneering at Lewis. 'So, before you're charged and convicted, take consolation... knowing that because of you, everyone, everywhere, will get an implant and surrender their freedom to me. You just confessed to every world leader that they have no choice—

they *must* connect their nations to the Grid. Think about it... if they don't, then they'll never feel safe... they'll never be sure that no one can get away with murder... not even attempting it.

'Don't look so worried, Wyatt... once you've been given your chip, Rowly here will look in on you... won't you, Rowly?'

'Mr. President?'

'For now, Rowly... it's just a role that I play... for now....'

16

DOMINATION

The capture of Lewis and the exposure of the highly publicised assassination plot was exploited to the full. Now the master of manipulation, Edgar regularly attended the United Nations and spoke of the challenges that came with trying to appease the terrorists; his hopes of how together, the leaders of the world might help prevent what had happened to him from ever happening to any one of them. It was a convincing argument, and one that was easily sold, which meant that there were now no criminals in jail anywhere, because jails no longer existed, and the world was seemingly all the better for it.

As governments praised The DOGMA Program, they also celebrated the monies that were liberated from fighting what was once considered ordinary everyday crime. The truth, however, was in fact quite different, and they continued instead to pay most of it back in one way or another to DomiGen Labs. DomiGen itself had grown into a complex maze of numerous offshore and international holding companies; essential to remove the concerns of an organisation, that was in reality, far beyond any form of control. Everything in

DOGMA: the contracts, the processing chips, the implants, the systems, the monitoring, the analysis—everything—it was all owned by DomiGen. For all intents and purposes, the program may have appeared to be serviced around the globe by hundreds of smaller independent operations. Nevertheless, all streams ran to the sea, and Edgar Spear owned every last drop. As a result, his fortunes now outweighed the combined economies of many of the world's nations. Such wealth was not to be squandered, and Edgar put it to good use.

Edgar had learned much about the power of persuasion from Abelman and had witnessed the art of showmanship from Munro. Alone, each had their merits and were powerful tools. Even so, by combining the two with his own perpetual storytelling—his ability to lie and mislead—or "marketing" as it was called; he was not only able to generate the public's enthusiasm for implants, but more importantly, fuel their desires to want them.

While Edgar's plans for DOGMA continued under a pyramid of corporate aliases, the home consumer was allowed to experience only one unambiguous brand. Bombarded with advertisements and the power of consumerism, DomiGen was not only fashionable, it had been made absolutely necessary. Within a few short years, its name had spread and become the single most recognised label in the world.

Despite the ambitions of Edgar, governments elsewhere were still foolishly elected by their people. Any political party seeking to govern must first understand that favour comes from giving the people whatever it is the people want. What the people wanted now, were governments who supported DomiGen; leaders who pledged and promised access to the DomiGen Grid. Over time, as various international elections took place, those elected were those who gave into public demand, because the people not only wanted an implant; they needed one.

Implants were the means to an end and the manner through which Edgar was able to rise to power. They had been given freely to every civilian in America, but the rest of the world would not be so lucky. Any government wanting access to the Grid, had to carry the expense of doing so through their own national budgets and taxes. Perhaps unsurprisingly, those who were able to join at the outset, were those who had enjoyed greatest success from DOGMA. The United Kingdom, France, South Korea, India, Australia, Germany, Sweden, and Canada. One by one, nations who paid DomiGen to implant their populations, and offered their citizens the gift of being: *Truly Connected.*

As the numbers of countries that joined the DomiGen Grid progressively increased, the pattern was always the same. First to receive their implants were those most vocal in their advocacy of them. News and media would focus stories for weeks promoting the benefits of the technology, as the voices of sceptics fell ever more silent. Then came celebrities and the younger generations seduced at the prospects of being able to connect with their idols on the Grid. Other family members would join over time to make communication simpler, until those who remained without an implant were those few determined to stand against them. There was simply nothing that could stop it, nothing that could slow it, and Edgar's kingdom increased its reach across the Atlantic, Pacific, and Indian oceans.

In war-torn countries where money was scarce and sustenance scarcer still, DomiGen could never hope to get populations connected or under their subconscious control, not unless it was willing to do so by itself. Still, the problem remained, how could Edgar legitimise implants for those without the means or ability to pay? The answer was surprisingly simple, and to do what has always been done to victims in greatest need; those unable to support themselves. The creation of DomiGen Care would allow Edgar to provide the casualties of war, the poor and the impoverished, with an implant for free. It was the cost of precision, and moreover, would be seen to be done with good reason through a selfless act of humanitarianism. In those destitute places, the DomiGen implant would not only offer comfort, but provide a release from the torment and suffering endured of survivors. The ability to re-connect, to communicate with other loved ones, those who were lost and displaced by conflict, was of course a lie. It was a disingenuous claim that was sold with the sole purpose to deceive and mislead the public. People were, and would always be, nothing more than pitiful, insignificant little ants. To Edgar, their only value was the influence that he could hold over them, and his only interest, the power that would come from controlling them all.

However difficult it may be to sell an ugly truth, it is arguably easier to lie and repeat the lie until it becomes the truth; until everyone believes the lie, and no one can deny its truth, when the truth itself is grotesque. The truth now was that Edgar had become a philanthropist, public-spirited and for want of a better word: a humanitarian. He was seen as a benevolent man, whose compassion and generosity to help others, those less fortunate and caught in the crossfire of battle, was all that he asked. The champion of innocent victims, those without a voice. The indigent who simply had to open their minds, accept an implant, and unknowingly give up the most precious of all freedoms: the right to express their own free will and ability to choose. Yet once the ability to think is lost, then slaves are made, and even dormant slaves must give praise to their master. The president of the United States was now Time Magazine's Person of the Year, Nobel Laurette and Peace Prize winner. His stature, like the awards and accolades bestowed upon him, continued to grow, and Edgar was fast becoming a god amongst men. Nevertheless, a lie by any name is still a lie, and a lie that masquerades as the truth can never really be true. For the real truth behind DomiGen Care was far more sickening, more calculated and depraved than anyone could have imagined. It was DomiGen Care itself that instigated the very wars it supposedly provided aid to alleviate. Their deliberate course of action financed conflict, then provided the arms necessary to sustain it, allowing Edgar to pray upon its victims and gain access to new regions that he sought dominion over. The cost of a few thousand weapons and a few hundred thousand implants here and there, was nothing but a tiny investment to keep the domino effect rolling. A small price worth paying to achieve his plan and realise the bigger picture.

Outside the hostile regions, any independent states that ran under dictatorship became targets for DomiGen. These were lands in which no amount of advertising and no measure of diplomatic pleading could ever make their leaders more liberal. In these places, where progress was seen as displeasing and implants as dangerous, armies remained, national laws were enforced, and judicial systems stood firm. These were the citadels, the obstacles to Edgar that refused to yield and refused to recognise the demands of their people. They had no users, and without carriers of implants, no means to manipulate. How ironic that these nations, renowned for their lack of democracy, for their repressions of freedom and unwillingness to allow people to think for themselves, became the only ones who could; remained the only ones outside of Edgar's control. In these bastions, these final fortresses of freedom, there was no option other than to declare war outright.

The business of war is a bloody one, and just as each coin has two sides, so too does each war with its dimensions. Perspective is relative: dependent upon camp and the view that is taken. So, while these lands defended their freedom with honour and vigour, fought back through bravery and courage, Edgar was not in agreement or able to share such opinion. He saw only suppression and the minds of dishonourable men; fundamentalists whose anti-democratic rule formed uncontrollable provinces that had to be dissolved. It was they who sought to undermine the very fabric of a society that he had strived so hard to create. And precision, like war, was a perspective, where Edgar was uninterested in anyone's stance or point of view. He was in the business of perfection, and their refusal to submit was a blot upon his otherwise flawless design. With one line of code and simple instruction, the rest of the world agreed. It was not the environment or the climatic changes, but these lands of persecution that represented the greatest threat to mankind. These impenetrable kingdoms without implants were the enemy, and their failure to understand was an intolerable imperfection to the inevitable utopia. They were more than a stain on the landscape; they were the sanctuaries in which Grey, along with his Remnants, most likely found their support. As the world now knew only too well, there could be no refuge for rebellion. There would be no place to harbour these outlaws, no territories left to protect these terrorists.

Like dominoes they fell, unable to withstand the onslaught; unable to match the numbers that the armies of the free world had sent against them. Their walls collapsed then crumbled, and as they did, the process of abolition began. With their leaders expunged, Edgar stepped closer to absolute control, and the world was now closer... closer than it had ever been... to the day when everyone would be joined together in progress. When anyone, anywhere, could connect to the Grid and experience paradise.

Edgar savoured his triumphs and the world rejoiced at the peace within reach. Yet peace was a concept for compliant minds, and the Remnants called those without implants to arms once again. They refused to be silenced so long as those like Grey continued to fight. So long as hope remained to resist and rebel, until the final free thought had been stolen. There would be no surrender because peace, much like war, is simply a matter of perspective; a fragile position that for some draws concord, while for others, its misgivings ferment their discord. Resistance or rebellion, the fact was the same: the hand that once rocked the cradle now rocked it no more. It was held instead, firmly in its grasp, and with each day his grip grew ever tighter.

The last of the dictators, an African general called Wekesa who had stood his ground, now found himself in the crosshairs of the mighty DomiGen. He had called his people to arms in order to fight off the growing influence of the west. However, Wekesa's mistake was believing the battle was against a conglomerate; a company who had created a private army of former criminals, led by the ruthless Commander Reams. Such an assumption would prove to be fatal, and on the day of his reckoning, Wekesa discovered that DomiForce was more than just a band of disciplined hoodlums. Backed and supported by every government from around the globe, Reams and the DomiForce travelled east to meet their opponent head-on. There in defiance on the fields of sand, as wide and as open as possible to imagine; the baking sun of the Danakil desert fell behind a vast surging cloud of red. To Wekesa and his warriors, the winds of the desert were the souls of their ancestors. They would join them in battle to aid in their victory on the ground that had borne witness to countless contests throughout the ages, and the failed attempts to conquer its people. Under cover of the howling tempest, barefoot on the dunes, they sneaked into position to gain their advantage on the higher ground. There, they waited. Wekesa at the head of over a hundred thousand of his painted braves, each taking cover behind their long woven, oval-shaped shields. As the pelting grains relented in their fury, the brilliant blue sky that was dulled through the air became eager to clear. Wekesa and his men released a deafening war cry, banging their spears against their shields to strike the fear of surprise into the heart of their enemy. The light steadily brightened, but the sands did not, as Wekesa stared out across the waves of black uniforms that laid siege and surrounded his every turn; their tactical visors enhancing their sight to see through the storm, straight into the eyes of their adversary. A warrior's spear trembled behind him, and Wekesa looked at the hand that clutched it. His warriors would fight for him, were ready to defend their way of life to their very death, and he smiled at the boy determined to remain dutiful.

'Don't be afraid,' he said, 'you are not alone, my brother.'

As a leader, Wekesa was young, although wiser than his years, and he turned again to look out across the hordes of DomiForce Rangers. He stared in wonder, then lowered his head, before turning again to the boy.

'Remember… courage is not found in battle… real courage is found within…. To do what is right, that is the only real test of courage. The only true battle you will ever face.'

He smiled, then did what any selfless or loving father would do. The weapons that he carried were laid down, peacefully. No shots were fired, no spears were thrown. Wekesa did not resist. He did not oppose nor defy the incursion; he capitulated and surrendered for the sake of their bloodshed. In the face of unsurmountable odds, he dropped to his knees and sacrificed his pride in exchange for their lives. They followed their general and lowered their weapons, as the rest of the world had done so before; yielding to Reams for all to see.

In suffering humiliation, such a damning defeat, the awesome terrible might of the global DomiForce was made conclusive. The leaders of the free world gloated at his downfall, unaware that success, like the spear of Wekesa, is a double-edged blade. That the giving of hope at the taking of dreams, and the winning of freedom at the loss of all liberty, is no cause for celebration or a future at all.

The end of Wekesa spelt the end of pretence. His presidency, like DOGMA and Operation S.H.R.O.U.D, had fulfilled its objective. There were no more tables or games to be played. There was only one seat and that was the throne; a place destined for one that was not to be shared. Edgar was without question the greatest dictator the world had *never* known, and unlike those who had tried to conquer it before him, he had not failed, succeeded only halfway, or been forced to suffer the losses of legions. Edgar's rise came not from the strength of the sword, but through the power of the mind: the ultimate weapon.

The four corners of the Earth and all that lay in-between were now his. Under his rule, it was his to change, and change quickly it must. Borders that once defined political regions began to blur. Nations merged, and geographical areas defined as countries disappeared. Maps were redrawn and names were removed to make way for perfection. Our planet, imprecise as it was, was now no more. Its new name: *DomiNation.*

Former continents were replaced by DomiGen Districts, arranged in order of their value and business potential. There was DomiNation Alpha, formerly known as the continent of North America; the home of DomiGen itself. There was DomiNation Beta, formerly known as Asia. DomiNation Gamma, formerly known as Europe. DomiNation Delta, formerly known as Africa. DomiNation Epsilon, formerly known as South America. DomiNation Zeta, formerly known as Oceania. And finally, DomiNation Eta, a region that was once called Antarctica.

Monuments were destroyed, buildings demolished, and national symbols desecrated without risk of repair. All relics of antiquity were smashed and then purged, as everything that culture had tried to express or shape with identity was torn down. The artefacts of eras, the galleries and museums, were razed overnight; unwanted reminders of creativity and free thought from the centuries of life that were idly wasted. The Seven Wonders of the World: Petra, the Great Wall, Machu Picchu and the rest, were wonders no more. History toppled and split into rubble, it burned into ashes and broke into dust. Sacrificed for perfection, for a world of precision and the domino effect. The implants of DomiGen erased the memories of landmarks from existence, as the skylines once filled with the mosaics of iconic silhouettes were cleared and laid bare, like a blank canvas that awaits the artist's brush. Gone now was anything of historical importance. The palaces of royalty and homes of the presidents, the foundations of society and the offices of democracy. Capitol Hill, the White House, Westminster, Reichstag, even the United Nations. Everything that was rooted in a former age, that could be traced to a former governance, had all fallen, and with them, the sentiments of vestige.

The analogy of Abelman to symbolise life was more relevant now than ever. Yet it was Edgar, not Abelman who was the architect; the man who designed and saw the bigger picture. As the bricks continued to fall, the results were spectacular, and the show continued towards the grand finale.

After the old towns were demolished, and the cities were cleared, construction of the DomiCentres began. Advancements in engineering turned vision into verity and allowed for high-rise buildings such as the world had never seen. These colossal superstructures with their system of sectors, meant cities could be practical, with populations efficient and no longer dispersed. A DomiCile, or apartment as they once were called, more spartan and impersonal, with rooms less generous; designed for moderation, not exorbitant lives. Four of these megacities would be built in each DomiNation District: one to the east, one to the west, one to the south and one to the north. With such efficiency, all of DomiNation's eight billion human inhabitants, would now be housed in just twenty-eight DomiCentres around the world. Twenty-eight monstrous mounds of concrete, glass, and metal. Twenty-eight structures of such sprawling magnitude, that each was forced to rise hundreds of metres into the air and span thousands of square miles in order to accomplish its task. It was not the price of precision but the cost of perfection that would assure a new world order. One without the need for senates or parliaments, for councils or governments, where all that was needed was a single supreme leader. An absolute ruler, who was willing to wield his absolute power.

DomiNation Alpha 1 was the first megacity to be built. If size and materials were a challenge, then they paled in comparison to the demands of labour: the numbers required to erect the monstrous metropolis. There were simply not enough trained workers involved in construction throughout the whole of DomiNation Alpha. So, the ones who were, functioned as supervisors, as foremen and forewomen, as Edgar set to work more than a hundred million citizens in addition. Simple, ordinary, everyday users of the Grid, who were programmed to perform their tasks to ensure that construction was completed within a year. One hundred million pitiful, insignificant, little ants who worked tirelessly and slaved without complaint to obey the will of their master.

Alpha1, the capital of all DomiNation, covered an area close to forty-eight thousand square miles: one hundred and twenty-four thousand square kilometres, to be exact. Simply put, it was roughly the size of the former state of Mississippi and was to become home for more than fifty million people; to all who had lived in New York, New York City, Maine, Vermont, New Hampshire, Massachusetts, Pennsylvania, and Rhode Island, before the rise of DomiNation. At its heart, was DomiGen Labs. The facility was now so immense that it crossed the former states of New York, New Hampshire, Vermont, and Massachusetts. From its centre, the Great DomiGen Tower soared to the skies. It was the wonder of the new world and reached to nearly a thousand metres above the city far below.

However, the demolition of so many buildings, and the clearing of the world that stood from before, had created vast clouds of debris. Dust now hung in the air like a smoke or a fog, unwilling to move or give way to the light. Obscured by the thick encumbering grey, the weak rays of the sun no longer touched the ground beneath. Those in the lower sectors, where temperatures were cold, much colder than before, lived lives in the gloom and the darkness of the overcrowded streets. As seasons blurred, it was never quite winter and long since summer, longer still since spring, so long in fact that any optimism of springtime could never be felt, and who knew if it ever would ever be again....

'Then end it. Bring Woodville online,' said Edgar, as he sat alone in his palatial office at the pinnacle of the tower.

He tapped his fingers impatiently upon the desk, then turned to one of the enormous white walls and blinked. The panels, like digital split-flap shutters, revolved to reveal a large display; a chequerboard of video feeds that completely covered the wall and offered a window into his world outside. Each feed was a broadcast, a live camera that surveyed and observed as it sent footage from across DomiNation. The blueprint that Alpha1 had set was now being followed, and every District was busy finalising the completion of their first DomiCentre.

Beta1 and Gamma1 were close to completion. Delta1 and Epsilon1 both nearing operation. Eta1 and Zeta1 followed closely behind. Edgar's plan was proceeding precisely. Within five years, the remaining twenty-one megacities would all be in place, and the population of DomiNation housed perfectly. It would be the crowning jewel, the grand finale, the point at which Edgar would have conquered and destroyed all; re-established and rebuilt all—only better.

Suddenly, a virtual display appeared in mid-air in front of Edgar, projecting a feed from the video wall. He rested his elbow upon the arm of the chair, then flicked his right index and middle fingers as he browsed for a specific signal. He skimmed through dozens of screens before stopping and tapping the air. The feed filled the entire chequerboard display with one gigantic video image. It was from Alpha3, where the third DomiCentre was to be constructed in DomiNation Alpha. For now, they were simply demolishing buildings, clearing a path for the future, and it was a day much like any other of recent times. Nevertheless, today was no ordinary day. To Edgar, today was a very special day, a day he had long waited for, and he followed intently.

As he watched the Golden Gate Bridge fall into the San Francisco Bay, the island of Alcatraz suffered the same fate, descending slowly into its icy waters. Edgar smiled a dry, albeit wry smile, and extended his fingers as if to catch a ball. He twisted his hand in the air, like he was turning a wheel; searching to find a specific camera angle, until eventually he found whatever it was that he was looking for.

The wrecking ball slammed hard, filling the view with a blanket of dust. Edgar pulled his fingers further apart, and as he did so, the camera tracked, zooming out to reveal more of the demolition taking place. The majority of the building was already destroyed, and as the cloud began to dissipate, the view from the camera was perfectly clear.

'I told you…. Finished.'

It was the University of California, the place where James Munro had chosen to humiliate him all those years ago. Now, with each pass, each blow from the crane, the bricks of its hallways collapsed in rapid succession. But unlike the bricks of a domino show, these were not simply knocked to the ground: they were smashed into smithereens. Edgar watched and smiled, embracing the fulfilment of a promise; the end of a memory that pained him, and the beauty of it all. He tightened his fingers and zoomed back in to inspect the site, until all that remained was rubble. His only regret, that the students who had stood and mocked him were not inside as the buildings crumbled. He had never forgiven, nor had he forgotten. Such was the nature of Edgar that he could not forgive or ever try to forget. His justice was swift, delivered without mercy, and his vengeance was taken, not partially or in part, but wholeheartedly with pleasure. The vendetta was settled, and he awaited fulfilment, yet Edgar found nothing. Nothing to fill the void within his empty, callous heart.

Disgruntled without feeling, or gaining satisfaction, he flicked his fingers to dismiss the screen, pausing on a thought before rising to his feet. He nudged his chair back across the gleaming white marbled floor, striated with its myriad of golden veins, and made his way towards the imposing glass window: unique by any design. Curved and over eighteen metres tall, it was more than eighty metres wide. For the lonely reclusive God, the stunning panorama offered an adequate view to look down upon his creation. To see, as far as the eye could see, and Edgar's eyes could see superhumanly far. From here, he could marvel at his mastery, at the breadth of his dominion and gaze upon its wonder. Edgar drew a jaded breath, as he glanced upon the flecks of light, the busy little ants performing their everyday tasks. He stared into the horizon. His implant enhanced and sharpened his sight as he looked beyond the sea waters; out across the three and a half thousand miles, the five and a half thousand kilometres, towards the borders of Europe—to London—and to what one day would become DomiNation Gamma 3. He watched as the Tower Bridge fell into the River Thames, and he stared at the mindless faces of those performing only as they were told. Everything was as it should be, yet his eyes were stolid; blunted by dreariness and unable to hide the one true flaw of perfection. With control of all things, of all thoughts when he needed, what more was there or what more could he want? What else could satisfy the insatiable desire of power; that which feeds off the hunger for more, when there is no more power left to be had. When there are no more cities left to control, no buildings left to ruin, or lives left to destroy. The sense of the inevitable was precisely that. Once accepted and understood, then only time remained. A wait with nothing more to expect and nothing else left to gain, not even the sport of resistance that once stood against him: the rebellion now fractured, and their leader in hiding, perhaps dying or dead.

Suddenly, a door closed behind him.

'I told you to send me the file on Whitlock,' snapped Edgar. 'I don't need an errand boy.'

Startled by the sound, by what the closing of a door meant, Edgar voiced his anger not with words or by talking to the unwanted visitor. He spoke instead to the mind of someone through his implant and awaited their answer. The delay was unacceptable, and Edgar was unaccustomed to being kept waiting.

'You dare to enter my private chamber!' he screamed aloud, before turning to upbraid his guest. 'How....'

'Stare into the darkness long enough, and eventually you'll see what isn't there,' said a very distinctive figure in the distance by the door.

A mysterious, yet strangely familiar looking man. He was older now and slightly more bowed, a little more crooked than Edgar remembered, but his gravelly voice was still dry and pronounced.

'It-it can't be.... You...?'

The man stood perhaps forty metres from Edgar on the other side of the room.

'How could...? How did you get in here? How did you bypass the Sentinels?'

He arched his back slightly, then slowly and most deliberately placed his old, shabby briefcase onto the floor. He was almost ceremonial in fashion, making sure that it sat just right.

'What do you want?'

The man straightened and was crooked once again. He raised his hand to tug on his hat; to pull it a little farther down and cast a little more shadow across his face.

'I... I'm warning you....'

He began to walk towards Edgar. It was closer to a shuffle than a stride; his feet almost scraping the floor. His head remained lowered, his face stayed hidden, and Edgar still unable to see beneath the brim.

'Stop...! Stop now! That's close enough....'

The man continued as he paid no mind and failed to heed. Edgar held his arm in front of his chest, and his wrist revealed a screen of sorts, like a translucent film that was integrated into his flesh.

'I'll shut you down... it's your last warning.'

Although he was older, much older it would seem, the man wore the same long black overcoat with the fur lined trim around the collar. It was bigger than Edgar remembered, loose-fitting, and it hung much more than he could recall; draped around the man's frail shoulders like a cloth, almost trailing across the floor. Even so, as he approached, Edgar could only stare at his hand, at the gap where a finger should be, and as he did, his heart began to pound—hammering in his chest. His eyes widened and his throat tightened. The colour fading from his cheeks as it drained into his stomach; clenched having felt something not experienced for many years. For the first time in a very long time, for decades in fact, Edgar was defied and challenged of his control. The associate of Abelman had returned. He was back to settle his account, to take what he was due, and the forgotten touch of fear fell again upon Edgar's soul.

'Do you hear me...?'

He raised his arm and swiped the screen. The display lit even brighter to project a map into the air above his hand, plunging the fears of Edgar deeper into darkness.

'It… it's not,' he gasped, stumbling back against the glass window. 'That's impossible….'

He gaped at the map that showed no hosts, with only Edgar visible on the radar. The doors to the room could not open without an implant; a security protocol to ensure that even if a Remnant should make it past the hundreds of DomiForce Guards that lined the tower, and the Sentinels of Spear who stood firm outside the penthouse upper floors, that they could never make it past the final barrier to Edgar. It was a safety provision, the last line of defence, and it meant that anyone inside, even an unwelcomed visitor, could be issued a kill code at will. Terminated if that's what was needed, or if that's what Edgar chose to decide.

'W-where's your implant…?'

The man continued, ignoring Edgar with every step.

'H-how did you get in here?'

His voice was weakened by dread. His mind was racing with doubt, losing each lap to confusion. How…? How could this be? How had he got here? After all these years, how was he still alive?

Edgar's breathing was short and grew shorter. A thousand needles stabbed his tingling palms that were pressed back, hard against the glass. There was nowhere to retreat, no place to escape. He was trapped by this ghost of his past.

'Reams, where are you…? Reams…? Reams!'

The man stopped short of Edgar. His head still lowered. His face still obscured. His voice still silent. His hat just the same: the black fedora with deep pinch creases, and the black silk band. He raised his hand and Edgar stared, watching as the man took hold and prepared to remove it. Four fingers expelled any doubt, and Edgar tried hard to gulp in a breath; something to stay on his feet.

As the man lifted his hat, Edgar realised that the shadow covering his face was actually a hologram. A projection of light from the underbrim that created a veil to cloak his features and provide a mask. Then, as he raised his head, he revealed the horrors beneath, and Edgar had every reason to feel panic; the right to be afraid.

'W… wh-what are you?'

His silence continued. His stare intense—deep into Edgar—down into the vacuous depths of nothingness. Unable to shield or avert his gaze, Edgar was pinned, terrified by the eyes that dissected him.

The man had been badly burned and his face lost to fire. His eyes were a piercing blue and their whites exceedingly large without eyelids to conceal them. They dominated his face and stuck out from their bony sockets like the cue ball on a billiard green. He had no eyebrows, no lashes, or stubble, and his head was bald except for a few long strands of thin white hair that hung down over a lump, perhaps a tumour, that protruded on the right side of his forehead. His skin was raw, pocketed in places, and there were large grafts where his nose and lips should have been. But the tissue had not healed, not properly at least. It was pinkish, redder in colour, with marks from the surgery and the carelessness of the knife. A long deep scar meandered like a river across his cheek. It ran from his left eye towards the hole where an ear was once found, before turning back and down to the corner of his mouth where it disappeared into an open sore that wept profusely.

'Wh-what…. What do you want?'

The man's refusal to comply focused Edgar's attention upon the brick that was out of place. A brick that in the business of precision had no business of ever being there. More importantly, it compounded the obvious truth. Exposed in the mirror of the man's eyes, Edgar saw the reflection of his own paranoia, and as the torture continued through silent denial, it stripped the command he believed that he had. Who was this man to take what was his? To steal what was earned after all he endured? Overwhelmed with emotion and resigned to desperation, he snatched at the collar of the man with both hands.

The act of a bully resorting to violence, to the loss of control and the very thing that his plan of perfection had sought to create.

'Tell me,' he screamed. 'Tell me!'

Edgar was humbled, and the God only human after all. He was far from threatening, even to a man so advanced in years.

'Tell me, damn it! What – do – you – *want!*'

The man stared, still silent as Edgar shook him. He seemed unmoved by violence or the tantrums of a spoilt child. Edgar's cheeks began to redden as his eyes and nostrils flared. His lips drew back into a snarl. Suddenly, the man's jaw moved, and Edgar saw his thin skin stretch across the muscles.

'An end.'

Confused by the words—the request or demand—Edgar's grip eased. 'An end…?'

'To all this, Edgar. An end to all this.'

'Then you know who I am?'

The man turned unimpressed, unchallenged by their encounter as he shuffled back towards a chair that was placed on the opposite side of Edgar's desk.

'I preferred the Resolute,' said the man, as he passed and trailed his fingers upon the marbled surface.

The contempt that he showed made Edgar forget for a moment and mistakenly believe in his power of control once again.

'How dare *you* turn your back on me!'

Such deliberate provocation was intended to incite; the man only too aware, as he sat, slowly, and placed his hat upon the desk. He leaned back into the chair and looked up at Edgar.

'You reek of fear… I can smell it.'

The man made a strange grunting sound as he inhaled through the cavities of his open nasal wounds.

'But you still don't know the meaning of fear… do you, Edgar? So, I'll offer you a choice.

'Forget – everything – and – run.

'Or.... *Face — everything — and — rise....*

'The path is yours to decide... but decide you must.'

'What...? Who are you...? I demand—'

'Who I am is unimportant.... What I am, is.'

'Tell me now or I promise... you *will* face the consequences!'

The man sat ready. Relaxed.

'You have *no* idea of who I am!'

He scoffed and shook his head at Edgar, as if disappointed by the threat; disheartened by the approach and his failure to see the obvious.

'*You* are the son of David and Olivia Spear. Grandson of William Calhoun. Graduate of the University of California, and not Harvard as you would have history believe.' The man paused, forced to wet his mouth. 'You were a resident at Massachusetts General Hospital who failed to complete the third year of his residency. You are an unqualified doctor with no right to the title. You were a laboratory researcher. A murderer at DomiGen Labs, who removed both his partners and became CEO. A man who has single-handedly destroyed civilisation and pretends to play God... or should I say, "supreme leader," as you prefer to be called.' The man paused again, and again wet his mouth. 'But you are better known by those you have been unable to corrupt as, Dr. E. Spear. A disgrace to your profession, where the E is justified and represents all that you are....'

Edgar stared, as the man wet his mouth once again.

'*Evil....* Evil by deed and evil by desire.'

'H-how.... Where did you—'

'Nomini tuo da gloriam.'

The hairs on Edgar's neck jumped to attention as his jaw fell suddenly in distress.

'What...? What did you say?'

'Nomini — tuo — da — gloriam.'

'Im-impossible....' murmured Edgar; his cheeks no longer red— now ashen.

'And yet....'

Edgar numbed from the ice-cold wash that poured down his spine and froze his open lips, until all he could feel was the weight in his stomach and the shards of the ice that pricked his paled skin. The words of the man were those of a memory, a long-forgotten past from a life long ago.

'Unto thy name—' said the man, before Edgar interrupted.

'—give glory.'

Still seated, the man reached for his hat and began to run the brim between his fingers. Edgar needed more.

'The pin…. What do you know about the pin?'

However, Edgar's place was not to ask questions, he was there to account for his actions, and the man continued to look down at the hat with his large expressionless eyes.

'What does it mean…? My grandfather… he—'

The man stopped and looked up at Edgar. 'W.A.T.C.H,' he said.

'Watch…? No, the pin… what does it—'

'Cerebus.'

'Cerebus?' Edgar asked incredulously. 'That's a bedtime story… there's no such—'

The man had no need for debate or engagement in discussion, and Edgar was silenced again.

'Throughout the ages Cerebus has stood watch. Maintained the balance and brought light to those who have seen only darkness.'

Edgar laughed, derisively. The man was not to be feared, he was a fool to be pitied. An old decrepit coot deprived of his senses. Most likely another of Grey's fanatical followers. One who had torn out his implant to leave a mind beyond repair.

Caught off guard, not expecting such a ludicrous revelation, the ghost of his past had become a clown in the present. Now free of anxiety, Edgar's anger found focus on the man's defiance. He stepped away from the glass, his fists clenched. Enough of the games, of evading the questions. It was time to reveal the identity of the man, even if forcibly so.

'Beware,' he said, unconcerned by the swagger and the aggression that Edgar showed carved on his face.

'Of what…? *You?*' replied Edgar, laughingly, as he approached.

'Soon the time will come when you must face your fears.'

'My fears…? It's not *me* who should feel afraid, old man.'

'Embrace your destiny, Edgar, for a war is coming. A war you cannot escape.'

Edgar stopped. His face scrunched.

'What did you say?'

'We are everywhere and nowhere. Everyone and no one.'

'Where did—'

'The shadows that safeguard all freedom.'

The man's persistence for drama wore thin with Edgar and quickly erased his bewilderment. Alone for so long, tetchier and less tolerate of others, he not only tired of the man's evasiveness, but had now lost all patience with it.

'You are someone—and you are somewhere… somewhere you're *not* supposed to be. Still… don't worry, because I intend to find out who you are and how you got here… even if it takes all night.'

Edgar grabbed the man by the arm, knocking his hat to the floor as he pulled up his sleeve.

'Did you think I'd forgotten…? Where is he? Tell me where he is!'

The man looked up again at Edgar, unable to show emotion, and Edgar unable to read or sense the man's thoughts.

'What is this? This tattoo… what does it mean?'

Edgar squeezed the wrist tighter, straining his hand as hard as he could. Nevertheless, the man failed to react. He had lived a long and troubled life, a life with pain, and become accustomed to it. He was there to speak, not answer, and he had come to deliver a message.

'We are the Knights of Cerebus.'

'What?' Edgar asked dismissively.

'Those empowered to wage *war – against – tyranny, control,* and *havoc.*

Edgar loosened his grip and eyed the man with sarcastic disbelief. 'War…? You…?'

'The W.A.T.C.H, Edgar. We are the W.A.T.C.H. The balance of order.'

'So, the pin? My grandfather's pin…? Are you trying to tell me…?' Edgar stopped and scoffed. 'No, wait… let me guess…. You're here to warn me? To threaten me, and I'm supposed to be scared…? Tell me I'm wrong… tell me there's something more….'
Edgar began to laugh again, and again the man was silent.

'Let me give you a little advice… something you can take back to your friend…. You don't want to go to war with me, old-timer… I'll wipe you out… you, him, and whatever group you claim to represent…. You have no idea what I'm capable of!'

The man simply stared in reply, then reached down and picked up his hat.

'Oh, but I do, Edgar. I know only too well.'

He began to brush the brim with his hand, unperturbed by the attack or by Edgar looming over him. Suddenly, he stopped, cocked his head to the side and looked up.

'The hope of the future has always resided in mortal hands, Edgar. And now they will come… heroes… to destroy your world and put an end to your DomiNation.'

It was the way that he looked, decidedly and without care, that made it disconcerting. The way that he spoke, articulate and eloquent, that made him so convincing. The message was absurd, yet its delivery was not. Not like the crazed ramblings of those who experienced cell death and brain injury. It gave cause for concern, and for Edgar, it gave doubt.

'W-who are you?'

The man leant forward, slowly placing his hat again upon Edgar's desk, then leaned back and sighed heavily in the chair.

'You're not a Remnant... you can't be... so where's your implant?'

Edgar's voice held an anguish in its tone; a helplessness at the man's defiance and refusal to obey the supreme leader. Like the little bricks that he pushed, the little patience he had left now toppled over.

'I *won't* ask again.... Who — are — *you?*' he screamed. 'You tell me now and I'll make sure it's quick.... Drag this out, and I promise— you *will* suffer.'

The man looked up and met with Edgar's fury. 'And you,' he said, 'who once took pride in keeping control... how quickly you lose your temper now. How swiftly you turn to foolish threats.' He stared at Edgar and paused. 'I don't waste time threatening people... I remove them.'

Edgar blinked several times; a pause between the man's words and when his head began to shake.

'That's... that's impossible....'

'So you say, and keep telling me.'

'But how...? I was alone with Lewis. There was—'

'You are never alone, Edgar. I am the shadow of your past.'

'My... my what...? What past?'

'The past you cannot escape.... No matter how high you build your tower.'

Edgar looked down and closed his eyes tightly. He shook his head. The man was no ghost and was far from a clown. He offered only torment and delivered persecution.

'A man who does not embrace his past, has no future.'

'Did *he* send you? Is that what this is...?'

'And I have seen your future, Edgar.'

Talking over each other and no longer listening to the man, Edgar now only cared to make his point.

'*Where* is he? Why doesn't he show himself? Why send you...? A broken-down man of broken-down dreams....

'Whatever your plan—whatever he wants—he failed. Look. Look out there. Look and see…. Everything is built by *my* design… *mine!*

'I am everything, and *everything* belongs to me…. *To me!* Not you… not Abelman… Abelman did *nothing*… Abelman—'

'Worked with your mother and your father,' interrupted the man.

'No! Abelman *betrayed* my mother and my father. He sent them to an asylum. To—'

'Santarillo State Mental Hospital. Yes, I know… but Abelman never sent them there. It was Abelman who freed them… who brought them to Cerebus and saved them.'

'To Cere…. No, no that's not… Abelman… he—'

'Was your guardian, Edgar. An elected Guardian of the Council who was tasked with your protection after your parents disappeared. You were just a child—an infant—less than a year… and Abelman travelled with you under cover to the Table Mountains of the Sudetes. To the birthplace of your mother and the sanctuaries of our heritage.'

'Sudetes…? I've never even…. I grew up in Renfield with my—'

'No, Edgar…. You grew up in the mountains of Central Europe, outside a small remote village called Ukryty… or as you would have known it, Occultatum. There you were trained by Cerebus. By warriors and scholars once descended from the Rytterne: *De Ordine Matutinus.*'

'The Aurorean Order?'

'And they trained you well…. How else do you suppose that you became so fluent in the words of our language?'

The man paused to wet his mouth again; the grafts of skin that acted as lips in need of constant moisture.

'You began to train as a Ceren. To begin your journey towards becoming a Knight of Cerebus… but the Order was infiltrated. Abelman had left to discuss your progress with the Council. He returned to find that all was lost… all had perished… poisoned at the hand of a traitor.

'When he found you, you were barely alive… so weak and your life almost drained. He took you to the Council where it was decided that fate had intervened and surely kept you alive for a reason.' The man paused again. 'It was for this reason that your training would end, and you would be granted your freedom. The chance to discover your own path.'

Edgar shook his head in bemusement. He floundered backwards slightly, touching upon a chair. 'That's impossible… I never met Abelman until I moved to Boston… and it was an accident when—'

'There are no accidents, Edgar.'

Edgar slumped into the chair. His face pale and uncomfortable.

'We believed that a member of the Order had turned to O.D.I.U.M, but never suspected it could be one of our own Council…. That Cerebus had been compromised at the highest level.

'You had witnessed the massacre at Occultatum, and that made you our only hope to find the conspirator in our midst. But that same hope had also placed a target upon you, and we could not let you remain in peril… it is our solemn oath to protect the innocents.'

'Protect the innocents…? Protect them from what? From this… this Odium? I've never heard of—'

'A syndicate. A cartel network whose only goal is the very subversion and destruction of civilisation itself. We don't know their true name… who they are… or how many of them exist. We know them only by what they have sought to achieve through the ages and what they aim to accomplish.'

The man paused again and wet his mouth.

'They are the *overlords* of *decay* and *implicit, untold, misery.*

'When Abelman brought you to us, you were young, shocked by what you had seen. Your mind was caged. Yet the Council knew that you would never be safe… not as long as the identity of the traitor remained unknown. So, they voted to appoint one who would keep you safe. A Guardian of the Council.'

Edgar sneered at the man. 'Overlords...? There are no overlords... there is no Council or guardians... the only thing that awaits you, is an implant.' Edgar touched his ear. 'Reams... Reams?'

'It was Abelman who again risked all and asked the Council to allow him to protect you. He knew that if O.D.I.U.M found you, it would mean certain death for you both. So, he did what no one expected... he took you to America. Convinced that O.D.I.U.M would never look for you there.'

'Reams... where are you?'

'He gave you memories of a childhood that you never knew, of parents you had never met, and hoped that one day you would find your rightful place in the world... answer the call that fate had made of you.'

'No!' snapped Edgar. 'Don't speak of my parents... there was an accident, and my grandfather, he—'

'Died long before you were born. You have no grandfather. William Calhoun was a Knight of Cerebus.... A member of the W.A.T.C.H, charged by Abelman with your protection. Why else do you think he was so hard on you? He had to be. To prepare you. It was his task. His mission to do as the guardian commanded.'

'My grandfather owned a shipping company and had men who worked for him....'

'Centors, Edgar. A legion of Cerebus Centors. Each a soldier, sworn to protect your life with their own. There if the Knight should need them. If you should fall into danger.... If O.D.I.U.M should find you.'

'*What!*'

'Try to think, Edgar... think back.... You know what I speak is the truth.'

But Edgar couldn't think. He couldn't believe what he was hearing, and yet the man was able to interrupt and provide response to every comment; to speak without pause if only for the sake of his injuries. How could he do so if he was not telling the truth?

'Melvin Abelman was the greatest friend your parents ever had. When all hope was lost and the Council lost theirs, it was Melvin who clung to the belief of finding them. He never gave up—he never stopped searching—until he found them... at Santarillo.'

Edgar leapt to his feet. 'It's a lie... it makes no sense... none of this.... None of what you say....'

'Tell me, Edgar, did you ever see Melvin holding a scalpel? Did you ever once see him actually operate on a patient? Ever see him do anything more than watch over you...?'

The man paused again to moisten his scars.

'Melvin was a scientist—not a surgeon. He worked with your father. Did you never stop to ask yourself why he needed you...? Why you were so vital for DomiGen?'

'Of course, I did. Abelman was the money, he just put up—'

'Melvin was a Guardian of the Council. A Council who used their influence to place him at a hospital in the position they needed him to be in. A position for one purpose, and one specific purpose only.... To safeguard, you.'

Edgar tried to recall, to remember a time at the Slaughterhouse when he saw Abelman in surgery—even holding a scalpel... he couldn't.

'W-well where is he now...?'

'We don't know. No one does. Underground...? In hiding...? We know he's out there... perhaps believes that Cerebus has betrayed him.... He may even have turned to the only force willing to stand against you....'

'There is *nothing* that is able to stand against me!'

'Are you so sure, Edgar...? Even a sleeping dog can bite.'

Edgar paused. 'What...? The Remnants?'

'We never thought that you would try to take the life of your protector. That he would need protection from you.'

'But....'

'When Abelman found your mother and father, he knew that O.D.I.U.M would turn their eyes again to your family. To finding you… the missing child. The child who would now be a man… who would one day return to find and free his parents…. Perhaps regain his memory and expose the traitor in Cerebus…? Avenge the massacre at Occultatum.'

The man was forced to pause again, not used to talking at such length; his voice now rasping as he stretched his tongue and tried to moisten his throat with dry gulps.

'Your parents were helpless… weak from the years of torture at the hands of those creatures. And William, convinced that your wild fantasies were the results of the serum given to you as a child. Abelman knew that your grandfather could no longer protect you, so they conspired to get you into Massachusetts General. To a hospital where no one would suspect a doctor—not even a senior one—not when there's a staff of more than eleven thousand of them. Where he could be with all day and keep you under his wing.'

He paused again. 'But then… they found you… and Clydesdale—'

'Clydesdale…? No, he—'

'Did this,' snarled the man, as he raised the hand and pointed to his face. 'When he burned down the lab.'

Edgar shook his head.

'Before he took our bodies to Santarillo, to be disposed of….'

Edgar felt faint, weak at the knees, his life like an onion: peeled by its layers. It was he who now gulped and swallowed hard at the thought; his hand reached out to the desk, to steady himself. Yet he would not fall nor shed any tears, not for this man and his incredible fictitious tale.

'Instead of killing us… they kept us alive—tortured us—as they tried to get every last detail about ARC.'

'ARC?'

'The research project that we worked on. The Alliance Rule Concord.... It was meant to be the end of all wars, for all time... the saving of man from himself. That every leader would be given an implant... to share all thoughts... to remove all secrets... the stigma of weapons and nuclear arsenals. The end of international opposition. No more groups of industrialised nations. No more national economies and stock markets.... Instead, the leaders of the world working together for the benefit of all—united as one—finally able to achieve and maintain peace. A global alliance that would have been, if not for....'

The man paused. 'No one expected us to survive the agony they inflicted... and your mother... without her.... Well... when Abelman discovered where we were, he brought us to Cerebus.'

Edgar's hold on the desk did little to end his quivering. Filled with doubt, his fear of the unknown, his trepidation of revealing the truth.

'No. No... that's impossible.... It was Abelman who... because then... it would mean that you are—'

'The impossible, Edgar. By every right and law of existence, I am the impossible....'

The man gripped the arm rests and struggled to his feet. Edgar, choked by epiphany, recoiled backwards: away from the man and the desk.

'I am David Spear, and yes... you, Edgar, are my son.'

The man's revelations had reached like a hand deep inside Edgar to rip out what little remained. Not enough to simply strip him of command, to fill him with doubt and imbue him with fear; his perfect plan, his bigger picture, all taken away, and left in the cavern were only the words of the man, now his father.

'My... my mother?'

The man shook his head. 'At peace now... free from pain... from the suffering.'

'I... I don't believe you,' cried Edgar, his voice cracked like a teenager during adolescence. He could not believe. He would not believe. Because the truth he had known, that had forged his dominion, had to stay true, whatever the cost.

'You're a liar! You can't be my father... my mother and father died *long* ago. He couldn't be alive, if he was, then—'

'In the future, implants can do more than just control minds, Edgar. This is only the beginning... they will slow time—freeze it. Allow travel in parallels through it... at a cost. You have not even begun to understand the consequences of my work. Of what is possible... of what repercussions await.'

'Your work...?'

'Yes, Edgar. My work. You simply completed my work. The ARC.'

Edgar fell paler still.

'W-why are you here...? Why now... after all this time?'

'I told you. I have seen your future. You have brought the world to the edge of its ultimate destruction, and this madness must end... before it's too late.

'When Abelman informed the Council that you had perfected the implant, we knew that it wouldn't be long before O.D.I.U.M tried to take it. To try to use it against us... against everyone.'

'Abelman? That's impossible... I was with him the whole time after the implant coupled... up until—'

'Then how did he disappear?'

'That was after. I mean, there was confusion and....'

'You still don't understand, Edgar. Timelines are not linear. They are junctions connected through space. The past. The present. The future. They are all one. And at this juncture, you simply lack the ability to see it.'

'But Clydesdale said—'

'Clydesdale was O.D.I.U.M. His biggest mistake was believing that if Penelope Davis could get close to you—'

'Don't you dare.... Don't you dare say her name!'

'Close enough to stay with you. Then if you ever succeeded in perfecting the implant, you would reveal everything to her.... She was O.D.I.U.M, Edgar. Sent to seduce you. Abelman knew it and he tried to break her.'

'Abelman killed her!'

'No, Edgar, Penelope killed herself. She was taking a suppressant to resist Abelman's questioning. A highly concentrated form of Gamma-aminobutyric acid. By the time he found out, it was too late... she was gone.

'You must have noticed? Seen her become distant? Unresponsive.... She was a slave of O.D.I.U.M... loyal to the O.D.I.U.M Omertà.'

'No, it's not... it can't... I never started working with implants until years after I met Penny. How could you know...? How could Clydesdale know that I would start working with something that I knew nothing about?'

'Clydesdale knew Abelman. He knew that you were my son, and he knew that someone had rescued us from Santarillo. So, he knew that we had to be alive. We think that he planned to use you as a way to get us... to your mother and me... to find out if I had completed my research.'

'You mean Abelman's chips...? But then why did Abelman demand I go after Munro?'

'He had to mislead them... to feed false information for as long as he could... until you were safe... to make it believable. It had to be from the inside—to someone in O.D.I.U.M who believed they knew everything.'

'You... you're insane.... Nothing makes sense... and you're slipping, old man.... If Abelman was Cerebus and Munro was O.D.I.U.M, then why would Abelman ever want to let O.D.I.U.M close to the research?'

'We knew that Munro was a long shot. William had shared his concerns with Abelman about him on the day that you started university. That he took such an immediate interest in you seemed more than just coincidence. But we were never sure... never knew if he was O.D.I.U.M... so he was a calculated risk. Roberts was always aware of that.'

'Roberts? What does he have to do with this?'

'Roberts was Cerebus. The first trial you did for him at Saven—the first implants—where do you think they went? Why do you think I was there...? To ensure they were brought to the Council. We had to see for ourselves... be certain that the implants worked. The Council needed to know that you could control the minds of even the world's most hardened criminals before Roberts would be allowed to go ahead... that's why we chose Saven.'

'Ahead?'

'With the control of DomiGen, of course. We could never allow it to fall into the hands of O.D.I.U.M. But you chose to keep it. To do with it as you pleased... to create all this... this misery and destroy all these lives—these innocents who have fallen beneath your hand....'

The man paused again and again tried to moisten his mouth. Edgar's questioning continued.

'But the first time I saw you... with Abelman... that was years before the trial... and you were older....'

'Like I said, Edgar, travel... at a cost.'

'I... I....'

Edgar's eyes glistened, fighting back tears. The first sign of humanity in a man so inhumane for so very long.

'My son... you are not a god... no man is... and your time of worship must end. We have watched as you have violated our work, torn this world to pieces and rebuilt it in your own image. You have fashioned it with such selfishness and voracity as if you were the very head of O.D.I.U.M itself!

'You must stop this insanity and come with me now.'

'With you...? Where?'

'To the Council of Cerebus. To answer for your crimes. I will do all that I can to help you... I know that I have not—'

Edgar shook his head. No longer pale, he was furious. He no longer needed to steady himself with his desk; wrath emboldened him.

'Do you think you can just walk in here... walk through those doors... tell me some... some fantastic story and think that you can deny me of my destiny?'

'Edgar, I beg you—'

'Beg...? No... you – should – *kneel!* Drop to your knees... because I – *am* – God... and you will bow before me!'

'Please, Edgar, as your father—'

To hear those words, a parental right claimed by a man after all these years, meant everything, yet nothing. It was more than Edgar was able to bear. His face was a glowering flame, and he stormed back towards the man, halted by the obstacle of his desk as he prepared to deliver his judgement.

'Who are *you* to call yourself my father? To deny me *my* birthright! I have no father... I have no mother. You said yourself, even my grandfather was a lie... just like Abelman or Groy or whoever he was.... I'm giving the world the justice it deserves—cleansing its past—ridding its lies....' Edgar's eyes narrowed, and his voice calmed as it deepened. 'Granting it truth. My truth—the only truth it will *ever* know.'

'Groy?' asked the man, his parched voice clearly concerned.

'Abelman's real name.'

'No, Edgar. Melvin... he....'

The man seemed alarmed; shocked, almost wavering.

'You think I didn't know...? Clydesdale warned me... he sent me a letter... he told me the real reason why Groy murdered Penny and why he killed him... to keep his past a secret.'

'Edgar, Abelman had no alias.'

'Of course he did! Once Clydesdale told me about Roberts, it was obvious that he and Groy were in on it all along... that's how he got the government contract... with Roberts as president, and Roberts had to pay... for his part in killing my parents, like you will....'

'I'll admit, you had me going there... I even bought it for a while, but now—'

'Groy is a... it's a name I've not heard in a long time.... It... it was our family name before we began work on ARC... before your mother and I assumed new identities to protect our children.'

The man was despondent. Edgar stared; his eyes were blank.

'Children...?'

'Then they know....'

'Know what?'

'About your.... Edgar, please, don't make this harder than it needs to be. I am charged by the W.A.T.C.H to bring you to the Council. You must end this now. You must give up this throne and come with me.'

Edgar slammed his fists down upon the desk, as he did on the day of his graduation, and just as he did when Munro made a fool of him, Edgar ground them harder still, until his knuckles began to bleed. Until there was no pain or feeling, nothing except his bloodlust.

'It's over, old man.... The world you claim to protect is *gone*— long forgotten. The new world—the world that I have created—is DomiNation. And in this world, I do not answer to your charges, or recognise your court, because I am destiny. I am the *voice* of destiny... I am its Spear.

'I am the weapon that extinguishes the light.... The lance that kills all hope.... The darkness that removes all shadow.... And I will *not* yield to a cripple.'

The man, still troubled, appeared unsurprised.

'Then you are lost. You are truly lost, Edgar... in a place where no one will find you.'

He bent down to pick up his hat. The holographic projection became active as he put it back on, disguising his face in shadow once more. Edgar stood behind the desk, his fists still buried into the surface, his stare still fixed upon the man as he glared into the featureless darkness. The man bowed his head slightly, then turned and shuffled back towards the door. He stopped unexpectedly.

'I am sorry, my son. Sorry that I could not spare you from this... from the pain that has made you do such terrible things....'

The man raised his hand with four fingers.

'You of all, Edgar, should remember... to take down the house, you must be willing to sacrifice.'

He nodded, only once, as if to acknowledge his son. Perhaps it was a sign of respect, perhaps an admittance of guilt, but the words of Abelman, the words that Edgar had used for so very long to exact revenge upon those who had stood in his way, were able to stun him again into silence.

'Remember, Edgar, the world of men will only fall when brother turns upon brother.... Father upon son... and son upon father.'

He placed his hand in front of the control pad, a hand scanner programmed to recognise the fingerprints of Edgar. The door opened, and the man stepped outside. Edgar glanced at the floor and noticed a forgotten item.

'Your case! You forgot your case, old man.'

The man stopped and turned around to face Edgar from the hallway. 'No, Edgar, I only forgot my son... the briefcase is for you. A gift that may help you find the light, now that your world has fallen into darkness.'

The door closed, and the man was gone. Edgar walked towards the briefcase, curious to examine the contents and the gift that was left behind. Perhaps it was a letter, some form of explanation? A photograph or an object from his childhood: something that might illuminate his past or help him to remember. Whatever it was, it would not end like this; the supreme leader denied the final word, and not until the man had at least explained how he was able to get into his office. Edgar stopped, halfway towards the door, and touched his ear lobe.

'Reams…. Where are you…? Reams…? There's an intruder. I'm sending his face to all guards and sentinels now… bring him to me… he's not to be harmed… I need—'

Suddenly, the order was interrupted, and Edgar silenced once again. Not by his anger or the man who claimed to be his father, but from the blast of the explosion; one that tore the briefcase to shreds. The bomb threw Edgar across the room with such force that the enormous glass window had already shattered from the impact. Deafening gale winds howled through the aftermath, fanning the flames of the inferno that roared out and lit the thick smoke-filled sky high above DomiNation Alpha1. The wall of screens once covering his kingdom, were torched in an instant; vaporised into dust. There was nothing left standing, nothing except carnage. Even the desk had fallen—the stone cracked into pieces—now blazing in the fires of the scorching heat. This was no show or assassination performance, because there in the rubble, surrounded by ruins, lay a crumpled burning heap. His clothes were on fire, his body bloodied and blistering; punctured by the shrapnel, by the slivers of glass, and the searing molten metal that dripped from the ceiling girders onto his lifeless corpse.

The grand finale was not to his plan, now that the truth had finally set him free. Relieved from the burden of its design, death had brought his release. Edgar was dead. The Spear of Destiny, slain. With him would fall dominion, and surely the dream that was DomiNation?

17

THE RISING

The explosion was thunderous. It not only lit the evening sky, but rang out like a siren would an alarm, alerting all to the atrocity of the attack. The Sentinels of Spear were the first to react, storming the stairwells as they raced to the scene. The wind, however, was ferocious, unforgiving at that height, even from the entry at the opposite end of the floor. It blew wildly through the tower, like a growling hurricane through a barn, whipping up wreckage and unleashing it violently. With their visors pulled down and their shields held up, the Sentinels were blocked, struggling to progress through the blizzard of dust and ash.

'Take cover!' yelled a Sentry, as a large piece of debris hurtled towards them like a train through a tunnel.

They moved to the sides, behind the pillars still standing, before an all clear was given to push on towards Edgar. These elite warriors were ruthless; ordered to kill on sight rather than detain or interrogate, and they showed no mercy to those in their way. Grouped into two, their roles differed slightly, and on the rare occasions that Edgar left the tower, the Sentinel Sentries were those sent on in advance. Their duty was to scout—to survey the area—before the Sentinel Setorians moved in to ensure its safety and accompany his arrival. It was the Setorians who stood guard before the attack; their body armour heavier, designed to protect, though their uniforms identical apart from the navy-blue shoulder sash and helmet markings of the Sentries.

The Sentry who stood ahead of the troop, raised his head above his shield and gave a signal. They approached the opening, the heart of the blast where the door had been; now just a hole and a mound of burning rubble, where only fragments of the surrounding walls remained.

'We must turn back.' The strength of the winds were too strong and the Sentry unable to withstand the assault. 'Sir, we must—'

'Hold firm, Sentinel. That's an order!' barked a voice through the helmet intercom.

Lord Sentinel, the leader of the Sentinels of Spear, forged his way to the front of his men.

'Do *not* abandon this position…. We must contain the area. Is that understood?'

The Sentry stared at Lord Sentinel, his face disguised by the storm and the billowing dust clouds that filled his visor; his voice drowned by the thundering wind.

'Do – you – read – *me?*'

Lord Sentinel reached out to the Sentry and pulled him in close before repeating his order. He turned his back to the opening to offer shelter and give respite to his subordinate, as the lumps of rock and metal pummelled him from behind.

'I'm going in!' he declared. 'Contain the area… wait for my mark.'

The Sentry signalled with his thumb and Lord Sentinel turned to face the tempest, instantly struck in his visor by debris. He crouched—half to his knees—and edged into the room with his head turned down to the side, as he tried to avoid the flying projectiles that bombarded his body and helmet.

With no visibility, Lord Sentinel switched to his scanner as he tried to locate the position of Edgar far inside the room. He followed the finder, stumbling and falling constantly as he struggled across the broken terrain; until the sound of the radar was almost audible and the dot on the finder became steady and bright. He turned to face forwards and dropped to the ground, then doused the flames of Edgar's burning robe. He looked back to the hallway, or where he believed it to be.

'MediTeam... do you read me? MediTeam, come in.... MediTeam, do you copy? Follow my signal.... Follow − my − signal....'

He glared at the badly charred body. His head bowed in shock, in quandary at the smoke that encircled the corpse. No intruder had been detected, and no scanner had registered any other lifeform on the upper level, so how had this happened? The Sentinels of Spear were the personal bodyguards of the supreme leader who were tasked with a single directive; a mission they had failed to achieve. Questions would be asked, and their integrity was at stake, but for now, all that Lord Sentinel could do was wait.

The wind was relentless: it howled and roared, pelting Lord Sentinel with wreckage from the ruins. In the distance, flashes of white tore through the dust as the medical team finally began to close in. Lord Sentinel rose to his knees, raised his arm against the wind, and clenched his fist as tight as he could. A brilliant light shot from the bracelet of his armour, up through the air like a beacon to follow. The medical team quickly examined Edgar, and the doctor gave what Lord Sentinel interpreted to be an indication; what he hoped, what he thought, was a promising sign of life. Impossible to hear or be heard above the roar, the doctor offered instead a signal; his swirling index finger, then pointed up and out towards the shattered window. Lord Sentinel shook his head and cut his hand through the air; his response was no. The doctor repeated his signal, nodding insistently to Lord Sentinel, who denied the request once again. He could never explain that the crosswinds at this height would prevent such a manoeuvre. The doctor, however, was adamant....

Lord Sentinel had failed his command, and whatever the risk or the danger to others, the duty of the Sentinels was explicitly clear. If there was a pulse it was undoubtedly faint, yet where there's a pulse there must surely be hope; a chance for redemption, to redeem reputation. He paused for a moment. The decision was made.

'The tower is compromised. I repeat... the − tower − *is* − compromised. Exodus is decreed.... I repeat.... Exodus − *is* − decreed. Execute by order of the Lord Sentinel.'

He shouted through his mouthpiece, uncertain if the order was received. Certain only that if it was, an army of DomiForce Rangers and Guards would arrive within minutes, and with them, armed air support to evacuate Supreme Leader Spear.

Lord Sentinel nodded. The doctor and his team carefully lifted Edgar's seared body onto the stretcher, securing it with restraints. Minutes later came confirmation that the message had been heard. Outside the tower, a DomiForce helicopter now hovered perilously. Thrown from side to side by the typhoon of turbulence, the pilot was unable to maintain steady course. Lord Sentinel raised his arm and clenched his fist once again, igniting the beam from his bracelet to signal the pilot. He stared at the stretcher, at the clear oxygen mask that covered the blackened flesh of an unidentifiable face—perhaps keeping it alive. Time was of the essence, and no need for a second opinion to realise that it was too far to the window. Simply too far to retrieve a line and return to the stretcher. Too dangerous to evacuate with so much damaged glass still hanging from the frame; partially shattered and ready to fall, to be blown into the room at any moment.

Near him, to his left, was a sheet of corrugated metal. It was warped from the fires, although largely intact, and Lord Sentinel pulled it in front of the stretcher; his glove igniting, then melting from the heat. He nodded again to the doctor, and the doctor nodded remorsefully back; a mutual understanding of what needed to be done. The doctor signalled for the MediTeam to retreat. He looked once again to Lord Sentinel who pointed at the ground, at the space beside the stretcher that gained cover behind the sheet.

'Hurry,' he yelled, and the doctor acknowledged, nodding in reply after crouching for safety.

The flames raged around Lord Sentinel as the heat scorched his visor and the putrid black smoke choked the air. He drew in a breath, it was long and slow, before he turned again towards the window. He closed his eyes as something hit his chest, something else struck his arm that caused him to jolt, and he imagined a place that was far from here. He had failed his master once, he would not fail him again, and he reached to his side, raised his weapon, then fired.

The glass that remained in the wake of the blast, had afforded some refuge from the merciless winds. It exploded in an instant from the impact of the bullet, clearing the exit and a gateway to safety. The shards flew back at incredible speed, slicing through his visor as it split into two. Stabbed by the fragments of the knives that cut him— impaled by the slivers of a thousand shining spears—the Lord Sentinel's body wrenched. He struggled to stay standing, releasing his breath, now heavy and strained, as the weapon fell from his skewered open hand. He signalled for the line, and waiting to cast, the co-pilot hurled it at the beam of light. Nevertheless, his senses were numbed, his vision was blurred, and the Lord Sentinel unable to see through the fumes or take hold. He dropped to his knees, the blood seeping from his punctures; the atonement for his failure in protecting his master, and his life worth the sacrifice to not fail him again. The line was reeled back and each second eternal as he mustered his strength for one more attempt. He raised his hand, the beam quivering as he did so, and the co-pilot threw as hard as he could. It landed somewhere, deep into the distance, while the co-pilot watched the beam fall in the dark.

Time was running out, the metal sheet melting in place, and the doctor spied from behind the defence. With no idea of what was happening, just the flickers of broken light that traced through the rubble, he crawled on all fours towards the Lord Sentinel. There was nothing he could do. The line was clutched beneath his chest, and he rolled him on his side, to prise the hook from his flaccid hand.

'I can't hold her,' screamed the pilot. His voice filled with desperation as he wrestled with the cyclic control. 'He's got to hurry… he's got to hurry!'

The co-pilot waved feverishly, hoping for a signal, as the doctor dragged the hook back towards the stretcher. He tugged hard on the line—three times once attached—and the co-pilot began to reel it in. The stretcher jarred suddenly, as the winch took up the slack, pulling it in bursts as the debris fought to prevent its escape. The line rewound and Edgar was dragged over the mounds of burning rubble; followed by the doctor who was blinded by the dust, his hand shielding his eyes, his face bloodied and cut from the glass.

'You've got to cut the line!'

The pilot's struggle turned to the fear of certain collision and his inability to prevent their crash.

'I can't keep her steady. You've got to cut it—'

'Almost there.'

'Cut the line!'

'Almost….'

Suddenly, the stretcher jammed, lodged against a fallen block of concrete. The helicopter jerked violently at a tilt towards the flaming devastation, then began to edge nearer as the winch continued to reel.

'Cut it…! Cut it *now!*'

The co-pilot slammed on the controls and the winch stopped. He grabbed the pilot by the shoulder. 'We can't!' he yelled. 'What do you think they'll do to us if we fail?'

'I don't care,' replied the pilot, his face drenched with perspiration. 'This is suicide. I'm not dying for—'

'Here…. Over here!' shouted the doctor, precariously close to the ledge.

His eyes were closed tightly, to shield them from the smoke. His bloodied hand gripped the frame of the window, as he waved one arm frantically, leaning out in the hope of attracting attention.

'It's free... the stretcher... it's free!'

The crew heard nothing but the wind, and the pilot committed to cutting the line himself.

'Wait!' screamed the co-pilot. 'Look... look!'

He pointed at the doctor who was waving his thumb in the air. The co-pilot hit the winch control and the stretcher moved again. Forced out onto the ledge, it pulled slowly and rested for a moment: balancing on the edge.

'A little more... a little.... Gotcha!'

Freed from the tower, the stretcher swung in mid-air like a pendulum beneath the helicopter, thrashing to the sides and spinning in the frenzied winds on the line beneath the whirling blades.

'Go. Go. Go!' screamed the co-pilot, and the pilot plunged forward on the stick.

The doctor squinted; the slightest glimpse as the helicopter dived hard, then banked as it disappeared into the smoke-filled dusk. He turned to the blazing scene of desolation, uncertain if Edgar was alive, or if fate had finally held him to account.

Weeks turned to months, with no news of the supreme leader. Edgar was nowhere to be seen and no details were released about his condition. Not a single public statement concerning his health, with no announcement of a burial to mark his death either. The dream of DomiNation had succumbed to its flaw, and the frailty of a plan, no matter how prepared or precisely applied, will always exist if a weakness is found. In Edgar's perfect world, where power was control and control created order, his absence was the weakness and the hole in his plan. In no time at all, not a year since his death, it had widened so deeply as to cause a divide.

Each DomiCentre could easily exceed a quarter of a billion people. A metropolis of such epic proportion that it housed a community three times the size of Germany and ten times that of Australia. Two hundred and fifty million human beings, living together within a single, solitary city; all crammed within its outer walls. Yet without the presence of its supreme leader, the temptation for personal prosperity and a life of betterment became the paradigm of the majority. The seduction of advancement and the climbing of social classes, of treading upon those necessary in order to ascend the ladder of success, promoted transgression. Transgression led to corruption. Corruption led to crime. Crime led to cruelty, until gradually, almost invisibly, immorality for many had become the new norm. The utopian urban design that was structured for control, now lent itself as easily to lawlessness with all of its moral turpitude, and it began to spread like a plague. A handful fled and escaped to the sequestered outer regions. To the small, abandoned townships; to remote homesteads and places that remained under the radar of DomiGen. Even so, without power or food, and with nothing except the hope of survival, life for these would be hard at best, which is why they were called: *The Forsaken.* For all those who remained, the ideological imperious state was equal no more; now a dog-eat-dog world, it was hard to maintain one's own self-respect when society itself demonstrated none.

With implant instructions no longer updated or issued as before, the ones most exploited had begun to regress. Why it began with the DomiForce, was a mystery to all. However, a theory persisted, that their minds once repressed, more extreme than the most, needed continual command and a program to conform. In the absence of both, and the benefit of hindsight, it was never a question of probability or if; just a matter of time before those most conditioned returned to their old and erroneous ways. The few who were willing to speak out, claimed it began with a flashback; through unaccounted recollections and memories that at first seemed out of place, then felt stronger over time, undeniable in the end. Before long, these former convicts reverted to the only life they had ever truly known. Crime, with all its malice, was allowed to flourish, and the very group of DomiForce Rangers and Guards put into place to subdue it, were now the ones who endorsed it. With nothing to stop them and no one to defy them, the DomiForce were effectively able to govern.

Paradise was lost, not only in the mind, but in the lower levels of each DomiCentre. They descended into dismal, abject wastelands, and nowhere more so than the Districts of DomiNation Beta2, DomiNation Epsilon2, and DomiNation Gamma2. These were the areas that once represented New Delhi and the surrounding regions of India, Nepal and Pakistan. Santiago and the surrounding territories of Chile and southern Argentina. Sicily and the surrounding provinces of southern Italy. All were especially hard hit, and each became a place where the hopes of young futures appeared to be lost. In fact, life for many in these vulnerable sectors was no life at all; a continuous struggle, a cruel vicious circle, and substance abuse the only form of escape. Those with no choice preyed on those who had, because those who had prospered took all that they could, and those who did not, lost all they possessed. Such was the cruelty this new world now offered, that the hatred of millions blamed fault for their suffering at the once worshipped deity and his failed DomiNation. In spite of abhorrence, on those grim troubled streets and impoverished corners, despair knew no depth in a world of its own. It was there in those murky dark waters, best left undisturbed for the fear of the terrors that lurk down below, that a poison was spreading, and rumours were stirring, of a vile secretive network that was growing in strength. No names could be mentioned, nor existence ever proven, when the cries of the helpless were heard as a canard for the whispers of evil. This was no handful of DomiForce officers returning to lives of corruption and crime. This was more sinister, systematic and cunning. A ploy to oppress and maintain depravity, ensuring indigence to those left behind.

They had risen from the darkness, from the chasms of the chaos, as they fed off the misery of the weak and the helpless. Born in the shadows, they had burgeoned in its gloom. A secret league that supposedly sought havoc, thrived off bedlam, and might one day prove a threat to more affluent DomiCentres. Perhaps even to the downfall of DomiNation itself.

Suddenly, everything that Edgar's father had foretold was coming to pass. O.D.I.U.M was real, and if it was, then the W.A.T.C.H must also be. So, where were they? Why had they not come forth? Where was this Council of Cerebus with their Knights and their Guardians? Their Centors and their Legions? What was the point of remaining vigilant at the ready, if when time came for action, they only tarried under cover and failed to act? Surely with their silence, just as Edgar in his absence, they too had failed to protect the innocents or deliver them to freedom; for whatever freedom or deliverance was worth.

After the fall of General Wekesa, the old world plunged quickly into total supremacy. With everyone able to connect to the Grid, the little brick masses, voracious to do so, stood in line with their eager consent to give birth to DomiNation. Gone was the need to stage terrorist attacks, to justify DomiForce and to tighten the reins. Gone also the need to place blame upon Grey and his anarchist Remnants who fled underground, now years since last seen. Their values and virtues were all but forgotten, and given more time, might well have been lost. Until Edgar's demise saw a newfound resurgence, as a dossier that was known, albeit never shared, had finally been brought to the incriminating light.

There had always been hosts whose bodies would experience rejection, the seldom anomaly who would suffer complications from having an implant. Their deaths were spontaneous, most often very violent. The result of organs shutting down as immune system defences fought against toxins that leaked from their circuits. This delicate information was never made public, not even when the world was confined by its governments and inapt regulations. An implant gave enhancement and not liability, they could never be responsible for the loss of a life. Their creation was simple, for benefit not injury, as research brought opportunity with the chance to improve and the means to correct. As the years passed after the Grid first came online, the power of an implant became more than connection, it was an instrument designed to improve upon nature, to restore what was damaged and remove limitation. Neural disfunctions and genetic disorders could all be corrected if a host sought a life more enriched than before.

Fatalities that occurred in the search of perfection—in the name of science—were always expected and therefore forgivable. An acceptable loss, and as Abelman once said, "You can't make an omelette without breaking a few eggs." In those early experiments at DomiGen Labs, Edgar had witnessed countless failures; the thousands of victims who had died by his hand. At the time of their suffering, when connection would fail or an implant implode, he reduced their affliction and disguised their rejection through a drug induced coronary with tragic results. A dose of amphetamine, concentrated and lethal, created the illusion of a fatal heart attack. Released from the implant as the chip and its casing dissolved in the bloodstream, the medical record would then be erased. Without trace of insertion or physical evidence, there was no chance to incriminate or argue against any "natural death." Despite his own measures, each loss was recorded, archived by Edgar and stored on a disc. It had stayed confidential, classified to all but a select chosen few, and they referred to these victims as: *DomiCides.*

During The DOGMA Program, procedures had improved. Even so, for every million Dominoes there were always new DomiCides: seventy at least—sometimes many more. Such few causalities were an insignificant price to pay, especially for precision and to realise the bigger picture. Yet the image was no masterpiece, it was rotten to the core; the artist himself now presumed dead for over thirty long and miserable years. Even after his disappearance, his legacy lived on, and generations had passed since the first trials at Saven over fifty years ago. During this time, the numbers of DomiCides had steadily declined: a result of new insertion techniques and the replacement of Edgar's first-generation implants. As the second advancement was replaced by the third, then the fourth and the fifth-generation technology, DomiCide rates were the least of the problems that the less ambitious leadership of DomiGen faced.

Without the authority of their once supreme leader, free thinking was rife and implants selective—a matter of choice, no longer compliance—as their use evolved beyond the DomiGen Grid. The form of an implant was just the beginning, again as his father had rightly predicted. They exceeded simplicity, the means of communication, for sharing information and controlling the mind. Applications were now endless for those who had money, and advancements unending for those who paid more. For the rest, there was always the consolation that the model they still hosted provided a function and addition to life; with the option to upgrade should the host acquire budget or need greater incentive to arise from the squalor of the lower levels. Regardless of status, those without means carried implants that were several decades old, and those who were affluent, who replaced and upgraded, had hosted an implant for equally as long. Time continued to pass, and the adverse effects of prolonged use grew increasingly clear. An evolution, once inconceivable in thought, was not without consequence nor willing to hide.

Cases were extreme, although few at the outset and quickly dismissed; why no probe for a pattern was examined or found. Nevertheless, mutations in tissue, in the genes of the new-born, began to emerge and diversify by kind. In the beginning, deviations were so small that they were often ignored, and their symptoms the result of rare medical conditions or a child that was said simply to be different than the rest. Despite such ignorant, flippant dismissals, the truth hid a secret more painful for all, and their emergence might once have been slowed, even thwarted, if only his voice had been listened to and heard....

With his final words on the day of his murder, former President Roberts had tried to warn Edgar; to tell him about Saven and the importance of something that he needed to learn. Overwhelmed by fury and his lust for revenge, Edgar gained nothing except the false satisfaction from the taking of a life that was based on a lie. The alarm went unnoticed—knowledge left unshared—the explanation for the signs that were there and quite obvious, might well have changed everything had it only been known.

While he ruled DomiNation, the occasional discrepancy that warranted attention was explained by Edgar as simply "misfortune." A chromosomal abnormality, or the result of a pregnancy that was beset by some problems, just an inconvenience of nature mistakenly ignored. Yet mutations in infants were more than coincidence and their existence were hardly a case of bad luck. Conspicuous from birth, they were special not ordinary, with all in possession of exceptional gifts. Some were more evident while others were subtle, but none had control over strengths that they held. These were more than mere mortals that DomiGen would aim to condition or control over time through an implant. These were powerful metahumans that could never be ruled, with no place in his world or precisely laid plan. However, he had lingered in ignorance, and since his dominion, the influence of DomiGen had decreased by the day. Edgar's empire had fallen, still progressively falling, and the grip of criminality tightened around the vacuum of its spiralling decay. Whether DomiForce or the mystic O.D.I.U.M plagued the poorer Districts that were ravaged and pilfered was impossible to tell, nor made any difference, as former DomiForce Rangers—bullies and thugs—most definitely ran dozens of outfits elsewhere. Always on the lookout, in search for new talent, they hunted individuals who could put their gifts to far better use. As infants became children, those who showed promise and signs of distinction, were often abducted for these criminal gangs. It took only a rumour, a careless word leaked from DomiGen, before the vultures came circling and the opportune moment eventually came; if not by fortuity, then by ways that were called for, and the child would then vanish with no hope to be found. Kidnapped by mercenaries who disappeared with their bounties to the shadows of the lower levels, these ruthless abductors had rightly earned their name: *The Shadow Seekers*. Lost amongst the millions of souls who were trapped there, those taken captive were raised in the factions; no memories of past lives and their abilities squandered for illicit gain. For the criminals, it was simple. Why take the risk of losing a footman, when one exceptional—"adopted"—child could settle a gang fight, subdue rival minions, or take what was coveted without being harmed. The Shadow Seekers were infamous, and fear was enough to suppress young abilities; to hide any gift and remove all suspicion or the focus of any unwanted attention. All the same, it was not only children that they captured, and in the sectors of the Districts there were people who had lived with mutated genes unbeknown their whole lives. Dormant in cells, they were suddenly triggered in extreme situations, resulting from stress or the predicaments of danger. They too became targets once their powers would manifest, though many would try to ignore and continue, it was never an option to keep those who they loved and their families safe.

DomiNation had become a darker, more dangerous place, and nothing had epitomised its downfall more aptly than the Great DomiGen Tower: it stood paralysed, crumbling and derelict. In the months following Edgar's death, the tower was sealed. No one dared venture inside, not without confirmation, for fear of repercussion or of facing his wrath should he still be alive. The months became years and the years turned to decades, as DomiGen continued with the need to make profit more than keeping control. Their squeeze on economies had long since been lost, commandeered by crime and the influx of criminal networks that now managed the majority of wealth in the world. There was simply not the level of funds in DomiGen as there were under Edgar, certainly not the kind required to demolish and reconstruct such a tower. So, it remained in ruins, a symbol of history and dominion destroyed. A reminder to all of an unforgotten empire.

With no supreme leader, chaos ruled supreme, and as conditions deteriorated within each DomiCentre, self-appointed ministries sought to take charge. Local leaders came to power, creating identities and rules they demanded to be followed. They squabbled over decrees and proposals for their charters that only persecuted citizens through their kangaroo courts.

Commander Reams was now pushing seventy-five, most likely closer to eighty. Strangely, he looked and had the physique of a man less than half his age, undoubtedly due to a number of implant enhancements, rumours he so vehemently denied. He was the first to challenge and then declare himself not only the leader of Alpha1, but of all four DomiCentres in DomiNation Alpha. A fearsome relic from an age gone by, many still believed he was best suited to a place in a museum rather than the throne of DomiNation. Be that as it may, after Edgar's death it was Reams who had tried to calm the storm, and despite everything that had happened, he was still the only criminal who had never received an implant; a secret that remained intact and strengthened his argument to lead. He was, after all, able to resist the temptation once the updates had stopped and free will had returned. The one with the strength to remain virtuous when so many like him did not. There was no question of his loyalty, his commitment and honesty, because the once most feared convict had been truly redeemed.

While Reams and his *new* DomiForce had authoritative control, in Alpha at least, the rebellion outside had been especially debilitating for the additional Districts where the mutiny in DomiForce had crippled its ranks. It was here that the criminal underworld, fuelled by the bowels of corruption, had experienced most growth and were buoyed in strength and by number; unlikely, nor willing, to accept any system that threatened the balance or the source of their power.

Micro regimes emerged across the Districts, within every level, and across every sector of each DomiCentre. DomiNation had become eclectic with nothing of unity, nothing beyond the need to survive. As the struggle to do so raged on between syndicates and the ambitions of so-called leaders with their illegitimate claims, a new kind of metahuman had come to the fore: one too powerful for the Shadow Seekers to overcome. Some had chosen to reject anonymity, while others—whose transformations were so extreme or pronounced—had never the option to consider the choice. Many had experienced aberration since childhood, their genetic mutations impossible to disguise; impossible to be anything other than what their powers had forced them to be. There were those whose gifts were endless, and those whose strengths were potentially monstrous. Those who had gained celebrity status, and those now revered through their acts of heroism or the deeds they performed out of kindness. They were followed by masses. By the minds of those impaired and made stagnant from the years of control by DomiGen. Those who had forfeited education over the lure of dissemination and of being *Truly Connected* to the Grid. They were more like automatons, easily fooled and the sheep still in need of a shepherd. Simpletons who saw the purveyors of such incredible gifts not as physical or physiological deviations from the norm. They were illustrations of the power, of the gods that now walked amongst them; the messiahs that were chosen to lead them into a fairer, more favourable world. These were the people who had never learnt, and who would never learn, because primitive are the minds of those choosing to follow; those unable or unwilling to reason for themselves.

Their numbers increased with each generation, yet the ones who found courage to reveal their true nature remained just the few. This advanced breed of mortal, terrifyingly prodigious with their copious gifts, continued to vary in dimension and scale. There were those who were able to transform matter, change time, conduct electricity, create kinetic energy, control water, reverse the elements, and even travel between the astral planes. In spite of their powers, the consequences to the planet playing host to these beings had come at a price that was obvious to all. As the surface became charged through unparalleled fluctuations, fields were reversed, before poles quickly shifted to alter rotation and axial tilt. With extreme climate changes, humanity adjusted in the face of extinction. Exposed to the effects of unearthly radiation and the abnormal rise of celestial energies, the consequences for DomiNation, for all who now dwelled there, were far from revealed; still mercifully unknown.

When the fighting first started, it broke out in DomiNation Alpha2: a place that was once called Mexico. Alpha2 was farther from the capital than the other DomiCentres of the District, and it was here, in opposition to Reams, that the authority of his new DomiForce was questioned. The violence spread quickly through unruly unrest. The doubt and distrust in his ability to lead, equalled only by the loss of any confidence he once had to control the clumsy, excessive methods of his rangers. What began as a routine check of a young girl with no papers or means of identification, manhandled with their typical tyrannical approach, was met this time by resistance. Objection came in the form of a rock; cast at the rangers along with the cry to leave her alone. However, one of rangers took exception to the challenge, and opened fire indiscriminately in the direction of the perpetrator. Several civilians were gunned down, including an elderly blind man; a man who sat helpless and whose only crime was to sit on a stool outside of his Domicile, listening to the world as it passed him by. He was no one special or of any importance. Just another bystander—one innocent too many—murdered by the overly zealous DomiForce.

The rock that was thrown became a barrage of stones, as a mob, now incensed and appalled by the act, were no longer tired, but unwilling to tolerate oppression any longer. A tall, raven-haired woman moved through the horde and emerged through their lines, holding the hand of a young child by her side. The boy was no more than eight years old. His clothes frayed, in need of repair. His skin, gaunt and stretched tight over his thin little bones.

'Get back!' yelled the ranger, as he pointed his weapon at the woman.

The boy looked up and she smiled affectionately at him. She dropped to her knees, placed a hand on his cheek and leant in close; to hold his attention away from the crowd and away from the barrel of the gun.

'In every battle,' she said, with a warmth in her voice, over the shouts of raging discontent.

'One will rise,' he replied.

She nodded. 'In every victory....'

'One must fall.'

The boy released the woman's hand, then looked at the ranger before taking a step towards him.

'Get back!'

He ignored the cry and turned to the crowd, his eyes gaseous and purple, flaming like fire behind glass. Suddenly, their missiles froze; suspended in flight and brought to a standstill as the child directed his glare upon the rangers. Aflame with a fury, his eyes burned brighter, and he reached out his hand, opened his palm, then stretched his fingers as far as he could. In the distance, the sound of a thud, heavy and dull, grew louder as a car hurtled towards the rangers at lightning speed. It compacted as it rolled, as if struck and fashioned by an almighty invisible hammer, until all semblance of the vehicle was lost. The rangers looked behind with no time to react, as the large, jagged metal sphere hurled them against a wall. Stopping abruptly, it lost all momentum less than a metre in front of the boy. Unfazed, the woman rose to her feet. She closed her eyes as she stood in anticipation, before a shockwave followed the loud crack of a sonic boom that pulverised the stones into powder overhead. It fell and rings erupted from around him, sending ripples of dust with such immense power that all were blinded within his range. In the midst of the haze, the boy lowered his hand and the fire in his eyes was extinguished.

The young girl, unscathed by the pounded hunk of metal, sat crouched and tucked on her knees. Her hands covered her face, without courage to look or to know it was over, as she trembled with fear after what she had witnessed. Desperate to avoid or attract further attention, she stayed down in the hope that she was somehow unseen, and able perhaps to make her escape. She peered through her fingers at the boy and the woman in the eye of the storm, then across at the rangers who lay broken and pale. This was not imagination, it was terrifyingly real, and she had to disappear into the crowd. She leapt to her feet, but her legs would not move; paralysed as the boy met her eyes.

'Please... please.... Don't... don't hurt me... I... I don't have anything....'

The boy took another step forward.

'Please... don't... please... m-my name is Ella, I don't—'

'Ella Lea, I know,' replied the boy, 'and with time, you too will choke on the same familiar dread.'

The young girl lowered her hands. Her knotted blonde locks blown in swirls across her grimy face.

'You... you know my name?'

The woman stepped forward and the boy took her hand. He looked up and again she smiled down at him. They turned and walked back through the thick, dust-filled air, disappearing into the heart of the confused mob.

'Wait!' the young girl cried, as the raven-haired woman weaved between clouded outlines, then suddenly was gone. 'Who are you...?'

A victory, even against two DomiForce Rangers, was a victory, nonetheless. While the first signs of rebellion against Reams could not go unpunished, word had begun to spread about a child with a very special gift. Unlike the rumours of those in possession of such powers, and the anxieties that followed from the bigotries of before. This time the boy was not to be evaded; the metahuman should be found, he was to be helped and to be kept unharmed. He was not one of those who were taken by the Shadow Seekers, consigned to servitude with only the prospect of a lifetime in crime. Neither was he one who sought adoration; a following or reverence for what he had done. There was goodness in the boy, a conscience that was noble, and perhaps there were others; perhaps many more like him? More who were willing to stand up for the helpless, restore hope to the hopeless, if only they knew how much they were needed?

From the humblest of beginnings, the first step to achievement was finding belief. Belief that now, the Dominoes themselves might stand once again after decades of DomiNation. Empowered by the act of an unknown child, through a deed that may come to forge the base of an alliance, the boy had achieved more in one selfless gesture than Grey and his Remnants had been able to do throughout their years of insurrection. For those free of the Grid, able to reason and willing to fight, there was nothing decided. Nothing except the need to do something.

Like a seal had proclaimed at the heart of Washington, on the ceiling of an office that once held power. Out of many come one, and the Dominoes were many, with a growing conviction to stay silent no more. It would be better to die, to die trying at least, than continue with nothing and living like this. It was the start of rebellion, and for them, the feeling that a time was approaching when all would need to face their fears; because destiny lies in the hands of the many and has the power to make heroes of us all. Heroes that should arise to challenge fate, not to decide it—that was the duty of war.

The words of the boy and the raven-haired woman now spread throughout DomiNation like a call to arms.

In every battle, one will rise.
In every victory, one must fall.

It was time to oppose the criminals that drained them. To retaliate against DomiForce and cut the head from the snake. Time to defend against those who had wronged them. Time to stand up and defy the metahumans who had chosen to stand out and take what they wanted. It was time to choose a side, to fight back against misery—against life itself—if only sides could be defined, become explicit and clear. Time to put an end to all that was past. Time to follow the lead, the virtue of a child; the example of one still a mystery to all.

18

AND ALL THAT WAS MINE

A midst the wrangling and the failure of the appointed DomiCentre leaders to appease their people or find an accord, a voice from DomiNation Eta2 shouted to be heard. It echoed from a place once called Antarctica, and a settlement once known as Queen Mary Land. Cut off from most of DomiNation, isolated by the harsh climate and conditions of nature, there was little understanding of the fighting that was spreading, only that it needed to cease. Even there, in the barren frozen wastelands, the effects of metahumans were already being felt as the glaciers shed their ice at an alarming rate.

Tensions continued to rise, and discussions continued to collapse. Under pressure to quell the rebellions against them, those chosen to represent the DomiCentres of each District finally agreed to meet at a group of uninhabited islands. Neutral ground that was far from the south, and far from the home of the voice so persistent to meet. On the fourth of March, and the eve of what should have been spring, in a territory that used to be called the Arctic Ocean, the leaders converged upon an old, abandoned ghost town, in a place that used to be called

Svalbard. All that remained were a series of derelict wooden huts, each torn by the blizzards and brutal arctic winds that wreaked havoc on the desolate settlements in the north. But it was here that the leaders had come, and it was here their abilities to lead would be questioned. That their differences would have to be set aside if unity was to be found, collaborations to be made, and war—even one impending— was to be averted. If only so the benefits they enjoyed and the kingdoms they each held should wish to be retained. Here where the ground was cold without favour; unwanted and wild, surrounded by mountains of snow. Where the sheets of ice formed the frozen fjords, where nothing lived because nothing could, and even the infamous polar bears that once roamed these lands, had long since been deceased.

The sun hung low beneath the horizon, barely sneaking its rays overhead. Before him, the landscape dipped into delicate shades of aquamarine and the eerie blue glow of its polished glass. Commander Reams sat back and checked the dial of his wristwatch, unable to read the numbers obscured by the blanketing fall of the storm.

'You need to put your visor down, sir,' yelled a DomiForce Guard, as he shouted through the mask of his helmet. It was camouflage white, like his thermal uniform, and protected his face from the blistering cold. Reams could barely hear a word, as the engines of their snow scooters spluttered beneath them.

'It's just over that ridge. We're on schedule... twenty-three minutes until the meeting.'

The wind howled around them, with Reams oblivious to whatever the guard had said. He lowered his visor once again and stared through the tinted lenses; the spectrums of blue were dulled and replaced, impossible to see into the grey. The guard revved his engine then pointed to the ridge before giving the sign for Reams to follow. He nodded and the guard sped slowly towards the climb, carving through the deep white untouched fields; Reams on his trail, following the faint red glow of the tail light. Ascending the drifts, before them in the distance the sky was lit with hypnotic swirls; like a rainbow of green and ebbs of pink watercolour softly bleeding into the edge of the heavens. The guard eased on the throttle and Reams pulled up alongside.

'There it is, sir,' he shouted, pointing at the only building below.

Reams nodded.

'Requesting that you respectfully reconsider, Commander Reams.'

The guard pointed at himself, then to the shack. Reams shook his head.

'Not this time, Ryan.'

The guard raised his visor, his disapproving eyes attempting to plead once again to his commander.

'I know, sir... but I wish... I'm just concerned about security.'

Reams rode down the hill alone. As he neared the dilapidated hut, he could see it was bigger and was more like a lodge. The scooter to a halt, and not wanting to announce his arrival, Reams trudged through the blizzard—twenty metres or more—his feet sinking with every step.

The corner of a frame stuck up from the ground, almost covered by the drifts. It leaned against the side of an old wooden post, and Reams bent down to paw away the snow. The paint was splintered into frozen shards and the little that remained was faded. It was hard to decipher, and yet it looked like writing, perhaps the form of a letter: T? Curious more than committed, he scooped away more before stepping back to read what was painted upon the sign.

HUSET

It meant nothing, at least not to Reams, and his eye was quickly caught by an orange glow that flickered from between the cracks of the crumbling exterior cladding. Hardly enough to see inside, and just enough to know that the flames belonged to a fire. He followed the light and spied a dark wooden door; a collection of planks—several broken or missing—where those that remained had slipped to a slant. He grasped at the edge and it crumbled in his fingers, sprinkling to the ground like shavings of chocolate. The door was rotten. There had to be another way in. On the ground, the snow had been moved, so he reached farther down and gripped the plank tightly. The door dangled from its hinges, held only by two screws. He pulled as it followed the shape of the arc. The loud, painful creak removed any hope of surprise.

Twenty-four leaders were present, all waiting to begin. All sat fixed on the door, as Reams stepped inside and pulled it shut. Now they were twenty-five. Everyone was here.

The sound of the howling wind sucked through the timbers as the flames of the fire danced wildly. Reams turned to the glaring eyes and stomped his feet; the snow falling to the piles already laying at the door. He raised his hands and lowered the hood of his parka. It cracked like the sound of glass shards; the white fur frozen stiff, reluctantly forced to move. He raised his visor then removed his helmet.

'Gentlemen,' he said. His eyes darted around the room. 'Ladies,' he smirked with a sardonic smile, nodding in acknowledgement of those present.

Amongst them was Peter Rubio, also known as "El Diablo," who had snatched control of Alpha2 from Reams. Lee "The Lyncher" Ling, who represented Beta1 and Beta3, was sat beside Ivan Petrenko, who had travelled from Gamma1. Tony Tratorri had made his journey from Gamma2, and to his right sat Arthur Cole, "The Aristocrat," from Gamma3.

Davu Dogo, who preferred to be called "The Gecko," was there from Delta3, along with Idi Aku from the harsh desert lands of Delta4. The chair beside him was empty, and then sat Javier Ortega, who represented Epsilon1. He appeared to be somewhat irritated by the presence of Felipe Trujillo, "The Professor", who was there representing Epsilon4.

Nikau "Cut-throat" Tan was infamous not only in Zeta1 but across all of DomiNation. He slouched as he whistled, bouncing his legs restlessly. While beside him, "The Outland Assassin," Charlotte Brown from Zeta4, sat idly crunching her knuckles.

From the colder regions of Eta came Sophie de Groot, Jean-Pierre Adrien, Fredrico Pais, and finally, Klaus Fischer.

They huddled in a circle, gathered around a makeshift fire, perched on twenty-four rickety chairs trying to stay warm. The room was dark, heavy and brown; the fire flashing traces of yellow shimmers to cast its transient shadows. Above them, the roof was partially intact, and the walls provided a degree of shelter; fairing slightly better at keeping the crippling winds out than they were at slipping them in.

Most of the room had collapsed, and the floor had sunk into an icy grave. There were tables and chairs upturned, more than to be expected for a lodge. Perhaps in better days, it had been a bistro or a restaurant; perhaps even a hotel? Whatever the HUSET had been was no longer of consequence as guests never came to fill its rooms anymore. From the look on the faces of those asked to attend, the only item on the menu was doubt. Served with suspicion and peppered with suspect.

'Well...? What are you waiting for?' asked Brown, her tone not unlike the arctic chill.

Reams raised his eyebrows; his eyes widened. 'Hmm,' he murmured, then tilted his head and nodded. He walked towards the fire and took his place: the empty chair between Aku and Ortega. The chair wobbled, almost buckled, and Reams spread his feet to steady himself.

They glanced at each other with sudden glares, their eyes colder than the room that hosted them.

'It was you... wasn't it?' Petrenko asked Adrien, his accent heavy and low. His eyes flamed like the fire, and the light caught the sides of the deep scar that ran from the side of his forehead down to the jawline of his square chin. He was from a place that would have once been called Eastern Europe, Ukraine or Moldova perhaps. 'You who bring us to this... this hell of a hole?'

'Non, monsieur,' replied Adrien, shaking his head. 'It was not I.'

'Then you? You're from Eta...' accused Petrenko again, as he pointed at Fischer through the flames.

Fischer shook his head. 'Nein,' he replied. 'Ich war es nicht.'

Petrenko snarled, growling like an angry dog.

Keen to exert his authority, Reams decided to remove any doubt of who was in charge. He stood, puffing his chest, then stepped closer to the fire.

'Let's get one thing straight.... I'm not interested in *anything* you have to say unless you speak the language of Alpha1.'

The room stayed quiet. Only the wind that whistled and logs that crackled rose to meet him with reply. Fischer turned to de Groot, and de Groot to Adrien. Each bemused, seemingly puzzled.

'Anglaise?' asked Adrien.

'Englische,' replied Fischer.

'Americano!' interrupted Reams. 'And don't you forget it. Now... enough of this nonsense.... Who summoned us here? Which of you brought us to this godforsaken place?'

Reams scowled at each leader in turn, before making his already public thoughts about their efforts and abilities known.

'We didn't need to come up here to play games—to reach the same conclusion we always reach... that none of you can—'

'Which is why we never get anywhere, Reams,' interrupted Cole. 'Because you don't know how to listen... and you don't know when to pipe down. Just look at the Alpha's.... Your DomiForce is half the reason we're in this mess.'

Reams was Commander Reams, and no one, especially some snooty, self-elected representative was going to talk to him this way. Certainly not someone from a place that once had a Commonwealth and power over the world. A DomiCentre that was once an empire with royalty that ruled; a country that had once been respected. Not now, now that the time of kings and queens were over. Now that the empire was gone and his voice nothing but an irritating whisper from a minor DomiCentre far away.

'Don't – you – *ever*—'

'Sit down, Reams,' interrupted Rubio. 'Sit down and shut up.'

Reams was furious. He glared through the flames. Rubio rolled his tongue inside his cheek, not caring what Reams wanted, liked, or heard. He looked up at Reams still standing and stared at him blankly. He licked his lips, then averted his gaze as he spat at the floor before staring back in contempt and repeating the sentiment.

'It wasn't an invitation.... I said... *sit!*'

Cut down and humiliated in front of his peers, Reams stared agape. The leader of DomiForce and the capital of DomiNation was ridiculed like a fool by El Diablo. He struggled for a moment with no jurisdiction then tried to appear as though the decision was his. Since respect is earned and he was shown none, it was not the time nor the place to begin earning points.

'Hmm,' he replied, as he sat boisterously. The chair wobbled again; the reason why no one sat in it. A snigger escaped from across the room aimed at the man who was stripped of authority, balancing on his chair, and forced to be sheepish all the same.

The air turned cold as the heat from the fire was trapped by the chill. Twenty-five faces froze to stone. They glared at each other with eyes of daggered ice, awaiting the confession of someone to break and acknowledge their weakness. There was one in the room who had called for the meeting. One sitting here who succumbed to the fear of losing control. Someone was desperate, eager for help from the others to retain it; not able or willing to return without support and a pledge of allegiance. No one moved a muscle, yet each was exposed with a fidget or twitch; the signs of anxiety as eyes cut between them, and their daggers of distrust inflicted the pain of the wait. Suddenly, a voice sounded from outside the room, as the wind howled without mercy and battered the walls.

'Did you know that they used to mine coal from these mountains over two hundred years ago? Back then, this place was alive... filled with life.'

Startled, the gathered leaders looked around them. Who had broken the promise to come alone? Where in the darkness had it come from; the voice disguised by the wind.

'Then came the second great world war. The allied forces needed this land for its resources—for its coal and their ships. But the enemy made plans for a strategic stronghold. So, here it was—caught in the middle—wanted by both sides. By those who sought this land for what it was, and those who sought it for what it had. A test of strengths.... A tug of war.'

The voice belonged to a man. It was distinctly familiar yet weak. Not old but with gravitas, and it had the attention of the room.

From the corner, the floorboards creaked, and the sound of a swing door screeched for oil then thumped. His heavy boots clattered across the floor, like five men stumbling together at once. He edged towards the flame, and the huddled half-circle broke ranks as they shuffled in their seats, anxious to find a face. The orange glow danced across his long, white winter cape, his hood pulled up to protect against the bitterness of winds. His head stayed lowered, face still hidden, and his hands were tucked from view.

'The allied forces evacuated seven hundred and sixty-five people from here to a place that they called Scotland... but then, you'd know that, wouldn't you, Cole?'

The Aristocrat, surprised at the mention of his name, was even more curious to know who stood before him. He blew a smoke ring as he pulled the cigarette from his mouth. Tratorri coughed and wafted it away.

'Soon after, the enemy forces sent two battleships and nine destroyers here to annihilate everything. And they did.... This place, the mines, the buildings... devastated... all destroyed... until in the end, only four buildings remained.

'Believe it or not, in the five years of occupation… throughout the bombing, the shelling, and liberation… not a single life was lost here. Not a soldier or civilian was killed. No one died in the conflict over this land and the resources that it had.

'When the war ended, they rebuilt. They came back and mined again. People lived and thrived again. Life went on…. Back to how it had been for generations.'

The man stopped and slowly raised his head. His face decked in the shadows as the flickers of light skimmed around the rim of the hood.

'Then came Spear, with his DomiGen. With his DomiNation and his Districts. With his DomiCentres and his DomiForce. And this place, deserted once more…. Destroyed and devastated yet again.

'But look around you…. Look at this building. It still stands clinging to life—holding onto the past… and now, in this moment, we are a part of its history.'

The man reached out and placed his hand on a large wooden beam. Split and decayed, neglected through time, it sprouted from the floor; somehow managing to support the ceiling above.

'When our time is over, and we are forgotten, others will come— others will rebuild—and this land will thrive again. You see, no one can own this place, and no one can control this land. No matter what is done, or whoever tries to mould it… after we are gone, it *will* survive. It *will* endure, and all that we can do is profit from it. Profit from each other while we are here… and share in our profits… together.'

The man turned to the assembled leaders and was met with muted gasps, as he raised his hands to lower his hood.

'I have asked you here for a purpose. To demand that you set aside your differences… put an end to your squabbling… and take this opportunity to join me.'

'Join you?' scoffed Brown.

'Yes. Join me. Join, O.D.I.U.M.'

'O.D.I.U.M?' questioned Ling. 'There are no cameras here, Munro. This isn't a stage for your drama. We have no need of theatrics…. Everyone knows that O.D.I.U.M does not exist.'

Many gazed in awe at the face not seen for so very long, a face that had barely aged a day. Ling's stare, however, was not of wonderment, or the unexpected pleasure at sitting this close to the legendary James Munro. In fact, Ling, was not impressed at all, nor was he called "The Lyncher" without good reason. Born in Beijing, before Spear tore it down, Ling's reputation preceded him. He was a man who took what he wanted and executed anyone who dared to say otherwise. A ruthless sadistic killer who was often misunderstood, he was not to be feared because of the numbers that he killed; people were terrified because of the enjoyment that he took in killing. He was infamous for carrying a switchblade. It was a gold and diamond encrusted knife that he would use to wildly stab his victims. Over and over in his unbridled frenzy, he would slice and wound, until their bleeding became profuse; until they fell, incapacitated, and ceased to struggle any further. After the initial shock of their injuries, having regained consciousness, his victims would find themselves tied to a chair. Life would not have long left, and Ling would sit aside them, enjoying their suffering as he awaited their final breath. It was said that he absorbed the souls of all those that he killed, which is why he stared into their eyes to take them from their bodies once they dimmed. That the spirits of his enemies could never reach heaven or ever find hell, because he kept them for himself. Locked inside to make him immortal.

Munro was more than aware of Ling's reputation and could feel the intensity of his stare. Nevertheless, he was not the West Coast surfer stereotype that he once pretended to be. Not the boy with the foolish façade that he wore in his act to befriend Edgar. Nor was he a clown, easily intimidated and here to perform for this circus.

'You can't know pain until you first feel hurt,' said Munro, glaring coldly back at Ling. 'And you won't know fear until you first become afraid.'

Munro stepped closer to the fire, and the flames burned within his eyes as he stared deeper into Ling.

'You should feel afraid… because you will know fear…. Question me again, and I will teach it to you.'

Ling looked away, not willing to test his immortality. Munro raised his arms as if hung on a cross, stretched open his palms, and looked up at the sky through the broken roof.

'We are everywhere!' he cried. 'In everything. We *rule* your Districts, and we steal your resources. We corrupt your power, and we *own* your world.'

He lowered his head, then his arms to his side.

'You *will* join us… you will join us and survive—or reject us and die…. The choice is yours, but your time has come. Your time to choose.'

The Gecko rose to his feet. 'Then I choose to kill you where you stand!'

He lunged forward and swung clumsily at Munro, who took a step to the side and easily dodged the outstretched fist. As he stumbled, losing balance, Munro kicked him from behind, sending him headlong into the fire. Dogo screamed as his clothes caught alight; a harrowing squeal, as he fell onto the flames and his arms flailed uncontrollably. Trujillo was first to stand and go to Dogo's aid.

'Touch him and you join him,' warned Munro. 'He made his choice… now you make yours.'

He stopped with all eyes upon him. Too scared to move forward, too afraid to move back. By no means a choice that he had been given, and this was no stand-off or attempt at a threat. Munro was clear and had taken his position; there was no backing down, or doubt of his intention of what would come next. Trujillo's face scrunched at the obstacle in his path. His face became redder, his breathing ever quicker, as he searched for the courage to leap through the flames. Brown reached to cover her nose from the repugnant burning smell, and suddenly, the screaming stopped.

'You cannot defeat the mutants alone.... This boy that you seek will unite many more. The rebellion is rising... your *only* hope to survive is to join me—to swear your allegiance to me now!'

Munro took a step closer to Trujillo, who yielded as he cowered back onto his chair.

'You will swear it, or I will take all that you have and leave you with nothing. None of your Districts will be spared.... None will survive. We will take *everything* and raze your cities to dust.'

Cut-throat Tan had heard enough. He clenched his jaw and bared his teeth, as he rose to his feet, fists clenched at his side; ready to charge.

'Never! None will accept your terms. You offer no choice, Munro. Only ultimatum.' Tan turned to the other leaders, drumming for support. Together they were strong. Alone they were targets to be picked off at will. 'And ultimatums *never* end well... especially for you,' he shouted, as he waved a fist towards Munro.

Unmoved by the outburst, seemingly offended by the disappointing show of resistance from the group, Munro was calm in reply. 'Of course, they do, Tan. Now, accept O.D.I.U.M – *or* – die.'

Encouraged by Tan's defiance, Ortega was compelled to speak out.

'You give us no proof.... No way to know that this O.D.I.U.M you speak of is real. Why would my men fair better with you than with me?'

'Well, why don't you ask them?' replied Munro, as he put his hand inside his coat.

A thunderous bang filled the air as Ortega's head jerked, and his face drew blank with confusion. He turned to face Reams as a stream of blood burst through the hole in his cheek. It soaked through his balaclava, spreading like a spill, before his mouth dropped in silence and he fell forward.

'And when you find out what they think, you can let me know.'

The floor around Ortega bled. The others, immediately pensive, were unable to conceal their intimidation. Two had already been executed and Munro had barely moved.

'DomiNation Epsilon1 is now under O.D.I.U.M.... Thank you, Javier. Are there any more who choose to oppose our reign?'

Tan stood speechless; aghast at the threat made effortlessly real.

'Erm... wh—'

'Thank you, Nikau. I accept your allegiance. You may sit down.'

Staggering back before falling into his chair, Tan's thoughts were the same as the rest. How could Munro show such disregard, such impudence to such powerful men? Fredrico Pais raised his quivering hand, not wishing to wait for the answer.

'DomiNation Eta3 is with O.D.I.U.M,' he blurted out fearfully.

'And Gamma2!' shouted Tratorri.

'Eta1 also,' cried de Groot.

One by one the leaders gave their loyalty, and one by one the DomiCentres surrendered themselves to Munro.

'I have no interest in leading your Districts. Our only goal is to push this planet into war. To destroy everything that stands within DomiNation.... Together, we will ensure that the Great Dominion Wars begin.'

'What...? No!' yelled Aku. 'We came here to avoid conflict, not to create bloodshed!'

'The Dominion Wars will cleanse our planet of all life that does not belong here. It will extinguish these metahumans and all who stand in our way.... All who oppose O.D.I.U.M, will perish. We will unleash the fury of chaos and through the misery of all those who resist us, profit from their defeat. In their suffering—through their pain— we shall start again... rebuild that which was built before the DomiNation.'

Suddenly, the wall was hit by a tremendous blast: a rocket-propelled grenade that shattered most of the remaining building, engulfing it in flames and decimating everything inside. Rubio, Petrenko, Trattori, Cole, Aku, Tan, Adrien, Fischer, all lay injured; perhaps fatally maimed. The others, partially conscious, dazed and confused, were scattered, unable to get to their feet or muster any form of defence.

Munro was face down, saved by a wall reduced to mere fragments of smouldering wreckage. His bloodshot eyes were filled with the dust and the ash from the explosion; unable to focus, as the vicious arctic winds froze the tears that tried to wash debris away. He blinked, but his eyes stung with fine arrowed splinters, and his efforts came to nothing, only weakened him further, as he failed to even raise his shell-shocked head. His fingers felt tentatively across the ground at his sides, as he tried to find footing and force himself up. He moved, then he gasped, as he winced from the pain and fell back on the floor. A large chunk of wood that was shaped like a stake, stuck out from his chest. Surrounded by blood, spreading out in a ring, it stained his white cape like the ink from a pen that had leaked. It drained him of strength as he lay like a prisoner, captive to his wounds. In the distance, across the icy landscape, a silhouette blurred in and out of his view. The figure moved towards the burning remains, and Munro lay powerless, unable to see who it was that approached. He stared through the flames outshining the sun, yet his body was cold and shivering. Writhing in agony, he battled to stay awake, until his eyes were too heavy as they fought against his failing resilience. He could not submit, nor concede to his wounds, not until he was able to see the assassin; the identity of the ghostly figure that moved ever closer. Through the high-pitched ringing that blared in his ears, he could hear the faint sound of snow trampling underfoot. The blurred figure grew taller as the trampling grew louder, then the sound: like a kite being flown in strong wind.

'W-who are you…?' Munro called with a whimpering murmur.

There was no reply.

The sun had stayed low behind the figure's silhouette, and the flames burned brightly before it. The ghost was a spectre, the reaper himself, come to claim Munro in person. Desperate to see, he wiped at his eyes to catch sight of the ghoul, but they were blind and thickened from haemorrhage.

'Who are you...?'

Still without reply, and without strength to prolong his torment, he closed his eyes and accepted his fate. Suddenly, he groaned, then screamed from the pain, forced over and onto his back. A warm breath rippled across his face, melting the frost for a moment. His eyes flickered to look up at the flames, and the shape that kneeled over him slowly took form. The long dark brown leather cloak was threadbare and worn with a hood that was raised. It covered a face that was wrapped in long strips of cloth, flapping violently in the gusts of the storm.

'Who are you...?'

Munro tried again to find clarity, as his eyes found those between the ribbons of rags; those that pierced the shadows from beneath the hood.

'No... no... it's not.... It can't....'

A glove reached up and pulled at the strips of white cloth, drawing them down over the tip of a nose to reveal the uppermost part of the killer's face.

'In nomine Patris, et Filli, et Spiritus Sancti.'

Munro cringed; repulsed by the sight, and in no doubt of the voice as he turned his tortured face to the side.

'You're dead!'

'Then death has come... and I have brought hell with me!'

The killer lowered the hood of his cloak, his bandages protecting the skin; shielding a face so badly burned, so dreadfully scarred as to be unrecognisable.

'But you... you're—'

'The weapon of vengeance... the echo of doom that will ring out across your wretched world.'

Munro coughed as blood splattered on the floor at his side. He sniggered, flinching as blood trickled from the side of his lips.

'You... you still don't get it... do you, Eddy....'

Edgar stared down into Munro's bloodied eyes with a coldness far worse than the icy ground upon which he lay.

'I got it. I got all of it. What else do you think did this...?'

His stare was unremitting.

'I have waited, and I have longed... and now I've returned to reclaim what was mine.... And all that was mine will be mine again.'

'Yours...?' scoffed Munro, faintly. 'It was your fathers... it was he who travelled back to warn Roberts... back to where it all began....'

'Don't speak to me of that man.'

'It was your father who tried to take them—'

'No. My father tried to take *my* destiny!'

'Yes... he did...' said Munro, as he coughed again. 'But not before he tried to prevent the future unfolding.'

Edgar's eyes narrowed with a withering stare.

'Mutation, Eddy.... It wasn't until years later that Cerebus discovered it all started at Saven. O.D.I.U.M knew but did nothing... it was your father who took the nine from the trial... he believed that the future was saved with Roberts to hold W.A.T.C.H.... Then you... you killed him and freed them all.... You implanted them all... and look at what you did... the great, Edgar Spear....'

Munro began to laugh. It was clearly painful to do so, as blood continued to fill his mouth.

'You created the mutant gene... three hundred and twelve strains of unstoppable mutant gene.'

He coughed yet again; his breathing laboured, becoming shallow. Wanting to smile but unable to hide his agony.

'You did more than we ever could.... We wanted chaos... you gave them cause.... You're the father of metahumans, Eddy... and there are thousands of them now... their genes passed down through generations.'

He winced as his chest heaved, his face contorting from the trauma of his wounds. He closed his eyes to try to hold on, to try as he could to continue.

'Now you've returned...? To reclaim your destiny...?' He wanted to laugh, amused by it all as the blood spilled from his lip.

'But you never truly fought the opponent who defeated you. It's not Cerebus, Eddy... and it's not O.D.I.U.M.... DomiNation is the world that your children destroy....'

Edgar swallowed. He shook his head; his eyes filled with uncertainty. 'Why...? Why did the genes mutate at Saven?'

Munro lay exhausted, barely conscious.

'Why?' screamed Edgar, as he grabbed the lapels of his cape and shook him. 'Tell me and I'll spare your pain.'

Munro opened his glazed eyes, his neck limp, unable to hold his head aloft.

'There's nothing you can teach me about pain... and you alone should appreciate the concept of betrayal.'

'What...?'

Munro sniggered again as he choked on more blood, faintly spying Edgar's reaction.

'He never told you, did he...?'

'Told me what? Who...?'

'Your father, of course. His name....'

'Groy... I know.'

'No, Eddy, you don't.... Your father was taken by the Rytterne from his home....'

Edgar said nothing.

'A place called the Rhine.'

'So what?'

'Your father never spoke the language of Latium... he learned it.'

Edgar was silent again.

'Groy, Eddy... in your father's tongue... it means Grey. Your father's name is Grey... like your brother's....'

His eyes began to dim, and his skin fell a deathly pale.

'Two sides of a coin... opposites forever joined and never facing each other.... More's the pity.'

He forced a smile, one last time in the clutches of his old friend.

'Tick tock, Eddy. Tick — tock,' he said, struggling to catch the air, as the bitterness of his suffering was eased by the sweetness of revenge. 'It's time... time to embrace your destiny. For a war is coming... and you will not escape....'

ACKNOWLEDGEMENTS

I would like to express my sincerest gratitude to everyone who has taken the time to read my book.

Although creating characters and telling their stories through imaginary worlds comes naturally to me, writing as an art form does not. These past two years have been enormously challenging, trying to translate my thoughts into words that I feel are strong enough to convey the images I would like to generate. In no uncertain terms, if I have been successful at all in achieving this, it is due to the help of my editor, Paige Lawson, and my strongest critic, Maria Kristin Strand. For your honesty and for not simply having an opinion, I am eternally grateful to you both.

Now that I am finally able to share with you the first book in the HeroPlot series, I hope that you will allow me to introduce new characters, share surprises, and craft unexpected worlds that will expand your experience of HeroPlot into an entertaining multiverse.

The future is far from decided, and whatever it may hold, may it bring you the very best. But if I may, like Abelman, have the final word....

We are each of us as capable of being a hero as we are of being a monster; as doing something heroic, as we are of doing something monstrous. Never let life or your circumstance define who you are or what you become, because the world will always need heroes, though many will never be known. While our paths are our own and each one unique, a time will come when a choice that we face is always the same. A time to remember that inside each of us a hero is only ever waiting to be born.

ABOUT THE AUTHOR

Scott Harvey lives in Norway with his wife and two small children. Although his family originate from Northern Ireland, Scott moved to the lands of Vikings and fjords after finishing university at the Kent Institute of Art and Design in England, twenty-five years ago.

An international award-winning designer, it is fair to say that Scott has always been a creative perfectionist, and that his determination is probably the main reason behind his long and varied creative career.

While his mind has always been on helping clients and creating new solutions to often age-old problems; his background and love of all things film perhaps best explains his journey into storytelling, and affinity for character development, dialogue, as well as the occasional twist.

In 2017, after twenty-one years within the design and communications industry, he chose to finally focus on creating a vision that he himself wanted to share. After plotting an entire array of characters and worlds, Scott is now finally able to release the first chapter of The HeroPlot Multiverse into the literary world.

Printed in Great Britain
by Amazon